Praise for The Holy Thief

'It is rare to meet a genuinely exciting new voice in
crime fiction. Ex-City lawyer William Ryan should definitely
give up the day job, because he is a writer through and through,
and in this first novel he establishes what promises to be a rewarding
series . . . Ryan writes with narrative drive and urgency, real sense
of place, and a central character who is conflicted, moral, and
above all likeable. Any one of these things is a rarity; the
combination is whodunnit heaven'
Times Literary Supplement

debut . . . The Great Terror's atmosphere of fear and
is well portrayed, and Korolev is an appealing hero'
Marcel Berlins, *The Times*

e, superb mystery, a wonderful central character and
sense of place and period to rival even the greatest
of the Russian masters. More please!'
Kate Mosse, author of *Labyrinth*

a tough, suspenseful premise for a debut, contrasting
rophobic atmosphere with personal optimism in a way
that can only intensify as the series continues'
Financial Times

'A lively, colourful debut'
Metro

'Excellently observed characters . . . an impressive debut'
Yorkshire Evening Post

'*The Holy Thief* is an utterly compelling and beautifully lucid novel,
in which murder, history and suspicion combine to create an
atmosphere of ever-increasing and constantly shifting suspense'
John Burnside

THE HOLY THIEF

William Ryan is an Irish writer who has lived in London for a number of years. He was called to the Bar in London, after university in Dublin, then worked as an in-house lawyer in the City. In his spare time, he wrote on an occasional basis for television and film before deciding to take writing more seriously. He completed a Masters in Creative Writing at St Andrews University in 2005.

William is married and lives in West London.

WILLIAM RYAN

THE HOLY THIEF

PAN BOOKS

First published in the UK 2010 by Mantle

This edition published 2011 by Pan Books
an imprint of Pan Macmillan, a division of Macmillan Publishers Limited
Pan Macmillan, 20 New Wharf Road, London N1 9RR
Basingstoke and Oxford
Associated companies throughout the world
www.panmacmillan.com

ISBN 978-0-330-50840-7

1 3 5 7 9 8 6 4 2

A CIP catalogue record for this book is available from
the British Library.

Typeset by SetSystems Ltd, Saffron Walden, Essex
Printed in the UK by CPI Mackays, Chatham ME5 8TD

Visit **www.panmacmillan.com** to read more about all our books
and to buy them. You will also find features, author interviews and
news of any author events, and you can sign up for e-newsletters
so that you're always first to hear about our new releases.

To Joanne

*IN THE still air of the sacristy the only sounds were the slow drip-
ping of her blood onto the marble floor and the faint whisper of her
breathing. In, out, in, out — then a lengthy pause before the ragged
rhythm began again. She was nearly gone.*

*It had been a messy business. She'd bled a lot, which was to be
expected, although it still made him uncomfortable. But what else could
he have done? When there wasn't time to unpick a person mentally,
to grind them down — then you had to use pain and terror. Even if
it wasn't necessarily the most professional, or even the most effective,
approach. He'd hoped he could shock her into submission, but, in the
end, she'd simply outlasted the time he'd had available. It was a shame.
Sometimes he only had to put on one of the gauntlets, slowly, perhaps
making a fist so that the stiff leather creaked as it stretched across his
knuckles, and that would be enough. They'd start gabbling so fast the
only problem was having a typist quick enough to keep up with them.
He preferred it that way, of course — they were more pleasant, the
straightforward interrogations. But for every gabbling goose there was a
rock — and the girl had been of the granite variety.*

*Everything he'd tried had failed. If he'd had more time, maybe he
would have succeeded, but he'd only had these two hours. Two hours
for a mind like that? Strong — closed tight like a metal box. It wasn't
enough. They wouldn't be happy, but what did they expect? He'd
warned them after all. If he could have softened her up first — no sleep
for a few days, a hot cell, a freezing cell, complete darkness, complete*

1

silence. Well, then he could have made some progress. With time and the right tools he could have found out things from her she didn't even know she knew herself. Instead, he'd had nothing to work with, really — just his leather apron, his gauntlets and a couple of hours in the back of some church.

He didn't like that either. It was sanctioned, of course — at the highest levels they'd said. But even so. If he was disturbed, the situation would be difficult to explain — particularly now, with her blood pooling underneath the altar. Anyone coming in off the street would think he was a madman.

Her breathing slowed again and he looked down at his evening's work. Her eyes, two huge black pupils surrounded by a narrow halo of gold-flecked almond, had accepted what was happening to her, and the light was slowly dimming in them. He looked for fear, but there was none. It often happened that way; at a certain point they went past fear, and even pain, and it was the Devil's own job to bring them back. He leant in closer, wondering if one of these days he might catch a glimpse of the next world through eyes such as hers. He searched, but there was nothing — her gaze was fixed on the ceiling above them and that was all. There was a painting up there of the saints in heaven, and maybe her gaze was fixed on that. He moved his head forward to block her view, but her eyes just looked straight through him.

At least when he was this close to her the stench was less oppressive. He could still detect the damp syrupy smell of her blood, but there was also the scent of soap and wet hair and something about the mixture that reminded him of a child. He remembered it from when his son had been newly born — a warm, happy aroma that had filled his heart. He wondered where she'd found the soap — there was little in the ordinary shops this year. You might get some in a closed shop or a currency shop, but even then it wasn't always available. He puzzled about the soap for a moment, and then remembered — she'd probably brought it with her. American soap. Of course, that made sense. Capitalist soap.

Still, he was surprised to feel something approaching sympathy for the girl. Tears had washed away some of the blood from her cheeks and she looked quite beautiful, her delicate nostrils dilating minutely as she breathed. He held his own breath for a moment, irrationally concerned that exhaling might fog those bottomless eyes of hers. He swallowed and then put the emotion aside. This was no time for self-indulgence. From the very first day, they'd drummed into him the dangers of misplaced pity, and the mistakes it caused. He'd have to revive her, make one last effort.

He put a finger to her neck: the pulse was still there, but barely detectable. He stood up and reached for the smelling salts. There was blood on the bottle – he'd used it twice already – and a part of him wanted to let her go in peace, but he had his instructions, and even if the likelihood she'd tell him anything was remote, there was still a chance. He uncorked the bottle and pulled her head towards him. She tried to twist away from his hand, but the movement was weak.

There seemed to be no change at first, but, when he turned to put the bottle back in his bag, her eyes followed him and, what was more, she seemed to be trying to speak. He picked up his knife and ran the blade down along her cheek, cutting skin and material together in his hurry to remove the gag. She coughed as he pulled the cloth away – blood had smeared her white teeth and he noted how thin and grey her lips were. Her breathing had quickened with the effort, but now she calmed a little, swallowed and focused on him. He leant slightly to the side to hear what she might say, without breaking eye contact, and she whispered something indistinct. He shook his head and leant further forward, waiting for her to try again. She took a deep breath, her eyes never leaving his.

'I forgive you,' she said, and it was almost as if he amused her.

Chapter One

IT WAS later than usual when Captain Alexei Dmitriyevich Korolev climbed the steps in front of Number 38 Petrovka Street, headquarters of the Moscow Militia's Criminal Investigation Division. The morning had started badly, wasn't getting any better and he still hadn't shaken off the pounding vodka headache from the night before, so it was with weary resignation rather than Stakhanovite enthusiasm that he pushed open one of the heavy oak doors. It took his eyes, dazzled from walking into the flat morning sun, a moment to adjust to the relative darkness of the vestibule, and it didn't help that thick clouds of masonry dust swirled around where he'd expected to find uniformed duty officers and bustling activity. He stopped for a moment, confused, wondering what on earth was going on and looking for a source of all the dust and debris. He was rewarded with a blurred movement that shifted the billowing haze on the landing – up where the statue of former General Commissar of State Security, Genrikh Grigoryevich Yagoda, stood. The movement was cut short by the crash of something very solid hitting what he strongly suspected was the plinth on which the commissar's statue rested. The noise, amplified by the marble floor and walls of the atrium, hit Korolev like a slap.

Korolev moved forward warily and began to climb the staircase towards the landing where the statue stood, fragments crunching underfoot. The commissar, swathed in blankets, was a muffled shape around the base of which four workers, stripped to the waist, toiled with crowbars, hammers and a mechanical drill which now thudded into action. Their objective appeared to be the statue's removal, but the plinth appeared to have other ideas. As Korolev approached, a worker looked up at him and smiled, white teeth cracking open a face plastered with grey dust.

'They meant the Comrade Commissar to stay here until the building fell down around him,' he shouted over the racket. 'He's cemented into the floor itself. We'll be lucky to get him out in one piece.'

Korolev saw the sledgehammer, wielded by one of the worker's comrades, arc through the air once again, hitting a metal chisel that scattered debris in all directions as it wedged itself further underneath the marble block on which the commissar stood. Korolev swallowed several times in an attempt to return some saliva to a tongue that felt like he'd eaten sand.

'There. He shifted. We'll have him out yet,' the hammer-wielder called to his fellows, spitting. The gob landed black on a piece of rubble at his feet. Korolev nodded thoughtfully, a stratagem he found useful when he'd no idea what was going on, and took a tentative step forward. As far as he was aware, Yagoda was still a senior Politburo member and entitled to the respect such a position was due – but clearly something had changed if his statue was being removed.

Korolev mumbled a gruff but firm, 'Good morning, Comrades,' as he passed the workmen, thinking that in Moscow, in October of the year of our Lord nineteen hundred and thirty-six, it was best not to comment on such things, particularly not if one had a hangover.

§

Korolev was a man of well above average height, at least according to the norms published by the Ministry of Health the week before, standing close to six foot tall. He was also above the average weight for a Soviet citizen, but this he put down to his height and certainly not overeating, as if such a thing were possible in this period of transition to full Communism. Anyway, being his size had its advantages when a little muscle was needed.

He looked like what he was, a Militia detective of considerable experience. It probably didn't help that he had a solid face, the kind that policemen often had, with a broad jaw and wide cheekbones and skin raw from years in the sun and the snow. Even the short brown hair clinging to his scalp like dead grass marked him out as a cop. Curiously, however, the thick ribbon of a scar that ran from his left ear to the tip of his chin, a souvenir of an encounter with a White Cossack during the Civil War, made him seem more genial than ferocious, and his eyes, kind and warily amused, saved him from looking like a bruiser. For some reason those eyes made citizens consider Korolev a good sort, even if he happened to be arresting them, and more often than not they found themselves disclosing thoughts and information to him they'd really have preferred not to. But the eyes were misleading; Korolev had fought his way from the Ukraine to Siberia and back again for seven long years, against Germans, Austrians, Poles and anyone else who pointed a gun in his direction, and come through all of it more or less intact. When necessary, Captain Alexei Dmitriyevich Korolev wasn't soft – on the contrary.

Korolev scratched his neck as he mounted the stairs towards the second floor and considered what the removal of Commissar Yagoda's statue might mean for the Moscow Criminal Investigation Division. Up until now the Workers' and Peasants' Militia, to give the Soviet Union's regular police force its full title, included among its responsibilities maintaining public order, directing traffic, guarding important buildings, and sundry other tasks, not least of which was, of course, the investigation and prevention of criminal activity – which was where he and the rest of Moscow CID came in. Most of the political work was left to the NKVD –

State Security – although, when you lived in a worker state, almost everything was political to some extent. In some people's eyes, any crime was an attack on the entire socialist system, but the distinction between traditional crimes and political crimes still remained, for the moment at least. Of course, the Militia uniforms often helped the NKVD with political matters – even the Red Army did that from time to time – but generally Korolev and the other Militia detectives had been left to do what they were best at, which was tracking down and catching the perpetrators of serious crimes that did not stray into the political realm. As a result, when a Muscovite referred to 38 Petrovka Street, the home of Moscow CID, it was in the same way a Londoner might refer to Scotland Yard, and was completely different from how they might speak of the Lubianka, if they even dared mention the feared headquarters of the NKVD. Korolev hoped the positive perception of Petrovka Street would persist in these times of change.

The awkward truth of the matter, however, was that now the Militia, and therefore Moscow CID, formed part of the Ministry of State Security, and when these days citizens referred to the 'Organs' – the Organs of State Security – they meant both the NKVD and the Militia, and everyone knew the Militia's role might well be changed to a more political one by the new commissar, Ezhov. What was more, judging from his statue's removal, Ezhov's predecessor's arrest might well be imminent, if it hadn't happened already. And if that happened, then a purge of the Organs would be likely to follow. Korolev knew the pattern by now – he had one of the highest detection rates in the department but no one would be safe if there was a purge. He'd seen too much in the last few years to be in any doubt of that.

Korolev entered Room 2F with a greeting that was closer to a grunt than a pleasantry, turned towards the coat hooks on the back of the door and began to manoeuvre himself out of his winter coat, which was tighter across the shoulders than was comfortable since he'd last worn it six months before. The room was painted battleship grey and furnished with four desks, two facing two, and eight filing cabinets that lined the walls. It smelt of men and cigarettes, and the light that streamed in through the window struggled against the smoke that the three other investigators already present were furiously producing. For decoration the walls had a functional map of Moscow and a portrait of Stalin. Up until yesterday there had also been a photograph of Commissar Yagoda, but now there was only a square patch of lighter paint. That fact alone was enough to make anyone light up a cigarette.

Korolev finally succeeded in peeling the coat from his body, revealing his seldom-worn uniform. He turned and found he had the complete attention of his colleagues' pale faces and round eyes. Three cigarette ends flared as one as they regarded him. Korolev shrugged, noticing that his uniform was also tighter since the last time he'd worn it, and nodded to them.

'Good morning, Comrades,' he said, once again, but this time more distinctly. Larinin recovered first.

'What time is this to come to work, Comrade? It's well past nine o'clock. It's not what the Party expects. It's my duty to raise it at the Works Council.'

Larinin looked like a pig in Korolev's opinion, and the chipped and broken grey teeth that snarled between his fleshy lips looked like a pig's teeth. His voice was higher than usual today, however, and Korolev noticed how the podgy fingers that held his cigarette were shaking slightly. He's rattled, Korolev thought, looking at him, and wasn't surprised. He was always careful of the bald investigator with the belly that spilled over the desk like a tidal wave, but today he'd be especially careful. The hammer blows still echoing up the stairwell might mark the end for a political man like Larinin. The desk, after all, had belonged to Knuckles Mendeleyev until a short time before, and Larinin had won no friends with the way he'd gained it. Mendeleyev had been a hard and effective investigator who'd been the scourge of the Moscow Thieves until Larinin, a traffic policeman, had denounced him for spreading anti-Soviet propaganda. Now Larinin sat amongst Mendeleyev's former colleagues, filling Knuckles' space, if not his shoes, while no one knew for certain where Knuckles had gone except that it was probably somewhere in the far north and against his will and all because of a stupid joke about the Chekists that the traffic policeman had overheard and exploited. So it was no wonder that Larinin looked nervous, knowing as he did how quickly the wind could shift these days, and conscious that after three weeks sitting amongst them he had not resolved a single case. It was hardly an achievement to boast of to his Party friends.

'I know what time it is, Grigoriy Denisovich,' Korolev said. 'I had to visit Staff Colonel Gregorin at the Lubianka. He kept me waiting. Would you like me to give you his telephone number so that you can check?'

Looking down, he noticed that moths had been at his sleeve over the summer. He rubbed the chewed fabric and sat down at his desk, placing his fur hat in the bottom drawer where it belonged. He turned on his reading light and began to look through the papers in the file he was due to forward to the procurator's office later that day, but paused as he became aware of the strange silence that had fallen over the room.

'Comrades?' Korolev asked, looking up. The other investigators were staring at him in open-mouthed fascination, a mixture of terror and pity on their faces. Larinin was wiping sweat from his hairless scalp with his shirt sleeve.

'The Lubianka, Alexei Dmitriyevich?' Junior Lieutenant Ivan Ivanovich Semionov said. Semionov was the youngest of the investigators, only twenty-two, although sometimes, as now, he seemed even younger. He resembled a Komsomol poster boy with his floppy blond hair, almost feminine good looks and straightforward demeanour. Semionov had only been with them for two months – most of it spent assisting Korolev with simple tasks and learning the ropes – and had yet to learn when not to say what was on his mind.

'Yes, Ivan Ivanovich,' Korolev replied. 'Comrade Gregorin wants me to give a lecture to the final-year cadets at the NKVD Higher School.'

The three men relaxed. Larinin's pasty face seemed suddenly a little less pasty, Semionov smiled and Dmitry Alexandrovich Yasimov, a wiry fellow of Korolev's age with a professor's face and a cynical wit, leant back in his chair, wincing as the movement stretched a stomach wound, and pulled at the end of his thin, barbered moustache.

'So, Lyoshka, *that's* why you're wearing the uniform. I suppose we thought there might be some other reason. It's rare to see you in one.' Yasimov used the familiar form of Korolev's name, as was his right after twelve years of working and drinking with him. Korolev looked at the chewed sleeve and scowled. It was true; he preferred to wear civilian clothes. Nothing stopped a citizen confiding in an investigator more surely than a brown uniform, in his opinion at least.

'It needed an outing, mind you. Look at this – the damned moths have been at it.'

'And it looks a little tighter now. Putting on weight, are you?' Yasimov's eyes twinkled and Korolev smiled, the old sabre scar that ran along his jaw drawing his left eye to the side and giving him a dreamy look, accentuated by the way his eyes lurked indistinctly under his thick eyebrows. Yasimov would joke that Korolev's eyes seemed always to be focused on his dinner. But Korolev, while acknowledging an element of truth in the assertion, thought that this dreamy quality made people trust him, and that was certainly useful in their line of work.

'Muscle, Dmitry. I've been in training. Keeps me sharp, stops old ladies from stabbing me.'

Semionov snorted behind a hastily opened file and Larinin forgot his troubles enough to laugh openly. Even Yasimov had to smile as he rubbed at the spot where an elderly woman had placed the business end of a pair of scissors when he'd tried to help her across the street. It was the uniform, she'd told them later, and Korolev hadn't been surprised; uniforms made people nervous these days. She'd thought Yasimov was going to arrest her, even though she'd done nothing wrong, and Korolev had had to lift her gently by the arms to stop her puncturing Yasimov for a second time. Even the innocent were jumping at shadows these days, and she'd just happened to have a pair of scissors in her fist when she did so. Korolev tried not to laugh, but to get the better of his friend was such a rare event that he had to put his hand in front of his mouth. Yasimov shook his head in admonishment.

'Very funny. But yes, I'm following your example now, Lyoshka. Strictly plain clothes after that experience. Anyway, tell us, if you're passing on your wisdom to young Chekists, on what subject will you be exhibiting your pedagogical abilities?'

Korolev had found the file he was looking for and now it lay open in front of him; the perpetrator's arrest photograph staring up at him, bruises dark on his pale young face. It hadn't been a pleasant case, but still he felt his conscience shy at the sight of the man's battered features. Korolev hadn't been in the room when they'd roughed the youth up, and he couldn't really condemn the uniforms who'd done it – they each had sisters and daughters, after all. Nonetheless, punishment was best left to the People's Courts – otherwise things would be no better than before the Revolution.

Distracted by the photograph, he wasn't really paying attention to Yasimov and when he looked up he cursed under his breath, half-smiling, seeing that Semionov and even Larinin had warmed to the game.

'Come on, Comrade,' Yasimov said, 'it's a great honour. You must share the news with your fellow workers. In what area of expertise are you so pre-eminent that a staff colonel should have picked you, an ageing captain in Moscow CID, to address the bright young Chekists of the F. E. Dzerzhinsky Higher School of

State Security? The cream of Soviet youth, no less. Even our boy hero here wouldn't get a look in with that lot.'

He nodded his head towards Semionov, who smiled good-naturedly. The three of them waited for Korolev's answer, knowing it already.

'Case file management, you rat,' Korolev said in a rush, unable to stop a smile at his own expense. He was rewarded with a burst of laughter from the other three men.

'A worthy topic, Alexei,' Yasimov said, pleased that the natural order of things had been re-established. 'The little Chekists will learn a thing or two from an old hand like you.'

'I hope so, Dimka, although I'm surprised they didn't think to ask you to give a lecture on self-defence.'

Yasimov wagged a warning finger at Korolev, who was somewhat surprised himself to score off his friend twice in the same morning. Semionov was coughing behind his file and Larinin was looking for something in his bottom drawer, shoulders heaving. Yasimov was about to respond when a loud crash echoed up the stairwell. It sounded like a former General Commissar of State Security's statue collapsing to the floor and breaking into several pieces, blankets notwithstanding. In the silence that followed the four of them looked at each other. The noise was a reminder, particularly to Larinin, that now was the time for results, not for idle laughter. Soon the only sounds in the room were the rustle of pages being turned in case files and the scratch of Soviet-made nibs against Soviet-made paper. Comrade Stalin looked down on them with approval.

§

It was Korolev's habit to review every page of his case file before it went to the procurator's office. On the one hand, the purpose of the exercise was to ensure the file contained everything the procurator's office needed to ensure a successful conviction, but Korolev also performed the task to see if he could identify anything he'd missed in the course of the investigation that, with hindsight, might have brought the matter to a close sooner. It was a practice that often yielded interesting results and was never entirely a waste of time. Sometimes Korolev found patterns of behaviour repeating themselves that he found intriguing and stored away for future reference. Now, as he looked at the student Voroshilov's photograph, Korolev wondered whether the rapist would ever have committed his crimes if he'd stayed in the small town near Smolensk where he'd grown up. Obviously, he must have had an inclination towards this kind of violence, but, perhaps, if he hadn't been sent to study in Moscow, he might have settled down, married a nice girl and contributed usefully to society. Instead, when he'd been accepted at one of the new Moscow engineering academies, he'd discovered the anonymity, and opportunity, at the heart of a Soviet city in transition, where people, buildings and even entire neighbourhoods were in a constant state of flux. Workers coming and going, factories opening, new construction projects: the development of Moscow into a capital worthy of the great Soviet Revolution had given young Voroshilov the space and opportunity to rape six young women over a four-week period, and he'd taken advantage.

It hadn't been reported in the newspapers and yet the word had spread. Moscow was a dangerous city at the best of times – long hours, short rations and vodka were a combustible mix – but a violent rapist striking again and again in rapid succession was unusual. Women had been careful walking alone at night, especially in the streets that had no lighting, but still Voroshilov had found opportunities. After the first one, he'd explained when he was arrested, the forced possession of women had become the only thing he thought of. With each attack the violence increased and it was only a matter of luck he hadn't killed someone. Korolev turned a page and came across a photograph of the bruised and bloodied Maria Naumova with her four missing teeth, her twisted nose and blackened eyes. Korolev wished he'd caught up with Voroshilov earlier, but sometimes to identify a criminal it was necessary for the dog to continue committing crimes. So he'd tracked him with a patient anger and extracted the information from each crime that had helped him slowly, but inevitably, bring the rapist to justice.

The first victim came from a town not forty kilometres from where Voroshilov had grown up and had recognized his accent. The second remembered his new knee-length leather boots – an almost astonishing fact in itself for a student, Korolev thought ruefully, moving a toe about inside one of his own battered boots and wondering if they'd last the winter. The third girl had seen enough of the rapist's face to give a good description of him, and one which turned out to be more accurate than most. The fourth victim, Masha Naumova, had barely remembered her own name by the time Voroshilov had finished with her, but the fifth had snatched a piece of paper from his pocket as he'd pressed down on her in a patch of waste ground near the Moskva. She'd rolled it up in her fist and hidden it beneath her. It was a list of lectures. But it had taken them a day to identify the academy he was studying at – time that allowed Voroshilov to attack his sixth and final victim.

They'd been waiting for him when he returned to the student hostel where he shared a tiny cubicle with three other young men. A youth like any other, it seemed to Korolev when he saw him, except for the blood-dotted scratch that ran down his cheek. He hadn't resisted and, when they'd taken him away in the black police car, he'd seemed more relieved than frightened. The Militiamen at the local station had scuffed their knuckles on him and then thrown him into a holding cell with a bunch of Thieves. By the time the morning came, Voroshilov had an idea of just how unpleasant ten years' hard labour could be for a rapist, and the beginning of an understanding of what the Thieves did to 'furry burglars' when they fell into their hands.

Korolev closed the file and wrote a brief summary in his elegant handwriting. A priest's hand, his mother had used to say proudly, dizzy at the possibility of young Korolev entering the tsarist bureaucracy, or perhaps even the Church itself. But then the German War had come and he'd enlisted and, when the Germans and Austrians were finished with, the Civil War had begun and so he'd fought the Whites, and then finally the Poles. By the time he'd made it home, his mother was dead and clerical jobs were few and far between in the new order. How could his poor mother have imagined that, twenty years on, all that would be left of the old regime would be a few well-mannered scarecrows scratching a living off what little manual work they could find, and selling the last of their possessions for food in the currency shops? And that there would be only a handful of churches still open in a city that had had one on every corner? He finished the note and took a stamp from the cluster that stood together on the windowsill. He marked the cover *For Attention of Moscow Procurator's Office* with satisfaction, and was thankful for the opportunity to contribute usefully to the creation of this new society, hard though the process was.

'A job well done, Alexei,' Yasimov said, for once not joking.

'He's Kolyma-bound for sure,' Korolev said, tucking the folder under his arm as he stood up.

'He won't last long there,' Larinin said, emboldened by the earlier laughter. 'The Thieves will have him at the train station. The burglar will be burgled before he even gets to the Zone.'

Waves of laughter rolled up his shirt front and his stomach heaved itself up a few inches onto the desk. His eyes, half hidden by fat at the best of times, were now mere slits of skin from which he wiped away tears, not noticing that the others didn't join in. Yasimov turned away with a frown and even Semionov looked as if he'd eaten something unpleasant. Korolev wondered how many years they'd given Knuckles on Larinin's evidence, and what the Thieves did to ex-Militiamen in the Zone. He left the room quickly, his fingers longing to squeeze Larinin's throat until it popped.

Outside on the landing Korolev took a long deep breath and heard the laughter come to a stop, then Larinin's uncertain voice asking was it not amusing that the rapist would be raped? He received no response. What *would* the Thieves do to a cop like Knuckles? You never knew. Their sense of honour was strange. And Knuckles had been fair in his own way. He might have a chance.

There was no answer when he knocked on the general's door, but he opened it anyway – being familiar with his boss's ways. Popov was looking out at the passing traffic – his back to the room and his massive shoulders filling the window, his three-quarter length leather jacket reflecting the sunshine.

'Comrade General,' Korolev said, holding himself at attention. There was something about General Popov that encouraged his men to behave like tsarist guardsmen.

'Does no one knock in this damned place any more?' the general growled, without turning.

'My apologies, Comrade General. I did knock, but perhaps not hard enough.'

After a lengthy pause, General Popov turned to examine Korolev, picking up his spectacles from the table to do so more closely. Even with his glasses on, he still looked every inch the Soviet hero, handsome as a statue and with hair and eyes as black as coal. Seeing that Korolev was the previously blurred figure in front of him, his chiselled features softened into a smile.

'Alexei Dmitriyevich, is it? Come to shut down the Voroshilov file? That rat. Ten years, would you say? If I'd my way . . .'

But the general knew Korolev was familiar with his preference for summary criminal justice and so made do with slapping a hand onto his desk with some force.

'On his way to Siberia soon enough, I expect, General.'

'He won't see the spring. The Thieves give fellows like him a taste of their own medicine. They don't last long.' The general smiled at the thought. 'Enough talk of that wretch. Sit, Alexei, and listen for a moment. I've some news.' The general took the file from Korolev and signed it quickly beneath Korolev's note. 'You did a good job here. An excellent job. Not the first time, of course. I give you all the hard cases, the crimes that look like they've been committed by ghosts, and yet you always find the devils and bring them to me. The highest conviction rate in the division and you don't even beat the confessions out of them.'

The general paused for a moment to look at Korolev with a hint of reproach, his unruly eyebrows drawing together in a frown as he considered the investigator's suspiciously liberal methods.

'I do my best, Comrade General,' said Korolev, and Popov sighed in response.

'And your best is very good. You're a terrier. Isn't that what the Thieves call us? Terriers? It describes you, you know. Once you're on the trail the bandit might as well hold out his wrists for cuffing. And excellent performance deserves recognition and reward. Comrade Stalin himself has made this clear, time and time again, and the General Secretary knows a thing or two about life. So I've had a word with Comrade Kurilova over at housing and asked her if she could find me something for my best man. I can't have you sharing a room with your cousin out in the back of beyond for ever, can I? I want you close at hand for when I need you. And in a way, as Comrade Stalin wants the best workers rewarded, I've no choice in the matter.'

Korolev found himself beginning to hope. Ever since his divorce two years before he'd been living with Mikhail, two tram rides and a long walk from Petrovka Street. He liked his cousin, but he wished he lived a little closer and drank a little less.

'Thank you, Comrade General. I'm grateful for your efforts on my behalf.'

'Efforts? I did better than efforts. She called me this morning

and said that for the man who caught the filthy rapist Voroshilov
– and how she knew about him, I don't know, but that woman
knows when a sparrow farts on the Lenin Hills, I'm sure of it.
Still, it worked in your favour – for the man who felt Voroshilov's
collar nothing less than a big room on Bolshoi Nikolo-Vorobinsky
would do. Fourteen square metres. Some furniture as well. Here.'

The general pushed across a requisition form from the housing
department signed by the sainted Kurilova. Korolev took it from
him, feeling his face grow warm. Forty-two years old and still he
blushed. He was glad Yasimov wasn't there to see it.

'I was only doing my duty, Comrade General,' he began, but
the general interrupted him.

'Enough. It's a shared apartment, so don't get too excited. But
you'll have your own room and as for the area – well, Kitaj-Gorod
is not to be sneezed at. Full of VIPs and Party cadres. It'll do
them good to see a real worker for a change.'

The general smiled at Korolev's discomfort.

'Don't worry, Alexei, I don't talk this way in front of Larinin
and his like. Not that Larinin won't be back directing traffic on
Tverskaya soon enough if he doesn't get off his backside and
catch a criminal. We've quotas here, same as everywhere else, and
he's not pulling his weight. Anyway, best get over there before
they change their mind – the head of the building management
committee has the keys. And as soon as you've finished, call in.
There's been a murder over on Razin Street; it sounds like the
work of a maniac – just your kind of thing. I'm going over to
take a look.'

Korolev got to his feet so quickly that for a fraction of a
second he felt dizzy.

'Comrade General,' he began and he could feel the gratitude
making him pompous, but the general shook his head almost
shyly, took Korolev's hand in a firm grip and held it for a moment
or two while he regarded his subordinate with affection. Then his

face became grave again, as befitted a Soviet leader of men, and he turned away towards the window, his voice rough when he spoke.

'I said enough, Comrade, no need for a speech. Go on, quickly now – get your belongings moved in. You deserve it. Hurry, before I change *my* mind.'

And in this way, Alexei Dmitriyevich Korolev acquired an apartment on the street of Great Nicholas and the Sparrows.

Chapter Two

PETROVKA STREET was only half an hour's walk from Bolshoi Nikolo-Vorobinsky, but it took Korolev three hours to make his way out to his cousin's room, pack up his few belongings and then travel back to Kitaj-Gorod by tram. Korolev's life possessions didn't amount to much. Zhenia had taken most of their joint belongings after the divorce, and with his blessing – she had their son Yuri to care for, and anyway there was little space in his cousin's room. All he had these days were a few clothes, bedding and some cooking implements, his books, a small leather armchair which had been all that had been left of his mother's when he'd returned from the wars, and a set of dumbbells. The armchair and the dumb-bells he'd left with Mikhail, who'd tearfully vowed to guard them with his life, and the rest he'd lugged across town in a large canvas bag. By the time he stood outside Number 4, looking up at the faded grandeur of a fine old house now cut and sliced into apartments for Party officials and the odd lucky nobody like himself, he felt as tired as if he'd circumnavigated the world. But he couldn't help a smile as he climbed the steps to the open hall door.

According to the requisition form, the head of the building management committee lived on the second floor, and so he left his bags at the bottom of the stairs and went up unencumbered. Reaching the correct landing, he knocked on a chipped and pitted door that had 'BMC' painted on it in sloping, ill-matched letters.

It was opened by a thin-faced man with the left sleeve of his ancient woollen pullover sewn at half mast, mourning a missing arm. He seemed to be not quite awake until he saw Korolev's uniform, at which his eyes flew open.

'Is there a problem, Comrade?' he said, looking anxiously into the corridor. 'Has someone been telling lies about me? I lost this arm in Poland, fighting with Budyonny, and now I'm to be persecuted? What a world we live in, what a world we live in. Who was it? At least tell me who it was. The lying scum.'

Korolev held up his hand to stop the man. 'Please, Comrade. I've a requisition form, from the housing committee. That's all. My name is Korolev.'

The head of the BMC let out an involuntary sigh of relief then recollected himself enough to smile and extend his hand in greeting.

'I apologize. Maxim Luborov. I look after the building. You know how it is: in this position you can't help but make enemies. Sometimes people threaten things and, even if you're innocent as a dove, you never know what might happen. Everyone wants a few square metres more and they don't care how they get it. The devils.' He put his hand to his nose and squeezed it, and in some strange way this seemed to give him relief. 'I'm sorry. My arm hurts today. I can't even wear the prosthetic, it hurts so much. That damned Pole. Slice. Down came the sword and off went the arm. Sssssssh-shushuk.'

Korolev shook Luborov's remaining hand and then raised a finger to the scar that ran along his own jaw. 'I was luckier. One of Denikin's Cossacks. I got him before he finished the job.'

'Good for you. An arm you can manage without – a head is more difficult.' Luborov took the form from him. 'Ah yes, the room on the first floor. Come on, I'll show you. There's some furniture. A bed, a chair, a table. I think there's even a wardrobe. It's not too bad, a good size. Well above the official norm.' He was already halfway down the first flight of stairs. 'If you need anything, let me know. No promises, but I might be able to help.'

He moved his hand from side to side to underline the speculative nature of the suggestion and the methods that might be used. Korolev nodded in thanks, although he wouldn't take advantage of the offer. It wasn't that he was averse to the idea exactly, but it wasn't sensible to accept a favour from a stranger unless he came with a recommendation. After all, you never knew what might be asked in return.

Reaching the first floor, Luborov led him along the landing.

'Here you go, Comrade,' he said, opening a door with a key which he handed to Korolev. 'Number seven. You share with Valentina Nikolaevna Koltsova and her daughter Natasha – not a bad child, quiet at least. Comrade Koltsova's husband was that engineer who got himself killed in the Metro accident last year. E. N. Koltsov? D'you remember him? They made him a Hero of the Soviet Union. Just for getting crushed in a tunnel. It wasn't that easy in Poland, I can assure you. They were tight with medals back then. All I got was a wooden arm for my heroics and I had to wait three years for that.'

The door opened onto a large shared kitchen into which the autumn sun splashed, tingeing the surface of a long, planked table in the middle of the room with a warm yellow. An ancient and much-scuffed chesterfield ran along one wall, above which hung a full-length portrait of an officer in turn-of-the-century cavalry uniform. Underneath the large windows a smaller table stood, on which a child's exercise books were neatly piled beside some knitting. It was positively luxurious compared to Mikhail's cardboard-walled shoebox.

'One of the previous owners – a count, I believe,' Luborov said, gesturing at the painting. 'Who knows where he is now, eh? Paris? Shanghai? The grave? Serves him right, wherever he is. Covering up the cracks in the wall is all his kind are good for now. Anyway, this is the kitchen: you share it with Citizeness Koltsova, of course, and the cooking area is in there,' Luborov pointed to a smaller room beside the front door in which a primus stove stood, as well as a stone basin, 'You have your own stove?'

Korolev nodded.

'Excellent, that makes life easier for everyone; this one belongs to Valentina Nikolaevna. Your room's through here.'

§

When Luborov left, Korolev stood alone in the room he'd been allocated. He placed his hat on the writing desk and looked around him. A narrow bar of light marked where the curtains met, leaving most of the room in shadow, and so he walked across to push them as wide as they would go, allowing sunshine to flood in. It was a good room, large, with high ceilings – it even had wallpaper. Of course, the wallpaper was a relic from before the German War, but it was in reasonable condition, and the mattress on the bed looked clean – there was even a worn Persian carpet to cover some of the wooden floorboards. He glanced out of the window at the alleyway below. A quiet street as well, he thought, looking to the left at the domes of the small church of St Nicholas Vorobinsky. He heard bells chiming for one o'clock and remembered he only had a few minutes to spare, so he looked over the room once again, but this time with a searching eye.

To start with, he examined the writing desk, opening the lid to the compartment where some nobleman had once no doubt kept a stock of fine writing paper, but which now contained only a browned edition of *Pravda* from 1928. The desk wouldn't do. He ignored the bed as being too obvious and, after a quick scrutiny, discarded the wardrobe as well. He flicked back the rug and paused, his focus gradually narrowing until it was entirely aimed at one floorboard and the infinitesimally wider gap between it and its neighbours. There were tiny signs of wear to the edges and he squatted, hearing the cartilage in his knees click, and took the clasp knife from his pocket. He inserted the blade at one end of the board and, sure enough, it came up smoothly.

The lifted floorboard revealed a small cavity in which lay a photograph of a half-naked woman, looking over her bare shoulder at the camera with a suggestive smile, her breasts pushed over a corset. She seemed to be milking the cow that stood behind her, its head out of shot but the udders fat between her fingers. Someone else had needed a hiding place once, it seemed. He placed the floorboard to one side and then raised himself to his feet. Underneath the other books he'd brought with him he found his bible, and put it in the hiding place with relief. He liked to have the book near him but it had to be hidden, and it made him sweat to consider the risk he'd run carrying it across Moscow. It wasn't that he was particularly religious, he told himself – he was certainly aware of the Party's line on the Orthodox cult and agreed with it – but the bible had stood him in good stead through nearly eight years of soldiering and now, more than ever, it gave him comfort when the world around him sometimes seemed even bleaker.

When he'd finished he looked down at the floorboards and was satisfied they'd stand up to most searches, then patted his pocket and felt the outline of the milkmaid. It would have been wrong to leave her with a holy book. He'd dispose of her when he got a chance.

§

Half an hour later Korolev was walking quickly along Razin Street, past the statue of the rebel Cossack for whom the street had been renamed by the Bolsheviks. An officer of the People's Militia couldn't be seen whistling in full uniform, not if he wanted an ounce of respect from citizens, let alone criminals, but, even so, Korolev was sorely tempted. If he'd been in plain clothes he might have allowed himself to attempt a few bars of something martial and uplifting, in keeping with his mood – the 'Internationale' perhaps – but the uniform prevented any outward display of satisfaction. In short, despite the morning's unnerving start, the new apartment had restored his usual cautious optimism and he was confident, for a moment at least, that things weren't so bad after all. In fact, things were getting better, as Comrade Stalin had recently stated. Things were definitely getting better.

He was looking for a telephone to call Petrovka Street when he spotted two Black Crows parked further along the street outside a church. Uniforms stood beside the Militia cars and he guessed this was the crime scene Popov had asked him to attend. It was a small church, adorned with a Komsomol banner that hung above the entrance and invited the members of the Party's youth wing to a dance in support of the Spanish Comrades. A rope was extended across the front of the building but it was unnecessary as most citizens were crossing the road to avoid the Militiamen. Only a starved-looking mongrel, lucky to have made it through a hungry summer without ending up in someone's pot, and three equally bedraggled street children showed any direct interest, and even that was from a safe distance. Popov came out, trailed by more uniforms, who listened as he gave them orders, his fist pounding into his palm for emphasis. Korolev was rewarded with a nod from the general as he approached.

'You got my message then?' the general said.

'No, General, I was going to call in from the booth on the next block when I saw the cars.'

'Just as well, just as well. This one's got your name on it, Alexei Dmitriyevich.' The general pointed behind him with the pipe, the gesture taking in the front of the church in a brief sweep, then he turned and scowled at the uniformed Militiamen.

'I want a statement from every citizen within a two-hundred-metre radius. We need to know the movement of every man, woman, child and mouse over the last two days. Send everything to Comrade Korolev here at Petrovka Street. He'll be dealing with this matter.'

The uniforms saluted and went. Popov looked after them.

'Probably a waste of time, but if you don't take every possible action these days, you leave yourself open to criticism.' He focused his irritation on the dwindling supply of tobacco in his pipe bowl, stuffing it full again from a small leather pouch with short angry jabs of his thumb. Korolev stood in silence, knowing better than to interrupt the general when he was thinking. Eventually Popov remembered his presence and pointed the unlit pipe towards the entrance once again.

'A terrible thing, Korolev. Some fellow got in there last night and . . .' He paused and then beckoned Korolev to follow him into the church. 'It's not pretty, anyway, and if we don't catch him soon he'll be at it again. He has the taste for it – I feel it in my bones.'

The interior was dark except for weak rays of light squeezing through the small stained-glass windows that circled the several domes. Each dome of the church offered a separate fresco representation of a scene from the Bible and the murky light picked out the gold-circled heads and silver robes of saints. Korolev felt his mouth harden as Party slogans loomed out of the darkness, painted directly onto the frescos and mosaics. The young brats should find better things to do with their time than acts of mindless hooliganism, he thought to himself, as he followed Popov from shadow to shadow towards the sacristy at the far end of the church.

Even the sacred templon, the wooden wall that separated the congregation from the mysteries of the altar and which would have been covered with icons in the old days, was now hung with banners exhorting greater efforts for the Soviet cause. Korolev made the sign of the cross in his pocket. Hadn't Comrade Stalin himself nearly become a priest? He'd have words to say if he saw what these Komsomol pups had been up to.

'She's in here,' the general said, walking blithely through the central doors of the templon and into the sacristy, from which white light poured out into the murky nave. Korolev hesitated and then made for the 'Deacon's Door' to the side. The 'Holy Doors' in the centre were forbidden to all except priests and, even if the holy fathers didn't seem to have been inside this particular church for a good ten years, he wasn't walking through their doorway.

Before he even caught a glimpse of the murdered girl, Korolev already knew something terrible had happened to her. He could smell it. Despite his years in the army, or perhaps because of them, he hated the smell of blood. He didn't much like the sight of it either and the white marble floor was covered with the stuff. The serene faces of the saints circling the room looked off into the distance, as though they were pretending the horrific scene beneath them had happened somewhere else – and he didn't blame them. It wasn't just blood – the poor girl lying on the altar had died hard. He swallowed an urge to retch and could feel his nails digging into the palms of his hand, grateful for the pain they caused. The body had been horrifically mutilated, and he struggled to control his stomach, saliva sharp and salty in his mouth. He reassured himself that if he could last another ten seconds he'd be fine; it was the first minute that was the worst. He took another step forward and, looking down at her, guessed her to have been pretty when life had coloured her skin. Only the Devil himself could be responsible for evil such as this. On the other side of the altar, the general sniffed angrily.

'In a church, of all places,' Korolev heard him whisper and looked up at the general in surprise. Two careless remarks in one day either meant he trusted Korolev more than he should or that Popov had grown weary of life. But then the savagery of the crime had indeed been amplified by the location. Korolev took another step forward, careful not to step in the blood, particularly not the congealed shoeprints that might give a clue to the killer.

She was laid out on her back, her arms extended at right

angles to what was left of her chest. Where the body was not hacked open or smeared with blood the skin was pearly white, as though it had never seen the sun, but he was aware this might be an effect of the arc light's intensity. The girl's legs were slightly spread, enough for Korolev to see that burn marks scorched the skin all around her pubic mound; indeed, most of her pubic hair was a smudged frizzle. He felt the nausea recede as he began to do his job. What kind of lunatic could have done something like this? He looked over at the general, who shook his head in disbelief, his mouth an angry straight line, nodding towards where a wrinkled ear and an eye that had been gouged from the girl's face sat, each in their separate frame of dried blood. The eye looked as calm as those of the apostles above it. It took a few moments for Korolev to realize that the last item of the grim arrangement was the girl's tongue.

'I think she may have been alive when he did some of this,' he said. 'Otherwise there wouldn't be so much blood. Who's coming from the Institute?'

'Chestnova,' replied Popov, his attention focused once again on his pipe. 'Did you see those marks?' He pointed at the girl's crotch. The charred welts were unusual and there were more on the breasts.

'Electric, do you think? She was clearly tortured. Dr Chestnova might be able to tell us the order of events, but if the tongue was cut out first then he did it for pleasure, not information. He's an evil one, Comrade General.'

Popov turned towards the girl once again – breathing deeply, the knuckles of his fist white around the pipe, looking down at the torn and mangled body. There was a savage expression on his face.

'Now listen to me, Alexei, and listen well. You don't rest until you catch this fiend. Do you understand? And if you break a few bad eggs along the way to making this omelette, so much the better. You have carte blanche. I'll assign Semionov to assist you. He can run errands, learn a thing or two perhaps – he's not stupid. But find the killer, and when you find him – when you find him, you give him to me.'

Chapter Three

THE FIRST thing Korolev did when he returned to his desk in Petrovka Street was to call Gregorin at the Lubianka. He wanted to ask the staff colonel's permission to rearrange the lecture, but was interrupted before he had a chance to ask.

'Comrade, may I take it you have been assigned to the murder on Razin Street?'

'Yes, Comrade Colonel,' Korolev said, wondering how Gregorin could possibly know about the murder already.

'One of my colleagues just told me about it. Shocking. I'm glad Comrade Popov chose you for the investigation – it sounds like a madman is at work in the capital. If we in State Security can be of any assistance, please inform me at once.'

'Thank you, Colonel. As a matter of fact, I was wondering whether I could postpone the lecture tomorrow. For a day or two, perhaps?'

'I understand, Comrade. You're keen to catch the killer: it's commendable. But you must remember that the security of the State takes priority over everything else in these dangerous times. We're surrounded by enemies, both internal and external, and the young Comrades you will lecture tomorrow are needed in the front line of the struggle against them. Comrade Popov will appreciate the need for your presence for an hour or two, even with such an important case.'

Korolev thought about arguing but he knew it would be pointless.

'Of course, Comrade Colonel. But, in the circumstances, if I could keep the lecture to an hour, I'd be grateful. Would that be acceptable?'

There was a pause and Korolev found himself drumming a pencil on the table. Yasimov, the only other person in the room with him, looked up and shook his head. Korolev smiled in apology and the pencil was still. Gregorin's tinny voice broke the resulting silence.

'An hour should be enough if you're concise, Comrade. After all, it's a useful insight from a Militia colleague, not part of their course work. Yes, an hour will do. Tomorrow morning at nine, then. I'll attend myself.'

'Thank you, Comrade Colonel,' Korolev said and then found his pencil was tapping the table once again. 'Actually there is something more practical that State Security could assist me with. Did your colleague mention that the victim had been tortured?'

Yasimov's head jerked up as if he'd been stuck with a pin. Korolev turned away, so as to avoid his colleague's shocked stare and waited for the colonel to answer.

Gregorin's voice sounded guarded. 'He mentioned she was mutilated. Tortured you say? The poor woman, I only hope you catch the killer quickly. A maniac by the sound of it.'

'Well, Comrade Colonel, it wasn't pretty. Not pretty at all. He used electricity to burn her – I've never come across that before. I wondered whether it was a method State Security had ever encountered.'

Korolev's question hung in the air like an artillery shell at the top of its flight and Korolev didn't have to look at Yasimov to know he'd now gone deathly pale.

Gregorin, however, after a long pause merely sighed. 'Comrade Korolev, you'll be well aware that torture is prohibited by the Soviet Criminal Code as a means of interrogation. You aren't suggesting that the NKVD would ever flout that prohibition, are you?'

'Of course not, Comrade Colonel.' Korolev felt sweat dampen the underarms of his shirt. 'I only wondered whether your colleagues might have come across something similar. In their investigations of terrorist organizations? Or foreign spies, perhaps? At least, if they haven't, it might allow me to rule out that line of enquiry. I hope you understand no other suggestion was intended.'

Korolev waited for an answer, the line crackling in his ear. He glanced over his shoulder at Yasimov, whose face was indeed as white as the murdered girl's.

'Comrade Colonel?' Korolev said, wondering whether he'd been cut off. Perhaps a van was already on its way to arrest him.

'Yes, Captain, I'm still here. I'm considering whether any of the questions you've asked or, should I say, suggestions you've made, can be responded to. I don't think they can. State Security takes precedence in all situations, you understand that, don't you, Captain?'

The colonel placed a slight emphasis on Korolev's rank, just enough to remind Korolev of the thinness of the ice under his feet. Korolev didn't need the reminder – he was a lowly Militiaman, a flatfoot, whereas Gregorin was a staff colonel of the heroic NKVD, the defenders of the Revolution – the armed wing of the Party no less. The colonel's driver probably outranked him in real terms.

'Of course, Comrade Colonel. I withdraw the questions. I tend to focus on the case in front of me and not take account of the wider social and political implications. It's a criticism my colleagues have made to me before.'

'I believe your intentions were proper, Captain. If, as the situation develops, the NKVD consider they have relevant information which can be released to you, taking into account our primary responsibility to protect the State and the Party, then I'm sure we will assist you accordingly. In the meantime, however, please keep me informed on a daily basis. What you've told me suggests a State Security element may reveal itself in due course and it would be as well to be kept informed about the situation in case we have to intervene at a later stage. You may give me your first report after the lecture tomorrow morning.'

'Of course, Colonel. Thank you.'

The colonel hung up without saying goodbye and Korolev turned back to face Yasimov once again. Some colour had returned to his friend's cheeks, but beads of sweat still twinkled on his forehead.

'Damn you, Alexei,' Yasimov said, rubbing his brow, the anger going out of him with the gesture. 'What the hell are you smiling about? If you're going to have a conversation like that with a Chekist colonel, can't you make sure I'm not in the room at the same time? In fact, if you don't mind, make sure I'm not even in the city.'

Korolev shrugged his shoulders and opened a new file on the Razin Street murder.

'I've three children,' Yasimov muttered, as he returned to his own work, 'and I look forward to them caring for me in my old age.'

§

Korolev was back in Razin Street an hour later and found Semionov waiting for him outside the church, along with the police photographer, Timofei Afanasovich Gueginov. The young Militiaman smiled when he saw Korolev.

'Alexei Dmitriyevich,' he said taking his arm, 'the general has assigned me to assist with your investigation. He told me, "Young Semionov, Comrade Korolev will need help on this Razin Street affair and you'll give it to him, or wind up directing traffic on Tverskaya with that idiot Larinin." Well, I'm against directing traffic and I'm against Comrade Larinin, so here I am and at your command.'

Semionov took a step backwards in order to give a half-salute, which seemed intended to be half-mocking. Korolev frowned and was pleased to see the salute stiffen into something approaching regulation standard.

'Good, I'm sure I'll find plenty for you to do. I see you've met Comrade Gueginov. Has he set up yet?'

'Not yet, Alexei Dmitriyevich, but is that fellow really a police photographer? Don't you need a steady hand for a job like that? With all the blood and everything? He's got something quite badly wrong with him, I think.' He looked over at Gueginov, whose head was twisting in spasm. 'See what I mean? Poor old fellow. Anyway, I had a look inside. Some mess, eh? I've never seen anything like it. Want me to handle anything in particular?'

Korolev suppressed a smile. Semionov's mixture of self-confidence, naivety and amiability was almost irresistible. If Semionov was the future, things wouldn't be too bad after all.

'Don't you worry about Gueginov, he's a first-rate man and experienced as well, which is more than I can say for some.'

Semionov looked abashed for a moment, but then grinned. 'That was the other thing the general said – that I needed experience and you'd give it to me. Or a kick up the arse. He said I needed both.'

'The general is a wise man,' Korolev said and tried to keep his face stern. Semionov looked perturbed for a moment before Korolev relented.

'Have the forensics team been?'

'Yes, they finished up about half an hour ago. A lack of cleanliness amongst my Komsomol Comrades, I'm afraid – they think they could have up to two hundred different people's fingerprints in the sacristy. It could take weeks to check them all out. The forensics boys think the killer might have been wearing gloves in any event, but they'll call you this afternoon to confirm. And they say there are no useful markings in the footprints, although they suggest you have them photographed anyway. They didn't look too happy when they left.'

'I see,' Korolev said, unsurprised. 'Well, the next thing I need you to do is go to the local station and see how the door-to-door questioning is coming along. Captain Brusilov is the man in charge and he knows his stuff, so don't presume otherwise just because he's in uniform. Be polite, listen, assist if you feel you can. But don't get on his nerves, because he's the type of fellow who really will kick your arse. My guess is that the murder happened early this morning, so ask them to focus in particular on the period from ten o'clock last night until when the body was found – at least until the pathologist tells us differently.'

'No problem, Alexei Dmitriyevich. I'll help the flatfoots out. Show them how it's done.'

Korolev inhaled deeply, ready to lambast the youngster, but Semionov held up his hands and smiled. 'A joke. I'll be a real world-class diplomat, don't worry.'

Korolev allowed his breath out slowly. 'Be sure you are.'

'I will, I will. Komsomol's honour.'

'Good and, speaking of your Komsomol's honour, get hold of the Komsomol committee that looks after this place. We'll need lists of anyone who had access to the sacristy. They'll need to be fingerprinted as well, but forensics are probably organizing that already. Still, check they are.'

Semionov produced a notebook and opened it, pointing over his shoulder into the church.

'There's a Comrade from the Komsomol committee in there now with a couple of young lads. They're in a side chapel. Demanded to be let in, crime scene or not: "The Komsomol movement must always move forward." I told them to keep out of the way, but I thought you'd want to talk to her anyway, as she's the one that found the body. What was the rest – lists of people, fingerprints?'

He started to write notes. Korolev was mildly surprised, but pleased.

'That'll do. Make notes of anything you come across on your travels, that's the idea. A note doesn't get forgotten. And when you've finished with Brusilov make sure you go and see the forensics team on your way back. Have a chat with them, keep them sweet. They'll work that bit harder on the case if they think the detectives are keen. Go on, hurry. Call me at the Institute if you need me.'

Semionov clicked his heels like a Prussian and gave another cheeky salute. Korolev made as if to kick him, but Semionov was already five steps away.

'At your command, Comrade Captain,' he laughed over his shoulder and then he was gone.

Korolev shrugged and approached Gueginov. 'I hope young Semionov wasn't any trouble, Gueginov? He's harmless, more or less.'

'Nuh-no trouble at all, Cuh-Comrade. He rolled muh-me a ci-cigarette, so he was ee-even quite useful.' Gueginov smirked and shook Korolev's hand. 'Sh-shall we get to wuh-work then?'

'Yes, please go ahead – I'll come through in a few minutes. I need to see someone first.'

He entered the church and looked around. White light from the sacristy cut through the dark like a searchlight, but there was a softer, yellow light coming from a side chapel on the left. He walked towards it and found a girl with a pretty oval face sitting at one end of a table, an abacus and an open ledger in front of her. At the other end were two hungry-looking youngsters – one of them cutting up small slips of paper and the other then writing on them.

Korolev looked at the girl's serious face and found himself strangely cheered by her rosy cheeks and down-turned mouth. She looked up, brushing a lock of black hair from her cheek, and he tried not to show the sudden warmth he felt towards her, this pretty little representation of Soviet youth.

'Good afternoon, Comrade. Captain Korolev, Moscow CID – investigating the murder.'

She was small when she rose, at least a head shorter than him, and he found himself leaning down towards her.

'You found the body, I believe?' he asked when she didn't respond.

'Yes, it was a terrible thing. She was on the altar in the sacristy. Excuse me, on the former altar in the social room.'

'The social room?'

'It's where we set up the buffet when we have a dance. We were meant to have one last night, but it was cancelled. We have a political meeting before the dance, of course, but the Party believes in providing healthy opportunities for enjoyment to its socialist youth, as well as political education. That's why we're here. You'll be out by Saturday, won't you? We're trying to make sure we don't lose momentum. This kind of thing could set us back if we allowed it to.'

Her voice was faint and her eyes didn't seem able to meet his. He saw the way her fingers pressed into the table, the tips white, and wondered if she was in shock. She lifted a hand and pointed at the slips of paper, the gesture seeming to cost her a lot of effort; the extended finger was visibly trembling.

'Tickets,' she said. 'For the dance. In three days' time.' One of the young men looked up at him without any interest.

'Can you tell me exactly what time you found her, Comrade?'

'Nine o'clock. I open the building every morning. I'm on the organizing committee. Lydia Kovalevskaya. Anything I can do to assist you – of course. Lieutenant Semionov said you'd have some questions. The door was open when I arrived – it had been forced – and then I found her. The blood was everywhere. Does it stain marble, blood? Will we be able to clean away the marks?'

Kovalevskaya rubbed at the table with the palm of her hand. The two young men exchanged a smile.

'Are you all right, Comrade?' Korolev asked, wondering should he take her somewhere quieter. She thought about the question for a moment and then nodded.

'Yes, I think so. I'm sorry; I know I shouldn't be upset – that I should be stronger. But what was done to her – it was horrible.'

'Your reaction is quite normal, Comrade.'

'Thank you, but your questions. Please ask me your questions.' She managed a tight smile as Korolev caught one of the young men raising an eyebrow to the other. Young scamps – hard as only the young could be.

'There was meant to be a dance that evening. It was cancelled. Why was that?'

'An electricity problem, Comrade. Our connection to the grid was damaged. It was a temporary problem. They fixed it in time for the dance, but we'd already cancelled.'

'Damaged? How?'

'Nothing suspicious. A workman cut through a cable on the construction site next door.'

Korolev considered her response and decided to have Semionov look into it.

'The thing is,' he said, 'I'm wondering how the killer picked this place. He may just have been lucky, walked past, saw the dance was cancelled from the posters and taken the opportunity that this provided. But even that would have had an element of uncertainty to it, do you see? Unless he knew something about the place, yes? The question is: how did he know he would be undisturbed? We think he came in about midnight. Is the church always shut then?'

'We prefer not to use the word *church*. It is a Komsomol recreational and political agitation centre. We have concluded that former church is acceptable, however.'

Korolev felt his hand clenching in his pocket. He knew she was correct in strictly political terms, but still. Sometimes you couldn't help but feel angry at the way some people spoke.

'Answer my question, please. The lectures can wait for a Party meeting.' She looked at him in shock. He realized he'd allowed some of his anger to show and then thought it wouldn't do any harm. She needed strong direction otherwise he wouldn't get a damned thing out of her. He tapped the table to get her attention.

'I'm investigating a murder, Comrade. I don't care how you refer to this building, it's just a crime scene to me – understand?'

'There is no need for uncultured aggressiveness, Captain. The dance was in support of the Comrades in Spain. When there isn't a dance or a special event, the club shuts at eight.' She spoke as if speaking to a child, and any warm feelings he had for her disappeared. The two young men had stopped working. He turned his head towards them and one didn't even bother to hide his smirk.

'You. Name, patronymic, surname,' Korolev barked.

'Grichkin. Alexei Vladimirovich.'

'And you?'

'Nikolai Alexandrovich Zoshchenko.'

'Well, Grichkin, and you, Zoshchenko – I want a list of every member of this cell, and everyone who has attended a meeting or event in this *former* church, for the last six months.'

'But—' Zoshchenko began, his eyes looking at the other two in panic.

'But what? I don't want to hear how difficult it will be, I want the damned list. And there will be no more public use of this church until I get it, and it's been checked, and I'm happy that it's accurate. And if it's incorrect in any way, I'll find a nice spot in the Butyrka prison for you two to spend a little time together. Six hours. That's what you have. Work on it together. And you can forget those blasted tickets until it's done.'

'I must protest,' the girl looked like she was about to begin a long-winded analysis of the murder's insignificance against the global scale of the Revolution when his hand slammed onto the table, causing the ledger to lift up into the air.

'Let me remind you, Comrade Kovalevskaya, that the Militia is part of State Security and that this crime was against a Soviet citizen in a Komsomol building. A crime against Soviet law takes priority here. And I'd be thinking very carefully about not cooperating fully, given the fact you and your Comrades here can't even secure a damned social club at a time when the entire Revolution is under threat.'

After which things went a little more briskly. When he'd finished, he left three pale-faced Komsomols no doubt wondering which of the others to denounce first to save their hides. Not that he would be following it up – it was clear they knew nothing. About anything, probably.

§

Inside the sacristy Gueginov was unpacking camera equipment from the two cases he'd brought with him. Looking at him, Korolev had to accept that Semionov had a point. The man didn't look well suited to his job. Aside from the stutter, which worsened in the presence of strangers, there was also the spasm that juddered through his whole body every minute or so – more often when he was nervous. It was strange then that he seemed relatively relaxed as he prepared to photograph the butchered woman, timing his movements to avoid the involuntary twitching.

'Scuh-scaring the yuh-young fuh-folk were you?'

'You heard me? Well, sometimes you have to shout to be heard.'

'Tru-true. Vuh-very true. Suh-so, ha-have you any ideas who did this yet?' Gueginov asked as he lined up a picture.

'Not yet. And those youngsters weren't much help. Perhaps the autopsy will tell us something. Can you take a picture of the clothes?'

'Of cuh-course, Comrade. I'm limited to ten photographs, however, unless I have the general's express approval. The film's imported, you see.'

This came as no surprise to Korolev, especially if it came from abroad. What little foreign currency the State had was needed to achieve the aims of the latest Five Year Plan.

'How many have you taken so far?' Korolev asked, wondering if ten would be enough.

'Fuh-four. A cluh-close-up of the face. Three location shots of the body from he-here, here and here.' The photographer pointed to where he'd stood to take the photographs. 'Now, I'll do the clothes, the body parts – anything else you'd like? I normally save a fuh-few for the autopsy.'

Korolev looked carefully at the body and then around the room.

'I'd like the footprints,' he said, looking at the bloody floor. 'Damn it. Listen, take all ten in here. I'll get the general to authorize the autopsy pictures.'

'Okuh-kay. On your head be it,' Gueginov said as he moved the arc light. He nodded at the ear, eye and tongue as he turned to Korolev.

'A savage. But it's strange, you know. The way the b-body is positioned. As though it might mean something, all the efuh-fort he went to. Look.'

The camera's flash sent black shadows flying across the ceiling. Korolev looked down at the body and saw it was laid out as though crucified. He wrote a quick observation in his notebook. It might mean something, or it could just be a coincidence. It would probably turn out to be a madman, but the electrical burns made him wonder.

§

After Gueginov had finished in the sacristy, the body was carefully lifted, wrapped in a canvas body bag, and then put on a stretcher.

Dr Zinaida Petrovna Chestnova from the Medical Institute arrived in time to supervise the operation. She was nearly as broad as Larinin, but today her jolly round face looked unusually haggard. As the body was prepared for removal, she began decanting the severed body parts into a series of glass jars she had brought with her, labelling them as she went.

'I'm sorry to be late, Comrade. We've taken on some new responsibilities. I've been working all night, I'm afraid.'

Korolev knew better than to ask what new work a forensic pathology department might be given that would involve such long hours. The dead were normally a patient clientele.

'Not to worry; we only finished the pictures a moment before you arrived. So, what do you think of this? Your first impression?'

The doctor turned to look at him and her eyes seemed drained of colour. The last time he'd seen her she'd been lively, despite being up to her elbows in a decapitation. Now she seemed ten years older and bone tired with it.

'Nothing surprises me these days,' she said, looking at the blood on the floor. 'She didn't die quickly, I can tell you that much. With the cold weather, it will be difficult to establish exactly when, but I suspect early this morning. Come to the Institute and we'll examine her immediately. I'll be able to tell you more then.'

'But you haven't slept,' Korolev said, looking at the grey pallor of her skin.

'I mightn't have slept tomorrow either, Comrade. Let's seize the moment.'

She smiled and they followed the body out to the waiting ambulance, the stretcher swaying stiffly to the rhythm of the attendants' walk. The same unkempt street children watched as the stretcher was loaded. One of the young vagabonds, a bony-faced redhead dressed in a padded jacket two sizes too big for him, ducked under the Militia rope and ran to the ambulance with his hand outstretched. Korolev reached out his hand and caught a lump of hair and the child came to a squealing halt. He'd meant to catch the jacket, but hair would do, he supposed, even if Dr Chestnova was looking at him in horror. He dropped his hand to the nape of the boy's neck and leant down to him.

'Well, what are you up to?' Korolev asked. The eyes which looked back at him were totally fearless.

'Just wanted to see what she looked like, the lady. They said she was beautiful, like an angel.'

Korolev reached his hand back to cuff the youngster, but caught Chestnova's glance from the corner of his eye and made do with a none-too-gentle push in the direction of his two friends, who watched with interest but not much emotion. Tough little lads, he thought to himself. So many parents shipped off to the Zone nowadays; there were kids like these on every corner. If they didn't get rounded up and taken to an orphanage, he wouldn't bet money on them seeing it through the winter. Not that the orphanages were much better, he thought, and found himself rummaging in his pocket for a few kopeks.

'Here, get yourself some cabbage soup, you rascals.'

The money was taken without thanks, but the redhead gave him an appraising look that made Korolev wonder what other men gave them money and why. He felt ashamed. What was he? Ten years old, perhaps? The same age as his own son, Yuri, yet his eyes were as knowing as someone ten times older.

Chapter Four

ONCE the ambulance started to move, Korolev and the photographer found themselves sitting on a bench across from the canvas-swaddled body as the wheels bumped along the cobbled stones of Razin Street. The ambulance had little or no suspension and the two of them were thrown around and against each other as it clattered round corners and rumbled over pot-holes. In the front, Chestnova shouted at the driver to avoid collisions and to pass slow-moving carts. Gueginov, on the other hand, spent most of the journey trying to make himself a cigarette and, what with his spasms and the roller-coaster ride, it was with a great deal of satisfaction that he put the finished product between his lips and lit it. Then he frowned and nodded towards the corpse.

'I huh-hope you ca-catch the fellow. It's unpleasant, ha-having to phuh-photograph suh-such a thing.' He extended the cigarette in the direction of the corpse. 'Before the Ruh-revolution, I took portraits of the living. Fuh-families, children, that kih-kind of thing. Suh-since the Revolution, I only photograph the duh-dead.'

It was difficult to make out the spirit in which the remark was made, as Gueginov's quiet voice was competing with the engine and Chestnova, and Korolev looked at him to see if he was making a terrible and dangerous joke. Oblivious to Korolev's scrutiny, Gueginov took another drag from his cigarette.

'The cuh-capitalists were a sight to see back then, you know,' he continued. 'One of their women's druh-dresses could feed a family for a year. Muh-maybe two. It was exploitation. I uh-uh-understand that, of course. It was bluh-blood beauty. Now, things are better. Fuh-fairer. I don't miss those days. And whuh-what I do now is of benefit to suh-society.'

Korolev wondered what the dead woman would make of such a statement.

'Huh-here,' Gueginov said, reaching into his pocket to produce a stainless-steel hip flask, 'ha-have a drink. My next-door neighbour works for a di-distillery. It's the real stuff. I did him a phuh-photograph of his wife. It made a nice chuh-change. I'd have done it for fuh-free, if the truth be tuh-told, but he guh-gave me a couple of bottles and I duh-didn't refuse.'

Korolev took the flask and the vodka warmed its way down his throat. The dead woman's hand slipped from the canvas bag with the movement of the truck and brushed against his leg. He reached down to move it and was surprised by the softness of the ice-cold skin.

§

When they arrived at the Institute, Korolev stepped down from the back of the ambulance with foreboding. Some of his dislike for autopsies came from the sheer brutality of the procedure. He couldn't help feeling victims of violence should be left in peace after what they'd been through, but instead they were chopped at, sliced, skinned and sampled. It was worse than butchering in some ways. The dead person, once entitled to all the respect properly due a Soviet citizen, was reduced to nothing more than a piece of meat for doctors and policemen to poke at. Surely the world owed them something more after what had befallen them. And then, of course, there was the fact that even after fourteen years in the Militia and seven years of war he still had to struggle to control his stomach.

With a dry mouth, he mounted the worn steps of the Institute and was struck, not for the first time, by the melancholy atmosphere of the place. Before the Revolution it had been a nobleman's mansion, a building built for pleasure. The ceilings still retained frescoes of naked cherubim perched on tufts of cloud, eating grapes and laughing across a cerulean sky, in stark contrast to the whitewash and plain floorboards beneath them. He wondered why they hadn't been painted over – perhaps there were no ladders available that day. At least they cheered the building up a little; otherwise it seemed reduced to despair by the use it was being put to. The feeling was at its most intense in the pathology department. The glossy white walls, the harsh glare of the electric lighting, the polished concrete floors – they all combined to distort sound, space and even time in some strange way. Whenever he entered the place he had the urge to sit down, cradle the impossible weight of his head in his hands and savour the stink of dead dreams and ruined hopes that permeated the place. He stumbled, nausea rising in him, and looked around for a chair, but the doctor marched on regardless, sweeping him along in her wake, down the corridor and into the main morgue, two walls of which were made up of steel squares, behind each of which lay cold corpses on smooth-running shelves. Formaldehyde, disinfectant and the sweet scent of dead flesh filled Korolev's nostrils. Somewhere a tap dripped.

'They're two to a shelf in there,' Chestnova said, pointing to the steel boxes. 'We've even got them piled up in Autopsy Room One.'

She pointed through a glass window. A two-high line of corpses lay on the floor, each wrapped in a sheet with a number tied to a bloodless toe. Chests of ice had been laid around them like waiting coffins.

'Too many bodies, not enough pathologists, and now we don't even have enough autopsy rooms. Citizens should travel to another city if they feel they have to kill themselves. The problem isn't so bad in Leningrad, you know. Maybe the Party could organize special tours there.'

She sighed and entered the second, smaller, autopsy room, leaning against the polished steel table and closing her eyes. Korolev wanted to do the same, but he reminded himself that if he leant against anything in this place he'd lose consciousness in moments. Even standing, he felt sleep licking his neck and his eyelids drooping down. He clenched his hand into a fist and punched back at the wall behind him, hoping the pain would wake him up. The punch sounded like a pistol shot against the steel. Chestnova's eyes flew open and she looked at him in terror. She was still looking at him uncertainly when the attendants arrived with the stretcher that carried the dead body.

Korolev spoke to cover his embarrassment.

'I'd no idea there were so many of them – the suicides. Perhaps it's the coming of the winter. Is that what brings it on?'

'It could be anything with these people,' Chestnova said, colour returning to her cheeks. 'All I know is it's un-Soviet to take your own life at a time of national threat. If you're unhappy, you should find solace in useful work. These people,' Chestnova said, waving her hand towards the mortuary and the other autopsy room, 'were selfish. Individualists. They all put themselves before the State.'

'That's right, Comrade Doctor,' one of the attendants said, as they removed the body from the blankets and laid it out. 'They make work for us when they should be helping. And most of them Party members, what's more – they should be ashamed.'

The attendants barely looked at the corpse as they worked, but their movements were efficient and quick. The girl was still caked with blood and excrement, but they showed no squeamishness.

'Shall I ask Comrade Esimov to assist, Doctor?' the second attendant asked.

'No, let him sleep. The captain here can take the notes. Is that all right, Comrade?'

'Of course,' Korolev said, thinking that at least he'd be able to read them for a change.

'Let's begin. Preliminary examination of unidentified female homicide victim commencing at three forty-five p.m., second of November, nineteen thirty-six. Am I going too fast?'

Korolev shook his head and the doctor began to clean the woman's body with a small hose, gently removing the thicker patches of dried body fluids with a brush. She called out details of the surface injuries to him as she uncovered them and then, when the body was clean, she stood back and reached for a large surgeon's knife. She smiled apologetically to the two men before making a deep and precise Y cut in the chest. Then, with practised efficiency, she peeled back the skin to reveal the girl's ribcage and internal organs. Korolev met the photographer's eyes for a moment before they both glanced away – it just wasn't right for a person to look like something you'd see on a meat-shop slab, ribs sticking out of their bruised white skin.

As always, the autopsy was slow going; the doctor, despite her tiredness, was thorough. After half an hour, Gueginov, who'd been taking pictures when instructed, suggested they take a break and a nip of vodka to fortify themselves for the rest of the examination.

'Have we guh-glasses?' he said, putting his flask down beside the girl's head.

'Sample jars. They'll do well enough,' Chestnova said, 'There are some in the drawer.' She pointed with her elbow as she scrubbed at her hands in the sink.

'Huh-here we go,' Gueginov said, splitting the remaining contents of his flask equally between the glass containers. Chestnova dried herself with the towel that hung beside the sink and then turned, stopping for a moment to look down at the girl. Korolev was surprised to see her eyes were filled with tears.

'The poor girl,' Chestnova said. 'A virgin, maybe twenty. No more than twenty-two. She saved herself, I suppose, and then this. Poor little one.' Her voice broke, and she looked up at them with a weak smile. 'Excuse me, Comrades, I haven't slept for too long. I'm ashamed of myself.'

Gueginov reached out an arm and put it round her shoulder and the large woman leant against her frail protector for a moment. Then she straightened herself and wiped the eyes that avoided theirs. She held her glass up to the corpse.

'I hope you were happy, for a moment or two at least, Citizeness. In your life. I hope so.'

The others raised their glasses in turn and then drank the vodka in a single gulp. Gueginov's eyes seemed moist as well and Korolev felt the sapping atmosphere of the mortuary dragging at him once more. He dug his nails into the palm of his hand.

'So how long did she suffer for, do you think?' he asked, his desperation to get back to the business in hand making his voice unnaturally loud. Chestnova and Gueginov looked up in surprise.

'Well,' Chestnova said, considering the question, 'I can't tell for sure – but the mutilation probably took place after death, just because of the relative lack of blood. As for the electrical burns, my guess would be they happened before death – he used a thin, lengthy object. Like a torturer might have used a red-hot poker in the past. She was restrained with rope and gagged – see the bruising and tearing round the mouth and the marks on her wrists and ankles? I'd say she struggled a great deal. And I think it was done by one man. Probably right-handed. See these bruises here?'

Korolev nodded and looked at the purple-grey marks on the girl's otherwise alabaster arm. The doctor explained how the bruises showed indications of being made by a right hand and that they probably indicated the hand the killer showed a preference for.

'And the mutilation? Do you have an idea why he cut her up?'

'No – I'm afraid not. That is something you'll have to ask the killer when you find him.'

Korolev nodded, more in hope than conviction, and turned to Gueginov.

'Boris Ivanovich?' he said, looking at the girl's head in profile, 'if we took a picture from here, the damage isn't so visible. Maybe we can find out who she was, if we can get it circulated.'

Gueginov nodded and positioned his lamp in preparation. Outside in the mortuary a door banged and then the younger of the attendants came in without knocking.

'Captain Korolev? General Popov wants to speak to you. There's a phone in the director's office. Follow me, please.'

§

Popov's call turned out to be nothing much, just a request for any new information, but the air in the director's office was fresh and a chill breeze from an open window rustled across the piles of papers on the desk, each weighed down with a pebble. The director, a middle-aged man with a wide, intelligent face, stood with his back to the window and his arms crossed, looking on as Korolev finished his report. He smiled when Korolev hung up the phone and offered him a cigarette. Korolev accepted it and then cupped a hand around the director's lighter. He inhaled the rough smoke deep into his lungs – anything to suppress the lingering smell of death. He felt the nicotine worming its way out to his extremities, and the sudden weakness it brought reminded him that he hadn't eaten since breakfast. He took a moment to savour the sensation and then nodded his thanks to the director, who waved it away. It was only when he was back at the examination room that Korolev realized they hadn't exchanged a single word.

In his absence, Gueginov had applied make-up to cover as much as possible of the damage to the girl's face. It was a trick Korolev had seen him perform before. The first time he'd been surprised at the garish colours, but as the photographs were taken with black and white film the end effect was lifelike. Chestnova was assisting him by positioning the head, using a towel to hold it in place. The head seemed loose in her hands and wouldn't stay in place. Gueginov and Chestnova looked up at him with welcoming smiles and Korolev detected the sharp smell of alcohol. Gueginov pointed at a beaker full of clear liquid.

'Duh-doctor Che-Chestnova fuh-found us some muh-medical spirits, Comrade. It's the buh-business. That's yours.'

'It's best with jam. A little bit of jam in the spirit and it tastes very good. But we have no jam today, I'm afraid.' Dr Chestnova seemed markedly more cheerful than before. 'See? We have made her beautiful.'

'I puh-put cotton wool in her chuh-cheeks, I think it works wuh-wuh-well.'

Gueginov looked down at the corpse with a pleased expression. The girl's hair was still wet from where Chestnova had washed it clean.

'She was good looking, the girl,' Korolev said, as much to himself as the others.

'Yuh-yes. Do you think we should huh-have the eye open or closed? I'll tuh-take her in puh-profile obviously.'

Gueginov opened the girl's eyelid with his thumb and looked to Korolev for approval. Korolev shook his head, disconcerted by the dead girl's gaze.

'Yuh-yes. I think, you're ruh-right.' Gueginov said and shut the eye once more. Then, satisfied with the positioning of the girl's head and the arrangement of her features, Gueginov picked up the camera and the flash lit up the room twice. Chestnova let the head fall back onto the table and the jaw fell open revealing the white teeth and the butchered mouth.

'Notice anything about the teeth, Comrade?' Chestnova asked, picking up the loose head and tilting it towards him once again.

'It looks like he broke a few,' Korolev said, then looked again. 'They're exceptionally white.'

'Indeed, which may be something to note in itself, but see these fillings? Amalgam. Well, Comrade, the Ministry of Health hasn't permitted our dentists to use amalgam fillings for the last ten years at least. And these fillings weren't done that long ago.'

'So the fillings were done outside the Soviet Union?'

'Perhaps the girl is a foreigner . . .'

'Huh-her clothes.' Gueginov's voice came from the corner where he was holding up her skirt. 'They look fuh-foreign to me. No luh-labels, but they feel like cuh-capitalist cluh-clothes. Perhaps she was a suh-saboteur? Fuh-fell out with her fellows and look what happened to her.'

Korolev ran the fabric through his fingers. It felt wondrously soft.

'Perhaps, or she could have worked abroad in an embassy or with a trade delegation. And, of course, there are plenty of foreigners in Moscow these days. Volunteers, industrial specialists, Comintern employees and so on. We may be able to match her teeth to dental records if she's listed as a missing person. We'll look into it. Thank you – an excellent observation.'

Dr Chestnova smiled proudly, although perhaps a little lop-sidedly. Korolev wondered how much medical spirit the two of them had drunk while he'd been out of the room.

'I always do my duty,' she said, reaching for a saw from the tray of instruments that stood beside the operating table. 'And now I shall look into the brain.'

Korolev felt his jaw clench. He took a quick look at his watch and gave a curt nod to the others.

'Please call me if there are any further developments. I have to get back to Petrovka.'

He decided to ignore the muffled giggle that followed him from the room.

Chapter Five

IT WAS past nine o'clock when Korolev finished combining his notes on the autopsy and the crime scene into a report for General Popov. While the autopsy had thrown up some interesting possibilities, not least that the dead woman was a foreigner, the forensic investigation team had come up with very little, as Semionov had predicted. There were fingerprints all over the room, but the fingermarks that were bloody had all turned out either to have been made by gloves, probably leather, or had belonged to the dead woman. They'd begin fingerprinting the Komsomol members who frequented the church in the morning, but the head of the forensic team thought it unlikely that they would come up with anything useful, especially as they had taken several hundred impressions from the sacristy alone. Korolev cursed under his breath as he finished writing and then began to read from the beginning for mistakes.

He took his time, considering the available facts from every angle. As he read, he began to form in his mind a very loose picture of the murderer and, indeed, of the victim. Nothing substantial, just feelings and impressions, but he'd been an investigator long enough to know intuition should never be ignored. Even though it was hard for him to be definite, he was beginning to think the killing showed an element of forethought that was unusual. For a start, the murderer's wearing of gloves and the lack of any forensic data indicated a care and detachment not present in the violent sexual murders he'd investigated previously. Usually the murderer was caught up in the fever of the moment and therefore careless. He might try to clear up evidence afterwards, but by that stage he was in a state of elation, fear or shock, and his efforts were affected accordingly. This fellow seemed to be different. Yes, there was blood and gore and lots of unpleasant detail, but there was very little evidence. He'd been careful and, as if to confirm Korolev's supposition, there were no signs of rape. There was torture, clearly, but the use of electricity, the way the body parts had been arranged and the deliberate nature of the injuries made him wonder whether the mutilations hadn't some significance outside the violent act itself. He was even beginning to suspect that the mutilations might be a smokescreen and that the murder might have a motive beyond the obvious.

He rubbed his eyes as he finished and looked at his watch. It had been a full day and it was time he made his way home. He smiled at the thought. His cousin's partitioned room had been tiny with only enough space for a bed for Mikhail and a mattress on the floor for Korolev, their clothes hanging from nails on the wall. They'd listened at night to their neighbours' whispered squabbles and even quieter lovemaking, whispering in turn to each other as they passed a bottle backwards and forwards. At least in the new apartment there would be space, far above the norm for the Moscow district, and a degree of privacy that most citizens only saw in films, and foreign films at that. He felt like pinching himself.

Zhenia would have liked it, he thought. His ex-wife had given up their old room in the Presnaya district a year or so after the divorce and returned to her people in Zagorsk. She'd never much liked Moscow, but as one of the first Soviet-educated female engineers, the capital had offered her opportunities for advancement, as well as the excitement of being at the centre of a Revolution that was transforming history itself. Indeed, she'd been a poster girl for the new revolutionary society; why she'd chosen

Korolev, when half the men in Moscow had been after her, had been a mystery to him. After three years of marriage it had been to her as well. It hadn't helped that he'd been an investigator, of course not, but then she'd worked even longer hours. They'd met in bed like strangers sometimes, and from one of those encounters Yuri had been conceived. The thought of Yuri saddened him; he hadn't seen the boy for six months. She had a new man now, a doctor, and it worried him. How long would it be before Yuri started calling the stranger 'Papa'? Would he even remember Korolev the next time they met?

Korolev put the handwritten pages in order, wrote a request for four copies, then took out his hat from the bottom drawer of the desk in preparation for the walk home. Zagorsk was just too damned far away – but he'd make the trip in the spring, no matter what.

On the way out he stopped on the first floor and knocked at a wooden window, which guarded the all-female typing pool as though it were an Ottoman harem. A moment passed before the panel slid back and a tired female face peered out at him. He couldn't remember seeing her before and he watched her examine his epaulettes, noticing the slight stiffening of posture that they brought.

'Yes, Captain? Something urgent?'

'A report for the general. He needs it for tomorrow morning. Four copies altogether.'

'Four copies.' The woman flicked back her grey-streaked brown hair from her eyes as she examined the papers. The gesture was almost sensuous. 'Captain Korolev,' she read. 'That's you?'

'Yes.'

'Eight o'clock in the morning?'

'Thank you.' He thought he saw the ghost of a smile lighten her features. 'One thing, though. It's not one for an inexperienced typist. It's a murder, a young woman – not very pleasant. Probably best to give it to someone who's been here a bit longer.'

She took a quick look at the first page, raised her eyebrows and nodded her head gravely in agreement, then smiled before sliding the panel shut.

He walked home, keeping to the main thoroughfares and maintaining a good pace. There were the usual queues outside the late-night shops and tired groups of workers, covered from head to toe in grime, were making their way back to their hostels, passing their replacements, only a little cleaner, heading in the opposite direction. There were students, hands bunching thread-bare coats around their throats, and, even this close to the Kremlin, beggars with the dead eyes of the starving. There were more of them recently – despite it being a criminal offence with a five-year ticket attached. Yet, for all the people, there was not much noise. The rumble of a truck passing drowned out what little conversation there was. It was as if the citizens suspected they were being listened to, and Korolev suspected they might have a point.

Turning a corner, Korolev saw two men with the strange pigeon walk that marked them out as belonging to the caste of Thieves. They recognized him for what he was as well, but showed no obvious reaction, except that one made a comment to the other as they walked by. Of all the people he'd passed they were the only ones who seemed relaxed. The Party believed in the principle of re-education for criminals, and so hooligans and bandits were receiving political lectures rather than lengthy sentences. What was more, Korolev, as a policeman, suspected the only real education the Thieves received in the Zone, as the camp and prison system was known, was from other Thieves. And the leniency to professional criminals meant Soviet cities weren't as safe as they should be.

It was a different story for political prisoners, of course – they were punished to the full extent of the law.

Still, the streets seemed quiet tonight, perhaps because it was cold, certainly below freezing point. He looked up at the dark sky lurking above the street lights and wondered if it would snow. He turned the corner of the Lubianka and, as usual, scanned the street ahead for trouble. It was more out of habit than from a perception of risk – after all, any sane criminal would stay well clear of the NKVD headquarters – so he was surprised when he saw black cars pulled up outside the Dzherzhinskaya Metro station and a crowd that swirled and jostled with excitement.

As he approached, the several hundred people seemingly laying siege to the station entrance appeared all the stranger. Perhaps it was a terrorist attack or an accident. He quickened his pace and patted his holster, checking the gun was secured in case there was rough stuff ahead, but the crowd seemed in a good mood, even cheering, as they surged forward and backward. A line of Chekists and Red Army soldiers, faces pale under the street lights, had joined elbows to hold the ever-growing number of citizens away from a convoy of black cars that was parked in front of the large illuminated M marking the station entrance. The line looked as though it would be brushed aside at any moment, but, despite the number of people, and Korolev estimated there were now close to a thousand souls waving thin hands and red handkerchiefs, he had the sense that the situation was under control.

The shouting slackened for a moment as the gleaming door of one of the limousines opened and a familiar face, pitted by smallpox and bedecked with a thick moustache, emerged, black eyes taking everything in. It was a powerful gaze, as sure of itself as a champion boxer's, and Korolev felt his own hand rising in salute. He joined in the growl of approval, which built into a roar that sent the hairs on the back of his neck shivering as his fist clenched above his head.

'Stalin! Stalin! Stalin!' the crowd cheered and Korolev bellowed along with them. Bulky Chekists gathered round the General Secretary, but they seemed small beside him, as though the world had to adjust to his scale because he clearly wasn't that tall, maybe five foot three. It must be the presence of the man,

Korolev thought, and then found himself shouting Stalin's name again as the great man smiled at the crowd, his moustache curling upwards. He touched his hand stiffly to his military cap in acknowledgement, but only as if to say, 'You aren't cheering me, you're cheering my position in the Party, and I accept the adulation on that basis alone.'

One of his bodyguards leant to whisper in Stalin's ear and the General Secretary nodded in agreement, then smiled at the crowd once again before disappearing into the Metro station. Other men stepped out of the cars now: Ezhov, Molotov, Budyonny with his cavalryman's twirling moustache, Ordzhonikidze, Mikoyan. It seemed as though half the Politburo had decided to take the Metro home. They smiled blearily from behind the collars of their greatcoats and leather jackets and followed Stalin inside. Some of them seemed a little unsteady on their feet, as though they'd been drinking. Their waves and salutes were friendly also, similarly dismissive of the adulation: 'We're all workers for the Revolution together, Comrades, no need to make a fuss.' And when the last of them had disappeared inside the crowd wanted to follow them, but the Chekists held firm and exhorted them to be patient, to give the leaders some room.

'Stand back, Citizens!' a man with a loudhailer instructed and the crowd reluctantly complied, stepping back as the Chekist cordon advanced. Now that Stalin had gone, they turned to each other and discussed what they'd seen – enthusiastic, like children. Korolev skirted the crowd, hearing snatches of conversation as he moved past.

'He wasn't tall, was he? But strong – like an ox.'

'Did you see his pipe? I smoke a pipe myself. I wonder what brand he uses?'

Korolev manoeuvred past them, feeling the same pride as his fellow Muscovites at the leadership's decision to come out amongst them.

He was nearly clear when he felt his elbow taken in a strong grip and he turned to find himself facing Staff Colonel Gregorin.

'Captain Korolev, are you only going home now? Working late on the investigation, were you?' Gregorin pulled a cigarette case out of his uniform's breast pocket; at some stage it had received a large dent and it opened stiffly. Gregorin saw his interest and closed the lid to tap his finger in the middle of the circular mark.

'A bullet. It saved my life – now it's my good-luck charm. If it weren't for the case, there would only have been a dead Corporal Gregorin rather than a live Staff Colonel Gregorin. I consider it a useful reminder of the arbitrariness of fate. And doctors tell us smoking weakens the chest . . .'

Gregorin chuckled at the well-worn joke and Korolev responded with an awkward smile. The colonel had taken him by surprise and he took the offered cigarette happily, relieved to have something to do with his hands. He reached into his pocket for the matches he habitually carried, but Gregorin stopped him, cracking open a lighter and moving the two of them away from the crowd.

'Comrade Stalin decided to visit the Metro on a whim. He's seen it in construction, and was at the opening, of course, but he wanted to experience it like an ordinary citizen. A spontaneous thought, so we were all called out at a moment's notice to provide security. A great responsibility.'

He pointed to a black car parked on the street about thirty metres further along the street, 'Can I give you a lift home? It will save you the walk.'

Korolev nodded, feeling he should participate in the conversation, but finding himself at a loss for words.

'Good. Bolshoi Nikolo-Vorobinsky, isn't it? Oh, don't look so alarmed, it's my business to know about those who interest me, whether for professional or personal reasons. It's a good building

– you'll like your neighbours. Babel lives upstairs. Do you know him? The writer? If not, you should make it your business to do so – a citizen has a duty to be cultured these days.'

'I know of him, yes,' Korolev managed to say, recalling the writer's all-too-vivid descriptions of the war against the Poles.

'I can introduce you, if you'd like. He may be useful to you. In fact, I'll make it a point to do so. He'll enjoy you, two veterans of the war in Poland – I can see you gossiping away like old women. Maybe he'll write about you. Who knows?'

'What could a man like Comrade Babel see in a humble Militia investigator like me, Colonel? And, for that matter, what is your interest?'

Gregorin opened the driver's door of a black Emka and Korolev saw humour flash in his dark brown eyes. The colonel's authority hung easily about him and his thick black hair, swarthy skin and strong features made Korolev wonder if he might be a Georgian, like Stalin, although there was no clear accent when he spoke. He carried himself like an athlete. Not a wide or tall man, but he looked as though he could handle himself.

'You underestimate yourself, Comrade,' Gregorin said, when Korolev was sitting in the car. 'I didn't choose you to lecture tomorrow for no reason – you get results. It will do our students no harm to learn a thing or two from such an effective investigator. And General Popov recommended you – he thinks highly of your abilities.'

'I'm pleased to hear it,' Korolev said.

'So, tell me. How's the case going? Making any progress?'

'It's in its early stages. We haven't much to go on just yet, but there are some indications. I've written up an initial report – I'll bring it along tomorrow morning.'

'Good. As it happens, it's a fortuitous coincidence that you're working on this case.'

'Why, Colonel?'

'Because the higher echelons have asked me to provide a State Security oversight.'

Sitting back in to the driver's seat, the colonel exhaled a perfect smoke ring, which hung round and still for a moment before gradually disintegrating. Gregorin observed the smoke ring with satisfaction.

'But why? The case has no political element, does it?' Korolev was mystified as to why the NKVD would be interested in a simple murder, albeit a nasty one. But then he remembered the possibility that the girl was a foreigner. He answered his own question in a whisper.

'Oh – but it does have a political element. The dead girl. She has foreign fillings, and her clothes . . .'

He let his voice trail off. He didn't want to criticize Soviet clothes in front of an NKVD staff colonel, but her clothes were clearly of a better quality than anything the USSR could produce.

Gregorin leant forward, the smile slipping from his face. 'What's this about the girl? Have you established her identity?'

'Not yet, Colonel, but we think there's a possibility she may not have been a Soviet citizen.'

Gregorin gave an abrupt nod of his head and motioned with his cigarette for Korolev to continue. He listened without interruption as Korolev told him all he knew about the girl and her death.

'Is that all? Anything else?' he asked when Korolev had finished.

'That's it, so far.'

'Very interesting. The higher echelons were correct.'

'So it does have a political element?'

'Yes, I believe it does.'

'But, if that's so, surely it will be taken over by State Security.'

Gregorin blew on the tip of his cigarette, the orange glow lighting his face for a moment. He looked pensive.

'There's certainly a political *element*, that's true. But it's still a murder.'

'I don't understand.'

'That's not necessarily a problem. Just investigate the matter as if it were an ordinary case. That's all we ask of you. Understanding is something you should leave to us.'

'But what *is* the political element, Comrade Colonel? Can I at least be permitted to know that?' Korolev couldn't help a note of frustration entering his voice.

Gregorin's mouth was a straight black line in the faint glow from the street lights. He regarded Korolev in silence and then he smiled, again relaxed. He turned back to look out of the window at the thinning crowd.

'What I'm about to tell you is secret. Understood?'

'As you wish,' Korolev said, and wondered what the hell he'd got himself into this time.

'Very well – you'll be aware of the State's ongoing efforts to raise finances for the current Five Year Plan, yes? I'm sure you, like most workers, lend a proportion of your salary in the form of State bonds to assist in the struggle to achieve the plan's objectives. Every citizen has tightened their belt for the greater good. And we're on target to achieve those objectives.'

The belt on the colonel's shiny leather jacket didn't look as though it was tighter than it should be, but Korolev held his tongue.

'It's a question of survival,' Korolev said.

'Indeed it is, and if we're to withstand the enemies of socialism, the State needs money to acquire the technology and to buy the weapons to defend what we've achieved since 1917. Borrowing money abroad is difficult, of course – why would capitalists lend money to a Revolution that seeks to bring about their end? So we have to earn the foreign money we need. We go hungry so that we can sell our wheat to whoever pays the best price – a temporary situation, of course, but vital until recently. Now, as Comrade Stalin says, things are getting better. We're turning the corner.'

'I often remember those words of his,' Korolev said.

'Well, one way we raise finance is through the sale of confiscated assets, such as works of art, jewellery, precious books and other valuables. The sales are managed by the Ministry of State Security – the NKVD, as it happens. Recently, however, we've become aware that there is a certain amount of "leakage"; items have been showing up in Europe or America that should still be here in Moscow. We know some of the people involved and it's possible your victim is connected to this conspiracy. In fact, based on your description of her, I'm sure of it.'

Korolev thought for a moment, digesting the information and coming to a conclusion. 'But that means . . .' He stopped himself in mid-sentence. Gregorin exhaled smoke calmly.

'We're investigating it, of course. No family, not even State Security's, is without an ugly member. Arrests have been made. But this is murder and that's an interesting development. It smacks of desperation.'

'Do you know who she was?'

'She could be one of two possible candidates. With a bit of luck, I'll be able to tell you for definite tomorrow. If you have photographs of the dead woman, that will help.'

'And you're sure it's one of these two because?'

Gregorin looked at his watch and shook his head. 'Nearly ten o'clock. I'd better get you home. You have a busy day ahead of you.'

He turned on the ignition and the car engine started immediately. Korolev was impressed – he'd heard the Emka's starter motor was unreliable.

'It's a good car, this. You see? Another great achievement of the Soviet State. We needed to produce our own automobiles, so we put our minds to it. We devoted the necessary finance, manpower and expertise and then we achieved the objective. That's the Bolshevik way.'

Gregorin paused while he concentrated on overtaking a slow-moving line of military trucks that was trundling along Dzherzhinsky Street, heavy canvas sides flapping.

'That's what we want you to do: put your mind to catching the murderer and devote all your resources and efforts to that aim. Investigate every lead, question every suspect, leave no stone unturned – treat it as you would an ordinary crime. We don't think the traitors know about our own investigation, so to do anything else might alert them. Understood? It's possible that the killing really was the work of a madman – but it's more probable it's the work of these saboteurs and the mutilation and torture are just a smokescreen. Pursue your investigation vigorously and perhaps you'll distract attention from our own enquiries.'

'I always investigate to the best of my ability,' Korolev said, feeling a little offended.

§

Five minutes later, Gregorin pulled up outside Number 4 Bolshoi Nikolo-Vorobinsky and switched off the car's engine. He turned to Korolev. 'Bring the autopsy photographs tomorrow, please. They'll help me identify her for you.'

'I have some questions,' Korolev began, but Gregorin shook his head.

'Perhaps tomorrow. Sleep well, Comrade.'

Gregorin's eyes were shadowed in the weak light, but Korolev didn't imagine they were anything other than cold. He stepped out of the car and watched the colonel drive away, knowing people were looking down from behind closed curtains. No one liked a car that had State Security written all over it to show up in front of their house this late at night, even if this time it had deposited a resident instead of taking one away. He made a silent apology to his new neighbours as he entered the building, feeling his tiredness with each step. He would think about what the staff colonel had said in the morning – there was nothing to be gained by worrying about it now. Reaching the door of the apartment, he rooted in his pocket for the key and then had a clear image of it sitting on the bed in his room, where he'd left it that afternoon. He cursed his stupidity and checked his pockets once again. He looked at his watch, past ten o'clock – he hoped Citizeness Koltsova would still be awake. He patted his coat one last time and then knocked gently, waiting for a response that didn't come. He knocked again, but this time with more force. There was a pause and then the sound of a door opening inside the apartment, footsteps and finally a woman's voice, suspicious but calm.

'Who is it?'

'I apologize, Citizeness, I'm your new neighbour. Korolev. I left my key inside this morning. On the bed. I know it's very late.' He sensed people listening from the other apartments and lowered his voice. 'Could you let me in?'

The door inched open and he found himself staring down the black barrel of a revolver. He took a step back.

'Captain Korolev?' her voice asked and he lifted his eyes from the gun's muzzle to find a pair of equally daunting blue eyes staring at him with unreadable intent.

'Yes,' he agreed.

The gun dropped a few inches, not that he felt any more comfortable with it pointing at his lower stomach. 'I'm sorry about the time,' he managed to say.

She was really quite beautiful, a narrow but firm jaw line below razor-sharp cheekbones and then short, bobbed hair that shone in the light from the hallway. If it hadn't been for the gun he would have enjoyed looking at her. 'I'm not normally forgetful, you can be assured.'

'I should hope not,' she responded, looking him up and down with a quizzical expression, as though not entirely sure how he fitted into her world. Her scowl relaxed, very slowly, into a smile as firm and uncompromising as a *Pravda* editorial and he found himself breathing again. She opened the door wider, slipped the revolver into her dressing-gown pocket and extended her hand.

'Comrade Korolev, we're pleased to have a member of the Moscow Criminal Investigation Division in the building; Luborov told me about you. Welcome. The gun wasn't loaded. You have to be careful in Moscow, even in a building such as this. So many bandits around. Although, of course, I'm sure that's not your fault.'

In fact, judging by the way she raised her eyebrows, it seemed she wasn't sure of this at all. Korolev shrugged his shoulders in apology, took the offered hand and wasn't surprised to discover her grip was as strong as a man's.

'Thank you,' he said. 'I hope you've a permit for the gun – there are severe penalties.' As soon as the words were out of his mouth, he didn't like the sound of them. Still, pulling a piece on your neighbour wasn't the way to start sharing a flat together either.

'Of course I do,' she said, with a protective pat of her pocket. She perhaps spoke a little too quickly, however.

'Natasha,' she called along the corridor, 'it's Comrade Korolev, our new neighbour, come and meet him.'

A small face appeared and disappeared in a doorway behind her. Koltsova laughed, her face lighting up for a moment, as though a switch had been turned on. Her skin seemed to glow when she laughed. She turned back to Korolev and smiled. 'She's a little shy, Comrade, and she doesn't like uniforms. Do you wear it all the time?'

He shook his head. 'No. Not at all, hardly. Normally I wear ordinary clothes. Just today, you see, and only because I absolutely had to wear a uniform. It was an exception. In fact the moths have been at it, it's so long since I've worn it. Look.'

He showed her the sleeve of his uniform jacket and was rewarded with a smile that seemed to express pity rather than empathy. He tried to collect himself, but his mouth had already opened.

'You see I'm a detective. Criminal. I mean I'm a detective who catches criminals, of course. A detective criminal would be absurd.' He put his hand to his forehead and closed his eyes for a moment hoping he would be somewhere else when he opened them. 'I apologize, Comrade. I've had a long day.'

'Come in, Comrade Captain Korolev,' she said, with a resigned tone to her voice. She followed him into the communal kitchen. 'Welcome to your new home.'

AN EASIER job this time, he thought to himself, as Tesak* the Thief began to tell him what he wanted to hear. Straightforward even. You just knew where you were with fellows like Tesak. He might puff out his chest, threaten and swear, but at the end of the day Tesak only believed in one thing and that was Tesak. So when he was really in trouble, when he faced the choice between oblivion and survival, he was always going to choose survival. After all, if there was an afterlife, someone like Tesak wasn't going to heaven – that was for sure.

They tied the Thief between two metal pillars, arms and legs spread wide, and then it was just him and Tesak, already feeling the pain of being hung up like a drying skin. At first there'd been the usual bravado; the fellow had thought he was just another cop looking for information. He could take a beating and had told him so. He'd even spat at him. But his swagger had begun to leave him when the gauntlets and the apron appeared and, by the time he opened his box of tricks, Tesak wasn't looking quite so confident.

'We live in a modern world,' he said to Tesak as he cut open his shirt, button by button. The buttons fell onto the concrete floor one by one, bouncing and rolling across the hard surface.

'That's a new fucking shirt, flatfoot.' Tesak was indignant, yes, but it was the indignation of a frightened man. So far, so good. Now was the time to establish the rules of engagement, so he stepped back a pace,

---

* *Hatchet*

71

looked Tesak in the eye, and then put his entire body into a back-fisted slap that spun Tesak's head hard against his upstretched arm. He had Tesak's attention after that.

'As if I care about your shirt. The very thought. Let's be clear – from now on you will only speak in answer to a question. Understand?'

Tesak just looked at him, a little confused from the blow to the head perhaps, but quiet now. He stepped closer once again, close enough to detect the stale alcohol on Tesak's breath. The Thief's eyes were now completely focused on the knife as it slowly climbed towards his midriff.

'Now, what do these tattoos mean?' he asked, looking at the rough blue etchings on the man's chest. He touched the blade to the skin underneath the ranked profiles of Marx, Lenin and Stalin staring across Tesak's chest from beneath a Soviet flag. 'You're not telling me you're a Bolshevik, are you, Tesak?'

'Not me. No way. That's so no firing squad will ever put Tesak in some shallow flower bed. Reds like you don't take potshots at your big men, do you? See? Not unless you want to end up in the same place.'

'You think I give a damn about Marx?' he said and then, taking hold of Tesak's neck for purchase, sliced Marx away with one clean cut. Then he punched him twice to stop the roar of pain. The comment about Marx was textbook, of course. Sudden changes in the expected parameters of a situation undermined defences. Tesak hung there whimpering, looking down at the bubbling rawness of his chest. He took the opportunity to gag him, whispering to him, as he did so.

'And I'm no flatfoot either. Tell me what I need to know and I'll make your death easy.' Tesak's eyes bulged as he lifted the blade once again. 'If not?' he continued, and to answer his own question he sliced Lenin away. Now Stalin alone stared across the mangled chest. Tesak was struggling desperately against the ropes and so he took the mason's hammer from his bag and hit his kneecaps hard, one after the other. Tesak mewled through the gag, but hung limply now that his legs couldn't support him.

'As I said, we live in a modern world, and one of the glories of Soviet power is the progress we've made in the field of electricity. Such a useful thing – and we're leading the world when it comes to electricity, you know. Every household will have a little Lenin's lamp soon, dazzling the peasants with four hundred watts of light at the flick of a switch. You'll have read about it in the paper.' He considered the likelihood of the Thief being able to read for a moment. 'Or perhaps not.'

He picked up the prod and showed it to Tesak.

'Anyway, every Soviet citizen should experience the reality of electricity. Theory is all well and good, but practical application is the thing.'

Then he'd attached the prod to the battery and he'd been surprised at how much noise Tesak had made, even through the gag. So he did know something about electricity. There were always surprises.

After a few minutes' work, he'd removed the gag and the whimpering Thief had bargained for his life, as was to be expected.

'What have you got to offer me? Money? I don't want your money. Love? I don't need it. What have you got for me? Come now, Tesak, you know what I want. Where have they hidden it?'

'I don't know. Count Kolya is the only one who knows. He's the one you want. I didn't even know it was real – I thought it was a fucking copy, believe me, Comrade.'

'The pig's no comrade to the goose, Tesak. You call me citizen.'

The Thief was hanging limply in the ropes, the bloody remnants of the clothes that had been cut away from him bunched around his ankles and shoulders. He looked ready. One final push perhaps. He almost felt sympathy for the Thief, but then he hardened his heart and put the gag back in place.

Chapter Six

KOROLEV awoke at five o'clock, as he always did. There were times he wished he could sleep for a few minutes more, but his mother, the tsar's army, and finally the Red Army, had trained him so that he had no choice in the matter. 'God gives to those who rise early,' had been his mother's mantra, but this particular morning he allowed himself a moment or two to savour the pleasure of the new room.

On the ceiling above him the floral pattern of the moulding was just visible in the pale creamy glow from the streetlamp outside and he found himself smiling with very un-Soviet, very bourgeois, very proprietorial pleasure at the beauty of it. Who else did he know who had a ceiling rose with plaster grapes and flowers and even what looked like apples? No one. Not even the general, he suspected. Nor did the draught from the window that nipped at his nose detract from the comfort of the new bed or the warmth of the quilt that had been leant to him by Koltsova. A strange woman, her. One moment she's pointing a gun at his heart and the next thing she's loading him down with bedclothes. Not from Moscow, of course. Odessa. Everyone knew they were different down there – the Odessians weren't Ukrainian and they weren't Russian either. They were just Odessian.

He lay there thinking how curious life was and how, at this particular moment and in this particular place, it had suddenly become quite pleasant. It was only with great reluctance that he reminded himself of the impending lecture. Some preparatory notes would stand him in good stead.

He swung his legs down onto the floorboards, found them cold to the touch, and crossed over to the window to look out. Snow had fallen overnight, sloping up against the wall opposite where the wind had pushed it. A solitary set of footprints marked out the middle of the lane – winter was early this year. The day before had had a bite to it, and the cold season had whispered its arrival in the chill breeze that had slipped through the streets as darkness fell. Personally, he greeted it as an old friend; the first snow was always welcome to him. Winters were hard, of course, but the snow masked Moscow's imperfections and, at night, silenced the city into a semblance of tranquillity. Moscow in winter was a beautiful, hard, breathless place where the only smell was the inside of your coat. He wouldn't miss the summer and the stench and swelter. How the People smelt in summer. He hoped it wouldn't be long before soap became a production priority.

His assessment of the snow complete, he turned from the window and knelt beside the bed and, his head upright, crossed himself in the Orthodox way, raised his eyes to heaven and thanked the Lord for allowing him to experience such a beautiful morning in such a fine apartment, then began to say the prayers his mother had taught him, adding, at the end, a plea for the advancement of soap to full production as soon as possible, feeling it his duty, both as a Believer and as a loyal Soviet citizen.

The point of praying to a God that the Party said didn't exist concerned him momentarily, as it did every morning. But then sometimes, looking back, it was clear that the Party made mistakes. After all, look how they'd nurtured that viper Trotsky for all those years. Perhaps it would turn out they were wrong about God as well. And even if they weren't, well, it wouldn't hurt to be on the safe side in the meantime.

Standing stiffly, he began his stretching. Wherever he was, and whatever his schedule for the day, he tried to spend a few minutes exercising. If that meant he had to get up a little earlier, then so be it. He moved on to some light callisthenics, then press-ups and sit-ups, reminding himself to bring his weights over from the old apartment later. He finished his routine with some more stretching and then, slightly out of breath and aware of a pleasant dull tiredness in his muscles, he forced himself to run on the spot for five minutes, the window rattling as his feet made the floorboards bang like drums. Finished, he went through to the kitchen, where he cleaned himself thoroughly at the sink, keeping an eye on the corridor when he washed himself below the waist. The water was surprisingly cold and it was with something of an effort that he resisted vocalizing his body's shock, but as there was a young girl in the apartment, and he had only just moved in, he thought it best to bear it in silence.

Clean-shaven and his morning rituals over, he put on a vest that had seen better days and went to sit at the writing table. Outside the first cockerel announced the new day, immediately answered by two more nearby. There were regulations about keeping livestock in communal apartments and residential blocks, but many of the new Muscovites were from the country and found ways round the restrictions. Even here, in Kitaj-Gorod, amongst the Party elite and the bosses, there were chickens pushed into small wooden runs on flat roofs or the corner of a courtyard. Once the winter really bit, they'd be kept inside, stepping over and around their peasant owners, who often slept in shifts.

He opened his notebook and began to write. 'Organization.' A disorganized file was not much use, in his opinion. There were times in Petrovka Street when he had to leave the room, so distressed did he become at Yasimov's sloppy approach to filing. He was certain that his friend's successful convictions were often not the actual perpetrators, although Yasimov argued that, even if they weren't guilty of the crime in question, the people he convicted were certainly guilty of something. Korolev shook his head, believing it was Yasimov's duty to identify the right criminal for the right crime, not just assign the crimes willy-nilly to which-ever criminal took his fancy.

'Subsections' was the next thing he wrote. He wrote it underneath 'Organization' as 'subsections' was itself a subsection. Then, in a column that reached halfway down the page, he added 'statements', 'photographs', 'evidence', 'autopsy/medical report (if any)', 'fingerprints', 'other forensic data', 'suspects', 'alibis', 'lines of enquiry' and 'miscellaneous'. Then he started on his favourite topic: 'Purpose'.

In Korolev's opinion, a good file should be like a mathematical formula from which, provided the necessary information was entered in the correct order, the solution would result as inevitably as night followed day. He was aware that some of his colleagues laughed at him when he said things like this, but it didn't change his view that the purpose of a file was, as with all police work, to identify and detain the perpetrators of particular crimes, Yasimov notwithstanding. A good file did this by providing a sound basis for logical deduction. A good policeman used the tools at his disposal to pursue criminals and serve them their just desserts and, when the time came, a good prison was one which kept the criminals secured for the period of time the People's Court determined they were to spend there. This was Soviet logic, beautiful in its simplicity and directness.

He looked again at the notes he'd made and wondered whether the skills he hoped to teach the cadets might possibly be used against innocent people. Yagoda had gone too far, that was clear, but the Central Committee had removed him. The Party had to take the utmost care to protect the State, of course, but within reason, and the expectation was that things would be different under Ezhov. However, now there were rumours that Ezhov had declared, on taking up his new position, that it would be better that ten innocent people should suffer than one spy go free – that 'When you chop wood, chips fly.' Korolev sighed and stood up from the table, imagining a host of innocent chips on a sawmill floor. Still, his filing techniques, clear and logical as they were, should operate to protect the innocent, or so he reassured himself.

With this happier thought in mind he put on the rest of his clothes. The image of the indiscriminate axe wouldn't leave him, but he did his best to brush it aside and, putting his notes in his briefcase, closed the apartment door quietly behind him.

He'd just succeeded in clicking the lock gently shut when he heard a cough behind him and turned to see a bundle of black woollen shawl on three legs swaying precariously from side to side. On closer examination, one of the three legs turned out to be a walking stick.

'So you're the *Ment*?'

'*Ment*? That's not a very polite way to refer to a Militiaman, Citizeness.'

'What are you going to do, arrest me? I'm eighty-three years old and, anyway, I've been to prison before. It's not so bad. They feed you quite well and the conversation is entertaining. Quite intellectual sometimes.'

Korolev looked for a means of escape, but she had the corridor blocked and, other than standing his ground, the only option was to retreat into the apartment, which he didn't have time to do. He pointed to his watch.

'Excuse me, Citizeness, I've no intention of arresting you, but I do have to go to work.'

'Work, is it? Well listen here, Mr *Ment*, what I want to know is this – how did you manage to get an elephant up these old stairs? I found it difficult enough to get up them myself. The elephant must have had a terrible time.'

'An elephant?'

'Exactly, an elephant. Which reminds me of a story about sheep. Have you heard it? Some sheep tried to cross the border to Finland. "Why are you running away to Finland?" the border guard asks. "It's the NKVD," the sheep say. "Comrade Stalin has ordered them to arrest all the elephants." "But you aren't elephants," the guard says. "We know," say the sheep, "but try telling that to the Chekists." It's a good one, isn't it?'

It was also the joke that had cost Mendeleyev a stretch in the Zone and Korolev put a finger to his lips, looking over his shoulder to get the point across. The old woman scowled in response, but said nothing.

'My exercises,' Korolev said, changing the subject as realization dawned, 'that was what the noise was. I apologize if I woke you.'

'Woke me? My dear Mr *Ment*, you woke the whole damned house and half the damned street. Can't you go to an athletics club or a gymnasium if you must undertake these dreadful exercises? I thought the Judgement Day had finally come, but then I reminded myself that God was a fiction of primitive man's imagination and concluded it was elephants. I'm sorry it wasn't – they'd make interesting neighbours. I believe they mate for life, like swans.'

'I apologize again, Citizeness. Allow me to introduce myself, Captain Alexei Korolev of the Moscow Criminal Investigation Division.'

'Yes, so I believe,' the old woman said, condescension colouring her voice. 'Maria Lobkovskaya. I live below you, although if you do too many more of your exercises you'll probably come through the ceiling and end up living downstairs too.' She regarded him with a keen eye. 'You look like an honest fellow, for a policeman, and not bad looking. Why aren't you married?'

'I was married, Citizeness, but it ended.'

'It was different in my day, you married for life, like the elephants. Now you sign a form and it never happened. Anyway, you must be on your way. You have work to do. All those hooligans on the street and you standing around talking to old women.'

§

Outside the air was fresh in the early light and his breath came out in a fog as thick as cigarette smoke. The temperature made him feel awake and strangely cheerful. He was glad he had his greatcoat to keep the chill off and that his feet were warm inside his soft felt *valenki* boots and, most of all, that there was no one else on the streets as yet. The only sounds as he walked along were the soft crunch of snow underfoot and an occasional early-morning voice from an open courtyard. He found himself humming the tune from the 'March of the Happy-Go Lucky Guys', and the humming soon turned into quiet singing.

> 'We'll grasp, discover and attain it all,
> The cold North Pole and the clear blue sky.
> When our country demands that we be heroes,
> Then heroes we will become.'

As he sang, his feet swung to its rhythm. He looked quickly at his watch – he had to pick up the report for Gregorin from Petrovka Street and he decided, having plenty of time, to walk past the Kremlin and see it in its first snowy coat since the spring.

§

In the end, the lecture went well. Colonel Gregorin met him inside the surprisingly plain entrance to the NKVD training school – there was no furniture apart from a metal table, and paintings of Dzerzhinsky and Stalin were the only decorations on the white walls, apart from the mandatory Red Flag. One of the two burly-looking sentries had given him a speculative look which had seemed more than a little hostile, so he was pleased Gregorin had been prompt in receiving him. He followed the colonel through a pair of large wooden swing doors into a wide corridor, along which hung revolutionary slogans on black canvas banners. 'Catch up and overtake the West!'; 'Defend against the enemy within!' and 'Make way for women!', although he noticed that in fact there were very few women amongst the students flowing back and forth from room to room, in an unhurried but purposeful rhythm that made it seem as though walking along the corridor was all they did all day.

The high-ceilinged lecture room itself was a little disorientating. He had to lean backwards to see the students on the highest level of the wooden semi-circles, which reached up almost up to the light fittings. At each desk a young face sat, scrubbed and grave above a spotless cadet uniform. He turned to Gregorin, who pointed him towards a wooden lectern, where, after taking a moment to open his notes and a further nod from the colonel, he began to speak.

He started slowly, perhaps because one of the banners at the side of the lecture room read 'Remain ever vigilant. Enemies surround you at all times!', which seemed, for a second or two, to be addressed to him personally, but he recovered and found himself moving through the presentation at a steady pace. Soon the scratch of the students' pens was the only noise, and he took breaks to allow them to catch up before he started a new point. The pauses also allowed him to observe his audience, and there was something in their concentration that put him in mind of the wolves that had hunted behind his column on that long winter retreat in nineteen. It was not a comfortable feeling. There were some memories you wished you could leave behind you for ever, like the corpses that had marked each kilometre on that terrible march.

Afterwards, however, when Gregorin had thanked him on their behalf, the young men and women's applause had seemed genuine enough. Perhaps he was just imagining they had the eyes of prowling predators.

'A keen-looking bunch, aren't they? Comrade Ezhov wants their course cut in half; he says they can learn on the job. Every day we discover a new conspiracy and he wants us to strike back – and hard.'

The colonel led the way into another corridor, this time narrow and empty.

'Incidentally, Captain, I think I may have something of interest for you.'

Korolev followed Gregorin, the heels of the colonel's riding boots sounding like pistol shots against the tiled floor. There was no natural light, just blank door after blank door. It was a relief when Gregorin stopped at one of them and opened it.

The room they entered was large, painted a bureaucratic cream and dominated by a wide desk, in front of which a chair stood on a carpet marked by several damp patches. There was a typewriter on a smaller desk to one side, which Korolev presumed was for the stenographer during interrogations because he had no doubt whatsoever that this was the purpose of the room. There were no windows and the lights were all arranged to focus on the sturdy metal chair, which the colonel now directed him towards. Gregorin himself sat down behind the desk and placed Korolev's typewritten report inside a buff-coloured cardboard folder. There was no name on the folder and it was the only one on the desk. The colonel put his hands under his chin, lifted his eyes towards Korolev and then indicated, with a drooping finger, the file.

'I read your report during the lecture. Very thorough.'

The colonel paused and Korolev found himself shifting in his seat, wondering about its last occupant and what might have become of him. After a moment Gregorin sighed and opened the folder once again. He turned a couple of pages and stopped at the photograph of the dead girl that Gueginov had been up half the night developing.

'We know who your victim is, anyway. Maria Ivanovna Kuznetsova. Born 1 July, 1913, here in Moscow. A Soviet citizen, in our eyes at least, although she emigrated to America at the age of six. Her father's factories turned out guns for the Whites, so he didn't hang around when the Civil War started going our way. We've kept an eye on the father, of course; he's done well in America but, as you might expect, he continues to have extensive connections with various counter-revolutionary and émigré groups. We hadn't heard much of his daughter but last week she entered the country as part of a tour group, under the name Mary Smithson. She disappeared soon after she arrived and that's when her real identity emerged. Smithson is a rough translation of Kuznetsova – here's her visa application form.'

Korolev picked up the form the colonel slipped across to him. A passport-sized photograph of the dead girl stared out at him from the first page. Although her expression was serious in the picture, her mouth had a curve to it that suggested a ready smile. Her hair was cut short, almost like a boy's, and her eyes seemed a brilliant blue despite the photograph being in black and white.

'Do the Americans know she's dead?' he asked, handing the form back to the colonel.

'We don't think so; at least, they've made no enquiries – which is how we'd like to keep it, for as long as possible anyway. Once they report her missing we can decide how to handle the situation, but until then we must keep things quiet. Very quiet. You're authorized to inform General Popov of her identity, but no one else.'

'I see. What about my assistant on the case, Lieutenant Semionov?'

'He's very junior . . .'

'Yes, but a Komsomol member and reliable – I'd stake my life on him.'

Gregorin examined Korolev as though he represented a rather tricky problem.

'You'll take full responsibility?'

'I will. He's a good lad.'

'Then I leave it to your discretion.'

Korolev nodded his agreement, feeling a little offended on his colleague's behalf. Semionov was a Militia investigator – he knew his duty. It was wrong for Gregorin to suggest otherwise.

The colonel, meanwhile, cleaned his nails with a letter opener and took great care about it. Korolev noticed his hands were trembling slightly and that both sets of knuckles were red, the skin broken in places. In the pause that developed, Korolev considered what he'd just been told and didn't like it. Investigating the murder of a foreigner – worse still, an American foreigner – it was just the kind of assignment that could explode in a fellow's face. He didn't understand why he was still being allowed to handle the case, it just didn't make sense. He found himself rubbing his palm across his chin, feeling a bristly scratch despite his morning shave. Well, if he was stuck with it, he'd better make sure he extracted as much information from the Chekists as was possible.

'Well, Colonel,' Korolev began, hearing the hoarseness in his voice, 'if she's from America – and rich – was she here to buy items like those you mentioned last night? Is that the connection?'

Gregorin shook his head, more in disappointment at the naivety of the question than disagreement.

'I can only tell you one thing more about her. We don't know much else, as it happens, so don't bother asking.'

'I'd be grateful, Comrade Colonel.'

'She is – or was – a nun. The Orthodox cult is stronger than you'd think in America. Even before the Revolution, it was strong. There's a convent near New York and, according to our information, she joined it three years ago. The Church is very active against us, as you might expect. They are usually more adept at infiltrating agents, so perhaps there is another explanation – but it's our suspicion that she was here on their instructions. Our people are working on it, of course, and they may turn up more information in time.'

'Do you have any idea what her instructions might have been? If she was working for the cultists, that is?'

Gregorin sighed. 'It's no secret that the Orthodox cult is interested in items of religious significance – icons in particular. If the murder is indeed connected to the matter we discussed last night, it might be a logical conclusion that she could have some connection to the "leakage". If you think some information about the sale of religious items might be of use to you, there's a man called Schwartz staying at the Metropol. He's an American and responsible for handling a very large proportion of the artefacts we send abroad. If you talk to him, remember that. Not that you would ever rough him up or anything.'

'I'm not that type of investigator. And if he does what you say, I can see his importance to the State.'

Colonel Gregorin tapped the folder. 'Good. Keep the reports coming and I'll be in touch. Be careful, Captain. You're dealing with people who'll kill to protect themselves – because if they're caught . . .' Gregorin left the sentence unfinished and rose to his feet.

Korolev stood up as well, 'Tell, me, Comrade Colonel, why, again, are the NKVD not investigating the case directly?'

Gregorin pointed towards the door. 'I'll walk you out.'

He said nothing more.

Chapter Seven

BACK at Petrovka Street, Korolev climbed the stairs to General Popov's office with the intention of passing on Gregorin's information and to ask for instructions on how to approach it. When he reached the second-floor landing, however, he saw Yasimov reading the Wall Paper. Every Soviet workplace had a Wall Paper, written by its Party activists to educate the workers politically and to publicize the Party line. Even from the staircase Korolev had no trouble making out the headline – the words were in lettering three inches high:

COMRADE POPOV'S FAILURE TO SUPPRESS
WRECKERS AND TRAITORS!

Korolev looked at Yasimov, opening his mouth to speak, but his friend gave a tiny shake of his head. He then began to read a different article with almost exaggerated attention while Korolev, taking the hint, turned back to the editorial. To his surprise, there was no mention of anyone else having failed in their duty to detect wreckers and traitors, which group must include his former colleague Knuckles Mendeleyev. Korolev guessed that it wasn't just sympathy for the general that was making Yasimov look grim – they'd both worked closely with Knuckles, after all, sharing a room with him for years, and if Knuckles had been a traitor to the State then surely they should have spotted him long before

Larinin's denunciation. He scanned the Wall Paper, but could see neither Yasimov's nor his own name mentioned – they were in the clear, for the moment anyway.

Yasimov finished the article he was reading, patted Korolev's shoulder and walked over to Room 2F's battered door – there was nothing that could be said out on the landing. Korolev stayed for a little longer, then continued up the stairs to the general's office, unable to shake the feeling that Yasimov's pat on the shoulder hadn't been meant to be reassuring, but rather was a warning.

Inside his office the general sat smoking his pipe and looking off into space. There was a glass of water on the table in front of him and two white pills beside it. The general followed Korolev's glance.

'Stomach ulcer. I can barely look at decent food these days, let alone alcohol. It's a hard life. I can still smoke though. Just about.' He puffed at the pipe and examined Korolev. 'You saw the Wall Paper, I take it?'

'Yes. What are they going to do, Comrade General?'

'As if they'd tell me. There'll be a disciplinary meeting in due course, no doubt, and then I'll be guided by my Comrades. If the Party believes I wasn't sufficiently active in my duties, then I'll accept that – it's my duty to accept it. But I'd never have thought it of Mendeleyev, and I can't help thinking . . .'

He didn't finish the sentence. Instead he sucked at the pipe and then focused his full attention on the glowing bowl that resulted. He seemed to have forgotten Korolev was there. When Korolev coughed into his fist, the general looked up, bemused.

'Alexei. What was it you wanted, anyway?'

'I'll speak at the meeting, Comrade General. I worked closest of all with Mendeleyev. If there was something wrong, I should have seen it before anyone else.'

Popov's brow creased, creating a series of deep Vs in his forehead.

'Don't even think of it. I'm grateful, believe me, but please stay out of this – you're not a Party member. Please, don't become involved.'

'But, General, no one's contributed more to our efforts than you have. Everyone knows it. Allow me to speak.'

Popov blew a gust of smoke out as he laughed. 'But I haven't done enough, Alexei Dmitriyevich, not nearly enough. They keep coming, the Thieves and the hooligans, the rapists, the murderers, the speculators, the whores and the bandits. According to theory, they should have been subsumed into the greater working class by now. And if they haven't been – then it must be someone's fault. Of course, you'd think my job would have become easier if the theory was . . .' He paused for a moment before continuing. 'I'm sorry. Let's stop talking about this – otherwise I'll say something stupid and we'll both be in the soup.'

'I'm sure the Party will come to the correct conclusion, Comrade General.'

The general shook his head as if to put the whole mess behind him. He looked round for inspiration and found it when his eyes met Korolev's report. He picked it up from the desk with one hand and put the pipe back into his mouth with the other.

'You're making some progress, Alexei Dmitriyevich. What did Staff Colonel Gregorin make of it?'

His voice was muffled by the presence of the pipe, but he was clearly more cheerful discussing the case than the Party meeting, so Korolev, after a brief hesitation, filled him in on Gregorin's information, leaving nothing out. The general's reaction was to give a long low whistle.

'The Devil – this on top of everything else? It's got trouble written all over it, but you don't need to be told that.'

'No,' Korolev said drily.

'What I don't understand is why they're leaving it with us.' The general considered the question, running the pipe's mouthpiece along his jaw. 'Let's see – Gregorin must think the killing is to do with the conspiracy behind the missing artworks, right? So he must think that if you poke around looking for your murderer, you'll distract the criminals from the investigation Gregorin's boys are carrying out. Yes. Not a bad plan.' The general nodded in approval.

Then he looked up. 'But what if they decide to knock you off as well? If there are Chekists involved, as Gregorin seems to think, you could be in an unmarked grave out at Butyrka before morning. They've killed an American and clearly didn't turn a hair, so why wouldn't they do the same to you? It'd be no problem for them to slip one more onto the production line; the investigations they're doing now are speedy, to say the least. Which makes me wonder why they didn't just do the same with the girl. Ah. American. Yes. Maybe they mutilated her to stop her being recognized.'

He flicked back the autopsy photographs and then shook his head.

'No. If they were worried about that, they'd have chopped off her face and hands. Old Thief trick. They get rid of the tattoos as well, if there are any. Perhaps they were disturbed?'

The general's rambling series of deductions were making Korolev uncomfortable, not least the part about him ending up in an unmarked Butyrka grave.

'All very interesting,' the general continued. 'Not least because there was another murder last night, out at Tomsky stadium. A Thief, it's true, but there might be a connection. It certainly sounds like it. The body was nicely sliced up, like your one. But what do a Thief and a nun have in common?' He stopped and half-smiled at the thought. 'It sounds like the beginning of a joke.'

'Tomsky?' Korolev said, trying to refocus the general on the matter in hand rather than suggest a punchline.

'Yes, Tomsky. They found the body there this morning. Larinin's taking it over to the Institute. Go and have a look

- ask the good doctor for her opinion. Maybe it's our killer, maybe not. Maybe the conspirators are falling out. Mind you, it was found in Spartak's stadium – anything could happen there.'

The general smiled, almost hopefully, looking for a reaction from Korolev, who, in his youth had played central defender for the Presnaya football team, the factory area he grew up in. The same team, led by the four Starostin brothers, had become the nucleus of the now famous Spartak.

'You know I'm too old to play for Dinamo,' Korolev said, pre-empting the general's usual teasing on the subject. Korolev, despite having been a useful defender in his time, had never joined Dinamo, Spartak's great rival, whose players largely came from the Militia, NKVD and other arms of State Security. The general found it amusing that he had a Spartak old boy in his command. 'Anyway,' Korolev continued, 'Presnaya boys stand together, thick and thin, and we wouldn't do in one of our own.'

Popov nodded, but the smile slowly faded.

'You know, Alexei,' he said in a quiet voice, 'you're a good man and people see that. But, for your own sake, be careful on this one. Promise me? And let's hope the Chekists take it off us. A good honest axe murder or something, that's what we need.'

The two men held each other's eyes for longer than would have been polite in other circumstances, then the general stood up from his chair and extended his hand across the table. Korolev took it and felt the general's grip hot and hard around his own.

'Don't come to the meeting. It won't do any good and if the bastards want my head, well, I won't drag a good man down with me. Anyway, nothing may come of it. It's only the Wall Paper, after all. Nothing official as yet.'

Popov stood back a pace and regarded Korolev for a moment, then nodded, as if to agree with his private assessment of the detective. Korolev also took a step backwards and, because the moment seemed to require the gesture, he brought his heels together and came to attention. The general's smile turned downwards into a scowl, but he didn't look particularly displeased for all that, and he waved his pipe at Korolev to dismiss him.

Korolev left the general at the window, looking down at the pedestrians, cyclists, horses, carts and occasional car that struggled along Petrovka in the slush and ice left by the snowfall. Perhaps the general was considering how so many people, moving in so many different directions and at such different speeds, managed to avoid collision. It could put years on you, trying to work out the answer to a question like that.

Chapter Eight

KOROLEV was still considering the significance of the Wall Paper's attack on Popov as he descended the stairs to Room 2F. Perhaps, after all, it was nothing to be worried about. Maybe it would be enough if the general was open and frank with the Party meeting and admitted to a lapse in the constant vigilance which Party members were required to exercise. Perhaps it was an offence that could be forgiven if Popov cleansed his character through public self-criticism. Or perhaps not. There seemed to be something in the air these last few weeks that didn't bode well. Nobody knew much about Ezhov, the new Commissar for State Security, except that he had to be better than Yagoda. After all, even Stalin had seemed to suggest, in the months before Yagoda's replacement, that the endless self-evisceration might have gone too far. But now, more recently still, Yagoda seemed to be in disgrace for not having gone far *enough*. If this was the case, then the public criticism of Popov, who'd discreetly, but firmly, prevented a wholesale purge of the Criminal Investigation Division, could signal the commencement of something far worse than had gone before. Gregorin's talk that morning of Ezhov wanting to hit back hard against the Party's enemies was alarming, after all it seemed to confirm the rumours that Yagoda had in some way been *soft*. Korolev cursed under his breath as he caught sight of the Wall Paper and the clutch of tight-faced detectives gathered around it. He hoped his instincts were failing him, but judging from his colleagues' expressions and the bubbles of silence surrounding each of them, he suspected he wasn't the only one who had a bad feeling about where things were heading.

Semionov was waiting in Room 2F and, unlike Korolev, seemed positively enthusiastic at the prospect of an autopsy, as well as apparently being the only person in the building oblivious to the portent of the Wall Paper. It took Korolev a moment to outline the events at Tomsky stadium and by then Semionov had gathered his flat cap and mackintosh from behind the door, and they were on their way down to the courtyard to pick up a car. As they walked, the younger man filled Korolev in on the details of the forensic investigation and the house-to-house interviews that the local Militia were undertaking. As far as Semionov could tell, the power cut had indeed been an accident – he'd spoken to the foreman on the building site and the worker who had cut into the cable was seriously ill in hospital. That seemed to suggest that the location of the crime had been opportunistic – which was interesting. Otherwise there had been no substantive steps forward as yet, but at least the process was starting and with a bit of luck it might soon begin to produce scraps of information that could lead to the killer. Semionov was excited at the scale of the investigation and the mysterious nature of the crime.

'This is just like Sherlock Holmes, Alexei Dmitriyevich. Really it is. Logical deduction, that's what we need here. "Logic, my dear Watson" – that's what will unmask the fellow.'

Korolev looked at his colleague with some amusement, although he was careful not to show it. He pointed at the mackintosh.

'That won't be much good when the cold weather comes,' he said.

Semionov took the hem of his coat between his finger and thumb and squeezed it, showing how thin the rubberized cotton was.

'Maybe not. But I've three vests on underneath my shirt. I

have an old winter coat, from before. When it gets really cold, I'll wear that.'

'At least it looks as though it's waterproof,' Korolev said.

'Indeed it is, and all the Arbat crowd are wearing them.'

Korolev could think of several responses to that, but he decided to restrain himself. In his opinion, the trend-setting youngsters who paraded up and down Arbat Street could jump into the Moskva River en masse and the city wouldn't be the poorer.

§

When they arrived at the small wooden hut that stood in the centre of the cobbled courtyard, the elderly Morozov, a bearded ex-soldier who'd lost an eye in 1914, came out to greet them. Morozov supervised the twenty or so cars that constituted the Criminal Investigation Division's transport pool from behind his pirate's patch, and was renowned for his grouchy demeanour.

'Let me handle him,' whispered Semionov.

'Greetings, Comrades,' Morozov said, as he slapped his gloved hands together and stamped his feet. 'Winter's early this year. Looking for a car, are we, Alexei Dmitriyevich? Taking young Semionov for a spin?' His good eye gleamed from under his fur hat. Despite his reputation, he had a soft spot for Korolev.

'Do you have something good for us, Comrade Morozov?' Semionov said, before Korolev could respond. 'I see a new Emka over there. Fine cars, I hear.'

Morozov looked Semionov up and down, turned to Korolev, and put a glove up to his face, adjusting his eye patch.

'You'll be driving, won't you, Alexei Dmitriyevich?'

Korolev looked at Semionov's hopeful eyes and relented. 'I might let the youngster drive, Pavel Timofeevich. Under my direction, of course.'

Morozov looked back at Semionov, grunted, re-entered the hut, and emerged with a set of car keys.

'The Ford,' he said and tossed the keys to Semionov, who caught them with a smile. 'A car's a means of transportation, young lad, not entertainment. It'll do the job. The Emka's not for the likes of you.'

'I'll look after it as if it were my own, Pavel Timofeevich.'

'Your own, is it? Look after it better than that, it belongs to the Soviet People, that car. It's no speedster, but it's reliable.' Morozov pointed the young man towards the end of the line of cars.

Semionov already had the engine started by the time Korolev squeezed himself into the passenger seat.

'Now, let's get this clear. I'm allowing you to drive, it's true, but take it slowly. The roads are icy and I'd like to make it home in one piece.'

'Of course, Alexei Dmitriyevich,' Semionov answered, with a look too innocent to be trusted. 'The Institute?'

'The Institute,' Korolev agreed, without enthusiasm.

'Excellent. And afterwards?'

'We'll see,' Korolev answered, having to shout the words because Semionov had inadvertently revved the engine as high as it would go, causing a flock of screeching black birds to fly up from the overhanging trees. Morozov emerged from his hut to give the younger man a one-eyed look that immediately reduced the engine's scream to a rattling growl. An abashed Semionov let off the handbrake and directed the car away from its fellows, while Korolev turned up the collar of his overcoat against the chill draught from the broken windscreen, and avoided Morozov's aggrieved gaze.

Semionov drove out through the front gate, saluting the wet-looking sentry and turning left into a stream of carts, cyclists and slow-moving trucks, before manoeuvring to the middle of the street, where he had a clearer run. It was strange, Korolev thought, how they never showed the carts and horses in the newsreels. It was almost as though they didn't exist in black and white; slowly fading from the picture and leaving only the speeding trucks and cars of the future. They weren't the only things that were being replaced, of course, and, as they drove along Gorky Street, Korolev found himself marvelling, not for the first time, at the extent of the reconstruction taking place in the city. Tverskaya Street had been a narrower, more intimate thoroughfare before it had been renamed in honour of the great Soviet writer, and now it was being turned into a fine wide strip of asphalt with pedestrian walkways along both sides, as well as giant new buildings, solid and practical, as you'd expect from Soviet architects. The car ran along the street's new surface as smoothly as its aged engine and bone-jangling suspension would permit, passing work parties who were clearing the remaining slush from the road and piling it up in banks that ran along the pavements' edges.

There were more motorized vehicles here: green and cream city buses coughing clouds of black smoke as they pulled away from the kerb; bustling red and white trams and a constant stream of mud-washed trucks; but theirs was one of the only cars to be seen. Forward planning was the key to achieving the economic development necessary for the Soviet Union to take its place amongst the great countries of the world. The cars would come in due course.

'We'll outstrip America soon enough,' Korolev shouted above the engine as they passed yet another construction site where iron girders were sketching out a new building against the grey clouds overhead.

'I hear they're going to build skyscrapers,' Semionov shouted back. 'Bigger than the ones in New York, bigger even than the Empire State building. Comrade Stalin himself has approved the plans, and they'll be twenty times the size of the Hotel Moskva.' He indicated the huge squat building with a dismissive nod. 'And they're going to move the buildings on rails, to widen the street.

It will be as wide as a football pitch, if not wider. What could be wider? Perhaps it will be as wide as a football pitch is long. Anyway, the plans are well under way.'

'A football pitch? And they'll move the buildings?' Korolev shook his head.

'On rails, like a tram. They'll get on at one stop and get off at another. My friend told me, but it's secret. Although everyone knows it, so it can't be that much of a secret. Apparently our engineers have it all worked out.'

'The Soviet Union, Vanya. An example to the world,' Korolev said, and meant it, but he spared a thought for the poky streets and familiar buildings of his youth, now being pushed hither and thither if they were lucky, but more usually flattened into rubble and used to fill in the foundations of the new city. The Moscow he'd grown up in had been a place of secrets and smells, courtyards and alleys, corners and hideaways. The reconstruction, however, would be about size and space and grandeur, as it should be, but he sometimes wondered whether he, like the old Moscow, had a place in the new world Socialism was creating around him.

The further they drove away from the centre of the city, however, the more the road narrowed and deteriorated – the surface holed and pitted by heavy trucks, and slippery with packed snow that had still not been properly cleared. The reconstruction hadn't reached this far out as yet, and tottering tenements leaned against multi-domed churches, shabby with twenty years of neglect. Most of this neighbourhood had been slated for demolition and some buildings had already disappeared, flattened to create a massive tunnelling site for one of the new Metro lines. A queue of young, mud-spattered workers was gathered outside underneath a banner that they had probably answered: KOMSOMOLETS, KOMSOMOLKA! HELP BUILD THE METRO! YOUR FUTURE NEEDS A GREAT RAILWAY! As they passed the queue, a heavy truck surged out of the site entrance, forcing Semionov to stamp hard on the brakes, the Ford's tyres slithering across unexpected ice before coming to a halt. The driver, looking as though he should still be at school, waved a good-natured apology as Semionov sounded the horn.

'We're Militia!' Semionov shouted at the driver as the truck swept past them, but the young fellow just carried on waving. Semionov was still muttering to himself when they pulled up at the Institute five minutes later.

'I'm Komsomol as well, Alexei Dmitriyevich, and that just wasn't good driving. I'm ashamed of him, if the truth be told. If I knew which cell he was from, I'd report him. He could have killed us and it wouldn't have been my fault. Believe me.'

'I believe you, Vanya. Come on, let's go and have a look at the body.'

§

The car parked, they entered the building with its familiar smell of disinfectant and damp and, as they approached the mortuary, they heard Larinin's voice in loud discussion with Chestnova.

'I have important matters to attend to elsewhere today, Doctor. Make no excuses for delay. It can only be inefficiency on your part. That's what we Party members must fight against. Inefficiency.'

As they opened the door, they saw Larinin emphasize his point by stabbing a fat finger at Chestnova. The two were of an even size and bulk, but Korolev's money would be on Chestnova if it came to blows and, indeed, she was giving a good impression of an angry bull about to charge. In the background, Gueginov was smiling nervously and, from the slightly lopsided slant to his face, Korolev deduced that he'd been at the medical spirit again.

'What's going on here, Larinin?' Korolev asked as they approached the two combatants. Larinin turned and then adjusted his eye line upwards to take account of Korolev's greater height.

'The doctor here doesn't seem to be aware of the Militia's priority when it comes to the performance of speedy autopsies,

Comrade Korolev. I've a very important case – the general himself asked me to make sure it was dealt with immediately – and now the doctor is telling me I have to wait. The criminal could be making his escape as we speak, all because she hasn't time to look at the victim. She's sabotaging our efforts to do our work efficiently, Comrades. She's a wrecker, if you ask me. I wonder what her class background is.' The last remark was made with a malevolent glare that would have terrified an ordinary person but seemed to have no effect on Dr Chestnova, other than to irritate her still further.

'Listen, you barrel of lard,' Chestnova snarled at him, her breasts swinging forward as she approached him, close enough now for her to spray his face with saliva when she spoke. 'I've told you I'll deal with your corpse in twenty minutes. At present I have to finish an autopsy for the NKVD. Would you like me to tell the Lubianka that you believe the Militia takes precedence over them? I'm happy to do so.'

Larinin looked for a moment like a man who'd swallowed a hornet. He blinked twice and then looked to Korolev and Semionov for assistance. Korolev shrugged his shoulders with a flat smile, while Semionov was oblivious to the drama, his nose smearing the glass window of the autopsy room where the suicides were piled. Larinin scowled at them and then waved his hand at Chestnova in a dismissive gesture.

'Well, why didn't you say so, Doctor, instead of wasting everyone's time? Of course State Security takes priority. Comrade Stalin himself has made that clear on hundreds of occasions. Possibly thousands.'

'Which is what I've been trying to tell you for the last five minutes, but you would only listen to the sound of your own voice. Drone, drone, drone. And who the hell are you to be casting aspersions around like your damned traffic tickets? Sherlock Holmes?'

Semionov gave an emphatically negative shake of his head at this suggestion.

'Comrades,' Korolev said loudly, 'remember the proverb: in any argument the wiser one's to blame.'

Which comment left both Larinin and Chestnova momentarily confused, before each looked at the other with a certain smugness.

'As it happens, I need to see the body as well. Come on, Larinin, I need an update on the murder scene – let's have a smoke outside. Your corpse isn't going anywhere and it will give Comrade Chestnova time to attend to her other duties.'

§

It was freezing on the Institute steps, and their breath and the cigarette smoke were indistinguishable in the cold air. Larinin explained briefly that the body had been found, mutilated, on the terraces behind the goalposts at Tomsky stadium. The large number of tattoos indicated the dead man had been a Thief and there'd been two sets of footsteps leading to and from the body. That was it, as far as Larinin was concerned. Whatever had happened, had happened elsewhere and the body had been dumped. In Larinin's view, a Thief had fallen foul of his fellows and good riddance. Korolev listened with as much patience as he could muster and then led the others back to the morgue.

Back inside the second autopsy room two attendants rolled a canvas body bag out onto the metal work surface without any ceremony. They quickly undid the cord that ran the length of the bag and peeled it open like a banana, revealing the grey corpse within and also letting out the damp smell of decay. The attendants expertly slipped the bag from under the body, assisted by its stiffness, then left the room without a word. Semionov whistled.

'He must have really got on somebody's tits, I'm telling you. Look at the poor fellow's family jewels.'

It was true enough: the Thief's face and body were battered and bloody from a beating and a smoke-circled hole in the middle of his forehead indicated the probable cause of death. Aside from the obvious violence of his last few hours, the dead man hadn't had an easy life – hard living, violence and drink had left their marks. A bite-sized chunk was missing from his right ear, his nose looked as though it had been broken several times and his remaining teeth were yellow and uneven. But the reason for Semionov's shock was the horrific damage inflicted to the fellow's genitals. Korolev had to look away to collect himself before returning his gaze to the Thief.

The dead man's face was broad and topped with brown hair that was cut short at the sides and allowed some length on top. Even now he looked imposing, however: his chest impressively wide and his arms, thick and muscled. But it was the tattoos covering his body that marked him out as a Thief as surely as if his police file were lying open on his chest; they gave almost as much information if you knew how to interpret them.

The door swung open behind him as one of the attendants returned.

'Here's his bits, the poor lad,' the attendant said and deposited two glass jars containing the missing body parts at the corpse's feet. The penis reminded Korolev of a discarded scrap of bread dough.

'It makes you feel ill,' Semionov said, and it was true that his pallor had a greenish tinge. Korolev, who was still fighting to keep his own stomach down, had no sympathy to spare.

'So what have we got here?' Chestnova said, coming into the room and picking up one of the jars. She shook the testicle from side to side as she examined it against the light. 'A testicle, by the look of things.' Then she looked up at Larinin. 'More than one, if I'm not mistaken.' Larinin scowled back at her.

'Reckon it's our killer, Doctor?' Korolev asked – hoping the question would distract Chestnova – he didn't think he could watch a testicle being rattled in a jar for very long without disgracing himself.

The doctor looked down at the body and pressed the calf muscle with a speculative finger. 'It could be. He's in full rigor mortis, but it was cold last night. Where was he found?'

'On the terraces at Tomsky stadium, in the snow. It looks like he was dumped there.' Korolev noticed Semionov's eyes following the jar in Chestnova's hands as though it were a snake charmer's flute.

'Hmm – well below zero last night. That makes it difficult to tell when he died. But there's some decay, so it could be as much as twenty-four hours or even longer. Ah. Look here. Recognize these marks?'

Chestnova pointed out the burn marks around the groin and nipples that Korolev had spotted as soon as the body was laid out on the table.

'The same as the girl?' he asked.

'Made with the same instrument, I'd say. At first glance.' Chestnova leant closer to examine the body. 'Quite impressive tattoos, Captain, if I'm not mistaken.'

Korolev grunted his agreement. Blackish-blue inked pictures covered most of the man's body – prison tattoos, etched out with a razor or a sewing needle, using ink made from coal dust and urine. Each image told a chapter in the Thief's life or confirmed his position in the Thieves' hierarchy; his criminal record, but told from the criminal's perspective. Ironically, tattoos were often more reliable than Militia files. Policemen could be bribed and official records changed, but a Thief's tattoos were written in stone – in a prison they were his calling card, and the first question he would be asked was whether he stood by his tattoos. An inaccurate tattoo, one that claimed a position or history that a Thief was not entitled to, would be burnt or cut off by his fellows. If the incorrect tattoo was considered sufficiently offensive, the wrong-doer could pay for it with his life.

As Chestnova began to clean the body, the flow of water revealed more. The largest tattoo, an image of the crucifixion, spread across most of the corpse's chest. A bearded Jesus stared down, the tangled crown of thorns embedded in his bloody hair and thick nails pinning his hands to the cross. It was beautifully done – each rib separately shaded, each tendon and muscle clearly defined. The pain in the Saviour's eyes seemed to reach out from the image and into Korolev's very soul. A craftsman made this, thought Korolev to himself, and made the sign of the cross with his pocketed hand. The tattoo was a living icon, or at least had been, but it was also the insignia of a senior Thief, an authority in the prison system and on the streets. The tattoo itself was a mark of the man; it would have taken weeks for the tattooist to produce a tattoo of this size and detail, and each insertion of ink would have caused pain. It was no disgrace in the Thieves' world to have an unfinished tattoo.

Beneath the Thief's left nipple, just under Christ's dangling fingers, Stalin's profile stared sideways at a bloody red patch where the skin had been sliced away; behind him a similar patch bubbled raw. Korolev knew the tattoo and the reason it was worn, and that the missing profiles were of Lenin and Marx. He was curious that Stalin hadn't been cut away, and wondered if it meant something.

The whole body was inked. On his left shoulder a skull was pierced by a crucifix, the crossbar of which supported weighing scales. It was a rare tattoo and meant that the dead man acted as a judge in the Thieves' internal disputes. There was also a tattoo of the Virgin Mary on the man's other shoulder, based on the icon of Our Lady of Kazan. The icon had a special significance for Thieves, although there was nothing strange in that, Korolov thought; known as Kazanskaya, it was venerated above all others by the Orthodox Church. There were other tattoos as well: the cat in the cavalier's hat signifying the Thief's happy-go-lucky approach to life; the sailing ship for a prisoner who'd tried to escape from jail; a knife entering the Thief's skin, telling Korolev this man had killed for his clan – he'd been a charmer, this fellow.

'It muh-may be nothing. Buh-but the girl's buh-body – it was luh-laid out in the same way as the cruh-crucifixion tuh-tattoo.' Gueginov pointed at the Thief's chest and Korolev nodded, making a quick note, then began to check the dead man's fingers. Two were missing, but had been for some time, probably due to gambling. A finger might settle a debt in the Zone if the loser couldn't meet his obligations some other way. The remaining fingers were decorated with blue tattoos, drawn like signet rings.

'See, Vanya,' Korolev said to Semionov, 'here's his life story.' Korolev picked up the dead man's left hand. 'The eagle on the thumb tells us he's an important thief, an "authority". See these two crosses in circles on the back of his hand – he's been in prison twice, so we'll have a file on him sure as I'm standing here. This one, on the forefinger, with the black and white diamond, means he refused to work in the Zone. The clubs and spades in the square beneath the domed monastery? Again that means he's a senior Thief, to be respected, at least among his own kind. This one – ' he pointed to a beetle with an orthodox cross on its back – 'means he was convicted of robbery. The plain cross on the little finger means he did solitary confinement during his stretch. Well, if he refused to work, what did he expect?'

Semionov's eyes were wide as he scribbled furiously in his notebook. Korolev picked up the other hand, the one with the missing fingers. He pointed to the ring tattoo on the forefinger – a square with lines criss-crossing it to represent prison bars. 'This one is called "My fate is in big squares" – it means he's destined to die in prison, looking at the sky through the bars of his cell. The church on the thumb tells you he was born a Thief and the scarab beetle on the middle finger is his talisman, a lucky tattoo. It brought him good fortune, until now anyway.'

'I never saw such a thing before, the way he's been cut up. To do this to one of their own? They're savages. Devils.' Larinin seemed more puzzled than angry.

Korolev looked at Dr Chestnova. She ignored him initially, concentrating instead on hosing down the body, but then she looked up at him and nodded.

'The burn marks are so unusual – there must be a good chance it was the same man as the one who murdered the girl.' Her eyes were red with tiredness, but her hand was steady and the hose slowly revealed yet more hidden tattoos and scars, old and new, from underneath the caked blood. One of the tattoos linked the names Lena and Tesak in a heart surmounted with a cat's head, a Thief couple. Now they had a name for the man, likely as not.

'Vanya,' Korolev said to Semionov, 'look at this. See the two names in the heart and the cat's head? The cat is the sign of the Thieves and the heart signifies a romantic relationship, as you might expect. As Lena is a woman's name, logic would suggest that the dead fellow goes by "Tesak". That should make tracking his file down a little easier.'

§

A long hour later Korolev and Semionov sat against the bonnet of the Ford enjoying well-deserved cigarettes.

'Two autopsies in two days. I hope we catch this fellow soon,' Korolev muttered as Larinin came out to join them. 'Well, Comrade Larinin, what do you think?'

'A dead Thief? We should be celebrating. That's what I think.'

'Not a great loss to the Revolution, it's true. Still, it looks like he was killed by the same person as yesterday's girl, so the investigations will have to be combined. I'm going to take young Semionov out to the stadium in case anything was missed.'

'You're wasting your time. He was dumped, as I said. There's nothing to be seen out there.'

Korolev swallowed his irritation. If it had been up to him,

he'd have had Chestnova visit the corpse where it had been found rather than just calling for it to be picked up. Larinin seemed to think their equal rank gave them equal investigative experience, but the fellow knew nothing.

'Comrade,' he said, 'if you wish to stay involved, that's your choice, and we can use the manpower. On the other hand, if you would prefer another assignment, I'm happy to recommend to the general that you pursue some other matter. Either way, I'll be making my own decisions as to how I investigate.'

Korolev could see Larinin calculating the political benefits to him of being involved in a successful investigation, even if Korolev did most of the work, and the likely fallout if he walked away. It was an easy decision to make. After all, if things went wrong, he could blame Korolev for the failure.

'Of course, Captain Korolev, it's a sensible idea to work together on the investigation, and if you want to check the crime scene then you should do so. Let us work in a spirit of comradely cooperation.'

Larinin held out his hand for Korolev to shake and Korolev, after a momentary hesitation, accepted it. It was a handshake neither of them committed to, the contact tentative and soft. Larinin's gaze slid off towards Semionov, on whom he bestowed a nod of his head.

'A partnership,' Larinin said to the younger man and then turned back to Korolev. His voice was a little too cheerful – the fellow couldn't even pretend to be sincere, thought Korolev, letting go of his hand. Still, it seemed fate, or perhaps the general, had thrown them together, and if they were going to work the case jointly, he'd better make sure he got as much use out of him as he could.

'Now tell me exactly where you found the body . . .' Korolev began once again.

Chapter Nine

SEMIONOV was silent on the way out to Tomsky stadium and his driving seemed to have lost some of its natural enthusiasm. Korolev hardly noticed, as he tried to work out what on earth connected the murders of a Thief and a foreign nun. Were the Thieves involved in the export of the stolen valuables? What was the murderer's motive? Or were the killings a psychopath's handiwork after all, and his victims random? Well, he must be truly insane if he'd murdered a Thief — that was like putting your head into a lion's mouth while kicking him in the balls. No. No one was that crazed.

If only he could put everything down on paper, perhaps he could begin to make some sense of the jumble of information that was making his head ache, but Gregorin would have him shot for that kind of breach of secrecy. What a complete mess this case was turning out to be. He groaned.

'Are you all right, Alexei Dmitriyevich?'

'I'm fine, just a little headache,' Korolev replied, wondering whether a bullet in the nape of his neck would actually hurt. Perhaps it would all be over before you realized what was happening. He swallowed.

'And a stomach ache,' he said.

'I don't feel so well myself. That poor fellow with his you know what. Normally I'd say good riddance to a Thief like him, but you wouldn't wish that on anyone.'

'No,' Korolev said, adding another worry to his list. What if he fell into the hands of the murderer? Given his victims to date and what he'd done to them it was unlikely that he'd go easy on some middle-aged, past-it gumshoe. A bullet in the head was beginning to seem almost attractive.

'Also . . .' Semionov said no more but gave a loud and deliberate sigh. So heartfelt was the sound that Korolev turned to look at him.

'What's up with you?' he said.

'Nothing. Really. It's just – do we really have to work this case with Larinin? I know he's well respected within the Party, but I'm not sure I like him very much. And what's all this about General Popov being investigated? He's been awarded the Order of the Red Flag *and* the Order of Lenin! He's as true to the Party as Comrade Stalin himself!'

There was a moment of silence in the car as both men thought about what Semionov had said. Korolev broke it.

'Perhaps . . .'

'Yes, I see your point. Comparing the General to Comrade Stalin . . .'

'While he's under investigation . . .'

'No,' agreed Semionov, his face flushed.

It wasn't easy for the young lad, thought Korolev. Being a good Communist these days was like following an arbitrary God who required you to believe that white was white one day and black the next. It only made sense if you remembered that the country was surrounded by enemies who were terrified by its very existence. Faced with such implacable foes, sometimes the Party took steps which seemed at odds with its long-term historical destiny. That could be confusing for ordinary workers like Korolev and Semionov, but everyone knew the Party had to keep going forward, no matter what the cost. Korolev believed in the Party line absolutely, even if it required a leap of faith to do so from time to time. After all, unity was as important as truth sometimes – you learnt that in the trenches, if nothing else.

Looking ahead, he spotted a small crowd in front of a familiar snow-topped kiosk whose sole advertisement was the word 'Snacks', spelt incorrectly. Still, even 'Snaks' would cheer up a growing lad like Semionov and, as it happened, the stallholder was known to Korolev of old. Each time he passed he felt relief that the stall had not succumbed to the reconstruction of the city or the continuing efforts to minimize private enterprise – the *blinchiki*, sometimes even containing meat, were amongst the best in Moscow.

'I'm starving, Vanya. Let's pull over and get some lunch. I haven't eaten all day.'

They came to a halt and Korolev stepped from the car and nodded to the stall owner. 'How are things, Boris Nikolayevich? Two, please.'

Several of the waiting men gave him angry looks, but seeing the car and the waiting Semionov drew the obvious conclusion, a couple even raising their collars and moving off. Korolev pretended not to notice – it wasn't his job to check people's papers – and as he prepared the *blinchiki*, Boris Nikolayevich told Korolev his news. He was now part of a nearby state canteen so his problems with bureaucracy had decreased, unfortunately along with his flexibility in acquiring ingredients.

'They keep the best stuff for themselves, but I make do,' the stallholder announced, wrapping the *blinchiki* and handing them over to Korolev in exchange for ninety kopeks. 'I'm blessed to be the son of a street sweeper. See poor Denisov across the street. The son of a factory owner. The troubles he has, you wouldn't believe, and we were both born in ninety seven. Who would have guessed then how things would turn out for us?'

The food paid for, Korolev got back into the car, handing Semionov one of the wrappings as he did so. It was only when he went to open his own that he saw that it had been wrapped in a vellum page and that ancient ink had impregnated his *blinchiki* with mirrored Slavonic writing. A holy book had been torn to pieces to wrap food in. He looked around at Semionov, whose cheeks were bulging as his jaw worked away at a huge mouthful. He hesitated and then took a bite himself, hoping he wasn't doing anything sinful. He chewed for a moment. If it was sinful, it was also delicious, and so he took a second mouthful, asking the Lord for forgiveness as he did so.

§

The red and white flag of Spartak hung loosely outside Tomsky stadium. It was dwarfed by the Dinamo stands on the other side of the road, but size wasn't everything. Spartak was the spirit of Moscow, as far as Korolev was concerned, whereas Dinamo represented the force that controlled that spirit. He might work for the Ministry, but Korolev was a Presnaya boy through and through, even if he now lived in Kitaj-Gorod. You didn't betray your birthplace, not in his book anyway. Semionov pulled the car to a halt outside the administrative building and Korolev saw a group of players approaching, their bodies showing every sign of tiredness and their breath trailing them like the smoke from a train. Beside them walked a familiar figure, dressed in a pair of old grey flannel trousers, a green hunting jacket and a red and white scarf. Thick brown hair tumbled back from the sharply cut face, and a pair of eyes the colour of old silver were already regarding him with amusement. Nikolai Starostin's face broke into a grin as Korolev raised a hand in greeting.

'Nikolai,' Korolev said, 'I see you're pushing the team hard as ever.'

There was a rumble of good-humoured agreement from the players, not least of which came from two more of the Starostin brothers, Aleksandr and Andrei.

'Go on into the baths, boys,' said Starostin. 'I must talk to this old player, even if he's long past it.'

Andrei Starostin waved a cheerful greeting but moved along with the others, several of whom also nodded to Korolev, being known to him, as he was to them.

'We haven't seen you at many games recently. Worried the supporters will give you a hard time?'

'I've been busy. Anyway I can look after myself, I'm not ashamed of my job.'

'Yes, I know that much. It's bad, though. When we play Dinamo it's "Kill the terriers", "Kill the filth", and when we play Red Army, it's "Kill the squaddies" or "Kill the horse washers". It worries people in authority, which isn't good these days, and when we're beating their pet teams it adds insult to the injury. Still, what can we do? They're a law unto themselves. They'll shout whatever they damned well please and the Devil take the consequences.'

Korolev smiled, knowing all about the rough bonhomie of the stands when Spartak were winning, and the rage when things were going badly.

'So who'll line up for you against the Army? They've a strong side: want me to dust off my boots?'

Starostin smiled and touched his finger to the side of his nose.

'All will be revealed, Lyoshka, in due course. But if you're coming to the game, let me get you a ticket – in the stand with the civilized people, not down on the terraces. You'll be able to see the game properly and, anyway, I need someone to keep an eye on my sisters. They can become a little obstreperous if things begin to go against us. Presnaya girls, through and through. Feel free to arrest them, it's better than them going up to Marshal Tukachevsky and telling him his boys are dirty cheats.'

'I'd be grateful,' Korolev said. He caught sight of Semionov staring at them from the car and was reminded of the purpose of his visit. 'Listen, Nikolai, there was a body dropped here last night and I need someone to show us exactly where.'

Starostin frowned. 'Ah, yes. The groundskeeper found him – I can show you myself. He dragged me out to have a look. Not pretty. Come on.'

Korolev signalled to his colleague and a grinning Semionov extracted himself from the car, stood to attention and saluted.

'Comrade Starostin!' he said, almost shouting, before reddening when the footballer laughed in response. However, Starostin stopped immediately when he saw the younger man's discomfort, stepping forward to put an arm around Semionov's shoulders then lead him towards the stadium.

'No, Comrade, don't be embarrassed,' he said. 'You were a little formal in front of my old friend, Alexei Dmitriyevich, that's all. So you're here to investigate our murder?'

'It's not as if he ever salutes me and I'm two ranks higher than him,' Korolev said to no one in particular. But he smiled at Semionov's delight in having the famous Starostin walk with him, arm in arm.

'Are you a football fan, Comrade? Spartak also?'

Semionov couldn't lie, but he had the good grace to look uncomfortable about his preference. 'I'm sorry, Comrade Starostin – Dinamo.'

'No reason not to support them, they're a good team. I toured with some of them a few months back and a nicer bunch of lads you couldn't meet.'

Semionov nodded in agreement, they were a fine bunch of lads. Not that he'd ever actually met them. But he had just met Nikolai Starostin. He rubbed his chin as he considered his dilemma.

'Perhaps now, having met you, Comrade,' he said, thinking aloud, 'I might support Dinamo *and* Spartak.'

Starostin laughed. 'We always welcome new supporters. Alexei, I'll have to give you another ticket for our new enthusiast. The

Red and Whites are always glad to have fine fellows cheering them on.'

'Well, Comrade, when you're playing those dirty Army bastards you can trust me to be behind you one hundred and ten per cent! Komsomol's honour – believe it!'

And there was something about the vehemence of Semionov's statement that made the two older men laugh for a little longer than was polite.

During the conversation, Starostin had led them through the open gates and now he pointed towards the Tribune area at the east end of the stadium, where the terraces were open to the elements.

'The groundskeeper found him just there, a few rows back. I waited with him until the Militia arrived so that nothing would be disturbed. He was very badly cut up, you know; the dead man. Some bastard had—'

'Yes, we know. We saw the body in the morgue,' Korolev cut in quickly, not wanting to be reminded. He looked at the spot to which Starostin was pointing. There was nothing much to indicate a body had been there, except the large number of footprints trailing towards it from several directions before meeting in a rutted, overlapping tangle where the snow was tinged pink.

'It's badly trampled, but do you remember whether there were any tracks when you got here? Any drag marks, for example?'

'Not really, but we can ask Sergei Timofeevich. I'll go and fetch him; he's down at the other end of the ground – wait here for a minute.'

Starostin walked towards the far goal post, where men were clearing snow from the pitch. Korolev looked at the muddle of footprints in disgust.

'God knows what happened here. At least Larinin had the sense to have some photographs taken, although I wish we'd seen it ourselves.'

'Why?'

'Because there's blood in the snow – not that much, but it might mean the man was dropped here quite soon after he died, or even that he was still alive when they put him here. If he was dropped after the snow stopped, the body wouldn't have had any snow on top of it and if it was dropped while it was snowing, we might have been able to work out what time it was left here by the thickness covering it. Still, the photographs might help. What time did the snow start last night?'

Semionov looked at him with wide eyes. 'Deduction! I see, like Sherlock Holmes. Excellent, Alexei Dmitriyevich – really excellent.'

Korolev lifted his hand to cuff the youngster.

'No, I'm being serious.' Semionov, half-offended, took his notebook out. 'Anyway, the snow. After midnight, I'm sure. I was out with some friends and didn't get home until then. It was very cold, but the snow still hadn't fallen. But I'll check with the meteorological office when we get back to the office. And what time it finished, yes?'

Korolev nodded agreement and turned to greet the grounds-keeper as he approached them, his felt boots moving quickly over the snow and his cap twisted in his gloved hands. Starostin followed behind him, smiling.

'I told them, I told the first lot, the footsteps, look at the footsteps, but they paid no attention. I made them keep away from them all the same, and my boys as well. Look over there.' He pointed to a set of blurred tracks that led towards them from the corner entrance to the north-east of the ground, the furthest away from the main road.

'A terrible thing, a terrible thing. I came in early to get the pitch ready for the reserve match tomorrow, but I always have a good look around in the morning to see if anyone's been in overnight. Local kids get up to the Lord knows what here in the summer, which is bad enough. I mean they're young and I was young myself once, but can't they find somewhere else? No, they can't, and I'm the one has to chase the little hooligans out all summer long. And only last March we found two drunks frozen under the away-team posts. Like this.' He stopped and contorted his face and body into an approximation of rigor mortis. 'Very upsetting. Their eyes were wide open, like fish in a tank. So I thought it was a drunk when I saw someone lying in the snow and, I'm thinking, here we go again, but no. It was worse.'

Only the recollection of the dead man stopped Sergei Timofeevich's monologue. His eyes glistened with tears, which he rubbed at with a threadbare glove.

'Oh it was a horrible sight, brothers. It shouldn't happen to anyone – a thing like that.'

Korolev seized the opportunity to interrupt. 'Sergei Timofeevich? I'm Captain Korolev and this is Junior Lieutenant Semionov. We'd like to ask you a few questions.'

'Ask. I know you anyway, Alexei Dmitriyevich, even if you don't remember me. A fine central defender in his time, Lieutenant; we used to call Korolev the Steamroller. If Korolev tackled you, you stayed tackled. That I can confirm. But always fair, always fair.'

Korolev looked carefully at the groundskeeper and detected a familiar face changed by drink and age. The eyes were the same though.

'Akunin? The referee?'

'Yes, yes, that's me.' The groundskeeper was delighted. 'Was me, I suppose. Akunin the referee. But then – ah well, now Comrade Starostin allows me to be Sergei Timofeevich the groundskeeper. It keeps me involved in the game and I enjoy the work. But enough – what are these questions you have for me?'

Korolev caught Semionov's smile from the corner of his eye and deduced that it wouldn't be long before his old nickname was doing the rounds in Petrovka Street. He turned his attention back to Akunin.

'It's good to see you, Sergei Timofeevich. We players always thought you were a fine referee.'

'I wasn't bad, it's true.' Akunin beamed with pleasure. 'So, how can I help you?'

'Well, for a start, could you show us how the body was laid out?'

'Of course, Captain. He was flat on his back, with his hands by his side, like this. The face, the poor face though. He looked terrified. His eyes were like this. I couldn't turn my head away for a full minute when I saw them.'

The groundskeeper did an imitation of the corpse lying in the snow, with crazed eyes and a wide open mouth. It wasn't dissimilar to his imitation of the dead drunks.

'And on his chest,' he continued, 'God forgive him his sins, were—'

'Yes, yes, yes,' Korolev said, cutting him off. 'We know all about that, thank you. But tell me now, was there snow on top of the body, Sergei Timofeevich?'

'A bit. We had about four inches last night, as you can see, but I'd say he only had a dusting. Did I mention how his clothes were hanging off him? It looked like they'd been hacked and cut nearly as bad as him.'

'Thank you, that's useful. Was there anything else you noticed? Anything at all?'

'Only the footsteps – they're blurred by the snow, but there were two of them, I'd say. Do you see? One behind the other?'

Korolev crouched down beside the trail Akunin indicated.

'But on the way out they walked alongside each other.'

'Look, Vanya,' Korolev said, pointing down, 'this fellow's steps are wider apart. So he was probably taller; quite a bit taller, by the look of it.' Starostin was looking at his watch and Korolev took the hint. 'Thanks for your time, Nikolai. We'll just follow the tracks out. There's no need for you to wait around – but if you could join us, Sergei Timofeevich, it might be useful.'

Starostin made his farewells and left the investigators to their work, along with their willing assistant, the former referee. Korolev looked with regret at where the body had lain.

'I'd wish I'd seen it. There might have been something, you never know.' He turned to the others. 'Come on; let's see if there's anything else.' They walked alongside the two sets of footprints, following them to the north-eastern entrance. Someone had taken a crowbar to the gate and it hung open, the lock disembowelled.

'Another job to be done,' the groundskeeper muttered.

'Wait a second,' Semionov said and pointed to the snow in front of them. 'No one else has been over here. Right, Sergei Timofeevich?'

'No, your colleague, the short fat one, said it was too cold to be running around in the snow on a wild-goose chase for a dead Thief.'

'Look, Alexei Dmitriyevich.' Semionov pointed to a half-covered empty packet of cigarettes. 'Doesn't that mean this would have had to have been left by the killers? Seeing as there's snow underneath it.'

'Good lad, let's get it out and have a look.'

Semionov stooped down and carefully picked the packet out, a small damp patch forming around it on the palm of his leather glove.

'Hercegovina Flor. Expensive. Restricted stores and restaurants. A friend of mine smokes them.' Semionov imparted the last piece of information with a certain reluctance.

'A woman friend?'

'Men smoke them too,' Semionov said defensively.

'I see. Got something to put the packet in?'

Semionov rooted in his pockets without finding anything suitable so he tore a page out of his notebook and wrapped it round the damp packet before following the older man through the gate. There were indeed tyre tracks, but the snow covered an asphalted area so no distinguishable markings could be made out, just tracks coming in and then going out, and a circle where the car had turned. They followed them to the main road anyway, just in case.

'A shame,' Semionov said, kicking at the snow.

'Well, nothing to take a cast from, but it looks like it was a car, rather than a truck. And how many people have access to cars in Moscow? Not that many. We'll ask at the local Militia station – see if one of their patrols saw any vehicles near here last night. Is there a nightwatchman, Sergei Timofeevich?'

'Of course, but he normally keeps to the office building if it's snowing.'

'Thank you. Ask him to call the lieutenant when he comes in. Ivan Ivanovich will give you the telephone number.'

§

Korolev was quiet on the drive back to Petrovka Street as he tried to make something of the visit to the stadium. The expedition had been useful he supposed. Now they knew there were two men involved, that one was tall and the other shorter, that they'd access to a car and that one of them possibly smoked Hercegovina Flor. Progress, sure, but unless the killer struck again not much to go on. He growled once more with the frustration of it all.

Semionov looked over at him.

'It's nothing. Keep your eyes on the road.'

The motive must be the key. Nine times out of ten with a murder, if you found the motive you found the killer attached to it. Gregorin had as good as confirmed that the murder was linked to someone in State Security flogging artworks on the side. So, if the dead girl was a nun, the logical deduction would be that she'd been after some item of religious significance or value. Gregorin had seemed to hint as much. A relic, perhaps. Or an icon? Many relics and icons had been destroyed since the Revolution, as had the churches they'd been displayed in. Still, it was worth following up. But what about the dead Thief? He didn't look like someone who'd have anything to do with icons, unless they were drawn in blue ink. It was confusing, but it seemed to him that if the killer wasn't a madman, or a pair of madmen now, then it was odd the bodies had been left in such public places. There weren't so many murders in Moscow that two like this wouldn't stand out. So, although the electricity burns and the signs of torture were the only definite links between the victims, he was pretty sure the killers were the same, but it was worth considering whether there might be different motives for the murders. He caught Semionov looking at him again, and pointed his assistant's attention back to the road ahead.

Hopefully Larinin, who'd gone back to Petrovka to see if he could find the Thief's file, would come up with something. There must be a file – he'd seen it on the fellow's fingers. If they knew which gang he belonged to, they could round up a few of his pals and give them a grilling. Not that Thieves talked to policemen willingly, given that cooperation with the Soviet State in any form was forbidden by their code. Even having a paying job was frowned upon, unless it was a front for criminal activity. He scratched his head in frustration – he felt like a dog in a field of rabbits, chasing after ideas that seemed to breed in front of his very eyes. And what was it Gregorin had said about the nun? That she was one of two possible candidates – did that mean there was another American wandering round Moscow? What on earth were they up to, these Americans?

'Alexei Dmitriyevich?' Semionov said.

'Yes?' Korolev barely succeeded in keeping the irritation out of his voice.

'He was a real gentleman, wasn't he? Starostin? And giving us two tickets for the final against the squaddies. Will we go? It should be a great game.'

'I don't see why not. I've a feeling this investigation is about to hit a brick wall.'

'Don't say that, Alexei Dmitriyevich. You told me yourself, my first day on the job – when it looks like there's nothing to be done, that's the time you go back to the beginning and start all over. One berry at a time, and the basket will be full. We still have avenues to explore.'

'Yes, there are certainly things to be done and berries to be picked.' He tried to sound more positive than he felt. They were driving along Okhotny Row and about to turn into Teatralnaya Square, when the Metropol came into view. And it occurred to him – hadn't Gregorin as good as told him to go and talk to this American, Schwartz?

'Pull over, will you, Vanya? I'll walk the rest of the way. I need to go and see someone.'

Semionov brought the car to a halt and noted his superior's changed demeanour. 'A berry, Alexei Dmitriyevich?'

'Maybe – we'll see. Start looking into the cars, Vanya. There are probably only twenty privately owned cars in the whole city, so you'll have to go to the factories, the big concerns, the ministries. See if you can find out who had cars available to them last night. It's a needle in a haystack job, but you never know. And take that cigarette packet over to forensics.'

It would keep him busy and away from the Metropol – full as it was of foreigners, bigwigs, speculators and the like – and, also, as a result, the NKVD.

Chapter Ten

THE METROPOL wasn't the tallest building on Teatralnaya, being a mere six storeys high, but it enjoyed a prime location across the square from the Bolshoi Theatre and on a dark, clouded day – such as this one – the hotel's many lit windows sent out a welcoming glow. The structure, an ornate mixture of the art deco and Russian imperial styles, still retained a *fin de siècle* elegance despite the more recent inscription that ran the length of the fifth floor: ONLY THE DICTATORSHIP OF THE PROLETARIAT CAN FREE MANKIND FROM THE CAPITALIST YOKE – V. I. LENIN.

The inscription always struck Korolev as a little unfriendly given that the Metropol catered mostly for important visitors from abroad and Western specialists, many of whom were presumably enthusiastic proponents of that same capitalist yoke, and very much against being dictated to by the proletariat. Still, whether the foreign capitalists liked it or not, even ordinary Soviet workers like Korolev could visit the Metropol and order a glass of beer – despite its splendours, it was owned by the State, and the State was the People. The thought buoyed him up as he crossed the road towards the entrance, conscious, as he was, that wherever there were foreigners there was danger, and that most ordinary people avoided the Metropol, leaving it to apparatchiks, Party cadres, famous actors and the like to fly the Red Flag on their behalf. The hotel might be owned by the People, but that didn't mean the People were crazy enough to visit it.

Korolev nodded to the tall doorman and showed him his identity card.

'Moscow CID. Militia business. Where's the manager's office, Comrade?'

The doorman, dressed in a uniform that had more gold braid and tassels than a tsarist general's and with a magnificent beard that looked like it might be supported by hidden wires, took Korolev's papers and examined them for a moment before smiling, as one worker to another.

'Up the stairs and ask at reception, Comrade. The duty manager's the fellow you need to talk to. Nikolai Vladimirovich. Don't be put off by him, he's a decent lad.'

The foyer was huge, lined with mirrors and paintings and more gilt and crystal than could be taken in immediately, all topped by a sky-blue ceiling, the corners and edges of which were decorated with painted clouds. Korolev had never been to the Metropol before and he was sufficiently taken aback by the grandeur of the interior to stop in his tracks and look around him like, he suspected, some village idiot at his first May Day parade. But most extraordinary of all was the long pool that graced the centre of the room, in which young women with unnaturally red lips and jewelled swimming caps were performing some kind of ballet, their tight black swimsuits stretching with their bodies as their legs rose from the water as one. Korolev found himself instinctively removing his hat out of respect, although the swimmers paid him no attention, their eyes being fixed at an indeterminate point somewhere in the vicinity of the chandeliers.

He felt his cheeks reddening, but pulled himself together enough to advance towards the ornate oak-panelled reception desk, hoping the foreigners paid through their noses for all this, the rats. A handsome fellow in a dinner jacket was waiting for him, looking like a film star with his oiled hair and carved cheekbones – it was enough to make a man want to kick something. Korolev placed his identity card on the waiting blotter.

'I've a few questions for the duty manager. I believe Nikolai Vladimirovich is the man I want.'

The receptionist examined Korolev's photograph with polite attention. No doubt the capitalist women just loved this fellow, Korolev thought, taking a quick dislike to him. If he was a member of the proletariat, then Korolev was a tangerine.

'Of course, Comrade, I'll go and fetch him. Please take a seat by the fountain and he'll be with you shortly.'

The film star pointed him to a cluster of red velvet seating, beside which water splashed and sparkled. Korolev walked over and sat down beneath a half-naked gilded nymph carrying an unlikely looking red star. He tried to relax, but he couldn't help noticing that his *valenki* were giving off a pungent aroma not dissimilar to damp horse. He looked down and saw melting slush spreading over the crisp marble floor around his feet. Well, at least it wasn't yellow, he thought to himself, feeling more and more uncomfortable.

After a few minutes, most of which Korolev spent wishing he was somewhere else, a small rotund man approached with an outstretched hand; teeth sparkling beneath his precisely sculpted, razor-thin moustache. A party badge twinkled on the lapel of his morning-suit coat.

'Comrade, I came as soon as I could. Nikolai Vladimirovich Krylov, Duty Manager. Please follow me. I wish to be of *every* assistance.'

Korolev followed Krylov's patent leather shoes as they clicked across the marble floor towards what appeared to be a mirrored wall. At Krylov's confident push, the mirror revealed itself to be the hidden door to a comfortably furnished office. Aside from a green-topped wooden desk, there were a pair of buttoned leather armchairs and a matching leather couch gathered around a glass coffee table. Krylov pointed Korolev towards the couch.

'Would you like a cognac, Comrade? French and very fine.' Krylov reached for a decanter.

Korolev was about to refuse the offer when he caught sight of a brass carriage clock on the chimneypiece. It was four o'clock already, and it had been a long day.

'French, you say? Well, why not?'

'Excellent,' Krylov said and filled two small glasses to the brim. He handed one to Korolev and sat down carefully opposite with the other, raising the delicate glass in toast.

'Your health, Comrade.'

'And yours,' Korolev replied and they drank a healthy sip, but not all of it. They were cultured Soviet citizens, after all, not beasts of the field.

'So how can I assist you, Captain?' Krylov asked, leaning forward, his pale face showing a concern that was perhaps a little exaggerated. Korolev decided there was no point in beating about the bush.

'You've a fellow called Schwartz staying here – I'd like to talk to him.'

Krylov nodded slowly. His eyes were very dark, Korolev noticed, and perhaps this accounted for the lack of visible reaction to his request.

'May I ask what your enquiry is in connection with?' Krylov asked, after lengthy deliberation. 'While we always cooperate fully with representatives of the Ministry of State Security, we do owe a duty of confidentiality to our guests.'

Korolev realized he had just very politely been reminded that he, a humble Militia captain, was treading on NKVD turf, and had better have some justification for doing so. He swirled the remaining cognac round his glass and finished it with a gulp, the heat of the alcohol warming his stomach.

'It's to do with a murder, Comrade Krylov. It's been suggested to me, by another part of the Ministry, that I should talk to this Schwartz fellow.'

Krylov stood up and reached for the bottle to refill Korolev's glass.

'We're under instructions to give this resident, in particular, a certain amount of discreet protection. Do you think . . .' he began and Korolev took the hint.

'May I use your phone, please, Comrade Krylov? I'll speak to a colleague at State Security, just to make sure I'm not stepping on anyone's toes.'

Krylov gave him a relieved smile.

'Of course, please be my guest. Ask the operator to put you through. And don't worry – she won't be listening in. They know better than that, but then, of course . . .' Again he failed to finish his sentence, giving a small shrug as he stepped through the doorway that told Korolev that if the operator wasn't listening in, someone else probably was. A good lad, despite the fancy dress. He picked up the phone on the desk, asking for the Lubianka and then for Staff Colonel Gregorin when the switchboard answered. Gregorin's voice sounded tired when it came on the line.

'Comrade Korolev? At the Metropol, I believe. Isn't it a little early for you to be out on the town?'

'Strictly business, Comrade Colonel,' Korolev answered, trying his best to hide his surprise that Gregorin knew where he was. 'I thought I'd talk to that American you mentioned – Schwartz.'

'I think you should, Korolev. But just talk to him, nothing more, you understand. Make it clear it's an unofficial enquiry and be discreet about the girl. We don't want to offend the Americans. You're dealing with Krylov, I believe. Put him on. By the way, I'll meet you at your building at seven-thirty this evening. I think you should be introduced to your neighbours.'

Krylov took the phone when summoned, agreed with the colonel twice in the one-sided phone call, then hung up. He turned to Korolev with a smile.

'Mr Jack Schwartz is the gentleman you want. He's a regular guest. American, from New York. He's been here for the last ten days. The profession he gives on his visa, which is a business visa, not a tourist one, is "antiques dealer".'

Korolev liked the way Krylov pointed out Schwartz was on a business visa. It meant that Schwartz was a friend of the State in case Korolev hadn't worked it out already, and an antiques dealer would fit in with what Gregorin had told him.

'I'll see if he's in. Is there anything else you would like in the meantime, a sandwich perhaps?'

'No thank you, Comrade Krylov. I'm not hungry,' Korolev said, the lie tasting like meatballs in his mouth.

'Are you all right, Comrade, you look quite pale.'

'It's nothing Comrade. Just a momentary dizziness. Perhaps my Soviet liver is reacting badly to this bourgeois cognac.'

'Well, your Soviet liver should be proud to prevent the cognac being drunk by foreign capitalists. A selfless act!' Krylov winked and left the room, returning moments later.

'You're in luck, Comrade, he's sitting outside at this very moment. Come, I'll introduce you.'

§

Mr Jack Schwartz of New York fitted in very well at the Metropol. Korolev had to acknowledge that the American's grey woollen suit was cut with a level of precision that was beyond Soviet tailors, even the one Krylov used. Disconcertingly, he found himself seized by a desire to run his fingers along the jacket's lapel – just to feel the fabric. Looking at it, he guessed it would be just as soft as the dead girl's skirt, but he put the thought aside, reminding himself that Soviet clothes would be its equal, and better, in time.

Schwartz was a young man, about thirty, good-looking with full lips, a long jaw and dark brown eyes that seemed large for his face. He sat reading through some typewritten pages, his overcoat and a briefcase taking up one of the other seats at the table.

'What can I do for you, Captain?' Schwartz said in perfect

Russian when Krylov introduced them. Korolev wondered whether his red tie was worn out of politeness or conviction.

'I'm investigating a crime, Mr Jack Schwartz, and I believe you may be able to assist me. My approach is unofficial, of course, and I hope if I ask you a few questions they will not interfere in any way with your enjoyment of your visit to Moscow and the Soviet Union, where you are most heartily welcome.' A little formal perhaps, Korolev thought, but better safe than sorry. Schwartz nodded his head towards one of the other chairs at the table.

'Pull up a seat, Captain Korolev. I'm always pleased to fulfil my civic duties. What's it that you're investigating? Must be something serious.'

'Yes, it is, Mr Jack Schwartz. A murder.'

'A murder?' At first Schwartz seemed almost amused but then, after he'd thought about it for a moment or two, Korolev saw the humour drain from his eyes.

'Who was it?' he asked in a flat voice.

'We're not sure. A young woman, in her early twenties we believe. Attractive, dark hair cut short. Blue eyes, slim build, about five foot four in height. Does that sound like someone you might know?'

Korolev thought he detected a reaction to the description, a momentary pause while Schwartz fitted the description together to make a picture, then an involuntary intake of breath, immediately suppressed, and covered up by a hunt through his pockets for a packet of cigarettes. Hercegovina Flor, as it happened. He pulled a cigarette out of the packet and then offered one to Korolev, before lighting both with a thin gold lighter.

'I don't think it sounds like anyone I know in Moscow,' Schwartz said, his face a picture of puzzlement. 'What made you think I might have? I come to Moscow a couple of times a year it's true, but I only stay for a week or so. Pretty much everyone I meet here is a business contact.'

'You speak excellent Russian, Mr Jack Schwartz. I would imagine a good-looking man such as yourself would find no shortage of female admirers in Moscow, even on such short visits.'

Korolev might not visit the Metropol, but he knew what went on here. He knew about the Russian girls who threw themselves at foreigners, desperate for a new life in a place like New York, where their dreams about capitalist life would no doubt be subject to a rude awakening. Schwartz frowned.

'I find my business here pretty much all-consuming, I'm afraid, Captain. But, like I said, what makes you think this woman knew me?'

'A suggestion from a third party. They also indicated you might be able to tell me something about the export of various valuable objects, some of them possibly religious. I don't know – icons, perhaps.'

Again Korolev watched Schwartz carefully for a reaction, but there was nothing this time except a quick glance at his watch.

'I'm afraid the description of the woman still means nothing to me, Captain. However, I'd be happy to tell you what I can about exporting art and so forth, but you'll have to forgive me. I've an appointment at five at the Moskva. Could we arrange to meet another time?' He smiled in apology and indicated the overcoat and briefcase.

'Of course. As I said, this is only an informal conversation. You shouldn't be late for your meeting.'

'I wish I could help you.' Schwartz looked at him for a moment, as though he were thinking something over. 'But listen, why not walk with me? You can tell me more about the case – maybe it'll jog my memory. And I'll tell you about the antiques trade.'

Once they were outside and walking across Teatralnaya Square, Schwartz turned to Korolev. 'So how did she die, this nameless victim?'

'Not easily. Are you sure you want me to tell you the details?'

Schwartz nodded, 'Yes, please do. If you're permitted, of course.'

'She was tortured, I'm afraid. Very badly. There was also some mutilation. Parts of her body were removed and it seems she was burnt with electricity.'

Schwartz slowed his pace and then stopped altogether. He carefully put his briefcase down beside him, put his hands in the pockets of his suit and looked over at the Bolshoi Theatre – he seemed lost in thought.

'Do you know who did it?'

Schwartz's reaction seemed genuine, so Korolev decided to give him some incentive to cooperate.

'We're at an early stage of the investigation, I'm afraid, and not making much progress. If it carries on like this, there's a good chance the killer will escape punishment – we're running out of leads to follow up.'

Schwartz seemed to consider this.

'It's very cold, isn't it?' Korolev remarked, after a pause, having come to the conclusion that the antiques dealer knew exactly who the dead woman was.

'Yes. To be honest, I didn't really come prepared. I thought I'd miss the winter this year, but it's started early.' Schwartz turned his gaze to Korolev and blinked. Korolev lowered his gaze, wondering whether he'd given his suspicions away.

'You know I'm an American citizen, of course.'

'Yes,' Korolev said, thinking this a strange statement to make.

'I come here twice a year to buy valuable objects of historical and artistic importance from the Russian State. Did you know that?'

'There's no one else here to buy them from, I believe.'

Schwartz smiled, as though at a hidden joke. Korolev noted the reaction.

'Perhaps not. Anyway, I pay hard currency, very large amounts of it, and I deal with the Ministry of State Security. Your Militia is part of that, right?'

'That's correct.'

'Well, I think I know who your dead woman was and I'll tell you here, out in the street, away from any recording device or witness – if you want me to. But I'll deny everything if I'm ever contacted in the future. In other words, I'm asking whether I can rely on your discretion. Of course, I could probably just make a phone call and you'd be instructed not to bother me any more, but I'd like to help you. If it's who I think it is, she was a good person. I didn't know her that well, but she sure as hell didn't deserve to get killed in the way you describe. What do you say?'

Korolev looked at the young man and then nodded briskly.

'Tell me what you know, please, Mr Jack Schwartz. I will keep it out of the file.' Korolev held out his hand to confirm the agreement and Schwartz took it.

'Well, first off, you can just call me Jack.'

Korolev nodded, although he thought this was a little informal, given that they had only just met. Still, everything was no doubt different in America. Capitalists probably had little need for politeness and refinement – they were unlikely to be as cultured as Soviet citizens.

'OK, Jack. And please – call me Alexei.' It felt odd, but he supposed reciprocation was necessary in the circumstances.

The American looked at his watch and appeared to be already reconsidering their agreement. He gave Korolev a quizzical look, sighed and then spoke very quickly.

'I think your woman is called Nancy Dolan, she's an American.'

'Nancy Dolan?' Korolev said, wondering who the devil Nancy Dolan was. He'd seen Mary Smithson's papers after all, and the dead girl certainly seemed to be her.

'Yes, Nancy Dolan, or at least that's the name she was using last time I saw her. Look, it works like this. I represent a number of clients on my visits here – art galleries, museums, collectors mainly – but I also act for some others. Your people know I act for them, and my clients know who I'm buying from, but it would be embarrassing for everyone if it became public knowledge.'

'I'm sorry, I'm not quite sure I understand.'

'I act for émigrés basically, former nobility, that kind of person, and I also act for the Orthodox Church. That's what you were hinting at, wasn't it? When you mentioned icons?' Korolev nodded, hoping he wasn't betraying his surprise.

'Well, sometimes I'm sent to look for a particular item that one of those clients knows is in Soviet hands. An heirloom perhaps, a painting, a piece of jewellery – if it's available, and the buyer is prepared to pay foreign currency and be discreet, your representatives are generally prepared to sell. With the Church it's a little different. They look for items of religious significance, often icons, but also other things – relics, books, churchware. I let them know what your people have available and they give me instructions accordingly. But it's rare for them to send me after a particular object. Are you still with me?'

It wasn't that different from what Gregorin had told him so Korolev nodded, although he was still a little perplexed that the State was selling property to former oppressors of the People.

'Good. Now, as I said, I often don't have a particular item in mind when I'm acting for the Church, unless it's already on offer. But this trip is different. The Ministry has a particular icon, at least according to the Church's contacts, and the Church want it. They want it very badly, in fact. And I think it's possible Nancy Dolan was here looking for that icon.'

Korolev considered what he'd just been told. What icon was worth two deaths?

'Tell me about the icon, please, Jack,' he said, the name feeling slippery on his tongue.

'I can't. I wish I could, but the information is sensitive to say the least. It's important – that much you can guess.'

'A miraculous icon?'

'Nice try, but I can't tell you anything more about it. Except that I'm ready to pay good money for it unless it's an obvious fake, but my contacts here won't confirm they have it. The only thing they've told me is that "they're aware of the rumours". I've told them I have the money for it. They asked how much. I named a figure – a damned big figure – and they said that that was very interesting and something they would bear in mind. Nothing more – I think the whole thing's a wild-goose chase.'

'But what did Nancy Dolan have to do with all of this?'

Schwartz seemed to consider how to respond and then he sighed.

'When I discussed the commission with the Church in the States, I'm pretty sure she opened the door to the house. She was a good-looking woman, so I remembered her, even though I only caught a glimpse. Then I met her ten days ago in Berlin – she was getting on the train to Moscow, same as me. I don't know if she recognized me, and I didn't let on I knew her – you know how these things are – but we were put at the same table in the restaurant for the entire journey and it was definitely the same woman. I knew she wasn't called Nancy Dolan back in New York, that's for sure, because she spoke Russian like a native. But on the train? Nothing more than "pozhalsta" and "spasiba". Anyway, we had a good time. I told her to look me up at the Metropol – she liked jazz and the Metropol's the place to come in Moscow if you like jazz. I got a call from her three days ago.'

'What did she want?'

'I don't know. The conversation lasted about thirty seconds – all she said was that she'd like to drop by. I told her to come over whenever she wanted to and that was the last I heard from her.'

'Three days ago. Did she say where she was staying? Anything at all?'

'Nothing. It was a pretty short conversation, like I said.'

'What was her official reason for being here, do you know?'

'She was on a tour, a Soviet organized one. Intourist, I think.'

Korolev pulled a notebook out of his pocket and then thought better of it. Schwartz nodded in gratitude.

'Thanks – I don't think I want any of this written down.'

'Understood. Did she mention meeting anyone in particular while she was here? Think back to the train journey. Anything you remember might be vital, Jack.'

He still couldn't get used to using Schwartz's first name; it didn't feel natural to him.

'She told me about some friends of hers working for Comintern in Moscow, but I don't remember their names or where they were staying. American I think.'

'Anything else?'

'Not really. Believe it or not, we spent most of the journey talking about the World Series. I saw the winning game – Yankees up against the Giants. She was a Yankees fan.'

'The World Series?'

'Yeah, baseball. You know, the game with the bat and the ball? American?'

'Yes, I think so. With the circle? I saw it on a newsreel once. Maybe the Ukrainians play it. We play football, of course, and every factory has an athletics team.'

'I think it's just us. Anyway, the Yankees won. She was happy about it. If you ever come to New York, let me know. You should go to a game.'

'Perhaps one day, Jack.' Korolev smiled at the unlikelihood of such a visit and then a thought occurred to him. 'But if you're still in Moscow on Friday, there's a big football game, Spartak against Central House of the Red Army. It will be an interesting cultural experience – you should come.'

They were nearly at the front door of the Moskva and Schwartz turned towards him and extended his hand with a smile. 'Why not?'

'Good,' Korolev said, already regretting the invitation. 'The game is at two o'clock. I could pick you up from the Metropol – say at twelve-thirty?'

'I'll look forward to it. Listen, I'm running late, but we have a deal? You keep me out of this?'

'Yes, of course,' Korolev said, shaking the American's hand. He watched Schwartz enter the hotel and shook his head in astonishment. What had he been thinking of? Asking a foreigner to a football game? He wouldn't have believed five minutes before that he could come up with a way to make things even worse than they were, but the answer was yes, he could. He'd better ask the general what he thought. And make sure Gregorin had no objections. Damn.

Still, Schwartz wasn't a bad fellow. Optimistic, self-confident, friendly, he seemed fresh and clean against the grey Moscow autumn. He wondered if New York was the same: shiny, a little brash. Perhaps things weren't quite as bad there as they made out. Things weren't that good in Russia: they couldn't keep the famines in the countryside secret, no matter how hard they tried. Hell, there were people starving in Moscow itself. The uniforms picked up bodies from the streets every day.

He looked at his watch. It was ten past five, and a ten-minute walk to the office. If he was lucky, he might catch Semionov. He started towards Petrovka and, as he turned, caught a glimpse of a face he recognized from the lobby of the Metropol: a young fellow, square of body and face, with short brown hair, sallow skin and a scrubby moustache. He appeared to be very interested in a passing group of Pioneers, their red neck-scarves poking from their winter coats. Korolev let his glance slide across the man – if it was a tail he didn't want him to know he'd spotted him. He wouldn't be surprised if they had been followed. Someone would be keeping an eye on Schwartz, given what he was in Moscow for, and they'd be interested in anyone who spoke to him. He had a nonchalant look round the square but couldn't see any others. Then again, if it was the NKVD, there'd be at least three or four and they'd be good at it too. He took a deep breath – they were either tailing him or they weren't. There wasn't much point in worrying about it, either way.

But when he caught a young woman observing him in the reflection from a Torgsin window five minutes later he cursed the day Popov had lined him up for this damned case. The investigation was beginning to take on a life of its own and he wasn't sure he was going to like what it might have in store for him.

Chapter Eleven

SEMIONOV rose to his feet with an excited grin when Korolev entered Room 2F. It almost made Korolev feel cheerful for a moment. He put his hat on the desk and sat down.

'Well?'

'Well,' Semionov began, and then paused as though to calm himself. 'Well, I may not have the car itself, Alexei Dmitriyevich, but I think I can tell you the make.'

'Go on,' Korolev said, shrugging his coat off onto the back of his chair.

'I've a hunch anyway. I went back out to the stadium. Every car has a different turning circle, you see, and I thought – well, why not measure it and see what it tells us? You see the new ZIS 101 has a turning radius of 7.7 metres, for example, whereas the Emka's is only 6.35 metres. The Model T we drove has a smaller one still. Anyway, I measured the tyre marks and, presuming they turned as tightly as they could – and I think they did because the tyre marks, if you remember, were within half a metre of the stadium wall – then I think the turning radius of the car they were driving was approximately 6.45 metres.'

'A bit bigger than an Emka's then?'

Semionov smiled and held his finger and thumb apart. 'Ten centimetres. Not much, really. But it rules out the ZIS 101. Anyway, listen to this. The nightwatchman was there when I went back and he told me he saw a new black car with a shiny metal radiator drive past his hut just after midnight. Coming from *behind* the stadium. The Emka has a chrome radiator facing, and we don't import many new cars these days.'

'I don't suppose he went out and had a closer look, did he, this nightwatchman?'

Semionov shook his head. 'He saw two men in a Black Crow, so he decided it was State Security business and none of his affair. He's about a hundred and five.'

'Did he come up with anything else?'

'He wanted me to investigate his next-door neighbour for currency speculation.' Semionov shrugged – everyone wanted to inform on everyone else these days. It seemed there was no class solidarity now that everyone was the same class.

'An Emka,' Korolev said to himself and wondered how many there were in Moscow. There was a knock on the door behind him and then the sound of it opening. He looked round to see the typist from the night before enter with a pile of papers. She looked at Semionov uncertainly, but then recognized Korolev as he turned.

'Comrade Korolev? Anna Solayevna – I have some interview notes for you from Captain Brusilov over at Razin Street. One of his men dropped them off. I thought they might be urgent, so I brought them up myself. Here they are.'

'Thank you.'

'It's a pleasure, Comrade. Particularly if it helps you catch that poor girl's killer.' She paused and gave a nervous smile. 'I'm sorry, Comrade, you said that the report was not suitable for the younger girls so I typed it myself. The poor child – what he did to her.'

She was about five years younger than him, light brown hair, a round face, brown eyes, a little careworn perhaps but still a good-looking woman.

'We're doing our best to track him down, believe me. We'll have a look through these; there may well be something useful. Thank you for bringing them up.'

She nodded and backed out of the door.

'Hmm, individual service. A little against the collective mentality, some people might say.'

Korolev turned towards Semionov and frowned. 'Well, is that all you have for me? Some wheel measurements and a drunken nightwatchman's hung-over recollection?'

Semionov's smile broadened.

'There's something else. The cigarette packet. No fingerprints, I'm afraid, but I know the outlets.' Semionov pointed at the piece of paper in front of him and Korolev held out his hand.

'You're a real shock worker today, I see,' Korolev said. Apart from the Metropol and the other central hotels, every other outlet was a closed shop, open only to senior Party members or privileged specialists attached to a particular workplace or organ of government. The NKVD stores were on the list, as were those of the Moscow Party's Central Office. 'Your friend must be very well connected or very well off to smoke such a brand.'

Semionov shrugged his shoulders. 'There are other outlets, of course, and they have a certain prestige, this brand. But the other outlets wouldn't be exactly "approved".'

'You did well,' Korolev said, relenting. He flicked through the list once again. 'It's good detective work, this. I'm not sure I much like the direction it's pointing us in, but it doesn't exactly come as a surprise.'

'It doesn't change anything, does it? If there's a bad apple in the Party then they need to be dealt with.'

'Of course, of course. It's just we'll have to proceed carefully: things are not always straightforward. I found out some things today as well, things that you need to be aware of.' And Korolev began to tell him about Mary Smithson, Nancy Dolan and the mysterious icon.

'The only problem is I'm not sure where we go from here,' he said when he'd finished. 'I know this is going to be a dangerous case to investigate. It may mean stepping on some people's toes, political toes. Whoever is behind this is probably a traitor of the worst possible kind. I've considered it carefully, Comrade, and I'd like you to consider stepping aside from the investigation. You're too young, Vanya. I won't take the risk.'

'Oh, come on, Comrade.' Semionov was indignant. 'How old were you when you went to the trenches? Surely fighting the Germans was a little more dangerous than a Moscow murder investigation, political or not. This is 1936, Comrade, in the Soviet Union, and we are Militia investigators. There's nothing we should be frightened of.'

'That's not the point, and it was a different situation back then.'

Semionov's jaw hardened. 'I don't know what's going on here, Alexei Dmitriyevich, but it doesn't matter to me who the criminals are. All the better, as far as I'm concerned, if they turn out to be Party members. A Party member who commits a crime is worse than an ordinary criminal because he's guilty not only of the crime, but also of betraying the Party. If I can help catch such a traitor, then I should be given the opportunity to do so. That's my duty and, as Comrade Stalin says, "Duty comes first."'

Korolev looked at his colleague and saw that there was no budging him. He'd known it would be this way, but he wouldn't have been able to forgive himself if something happened to the young fellow later on and he hadn't tried. At least he'd given him a choice. He shrugged his shoulders and waved Semionov to sit down.

'Then it's agreed, you stay on the case. Just trust me to handle some things alone until the situation is a little clearer. That's not an insult or a lack of trust on my part – just common sense. There's no point in putting us both at risk. I think I was followed here after I met the American. So you see? I may already be marked – no point in adding you to their list as well. Anyway, there'll be plenty of things for you to do, believe me. Just let me look after the political aspects for the moment.'

Semionov thought about it and then spoke quietly. 'I'll accept that, but let me help as much as I can. I'm not afraid of the consequences.' He held Korolev's gaze. 'So what's our next step?'

Korolev tapped the interviews in front of him. 'Well, let's work our way through these for a start.'

'Agreed,' said Semionov with a grin.

Korolev took the top half of the papers and slid them across to Semionov.

'Make notes as you go – anything remotely relevant or even just unusual. Remember, we don't know what we're looking for necessarily, so look for what shouldn't be there.'

Semionov nodded and opened his notebook beside the first interview. He was soon making notes. Korolev picked up an interview from his own pile and began to read, hoping a nugget might be hidden amongst the gossip and denunciations that made up the first few interviews. Why was it, he wondered, that if you put a policeman in front of a Muscovite these days they'd use the opportunity to denounce half the people they knew? Here was another one, a single man with no apparent job, out all night and possessed of a large room all to himself, while Citizeness Ivanova, her husband and four children were crammed into a smaller room that they had to share with a young couple and a baby. How had the rascal managed it? Citizeness Ivanova asked. A drug dealer and a male prostitute was her answer. Korolev was almost tempted to look into it, but then it would probably turn out the fellow's uncle was a senior Party member or the like.

He ploughed his way through the grimy reality of Soviet life from one end of Razin Street to the other. Primus stoves missing from the communal cooking area, drunkenness in Metro Workers' Dormitory Number 12, a single mother's string of male visitors: it would be better soon, he hoped, for the next generation anyway. A thought occurred to him and he flicked through the interviews to confirm it. No one had spoken to any of the street children who'd been outside the church. It might be worth tracking them down – children often noticed things adults took for granted. He made a quick note.

It was tedious work, but the best way to approach interview notes was to read with a sort of double focus. You obviously had to take in every detail, no matter how mundane it seemed, and then you had to fit that detail into the wider picture. As it turned out, Brusilov's men had done a good job. Korolev wasn't surprised – you didn't last long on Brusilov's beat if you weren't up to scratch. It was an uphill struggle for the Militia in Moscow at the best of times, but the last few years had seen huge numbers of peasants coming in from the countryside, driven by a combination of hunger at home and the prospect of work in one of the big factories or on one of the many construction sites. Getting a residence permit was tough, but that didn't stop them; if they got a job they'd probably get the permit. In fact, getting a permit wasn't that difficult compared to finding a scrap of dry floor to lie down on at the end of the day's work. There were people sleeping on stairs, on trams, in the Metro. The Militia uniforms moved them on when they found them, but there were so many. And the hardness of life led to other problems as well. The incomers made fools of themselves when they managed to get enough money together for drink, not that native Muscovites were much better, and the drunkenness led to violence, rape, sometimes murder. But Brusilov had a lid on things around Razin Street and mischief-makers avoided the area.

Perhaps as a result of this, Brusilov's men had found the local residents helpful or at least very talkative when they'd asked them whether they'd seen anything unusual on the night of the murder. Korolev suppressed a smile when one interviewee in a communal apartment claimed that her neighbours, recently arrived from some far-off village to work at the Red October factory, were keeping a pig in the shared bathroom. Korolev was fairly comfortable that this was both unlikely and unconnected to his case, although, on second thoughts, he'd heard stranger tales about communal apartments, where collective insanity, after years of living in strangers' armpits, was not unusual.

In amongst the gossip and recriminations, however, two interviewees mentioned a black car parked on Razin Street, close to the church. One remembered nothing more than the colour of the car, but the second, a teenage boy, was absolutely certain that the car was a GAZ M1. The 'M' in the car's name referred to Vyacheslav Molotov, the Premier, and so the car was known to all as the Emka, the car Semionov suspected the murderers might have been driving out at Tomsky. Korolev made a note. It was surprising anyone had mentioned a Black Crow at all, the nickname for the black cars associated with the security Organs, particularly the NKVD, who had production priority. He usually refused if Morozov offered him one; the old Model T might have a broken windscreen, but at least people didn't turn away when they saw it, not immediately anyway. Finishing the pile, he looked up at Semionov, who was waiting patiently.

'I've two people who saw a black car that night,' Korolev said. 'One of them, at least, saw an Emka.'

'I've a black car parked near the church,' Semionov said.

'It doesn't prove anything, of course, but I think we should re-interview those witnesses. Ask them if they remember anything about the number plate. This boy who identified it as an Emka might remember something. He seems something of an enthusiast. Anything else?'

'This one here might be worth following up: an old woman who lives a few doors away from the church saw a drunk girl being guided along Razin Street by two men in heavy overcoats – just after midnight. She knew it was after midnight because she'd just heard the "Internationale" on the radio and then, because she lives so close to the Kremlin, she heard the bells from the Spassky tower ring the time as well. What do you think?'

Korolev was too long a detective to be surprised that an old lady would be scanning the street at midnight.

'Two men – same as the stadium. Any description of the girl?'

'Black coat, short hair – it could be her.'

'Maybe the killers drugged her before taking her to the church. Where's the old lady in relation to where the car was parked? That's what we have to check. We'll have to go round to all of these witnesses again. Draw it out on a map.'

Korolev pushed the pile of interviews to the back of his desk. 'Well, a few things to follow up, at least. I'll ask Staff Colonel Gregorin if he can help us with the Emka, but a registration number is what we really need.'

'What about identifying the dead Thief?'

'Larinin's looking through the mugshots and files, but if you could look through them as well, that would help. We'll see if we can get a picture to show around the stations. He's been through the Zone so there should be something.'

'Of course, Alexei Dmitriyevich. And thank you. I won't let you down.'

'I know. Get on home now, I'll write up this report and we'll talk tomorrow.'

§

Semionov didn't need to be told twice and with a quick farewell was on his way. Korolev looked at the younger man's empty seat, put his concerns about the lad behind him and started to write down the latest developments. It didn't take long: after all there were only so many of the day's revelations that he could put in writing. The rest would have to be communicated verbally.

He'd just finished and was checking over it for spelling mistakes when he heard a gunshot, muffled, but sounding as though it came from inside the building. He stood, slipped the Walther from his shoulder holster, pushed a round into the chamber, flicked the safety catch back and opened the door very slowly. Across the hall he could see the occupants of 2C and 2D also manoeuvring out into the corridor, guns first. He held his automatic up towards the ceiling and whispered across to Pauni-chev from 2C.

'Hey, Semyon. What the hell was that?'

Paunichev kept his eyes on the corridor he was slowly moving down and whispered back, 'We'll find out soon enough.'

Then a loud voice came from the stairwell up ahead. 'It's all right, boys. Just an accident.'

Korolev recognized General Popov's voice and slid his safety catch back on, the click it made echoed by several others along the corridor. Korolev stood upright and walked towards the stairwell, which was ringed on every floor by curious faces, some in uniforms and some not. The general looked down from the third-floor landing.

'Andropov had an accident, nothing to worry about. An ambulance is on its way.' His face looked pale in the electric light. 'Go on, back to work or off to a bar. If you all stand on the staircase at once, it might give way.'

There was a low rumble of laughter and the Militiamen started to disperse. Korolev took the opportunity to pick up the report he'd written and take it down to typing. Anna Solayevna was leaning out of the hatch to the typing harem, her face white in the shadows.

'What happened?' she asked in a whisper. 'I heard a shot.'

'It was nothing. An accident I think.'

But neither of them believed it.

§

He returned to his office and read through the interview notes once more, in case they'd missed anything, until the clock reminded him that it was nearly seven and time to go home. He collected his coat and hat and stopped at the canteen on the first floor for his weekly food parcel, which he slipped under his arm, where it was joined by the freshly typed daily report, handed to him by a proud Anna Solayevna as he passed the typing pool. She must have typed like a demon to have it ready in time, he thought to himself as he thanked her.

The temperature outside was so cold it hurt his eyes. He was turning up the collar of his coat when he saw the general standing beside an ambulance, watching a stretcher being loaded. A blanket covered the body but Korolev presumed it was Andropov – a fatal accident then. He walked over, murmuring a prayer for the dead man and removing his hat as he did so. Other people leaving the building had stopped, and five or six of them came closer to form a clump of dark solemnity on the wide steps that graced the front of the building. They waited until the ambulance pulled away. No one said a word – there was nothing to be said. Perhaps it really had been an accident, but now it had become yet another hole in the chronology to be carefully avoided. Korolev replaced his hat and walked away, not looking at the others. As far as he'd known, Andropov, a colonel, had been a happily married man with two children and a good apartment. A lucky man. Something had happened to change that, he supposed.

He watched the ambulance turn a corner, then walked out of the gates to join the dark crowds of silent pedestrians walking into the Moscow night.

Chapter Twelve

GREGORIN'S Emka was waiting for him when he reached Bolshoi Nikolo-Vorobinsky and, as he approached, the door opened and Gregorin stepped out. He leant back into the car and spoke a few words to the driver, a large black shape behind the steering wheel. Gregorin looked at his watch and smiled.

'A few minutes late. Busy day?'

There was something in his cheerful demeanour that infuriated Korolev. The feeling was so intense that he could feel it twisting his face into a snarl. He tried to suppress it but Gregorin was already giving him a quizzical look.

'Is there something wrong, Comrade?'

'Nothing. I watched an ambulance take away a colleague's body not thirty minutes ago. Perhaps it's that.'

'I'm sorry to hear it. What happened to him?'

'An accident, they say.'

'I see. There are a lot of accidents these days. Your friend Chestnova is kept busy.'

'Yes, it seems so.'

Gregorin shrugged his shoulders. Korolev knew what he was thinking – this was just the way things were these days.

'Have you brought today's report?' the colonel asked.

'Yes,' Korolev said, patting the front of his jacket with his free hand.

Inside the car, Korolev placed his food parcel at his feet. Gregorin switched on a small roof light, gesturing towards the driver as he began to read.

'This is Volodya, my driver. We can talk in front of him.'

Volodya turned his head towards Korolev. Everything about the face seemed to bulge, except for the eyes that peered out at him through pillbox slits. A massive hairy hand gave Korolev an incongruous thumbs up. Korolev nodded back, aware of the smell of sausage wafting up from the parcel on the floor. Krakow sausage. Korolev hoped this wouldn't take too long.

'Interesting, the tattoos. You'll have a full autopsy report tomorrow?'

'Yes, and hopefully an identification as well. There's bound to be a file on him – probably has a filing cabinet all to himself if the tattoos are anything to go by.'

'And the car?'

'If it's an Emka – well, they're not easy to get access to.'

'No,' Gregorin said, with a smug smile.

'We'll do our best, Comrade Colonel, but it might be that the NKVD would have more success tracking it down.'

'We'll certainly be looking into it,' Gregorin said, turning the last page and then switching off the light.

'What about the American?'

'It was an off-the-record conversation, for what that's worth.'

'Don't worry, Schwartz is useful to us. We leave the Americans well alone, particularly those who are, as I said, useful to us.'

There was something contemplative in the way he said the word 'useful' which made Korolev wonder if Schwartz did more for State Security than just buy a few icons from time to time. He hesitated, pretending to himself for a fleeting moment that he had a choice, and then repeated to Gregorin everything that Schwartz had told him. Maybe Korolev would have withheld something if he'd had an American passport and a return ticket to New York in his pocket. But he didn't and so discretion was a luxury he couldn't afford.

When Korolev had finished, Gregorin reached inside the inside pocket of his coat and produced his battered cigarette case, taking one out for himself, and then one each for Korolev and Volodya. Soon the car was a thick fug of cigarette smoke.

'Well, you're right,' Gregorin said after a while, 'Nancy Dolan isn't Miss Smithson. Lydia Ivanovna Dolina is her name. You remember I thought the dead girl could be one of two possible candidates? Well, Citizeness Dolina was the other candidate. A similar White Guard background.'

'Not a nun?'

'We don't know, but Schwartz's information seems to indicate she has religious connections at the very least. We have people working on it – I'll pass this on to them.'

'Schwartz said she was with an Intourist group.'

'Yes, it was when she went missing from the group that her cover story began to come apart. No one at Comintern has ever heard of her, although we're keeping an eye on the Americans there just in case. It's possible she has ended up the same way as Miss Smithson – if not we'll find her sooner or later. Moscow isn't such an easy place to hide.'

'You're looking for her?' Korolev asked through a cough – by this stage there was enough smoke in the car to cure fish.

'Only as a visa violator. We don't know how she fits into the picture, so we're keeping it low key. I'll let you have a photograph, in case you come across her.'

Korolev nodded his thanks.

'And this icon? Can you tell me anything about it?'

Gregorin let a small leaf of smoke curl out of his mouth and then exhaled the rest through his nose.

'There is a particular icon – one that went missing from a Lubianka storeroom two weeks ago. There might be a connection.' His words seemed carefully measured.

'The Lubianka? Christ,' Korolev said and would have pushed the word back into his mouth if he could, but Gregorin only laughed.

'No, I don't think it was him, he hasn't got the clearance. Other people have, though.'

'Is there a connection? Between the murders and the icon going missing?' Korolev was surprised his voice sounded relatively calm, given his entire body had broken into an icy sweat. To mention Christ in front of a Chekist staff colonel – he felt his toes curl into a cramp.

'It seems certain Nancy Dolan knows about the icon, if it was her who opened the door to Schwartz in New York – therefore it seems reasonable to assume she's here in connection with it. I think your dead nun must have been as well.' Gregorin spoke slowly, seeming to weigh each word. 'And if she was, then the Thief also – after all, it seems they were both tortured in the same way.'

'What icon is this – that people are dying for it?'

Gregorin shook his head after a long pause. 'I'm sorry, Comrade. There's no need for you to have that information at this stage. You must now concentrate on identifying this fellow Tesak and then any associates of his who might be involved. If you find Nancy Dolan along the way, so much the better. But leave the icon to us.'

'I see.' Korolev didn't really, but he saw enough to keep his mouth shut. Gregorin leant across and opened the door for the detective.

'You're expected.'

'I'm sorry?'

'Babel, the writer, your neighbour. He has good connections with the Thieves. He may be able to assist in your enquiries. I'm afraid another matter has come up that Volodya and I have to deal with. But I'll see you tomorrow evening, if not before.'

§

It was only after he entered the building that Korolev remembered he'd no idea which apartment Babel lived in, so he left his food parcel in his room and climbed the stairs to the second landing, hoping that the one-armed BMC chairman, Luborov, would be able to direct him properly. He knocked on his door a little out of breath, and waited, hearing movement and then the hollow sound of footsteps approaching on the wooden floorboards.

'Who's there?' Luborov's voice sounded strained.

'Korolev. I moved in yesterday.'

The door opened and Luborov looked out at him.

'It's nearly nine o'clock, Comrade. Do you need me as a witness?' Luborov was referring to the practice of having two independent witnesses present for arrests, particularly when it was a political matter.

'No, I just need you to tell me where the writer Babel's apartment is.'

Korolev knew some people made a living from being witnesses, but it was generally night work and often meant going without sleep if you worked in a factory or on a building site. He supposed Luborov's condition and his position on the BMC made it easier for him than for most people, but it wasn't a pleasant way to pass your time.

'Babel? He has rooms in the Austrian's apartment. I'm glad you weren't calling me out, I could do with a good night's sleep. It's become busy all of a sudden – it hasn't been like this for a while. Anyway, big black door to the left on the next landing up. Comrade Babel entertaining, is he?'

'I don't know, I've an appointment.'

'I thought I saw some people go up earlier – he likes to entertain. He never asks me, of course. Well, remember me to him. Goodnight, Comrade.' Luborov shut the door.

Korolev stood for a moment, considering what Luborov had said, and then turned to climb the stairs. So the witnesses were busy again. No one had thought things would change completely, of course, Muscovites knew better than that, but it seemed the quiet optimism of the last few months had been misplaced. He shrugged – it wasn't as if he could do anything about it, after all. It was like poor Andropov's accident: you just had to accept that these things happened and then forget about them.

He knocked on Babel's black door, which was indeed a fair size, and heard laughter and music inside. It sounded like Melkhov's band performing 'Girls, Tell Your Friends!' He knocked again in case they couldn't hear him and the door opened. A small woman in a black dress with a white handkerchief over her grey hair looked up at him, her sagging sallow face speaking of troubles endured, as much as age. Two sad brown eyes started at his waist and worked their way up. He took off his hat – there was something about the old woman that made him feel like a small boy.

'Who are you? What do you want?' the woman said, her voice rumbling with quite astonishing depth for such a small frame. The jazz record came to a bumping stop in the background.

'I'm Captain Korolev, Criminal Investigation Division. I believe I'm expected.'

'A *Ment*? I suppose I shouldn't ask.' She stood aside with an expression of distaste. 'Come in, come in. You're letting the warmth out. You think we can afford to heat the stairwell, do you?'

'Thank you.'

'Give me your hat and your coat, come on. Don't worry, I won't sell them to a passing speculator. I wouldn't get much anyway, they've seen better days. There.' She took the coat and hat and dropped them in a heap on a nearby chair. 'You can leave your briefcase as well. Have you eaten?'

Korolev hadn't had anything since the *blinchiki* on the way out to the stadium, but it wasn't polite to eat other people's food. Not with queues for bread the way they were since the poor harvest.

'I'm not hungry,' he said, hoping his stomach wouldn't betray him.

'Of course you're not. I made some cheese dumplings this morning. Will I bring you a plate?'

He shook his head, but his eyes must have betrayed him and she squeezed his arm.

'Of course I will,' she said.

In the sitting room five people sat around a low table on which glasses, a full ashtray and bottles stood. Five pairs of eyes looked up at him through the layers of smoke.

'Who's this?' A short, balding, heavy-set man was sitting cross-legged on the daybed, squinting at them from behind a pair of round, gold-framed glasses. He wore a collarless shirt with open cuffs and a pair of old trousers held up with braces. The shirt was starched a dazzling white and all the light in the room seemed to be focused on it. He smiled at Korolev, his brown eyes mischievous. 'Some boyfriend of yours, is it, Shura?'

'Ah, Isaac Emmanuilovich, you do like your little jokes, I can't grudge you them, I suppose, you poor thing you.' The old woman's deep voice rumbled out from the kitchen she'd stepped into.

'It's Captain Korolev, our new neighbour. I was just telling you about him.' Valentina Nikolaevna rose from the soft chair on which she'd been sitting. She was wearing a cocktail dress with a neckline that plunged low enough to reveal chiselled clavicles and swan-white skin. She smiled at him; not exactly a friendly smile, but not unfriendly either. Babel uncrossed his legs and rose to his feet, as did the others, and his smile was, in contrast, as warm as the sun. He waved Korolev to an empty chair.

'Welcome, Comrade. Valentina you know, and Shura it seems. This is my wife Antonina Nikolaevna – Tonya – and this is Avram Emilievich Ginzburg, the poet, and his wife, Lena Yakovlevna. Shura, bring Comrade Korolev a glass. Would you like wine or vodka, Comrade? We've both, you see.' He laughed, revealing even white teeth.

'I'd drink a glass of wine, if I might,' Korolev said.

'Let me guess, Captain. You're late home after a long day wrestling with evil, heard our little party and thought you'd introduce yourself. Thank God you did – poor Ginzburg was getting bored.'

The small man with wary eyes and a grey beard waved the suggestion away with a half-irritated smile, not shifting his gaze from Korolev's. He looked ready to run, but that was a reaction you became accustomed to as an investigator. It used to mean people had something to hide, but that wasn't necessarily the case any more; although, on second thoughts, there was something about the man's pallor and frailty that suggested Ginzburg was no stranger to the Zone.

'I'm sorry to disturb you, Comrade, but I'd hoped you were expecting me. Staff Colonel Gregorin suggested I come by.'

'Gregorin, ah yes,' Babel said.

'He thought you might be able to assist me with a case I'm working on. A murder.'

'A murder,' Babel said, his eyebrows lifting. 'Did you hear that, Shura? I know you're listening. Shura loves a good murder – the more horrific the better. And my beautiful Tonya isn't averse to homicide either.' Babel placed a proprietary hand on the knee of the pretty, long-necked brunette, who shook her head in shy disagreement.

'Have you eaten?' Babel continued.

'I have cheese dumplings for him, haven't I?' a grumpy Shura said, coming from the kitchen with a plate and an empty glass.

'I told you she was listening,' whispered Babel, and Shura leant over and slapped his arm.

'Don't be like that, Shura. Sit down now, and we'll see what kind of a story Captain Korolev has for us.'

Babel poured wine into Korolev's glass before crossing his legs beneath him.

'I'm afraid I can't talk about this particular case,' Korolev said, feeling awkward.

'Don't worry, Captain, I was only teasing. Have some wine and food and when you feel refreshed we'll talk. Avram is telling us about Armenia.'

Korolev lifted the glass of red wine and enjoyed the warm taste of it, beginning to relax as the bird-like man began to speak. Korolev looked over at Valentina Nikolaevna and was struck by the sharpness of her profile and the way she listened to Ginzburg. Her look was benevolent, even motherly, as though she wanted to shield him from the times they lived in. His wife, Lena, regarded him with the same affectionate gaze, although when she looked up at Korolev her face became closed and careful.

When Ginzburg finished his tales of the sun-baked Armenian hills, the conversation wandered from talk of Paris, where Babel had spent part of that summer representing Soviet literature at a writer's conference, to the construction of the Metro, on which Babel's wife Tonya worked as an engineer. Without being aware quite how it had come about, Korolev found himself telling the story of the rapist, Voroshilov – the trail of clues, the relief on the young man's face when he was caught. Although Shura, leaning against the kitchen door, maintained her stony face, he couldn't help notice the way she stared at him. Not at his eyes, he thought, but at his mouth, so that she didn't miss a word he said. It was Babel, however, who asked what clothes the rapist had worn, how he'd managed to obtain such a fine pair of boots, which lectures had been on the list that led to his undoing, and so on.

'What happened to him, the dog?' Shura asked when he finished.

'He'll get eight or ten years I should think, depends on what the court decides. It doesn't matter.'

'How so?' Ginzburg asked, but Korolev was sure he already knew the answer. He'd been in the Zone, or close to it – Korolev was sure of that now. He had the prison pallor of a *Zek*. Babel coughed, then picked up a bottle of wine.

'Come, friends, let's finish this off and we'll open another.'

'Tell us, Captain, why doesn't it matter?' Ginzburg's wife asked now and there was accusation in her tone. Perhaps she didn't understand. He looked at Babel, who shrugged his shoulders and poured out the wine, his eyes on the stream of red. Korolev sighed. Well, if they wanted to know, why shouldn't they? There were no children present.

'There's a hierarchy in a prison, even in a police cell. At the top sits the ranking Thief, the "Authority", then his lieutenants, then down through the Thieves to the lowest apprentice. Then beneath the Thieves are the other prisoners and then the politicals. At the bottom, beneath everyone, are the untouchables. No Thief, nor any other prisoner, will touch them except to commit violence upon them, sometimes sexual violence. They sleep underneath the bunks in case they contaminate a bed. They have their own cutlery, as a fork used by an untouchable would contaminate anyone who used it after them and bring them down to the untouchable's level. They are given the filthiest jobs. And they don't last long. Voroshilov will end up like that, as a rapist, unless he's very lucky. It's the Thieves' morality.'

Shura nodded her head, a short jab downwards with a hard mouth. It was peasant justice also. Harsh, even brutal, but just in a peasant's eyes, and she approved. Babel gave a half-smile.

'They have their own rules. It's difficult for cultured people to understand.'

Valentina Nikolaevna looked at him in confusion. 'How could this be allowed to happen? The Thieves are not the law.'

'They are in the camps and the guards allow it,' Ginzburg said and his eyes burned. 'The Thieves are the guards' dogs, and the rest are the sheep. That's what the Thieves call us – the politicals and the rest – sheep. And they can shear us whenever and however they want. The untouchables are there to tell us that, no matter how bad it gets, it can get worse. And to make us complicit because we all conspire against the untouchables. After all, if we helped them, we would become one of them. It's a little microcosm of Soviet society, wouldn't you agree, Captain?'

Korolev looked at Ginzburg in the silence that followed and saw how his chin was lifted, as though expecting a blow. Korolev sighed and shook his head.

'I'm a criminal investigator, Citizen. I find bad people who have done bad things and I put them in a bad place. What of it? As for Soviet society, it's getting better. We know it isn't perfect. Comrade Stalin tells us as much. It's in the nature of Bolshevik self-criticism to recognize its current flaws. It's where we're going, not where we are.'

'We know where we're going, Captain. We're going to . . .' Ginzburg stopped and turned to his wife, who'd taken his arm and now shook her head. Babel passed a glass of wine to him and another to Korolev. He seemed comfortable with the break in the conversation, and when everyone had a glass in their hand he raised his own.

'A toast, friends. To our beautiful future.' He held the glass for a moment as though to contemplate the prospect in the colour of the wine. Each of them seemed lost in thought and Korolev wondered if they, like him, were imagining what such a beautiful future might be like.

§

'You've won Shura's heart, you know,' Babel said, when the other guests had left and his wife had gone to bed. 'She loves a man with a healthy appetite and a good atrocity up his sleeve. You'll have to come again – she'll want to feed you now. If you don't watch out she'll make you fat. Look at me. I was a stick when she took me on.'

'A fat stick,' Shura said, from the kitchen. Babel laughed and stood up awkwardly from the daybed.

'Now, Captain, come into my study – we can talk privately there.' Babel led him along the corridor to a room with a desk and a typewriter, a chaise longue and a great many books that were shelved and stacked on or against every available surface. He shut the door behind them.

'It's not really mine, this room,' Babel said. 'I share the flat with an Austrian engineer, but he's in Salzburg and we don't know when he's coming back. It's been eight months, so I'm gradually taking it over. I don't think he's coming back, if the truth be told – but I tell the BMC his arrival is imminent. Of course.'

'An Austrian?' Korolev couldn't keep the surprise out of his voice.

'Yes, an engineer. I think he decided he couldn't face another of our winters, so he's staying at home in the Alps, listening to Mozart and drinking hot chocolate instead. They probably have a different type of snow, a polite kind, very gentle.'

'I would have thought . . .'

'Yes. It is dangerous, but I need the space to write. I assure you I'm not an Austrian spy, by the way.'

'I'm sure of it.'

'Oh, you can't be sure of it. The Party may decide otherwise.' He winked at Korolev and gave him a slanted smile. Then he frowned. 'Pay no attention to Ginzburg – he's at the end of his tether. Highly strung poets aren't designed for Five Year Plans and purges.' He put the glass to his lips and closed his eyes as he drank.

'Anyway, what's all this about? What assistance can a poor writer offer the combined forces of the NKVD and Petrovka Street?'

'I can't tell you all I would like to,' Korolev began and Babel nodded.

'That doesn't surprise me. I guessed as much when Gregorin called. Tell me as little as you can, if you don't mind. I've a two-year-old daughter asleep down the corridor and a wife I plan to spend a lifetime with – but I'm happy to help if I can.'

It was Korolev's turn to nod. 'There have been two murders. One of the dead was a Thief. The other was a young American woman, although of Russian birth – it seems she was also an Orthodox nun. The two killings are almost certainly connected.'

Korolev looked into Babel's eyes for a moment, then opened his briefcase and extracted the envelope of case papers. He took out the woman's autopsy photographs.

Babel took his time with each picture, seemingly absorbing each pore of her skin, each crusty fleck of blood. He turned the images to see them more clearly and when he had reached the last photograph, the one Gueginov had taken of the girl's profile, he sighed.

'She was quite beautiful. You would think he must have hated her to do this. But maybe not – he's such a precise man. See the way the clothes are neatly folded, the body parts arranged in just such a way. I wonder. Perhaps he's sending a message.'

Korolev leaned forward to look at the girl's body, all shadows and light in the black and white photograph. 'I thought as much myself. The way the ear, eye and tongue are arranged?'

'Yes, I've heard of something like this, but I've never seen it. It's something the Thieves used to do. To an informer. Or a spy. It means that the dead person may have heard and seen but he will never tell.' Babel looked up at Korolev, his eyes blinking as though trying to remove the dead girl's image from his retinas. 'But the Thieves would be unlikely to desecrate a church. They might steal from it but they wouldn't do something like this. Well, not while Kolya rules Moscow, that's for sure.'

Korolev found himself blinking now, but with surprise. He'd heard of Count Kolya but Babel's offhand reference implied a personal knowledge of a man reputed to be the Chief Authority of all the Thieves in Moscow. It wasn't an elected position, it was open to challenge, but Count Kolya was never challenged. At least, if he had been, the challenge had been dealt with so quickly and savagely that it had barely rippled the surface of his reign. The Militia had been trying to track him down for seven years, but a wall of silence surrounded him and any time the wall looked as if it might be penetrated, the informant who'd seemed to be a promising prospect had either disappeared or shown up dead. Now that Korolev thought of it, one of them had been mutilated in just such a way.

Babel tapped the side of his nose. 'I was born in Odessa, Captain. Do you think I made up the stories I wrote about Benya Krik? I changed his name, but if you ask any of the old Militiamen from Odessa they'd tell you all about him. As brave and honest a Thief as ever broke a maiden's heart. It was just that his version of honesty was quite different from yours and mine, and most certainly from the Party's. They caught him in the end. A bullet in the neck, I'm told. But they probably needed more than one to finish him. And he was revenged by his fellows, you can be sure of it.'

'Do you know Count Kolya?' Korolev asked and Babel exhaled a long breath, then nodded.

'I talk to him sometimes when I go out to the Hippodrome. Horses are a weakness we share. You might not spot him straight away, except that if you were to look in his direction for a little longer than you should you'd find three or four handy-looking lads with blue fingers have surrounded you, and then you get the strong impression it's time to go and look at the horses for the next race.'

'You know Count Kolya.' Korolev wasn't asking the question again, just expressing a quite amazing fact.

'Why do you think Gregorin sent you to me? The NKVD use me as a line of communication from time to time, although I try not to know what they communicate about. I'll tell you this, though. Kolya would never desecrate a church in this way. He's not a Believer, at least not the way I suspect you may be, but there's a code he must live by the same as any other Thief. If this was done on his instructions or with his consent – well, he wouldn't be the Chief Authority for long.'

Babel seemed oblivious to the fact that Korolev's blood had concentrated in his toes.

'A Believer, Isaac Emmanuilovich? Me?'

Babel looked up at him and smiled.

'Am I wrong?' He leant across and put his hand on Korolev's arm, smiling. 'Comrade Korolev, I apologize if I've offended you. I must be mistaken.'

Korolev drank the rest of the wine in a single gulp and wondered, not for the first time that day, how the hell he'd got himself into this mess. He took a deep breath, put the glass down firmly on the table and thought for a moment.

'I think I agree with you. If it was a message, maybe it was a message sent to the Thieves. Maybe to Kolya himself. The dead Thief was tortured as well. See these electrical burns on the girl's body – they both have them.'

Babel whistled. 'Is that what they are? You hear things, of course . . .'

'What things?'

'Things. How people are interrogated these days. I've heard that electricity isn't only used to brighten Lenin's Lamp.'

Korolev suspected Babel was coming to conclusions about what kind of a person might be behind the killings.

'Look, Comrade,' Korolev said, emphasizing the word 'Comrade' and putting into it all the loyalty and hope that old soldiers like Babel and himself remembered from the bitter years after the German War, 'I know it's a lot to ask, but there's someone going round killing people and I want to stop them, if I can. Whoever they are.'

Babel rolled the red wine round his glass, let it settle and then drank. He pursed his lips in appreciation and then shifted his gaze to Korolev.

'There's racing tomorrow. Trotters and flat. A horse I follow is in with a chance so I'd have been going anyway. If I see him, I'll approach him. I presume you'd like to know his side of it, if he'll tell me. I'll have to let him know who's asking, of course.'

'It might be better if he were to agree to a face-to-face meeting. That way you wouldn't hear things you might not wish to.'

Babel shrugged his shoulders as if to say, 'Why not?'

'It might be possible and, of course, even a man like me would rather not hear some things. Although I am curious – my God, I'm curious.'

He paused and smiled a cat's smile, full of speculation and mischief.

'It will have to be quietly done, of course,' he continued. 'The first rule in the Thieves' world is non-cooperation with the Soviet state in any form, you know that. What Ginzburg said – it's not quite right. Even in the prison system the Thieves bark at the sheep for their own purposes not because they're told to. Is there something in it for Kolya?'

'The Thief's body, perhaps? His tattoos say he was known as Tesak.' It might be done. General Popov would consent if it bought them some information – the body would only be incinerated otherwise. 'What do the Thieves do with their dead?'

'Same as the rest of us, I think. Put them in the ground and remember them fondly, or not, as the case may be. But for Kolya to recover Tesak's body from the police it would have to be handled so as not to make him look like an informer.'

'He can steal it, for all I care.'

'I'll ask him. Anything else you can offer him?'

Korolev considered for a moment and then decided that if he was going to run the risk of being shot, he might as well be shot for a reason.

'It can be a two-way conversation. He may be as interested in my information as I am in his, particularly if the mutilation was a message with his address on it.'

Babel took another drink of the wine and sighed. 'Do you know, when they reopened the Hippodrome after the Civil War I practically lived out there. It's a place I feel very happy. It's all about the horses, which is not a bad thing at all.'

§

A little later, the rest of the wine finished, Korolev said his farewells to Babel and stumbled down the stairs, a paper bag of Shura's cheese dumplings clutched to his chest. He shut the door to the apartment behind him, taking all the more care when he heard the child Natasha's voice and then Valentina Nikolaevna's, quiet and reassuring, in response. He paused for a moment in the shared room and listened to the sound of a distant train's whistle then walked over to the window. It was snowing outside and a set of tyre tracks in the centre of the lane were already losing their shape. The lantern across the street cast its yellow glow and Korolev thought it seemed as peaceful as a scene from an old postcard.

He wouldn't have seen the watcher in the carriage entrance if the man hadn't moved. It was just a shift in the darkness, but when he looked more carefully, shielding his eyes from the streetlamp's glare by placing a hand down the side of his face and looking a little off centre – the way he'd learnt to do in the trenches – he was sure he detected the outline of a man there in the shadows. Then he noticed the disjointed footprints under the round arch. If there was a watcher, then the cold was making him stamp his boots from time to time. It would be difficult, Korolev thought, for whoever it was to see inside the darkened apartment, but perhaps they'd seen the light from the hallway when he'd entered. The watcher's eyes would be more attuned to the dark than Korolev's, and he wouldn't have made the mistake of looking at the single street lamp that served that part of the lane. Possibly he was looking back at Korolev at this very moment, seeing Korolev's face in the same street lamp's glow, which added a slight sheen of silver to the surfaces of the shared room. Another flicker of movement decided the matter. He considered going down and confronting the watcher, then thought better of it. He wasn't sure he wanted to know who was keeping tabs on him – at least they were only watching at this stage, and not carting him off to Butyrka.

But Korolev didn't turn the light on as he undressed. And when he lay down to sleep it was with the chair against the door handle and his Walther underneath his pillow.

IT TIRED you out, this kind of work, and it didn't help that he hadn't had a good night's sleep in nearly a week. Of course, it was always difficult when you came home after a job, and busy periods exacerbated the problem. You couldn't just lie down straight away when you'd finished — humans weren't light bulbs, after all. They couldn't just turn themselves off with the flick of a switch. They needed time to adjust to different situations. Like tonight, for example; the contrast between the sleeping domesticity of the apartment and what had happened out in the empty house was too extreme. As a result, he knew he'd have to let sleep come to him. He would have to be patient.

Over the years he'd become more accustomed to the late jobs. Of course, he'd had to; it wasn't unusual to work past midnight, in fact it was probably the norm. After all, it was ideal for his kind of work — being the time when people were at their lowest, mentally and physically. But he was human also, and it required enormous effort to remain alert and hard and show nothing but strength to a prisoner, particularly if he also was exhausted and at the end of his tether. When it was over, no matter how tired he might feel, turning off that effort was difficult. He'd be driven home — they knew how to conserve his energy — and sometimes he'd drift off in the car, but it was rare. Mostly he just stared out at the empty streets and thought about the human being he'd just broken.

Tonight he'd climbed the stairs carefully, avoiding the steps that creaked, and slipped a soundless key into the apartment door. Once inside, he looked in on his son and touched the curls of his head as he lay there. His fingers looked rough against the boy's porcelain cheeks, and he tried not to think of the blood he'd shed that night. He stepped back when his son stirred, his lips puffing outwards for a moment and a frown forming, but the boy didn't wake, and he was grateful – who knew what the boy might see in his eyes? He wished then that the boy could stay for ever just like this – innocent and safe. Who was to say that the boy might not find himself in just such an empty house as the one he'd just left? And what if he were there too? They might ask that of him some day – to kill his own son. They had asked everything else of him. He sighed and pulled the blankets closer round the sleeping child.

He was never hungry when he came home. He liked to have a drink, it was true, but he didn't have an appetite for food. Some did, but not him. Instead he'd sit in the kitchen, like tonight, pour himself a glass of vodka and read for a bit. Anything would do. For a while he'd read Shakespeare's plays but then they'd become difficult. There was too much right and wrong in them, and he lived in a world where such bourgeois considerations were unhelpful. What did so-called virtues like honour, compassion and justice mean in the context of a Revolution? Let their enemies get bogged down with such nonsense – they were meaningless in the prism of predestined historical change. And yet they left awkward questions, the kind of questions his wife had asked before the end. He poured another measure. She'd seen him late at night too many times to have any illusions as to what kind of person he might be. And now nor did he. It was the reason why there was no mirror in the kitchen.

Two more ruffians dealt with tonight – easier with two, as well. The driver had taken them out well past Lefertovo, then down a winding road, and then a track. The two Thieves were trussed like chickens in the boot, and had looked around in confusion when they'd been hauled out. He wondered if it had been the first time they'd seen the moon cut through a forest's bare branches – they certainly looked as though they'd never left the city before. It was the last time they'd seen the moon, anyway, if they'd bothered to take the chance.

Inside, the house had the penetrating cold of a long-empty dwelling, but it had three rooms, and doors to separate them, and once he started to work he'd warmed up soon enough. He'd played them off each other, used one's pain to persuade both, passed information from room to room. Having the driver there had been a help – and, for once, he hadn't had to worry about the noise. That had been useful too.

Afterwards he'd shot them in the cellar, and the driver had helped drag them back to the car. This time they wanted no traces – the Militia were investigating the first two, and there was no point in getting them all worked up with another couple of stiffs. That worried him, if the truth were told. When he'd done this kind of work before, investigations had been no more than paint jobs. The idea that this one might be more substantial – well, it made him wonder.

He reassured himself that he'd followed the orders that he'd been given, and that they were close now; that much was evident. It shouldn't be long – the two Thieves had given them useful information. Still – messy. It wasn't the first time he'd been involved in an irregular action, but normally, of course, there was a team, preparation and coordination, a clear aim. This time the support was almost non-existent – they didn't know who they could trust within the organization, so they said, and therefore the operation had been stripped down to its essential parts – the driver was the only active assistance he'd seen. They'd told him there were others acting independently, but he'd seen no signs. And there was no plan as such – they had an objective, it was true – to recover the icon, and trace it back to the leak – but everything was improvised, each step forward leading to the next, whatever it might be. That was not something he was used to either.

There was always a degree of trust and support amongst Comrades from the organization, a fellowship that accepted frailty and occasional excess. The organization understood all too well the pressure they placed on operatives like him and they made allowances. They looked after you, kept an eye on you, sent you for a break when it was needed, organized extra rations of vodka when you were busy, that kind of thing. Mostly he worked in the Moscow area – the Butyrka, the

Lubianka, Lefertovo, he was well known in all of them. His colleagues didn't look down on him for what he did, far from it; they understood that specialists like him were essential to their work. You could only get so far with ordinary forms of interrogation, they all knew that. For tougher cases you needed a man like him. He could take a prisoner to pieces and then put him back together again, but always as just one more step in a process. He was merely another cog in the machine and each cog relied on the others for forward momentum. It was Soviet power in action, no detail overlooked, no goal unattainable.

But it was strange that they wanted things done quietly now – it seemed a change of tactics since he'd been instructed to leave the mutilated body of the girl on that damned altar. If that hadn't been sending someone a public message, he wasn't sure what else it could have been. And the girl troubled him as well. Her last look was always there, lurking at the periphery of his consciousness, and only effort kept her from his thoughts.

The girl came to him now, despite his resistance, with that gentle look she'd given him just before she died, and it occurred to him, and there was a sweet dizziness to the thought, that this might not be an authorized action. That he might be out on a limb with no back-up, no protection. That if it blew up he'd be the hunted, not the hunter. It didn't bear thinking about. He'd followed orders, trusted his superiors, that was all he'd ever needed to do. He thought of his son asleep in the next-door room, his blond hair curling on the pillow and hoped this was tiredness playing tricks on him – this feeling that the girl had cursed him with those soft eyes of hers.

He poured the last of the bottle into the glass and drank.

Chapter Thirteen

THERE WAS only a slight disturbance in the snow outside the carriage entrance when Korolev passed the next morning. On the cobblestones inside the arch, however, he spotted three discarded *papirosa* tubes and an empty packet of Belomorkanal, the red star on the map of the White Sea Canal clearly visible on the crumpled box. He didn't stop to examine them, but kept on moving. It proved nothing, he reasoned. Even if someone *had* been there during the night, who was to say that Korolev was the target of their attention? He pulled his chin a little lower into his collar and put the matter from his thoughts.

By the time he reached Petrovka Street, work parties were already shifting the snow from the street and most of Number 38's courtyard had been cleared by a group of pale-faced cadets wielding wide-bladed shovels, who ignored him as he climbed the steps. Inside the foyer there was activity as well, workers in dirty overalls installing a freshly cast statue of Lenin where Yagoda's had stood. You knew where you were with Vladimir Ilyich, Korolev mused as he climbed the stairs – he, at least, was unlikely to fall out of favour, being safely dead already.

Entering Room 2F, he nodded to Yasimov and was promptly bustled out of the way by a harassed-looking young woman in a white headscarf pushing in the door behind him. He smiled as she placed several envelopes and circulars on the table and then rushed out. His smile ended up being directed to the closing door.

'No manners, these young people,' he said as he placed his coat on the rack.

'No sense, anyway,' Yasimov said, pointing at a report he was writing. 'Two students thought it would be amusing to give a half-bottle of vodka to the bear in Yaroslavl Market.'

'That old one on the chain? What a waste.'

'Oh, he wasn't too old to enjoy it. He broke the chain in two, helped himself to anything that took his fancy on the nearby stalls and gave one of the students a proper chewing. Some uniforms had to shoot the poor creature. The bear, of course – they took the student to hospital. Giving vodka to a bear? How can youngsters afford such extravagance? That's what I'd like to know.'

Korolev found an envelope addressed to him in the pile of post. It contained a short typed letter and two photographs, one of which was of Mary Smithson.

Dear Captain Korolev,

Further to our conversation yesterday, I attach the visa photographs of Citizeness Maria Ivanovna Kuznetsova (alias 'Mary Smithson') and Citizeness Lydia Ivanovna Dolina (alias 'Nancy Dolan'), in order to assist you with your enquiries. It has been confirmed that Citizeness Dolina is also a cultist nun. You will, as discussed, exercise extreme discretion with any investigation relating to these persons and, if in doubt, contact myself for instructions on how to proceed.

Gregorin
(Staff Colonel)

Korolev looked at the picture of Dolan. Pretty, like the other one – dark eyes, a long neck and pale skin. There was humour in her expression, and to judge from the picture she had a cheerful disposition. Her gaze was directed to the left of the picture, as if avoiding the camera, and her dark hair was cut into an elegant bob, something that would stand out in Moscow, where only the wives of specialists or party cadres had access to the quality hairdressers. It was said that Central Committee members had to intervene personally to arrange appointments at Master Paul's on the Arbat. If the truth be told, she didn't look much like any nun he'd ever seen – but he presumed Gregorin's information must be correct.

He reached for the packet of Little Star he kept in his top drawer for moments such as these. He was about to light up when the phone rang.

'Korolev,' he said, through the corner of his mouth, picking up his receiver.

'Alexei Dmitriyevich? Popov here.' The general sounded like he'd been rudely awakened from hibernation. 'I read your report. Come up with Semionov, please. Larinin as well.'

'They're not in the office at the moment, Comrade General.'

'When they arrive then – the lazy rascals. In the meantime send up Yasimov. Tell him I hope he's made progress on that damned bear.'

'Of course, Comrade General.'

The general hung up and Korolev lit the cigarette with a sigh that was more sadness than satisfaction. An angry General Popov was not an ideal way to start the morning and took some of the sweetness from the smoke. He caught Yasimov's eye and pointed the orange tip at the ceiling.

'The boss wants an update on the bear. By the sound of things they were related.'

§

Half an hour later it was the turn of Korolev and his two colleagues. Korolev summarized the developments from the previous day and, at the general's suggestion, informed Larinin of Mary Smithson's identity and the NKVD's involvement. As Korolev spoke, he saw Larinin's face gradually pale. He still looked like a pig, but not a happy pig. In fact, he looked like a pig who'd just discovered what sausages were made from.

'Comrade General,' Larinin began, but he got no further.

'Don't waste your time, Larinin. The Thief was yours, so you're not ducking out, and I'll be keeping an eye on you to make sure you don't try. Any questions?'

All eyes turned to Larinin. His mouth was slightly open as though still trying to speak, but then he shook his head.

'Good,' Popov said. 'Now, today – what have you in mind, Alexei Dmitriyevich?'

'It seems to me we need to try and identify the car. We think it's a black Emka, but perhaps Comrade Larinin could see if his former colleagues in the traffic department are able to narrow the search. If we had an idea of how many Emkas there are in Moscow and which organizations they've been allocated to, that would help. Then whether any identifiable vehicles were seen in the neighbourhood of the stadium or the church on the nights in question. Anything would be useful.' The general nodded his agreement.

'Also Comrade Semionov should follow up with the interviewees,' Korolev continued. 'And there were some street children around at the time the nun's body was discovered – I think I might see if I can talk to them this morning.'

'What about friend Tesak?'

Semionov and Korolev turned towards Larinin.

'I'm still going through the mugshots – nothing so far. I'll try showing the autopsy pictures round the other investigators when they've been developed – see if anyone recognizes him.' Larinin's voice sounded tired.

'And this new girl, Dolina? Or Dolan, is it?' Popov said.

'I'll show the photograph to Schwartz.' Korolev considered what he was about to say next. 'If she does have a link with Mary Smithson then we should start looking for her, quietly. She's an American, in their eyes anyway, but it's probable she'll have assumed a Russian identity. Even so, we could maybe have a discreet look at the places Americans frequent. The embassy, I suppose, the hotels—'

Popov cut him off with an upheld hand. 'No. Don't piss on the NKVD's lamp post – believe me they'll smell it straight away if we do. Steer clear of hotels and embassies. Get Gueginov to make bigger copies if he can and we'll circulate her picture to the stations as a missing person. That's as far as we can go. And keep it low key.'

Korolev nodded in agreement. 'I've already asked him. How about informers with cult contacts?'

'I'll see what can be done. Do you really think your writer friend will be able to arrange a meeting with the Thieves?'

'It's worth a try. If Count Kolya will talk, he might be able to explain some things. About the icon for a start, and perhaps why Tesak ended up as he did.'

'A Thief won't talk to you,' Larinin said. Korolev looked at him, expecting to see contempt, but Larinin's frown seemed to be from doubt more than anything else.

'I could offer him Tesak's body.'

Larinin's chin dropped the fraction of a millimetre it took to reach his neck. General Popov merely grunted and pointed at Semionov.

'If there's a meeting, take him with you. And keep your safety catches off. Only give him the body in exchange for good information. Anything else?'

Korolev thought of mentioning his overnight watcher and the tail he thought he'd detected the day before, but decided there was no point. After all, he'd nothing concrete to tell them, only a feeling which he wasn't too sure about himself.

'Off you go,' Popov said and the three investigators rose as one.

Larinin looked at Korolev as they left and shook his head in bewilderment. 'I'll keep on with the mugshots,' he said. 'First things first.' His sad, pale face reminded Korolev of a circus clown's.

§

By the time Korolev and Semionov reached the Razin Street Militia station, the clouds had darkened from white to grey and were becoming blacker by the minute. The remaining snow was being washed into clumps of dirty ice by the curtain-like drizzle and the broken windscreen in the Ford had left Korolev's coat soaked through. He nodded to Semionov as he stepped out of the car.

'I'll meet you back here,' Korolev said, wiping rain from his face. 'If the witnesses have anything interesting, ask Brusilov to hold onto them till I come back.'

Korolev didn't really mind the rain; after all, what could you do about weather? It was what it was. Maybe, in the future, Soviet science would be able to control it, turn it on and off or adjust it like a radiator, but for now it was something that only God could influence, and today God had decided to let it wash Moscow's skies clear of the factories' smog and drop it onto her streets as murky puddles and black sludge. Korolev suspected the chances of finding the street children would be few in this muck, but there was a Militia post near the church which was manned during the day so he decided to ask there just in case.

The Militiaman, a sergeant, looked at his identification with great care. Korolev had a suspicion that he was spelling the words out to himself one by one.

'Ko-ro-lev?' The elderly sergeant said with a frown, as though unsure of the pronunciation. Despite the roof on the small hut, it was open to the sides and his grey beard and eyebrows were greasy with rain. He looked like a damp St Nicholas.

'From Petrovka Street. I'm investigating the murder earlier in the week.'

'Ach,' the sergeant said in disgust, 'What's the world coming to, Comrade? When they kill a young girl in God's own house? Things must be bad. Well, we're all atheists, of course, but some things just shouldn't happen. It's the Devil's work. I remember you, now I think of it. You were here the morning we found her. In your uniform, weren't you?'

Another atheist like myself, thought Korolev. There are a lot of us around.

'That was me. Listen, Comrade, there were some *besprizorny* at the church that morning – have you any idea where I might find them? They were very young, under ten I'd say. One had red hair, blue eyes, a thin, bony face and a big padded jacket – ring any bells?'

'That little one rings all the bells in Moscow, Comrade Captain – a hooligan in the making of the first degree called Kim Goldstein. His parents got caught up in something or other, you know the way it is – who knows where they ended up and best not to ask I should think. Left him to fend for himself, anyway, and the rascal's been running wild ever since – I've felt his collar in my hand once or twice, but I haven't had the heart to hold onto it. Although maybe I should, maybe I should – he hasn't an ounce of flesh on him and won't last the winter if I don't, that's for certain.'

'Any idea where I might find him?'

'Yes, and I'll show you and willingly, Comrade. Let me just call in and tell the station I'm leaving my post.'

Korolev wondered whether the boy's parents had called him for the Kipling character or the Soviet acronym for the International Communist Youth Movement. He hoped it was the former, given where the young lad had ended up. A bit of resourcefulness would be no bad thing.

§

Ten minutes later, Korolev stood at the end of an alley, watching some dilapidated stables that were scheduled to be knocked down for a telephone exchange. In the meantime, it was the *besprizorny* hideout. He heard the sergeant blow his whistle as he entered the stables from the other end, and almost immediately ten or twelve young children burst out into the alley, rather than the three or four Korolev had been expecting. They came to a halt when they saw him, looking uncertainly behind them as the sound of the whistle came closer.

'Hey, old-timer! Don't get in the way of the Collective!' a voice came from the back.

'Listen to that, Grandad. There are no fortresses we can't storm!'

The voices were absurdly young, but their angry eyes were like searchlights in the wet gloom. Korolev almost reached for his pistol, but that would have been ridiculous. They were just a bunch of kids shouting slogans from the movies.

'Now just stay there, I'm a Militia investigator,' he said in what he hoped was a firm voice, but at that moment the sergeant appeared at the stable doors and then the whole bunch were pelting towards him. Korolev, bending down to their level, picked out Goldstein from the charge and decided it might as well be him as any other. He grabbed hold of the boy around the stomach, felt the padded jacket squirm in his hands as the boy nearly dropped out of the bottom of it, but managed to catch a leg. He'd expected the others to run on past, but instead he felt feet kick at him, hands pull at his hair and then the excruciating pain of a small fist punching him repeatedly in the testicles. He swung Goldstein around like a weapon and then the sergeant was roaring above him and laying into the slower children with his night stick.

'Rats! Rats! Rats!' the sergeant bellowed at the retreating figures and then leant against the alley wall breathing heavily. 'They mug drunks like that, Comrade. At night. A little swarm of them. Once the fellow goes down, he doesn't have a chance.

They'll kill someone one of these days. Look at your coat, if you don't believe me.'

A long straight cut ran downwards from beneath his armpit. He checked it quickly with his free hand. No blood.

'God above,' he said. 'How the hell will I get that mended?'

'Sew it yourself, you old woman.' The voice came from the bundle of legs and coat he had pinned to the alley wall. As if on cue, stones and pieces of wood began to thud into the ground around them as the children, regrouped, now advanced to recover the captive.

'Hey, hey. Stop that, you little shits,' Korolev shouted, allowing his annoyance about the slashed coat and bruised testicles to come through. 'I'm not going to hurt any of you unless I have to, and I'm not going to take young Goldstein in either. I just want to ask a few questions. I'm a detective, from Petrovka Street.'

Everyone knew about Petrovka Street and the boys, and what looked like one or two girls, stopped their bombardment. Korolev took the opportunity to arrange Kim Goldstein's clothing so that his face was visible.

'See? He's fine,' Korolev said, keeping his hands well clear of Goldstein's teeth and stopping his kicking by holding the boy's legs flat against the brickwork.

'Do you remember me? From outside the church where the lady was murdered?'

'What do you want, *Ment*?' the boy said, his voice low with indignation, but at least he'd stopped struggling.

'Information. There'll be a few roubles in it for you.'

'We don't grass people up, not us.'

A rare distinction, thought Korolev, in a city where so many denunciations came to Petrovka Street each day that they had a team of eight officers just to read through them.

'Look, I'm after a murderer who tortures young women to

death. He's a monster, not some regular fellow from the neighbourhood who buys and sells a few vegetables down at Sukharevka market. I need your help.'

The children looked at him, considering the proposal.

'Like the Baker Street Irregulars?' a small blonde girl asked. She had a dirty face and a filthy but well-cut woollen overcoat.

'You like Sherlock Holmes?' Korolev asked. Several of the children nodded and one of them produced a savagely mangled copy of *The Sign of Four*. 'Well, you can be the Razin Street Irregulars, if you'd like. A rouble for a prime piece of information.'

'A rouble? Forget it.'

Korolev looked down at the scornful face of young Goldstein, noting his obvious interest. He felt it safe to loosen his grip now it had become a matter of price rather than principle.

'I could go a little higher,' Korolev said, wondering how he would explain this to the general, who didn't approve of paying informers at the best of times.

'Five.'

'If it's very good, yes. Otherwise, we'll have to see.'

Two shrewd eyes stared up at him from beneath red hair, curled thick with grime.

'Well then,' the boy said, which seemed to constitute an acceptance of the offer. The others came closer, although the sergeant still kept his night stick ready and Korolev made sure to keep the children where he could see them.

'All right, Citizens. My name's Korolev. Alexei Dmitriyevich. First things first – this is the lady who was murdered. Does anyone recognize her?'

He showed around Mary Smithson's passport photograph, but there was no response apart from ghoulish interest and a quiet sob from the little girl. He tried again.

'Some witnesses may have seen her at around midnight on the day in question. Were any of you up then? There may have been a car parked further along the street. Anyone see that?'

'There was a black Emka, right enough. Remember? Near the cigarette stall?' This from a scrawny child in a flat cap and a stretched and worn jumper. Two others nodded agreement.

'I remember it, towards the Kremlin it was. On the same side of the street as the church.'

'Yes, and there was a fellow in the driver's seat smoking, remember?'

'Anyone get a look at him?'

'No, we thought it was some high-up's driver, or a *Ment*. Stayed well clear.' The other two nodded agreement with flat cap.

'He'd his collar turned right up. All you could see was the cigarette poking out.'

'Very good.' Korolev reached into his pocket and pulled out his wallet. He extracted two single rouble notes, thought about it and took out another three.

'There's someone I want you to see if you can find for me,' he said, taking out the picture of Nancy Dolan. 'Ten roubles if you track her down, and these five to share amongst yourselves in the meantime.'

Goldstein took the money from him and extended his hand to shake on the deal.

'We'll find her, don't you worry.' He walked over to the other children, nodded and then they turned as one to walk off down the alleyway.

'Waste of money, if you ask me,' the sergeant grumbled, but he had a smile hidden under his moustache. Korolev nodded in the direction the children had departed.

'What happens to them? In the end?'

'The Lord takes them to himself soon enough, if the State doesn't throw them into an orphanage. I don't know which is better.'

It was as Korolev had expected. He buttoned his overcoat against the floating drizzle and ran a finger down the cut as they walked back towards the Militia post.

'What's your name, Sergeant? So I know it, if you call?'

'Pushkin.'

'Really?'

The sergeant shook his head in resignation. 'Please, Comrade Captain. It wasn't my choice. I was just born to it. You can't change your family name, can you? I don't complain – a name's only a name. The Lord willed it. I mean to say – it's the way it must be. Comrade Stalin wouldn't change his name, now would he?'

'No, that's true enough, Sergeant.' Although, of course, the big boss *had* changed his name, the canny Georgian. Stalin sounded better than Djugashvili to Russian ears, after all.

Chapter Fourteen

KOROLEV splashed through a deep puddle in front of the Razin Street Militia Station and cursed. Brusilov was waiting inside the doorway, smoking a cigarette.

'Korolev. You look like you swam the Moskva to get here. What happened to your coat?'

Korolev shook Brusilov's shovel of a hand, holding up the edge of the slashed coat as he did so.

'A little brat tried to shave me with his razor. Is there a fire I can put it in front of for a while? It's wet through.'

The captain's face seemed formed from the same hard stone as the station's walls, but his eyes were friendly as he pointed to a cast-iron stove at the back of the room, and Korolev gladly shed the sodden garment. The station was even more rundown than Korolev remembered it. A mixed bag of citizenry sat on a bench that ran the length of one wall, their clothes wet and their faces sour, while in front of them uniformed Militiamen sat at three desks dealing with the endless complaints, notifications and attendances. A bare electric light bulb lit the scene. Brusilov followed his glance and shook his head.

'Half our time is taken up with bureaucracy – I've three of my boys stamping documents from morning to night and the queue gets longer every day. Anyway, your young fellow's upstairs with Citizeness Kardasheva, and a right one she is too. Mind if I sit in?'

'Help yourself, brother. The more the merrier.'

Semionov and Kardasheva were sitting facing each other across a pock-marked wooden table in the station's interview room. Paint peeled from the grey walls and the weak light bulb didn't seem quite strong enough to reach the corners.

'Ah, more of you, I see,' Kardasheva said, adjusting her glasses so that she could focus on Brusilov and Korolev. 'Am I under arrest?'

'No, Citizeness, we just have a few questions for you about what you saw the night before last.' Semionov looked weary; it clearly wasn't the first time he'd explained this to her.

'But this is a cell, is it not? It has bars on the window.' She pointed at the tiny window high on the wall facing the door. The window was so dirty Korolev was surprised she could see the bars outside.

'I'm not the architect, Citizeness, but this is an interview room, nothing more. And I've asked you to remain here so that you can describe exactly what you saw to Captain Korolev.'

'I thought it was you investigating the murder?'

'I am, but Captain Korolev is the senior officer on the case.'

The elderly lady snorted, then pulled her ancient brown coat closer around her, tucking her silver hair inside the frayed velvet collar. She was about sixty-five, Korolev guessed, with a once pretty face sharpened by hunger and chronic cynicism.

'Thank you for your cooperation, Citizeness Kardasheva. I'm afraid I'm at fault here. I wanted to hear what you had to say directly.'

'Well, it's just not right. I haven't done anything wrong and I'll be lucky if I get a crust at the bakers' cooperative now. There'll be a queue a *verst* long – all for black bread at one rouble and seventy five kopeks a kilo. It was easier with coupons. But go on, go on. Ask your questions. I'll tell you everything. I'm a loyal citizen – see no one tells you different.'

'Of course, I can see that.' Korolev spoke in a conciliatory voice. 'I'm sorry to have to ask you these questions yet again.'

Kardasheva's hard mouth softened into a grimace and she inclined her head in acknowledgement of his courtesy.

'You saw a young woman walking with two men on the night of the murder, heading in the direction of the church where the victim was found. Do you think you would recognize the woman from a photograph?'

'Perhaps. My eyesight isn't perfect, but I was wearing my glasses and the street is well lit.'

Korolev put the photograph of Mary Smithson on the table and pushed it towards her. A long thin hand extended to pick it up and then held it so as to catch as much of the light from the bulb as possible.

'I think so. It was dark, but I would think so. I wouldn't say it wasn't her, anyway.'

She pushed the photograph back and then refolded her arms. Brusilov leant forward and picked up the picture, examining it with the same care.

Korolev continued. 'Your description of the clothes matches those of the victim as well. So, for the purpose of discussion, let's presume the woman you saw was the victim. I'd like you to tell me as much as possible about the two men with her.'

Kardasheva's eyes seemed to refocus on the remembered midnight street.

'One of them was big. You know, not really tall, but very big, like a two-legged ox. I felt sorry for the girl. I thought he'd do something bad to her.'

'Why did you think that, Citizeness? You said nothing about that in the interview.'

'Well, it looked like she might be drunk. She wasn't unsteady on her feet as such, but the big man had his arm around her and I don't think she had much choice about where she was going.

He looked like he could lift a house with one hand. Just the size of him. And it wasn't fat either. He was solid muscle. You could tell from the way he walked.'

'How tall do you think he was?'

'I would say about five foot ten. How tall was the girl? I'd say he was half a foot taller than her.'

Korolev thought five foot ten sounded about right. The girl had been five foot four according to the autopsy report.

'The other man had a fedora, smaller, but a little taller than the girl, and he carried a suitcase. Both of the men had long overcoats. Dark. I couldn't see their faces, but the larger man had a very wide face, the same as his body. The other man I didn't notice so much, really. The big man caught my attention. They weren't ordinary workers, that's my opinion. But you'd know better than me.'

'What do you mean by that?'

'I mean what I say. They were Militia or State Security if I'm not mistaken – certainly the larger man was. Not hooligans or Thieves. I could tell, even from the other side of the street. The click, click, click of new boots on the pavement; not that many new boots clicking along Razin Street this year – you can't buy them in the shops, no matter who you know. And the way they walked as well – like they owned the place.'

Korolev knew the kind she meant – they deliberately made their presence felt, even in plain clothes. Sometimes they were detectives, it was true, but more often than not they were Chekists. Korolev looked down at his feet and then at Semionov and Brusilov's – both the other Militiamen wore new leather boots. Was he the only damned policeman in Moscow squelching round in felt this winter? She caught his disgruntled look and laughed.

'Yes, Captain, I'm not sure you're taking full advantage of your position.'

'A bit of respect, please, Citizeness.' Korolev didn't manage to keep the irritation out of his voice. How the hell *did* everyone else have new leather boots?

'Do you have any other reason for your assertion that the two men were investigators?'

'Oh no, I didn't say they were investigators. They were heavies. You're not a heavy, my dear Captain. Not at all. And nor's the boy.' She nodded towards Semionov in such a dismissive way that the lieutenant blushed. 'Comrade Brusilov here could be, but isn't. The other two – well, it was their profession.'

Chekists for sure, then. Korolev looked down at his notes and then at Brusilov, who shrugged his shoulders. Semionov nodded in agreement with the consensus. She'd nothing more to tell them.

'You're free to go, Citizeness, and thank you for your help. If by any chance you spot one of the men, please call me at Petrovka Street. The exchange will put you straight through. Or contact Captain Brusilov.'

'I'm not afraid, you know. Of saying two Chekists might have been involved in a murder.' She sighed, and then lifted her chin slightly, proud or perhaps just resigned. 'Maybe I would be if I were younger, Captain, but I saw what I saw. What can I do? It's my duty to tell the truth, surely. Weren't we all taught that in school?'

Before the Revolution perhaps, thought Korolev, and nodded towards the door. 'Lieutenant Semionov will see you out. Thank you, Citizeness.'

When the heavy door had shut behind them, he turned to Brusilov.

'What d'you make of that?'

'Not possible, surely? If the Chekists need to do something like that, they've got the Lubianka and the Butyrka and half a dozen other prisons. It just seems unlikely. What else have you got?'

Korolev told him about the Emka and the electrical burns and the dead Thief. Brusilov rasped a broad hand back and forth across his unshaven chin.

'I'm glad it's your case and not mine,' he said, after a long pause. 'It stinks. Still, we'll pass on anything we come across. We're still checking the Komsomol members who visited the church.'

The way he raised his eyebrows told Korolev he thought this was a waste of time.

'It's worth doing,' Korolev said and reached for a cigarette, offering the pack to Brusilov, who refused with a sigh.

'Did you hear the explosion last night?' Brusilov said, changing the subject.

Korolev thought for a moment before he shook his head.

'Another church. They've half of it cleared away already. To make space for the October Day Parade.' Brusilov's statement was neutral, betraying no feeling about the event, one way or the other. 'Maybe I will have one of those cigarettes.'

He was just lighting it when Semionov returned and handed Korolev a note with an expectant look.

Meet me at the Hippodrome at 1.30. Sit in the stands – in line with the winning post. I'll find you. Our friend wants to meet you. I.E.B.

Chapter Fifteen

IT ALWAYS struck Korolev that the exterior of the Moscow Hippodrome made it look more like a museum than a sports venue. With its columns and grandeur, the long white building seemed a relic of a time gone by – a building meant for princes rather than proletarians. Even the entrance resembled a triumphal arch, surmounted, as it was, by a bronze chariot team. It all seemed decidedly un-Soviet, despite the large banner exhorting the citizenry to early completion of the Five Year Plan. Perhaps the building's elegance was why, for several years after the Revolution, there'd been no racing there. The need for a suspiciously bourgeois-looking race track hadn't been a priority while the city starved and armies moved back and forth and battles were won and lost. Eventually, however, when the Civil War was over and peace had been reached with the Poles, it had been allowed to reopen. Muscovites still liked to gamble, after all, although these days the crowds wore flat caps instead of top hats.

Semionov brought the car to a halt a safe distance from the scattered groups of loungers and hawkers outside the entrance and turned to Korolev. 'Close enough?'

'This will be fine.'

Korolev had a quick look round to see if there was anyone near, then checked his Walther was fully loaded – chambering a round, just in case. Semionov followed his example. As always, the smell of gun oil sent a shiver of anticipation down Korolev's back. He didn't expect to have to use the automatic, but it was best to be properly prepared, just as Popov had instructed.

'You stay back. I'll pull out my handkerchief if I think I need help, but even then I don't want you barging in on your own. There'll be some uniforms around, so grab hold of them first – Kolya isn't likely to be on his own.'

Semionov looked at Korolev's white handkerchief as though memorizing it. 'You won't notice me, Alexei Dmitriyevich, but I swear on my Komsomol honour I won't lose sight of you.'

'Good. Now, give me a head start before you follow.'

§

Korolev levered himself out of the car and started to walk towards the main entrance, the Walther a reassuring presence in his armpit.

He handed over a fifty kopek note at the ticket barrier, then walked through into the ill-lit entrance hall, the high walls of which were decorated with mosaics celebrating the glory of the equine species – barely visible beneath twenty years of grime. Here was a cavalry charge, with Cossacks galloping out of the gloom, their mounts' nostrils huge and their teeth bared; there, a column of horse artillery advancing across a desert. Horses ploughed, carried, fought, marched, jumped and pulled, in dust-streaked image after dust-streaked image. He hadn't been to the races since before the German War, and was surprised how rundown the place was. It had been truly spectacular back then, and the smell of the aristocratic women parading themselves on this very spot had been that of a field of summer flowers. Now things were not so pleasant. Most of the light bulbs in the chandelier were blown, the roof seemed to be leaking and the tiled floor was pooled with rainwater. At least he hoped it was rainwater, although the smell made him suspicious it might be something else. Men's faces peered at him from the gloom as he went past, one or two turning away but others staring at him with a strange intensity. He kept moving, unsure what these men were waiting for, and shrugged off a hand that tugged at his sleeve.

The next room was better lit, with a rank of glass booths manned by morose, middle-aged women, alongside which a thin man on a stepladder wrote odds on a blackboard. There was also a stall selling food so he handed over sixty kopeks and received in exchange a *buterbrod* – a slice of black bread decorated with some thinly sliced sausage. He took a bite and, remembering he'd smoked the last of his cigarettes back in Razin Street, picked up a packet from the next stall along, then climbed the cracked grey marble steps that led to the front of the stands, brushing his way past a swaying sailor, who gave his slice of bread a hungry stare.

It was good to be back outside, despite the swirling drizzle, and he breathed a sigh of relief. The stands were busy: several thousand Muscovites had packed themselves into the tiered seating and were now letting loose a rumbling roar of excitement that was increasing in volume second by second. He turned and saw a clump of brightly coloured riders approaching, their silks all the brighter against the slate grey sky and the dirt track. A great spray of water and mud surrounded the jockeys as they urged their horses on and the roar of the crowd rose, drowning out the galloping hooves. Three horses detached themselves from the larger pack and a roar went up that mingled delight and dismay as the race splashed past, the jockeys' whips flailing as the first two battled for the win.

The race finished; much of the crowd began to disperse. Some happy citizens waved winning tickets, while others made for the bar at the back of the stand and the consolation of vodka. Korolev climbed to the second tier of seating and picked a spot in line with the finishing post, as Babel had asked. He sat down, made himself comfortable, finished the last of the bread and sausage and lit a cigarette, inhaling the smoke with quiet pleasure. He wriggled a little deeper into his damp but still warm overcoat and tried to spot the stocky figure of the writer.

He was still looking when Babel sat down beside him, smiling with pleasure.

'You didn't see me coming.'

'I wasn't looking for you,' Korolev lied. 'I decided it would be less hard work if you found me instead.'

'Got one of those for me?' Babel said, pointing to the cigarette.

'Sure.' Korolev offered the packet he'd just bought. 'So, tell me. How'd it go with Kolya?'

'Not too bad. It seems I'm a first-class matchmaker; you both can't wait for your first walk out. He knew all about you, anyway.'

'He knew about me?' Korolev repeated, mystified as to what a Thief like Kolya could possibly know about a run-of-the-mill investigator like him.

'It seems so.'

'Does he know about Tesak, perhaps? That I'm investigating his murder?'

'Well, he knows that Tesak's dead. I'll tell you how it went. I saw him by the parade ring and tipped my hat to him. He waved me over. "I wanted to have a word with you," I said. "Me likewise," he said. "Well, I've a proposal for you," I said. "Go on," he said, "I wonder if I can guess what it is." "Well,' I said, "mine concerns a policeman who wants to have a word with you." "Korolev," he said, "your neighbour?" At which point you could have tipped me over with a feather. But Kolya just gives a little smile, as if to say, "I know when you fart in the bath, Babel." Which was disconcerting, I can tell you.'

'I can imagine,' Korolev said drily.

'"You know about Tesak, how he died?" I asked, and Kolya nods, a slow nod which tells me he not only knows about it, but that he has plans to send a bit of what Tesak got back to the return address. "Well, Korolev wants to ask a few questions. He'll give information in exchange for information, and if you want the body, it can be arranged. And it will be safe for you, no trap. His word of honour." He looks at me and it's a hard look, the kind that reaches down into you and squeezes your stomach till it feels like there's nothing in it. He's wondering whether he can trust me and then he's telling me, with his eyes, what will happen to me if anything goes wrong. Eyes can be very expressive, you know. Anyway, "Where and when?" he asks, after a couple of hours, it seemed, of him looking at me like I'm going to be lunch for his dog. "Up to you," I say, as we discussed. "Korolev understands you'll want to feel secure, so you pick the spot and the time." At this he laughs. "I always feel secure, tell him that. Today. One thirty. Here. Then we'll talk." And that was that. I was dismissed.'

'You did well, Isaac Emmanuilovich.'

'Oh, please, call me Isaac. And, to be honest, I found it a very interesting experience. Have you a plan?'

'We'll see if he shows and then we'll play it as it comes.'

They sat in silence smoking their cigarettes, watching as the crowd began to return to their seats. It was a mixed card and the next race was for trotters. Jockeys on low-slung sulkies came out onto the track and picked up speed as they headed round the course to the start. Babel pointed to a jockey with a red star on his white silks.

'Ivanov should win this. Proletariat Strength is a banker – I can't see the rest of them getting close. Not very good odds, though.'

'Did you put something on?'

'A *parny* with number four. The odds were a little better.'

The stand had begun to fill up and Korolev became conscious of several likely-looking fellows taking seats around them. A large tough, his face obscured by the turned-up collar of his leather jacket and a peaked hat pulled low over his face, sat in beside Babel, but the hat didn't hide the tattooed fingers, burnt yellow by nicotine, that were lifting a *papirosa* to his mouth.

'Can I barter a smoke off you, friend?' a clear-skinned youth on Korolev's left asked, turning to him. Korolev nodded, put his hand into his pocket and offered him his packet of Belomors.

'Ah, the White Canal!' the youth said, tapping a blue finger on the map that graced the packet. 'Many a fine fellow dug his own grave in that drain. But not me, *amigo*, not me. Lovely smoke they named after it, all the same.' Korolev looked into the young man's sea-blue eyes; the pupils were the size of pin-pricks and there was no life in them when he flashed his chipped yellow teeth in a smile. The youngster's breath stank of decay and Korolev had to make a conscious effort not to recoil.

'Be so kind as to follow me when the race starts, *Señor*. When we get to the corridor at the back of the stand, you pass me your piece. The one in your armpit – I can see the bulge. Quietly, of course. The citizens don't like to see hardware being flashed around in a place of entertainment. You'll get it back, don't you worry.'

'Understood. You have your own light?'

'Yep.' A match appeared in the boy's hand, which he ran across his teeth. The match burst into flame, the flash of sulphur lighting up his face. He was almost good-looking, thought Korolev, but the eyes would warn away all but the blind. This child would laugh as he slid a blade between your ribs, and then he'd twist it just for fun.

'Backed anything? I know my chariots, I could set you straight.' The boy spoke with friendly insolence.

'We move when the race starts, right?' Korolev asked, ignoring his question.

'Hey, don't be like that. It's not often I get to chat with the filth in a pleasant social atmosphere. Perhaps we might end up pals, you know? Go to watch Dinamo together, hang out with all the other *Ments*? Maybe you could even reform me? Turn me into a world-class Komsomol choirboy? No more thieving for Mishka – I'd have a new way to get fat off the back of the citizens.'

His sniggering laugh didn't extend to his eyes and suddenly Korolev wanted to hold onto his gun very much indeed, but then the race began and Mishka was standing, and so was the *papirosa* smoker. Korolev hoped his face showed none of the nervousness he felt as three other burly ruffians stood as well.

'The scribbler comes too,' Mishka said and Korolev nodded to the wide-eyed Babel to stand. The writer rose to his feet, looking with open curiosity at the Thieves, the suggestion of a smile playing about his lips. He's enjoying this, Korolev realized with surprise, taking it all in so he can write one of his damned stories. There was something so ridiculous about the thought that it made him smile in turn.

'That's the spirit, *compadres*. Up the stairs and then we're on our way. Step lively – we don't want to be late.'

In the corridor at the back of the stand Korolev held open his jacket, and Mishka slipped the Walther out of its holster, flicked on the safety catch and then put it into his own pocket. Another man checked Babel, then Mishka inclined his head to the left, pointing them towards a door at the far end of the corridor. He fell in step beside Korolev.

'Nice piece. Reliable artillery, the Walther. Of course, the Americans make the best armaments. A Browning or a Colt, that's the kind of cannon gets respect from the dead, if you know what I mean. And the Thompson? Now there's something that stacks the odds in your favour – rat-a-tat-tat-tat and down they go. Still, the Germans make nice cannons too. Your German knows a thing or two about how to build a howitzer.'

One of the escorts knocked twice and the door was opened by a shaved head that Korolev recognized from the entrance hall. The man looked at Korolev with an unreadable expression, then spat on the floor as they passed.

'Pay no attention. It's his time of the month: he turned into a bitch in the Zone is what I heard.'

They descended the wooden staircase, their footsteps echoing down the stairwell, the shaved head bringing up the rear. At each turn in the stairs, Korolev cast quick glances at their escort, coming to the conclusion that they knew what they were about, and hoping Semionov would realize it and stay well back.

At the bottom, they left the building and walked across a deserted yard to a set of heavy doors already being opened by a waiting goon, then entered a dark corridor heavy with the warm, earthy smell of horses. Korolev could hear Proletarian Strength's name being shouted outside as the race reached the final stages and wondered whether Babel had landed his *parny*. He looked across at him and was unsurprised to see the smaller man's eyes bright with excitement despite the murky light. He doubted it was much to do with the horse race. The lead Thief stopped in front of a large double-width door and Mishka followed Korolev and Babel into a barn-sized room which had open stalls down either side, then the door was shut behind them. The only illumination came from the far corner, where a large man sat underneath a lantern, his shoulders stretching taut the black leather waistcoat he was wearing. The man's face was hidden in shadow, but he had a wrestler's physique.

'Not you, scribbler,' Mishka said. 'Just the strong arm of workers' justice, if you don't mind. You get to wait here with me.' Korolev put a reassuring hand on the writer's arm as he passed. From outside the tumult of the race's finish could be heard, but it seemed a long way from the stillness of the barn.

The waistcoat looked up as Korolev approached.

'I heard you wanted to talk to me.'

Korolev was surprised how cultured the voice was, its tone as deep and clear as an actor's. Perhaps that's where the 'Count' came from, he thought. Kolya's wide face was pale and clean-shaven in the flickering light, but his eyes were black and deep-set. His muscular neck emerged from a crisp white shirt that seemed all the brighter against the dark waistcoat. He was handsome in the way that athletes often were, with regular, well-defined features and charcoal hair cut close to his skull. The Thief raised a hand to his ear with fingers blue from prison ink and pulled at the lobe, returning the appraisal with interest. It felt as though Korolev was being calculated – added, subtracted and, finally, solved. An uncomfortable experience.

'And I heard you wanted to talk to me,' Korolev said. 'I was surprised,' he added when the pause became uncomfortable.

'You should be. A man like me talking to a captain of Moscow CID? I ought to shoot myself.' There was a hint of a smile. Korolev noticed an expensive-looking overcoat hung on a hook like an advertisement of the man's crooked ways.

'So why?'

Kolya considered his response, and then shrugged. 'We felt it was an exceptional situation.'

'Exceptional?'

'I think that's the correct word for the circumstances.' Kolya nodded, as if agreeing with himself, giving Korolev the feeling the Thief had made a rather dark joke.

'Your men agreed it was exceptional? You had a vote, did you?'

'They aren't *my* men, Captain. I *represent* them, it's true. But if I don't represent them the way they like, the job goes to someone else and I get a bullet in the head as a pension. But, yes, we had a meeting, the senior Thieves anyway – the "Authorities", as we say – and the decision was a collective one. Very Bolshevik – you should approve. You know the saying: if all your choices are bad, you choose the one that hurts the least. So we chose to talk to you.'

'Why me?'

'You have a straight reputation, unlike many of your colleagues. And then it turned out you wanted to talk to us, which is always a good starting point.'

Korolev took a moment to remind himself what he needed from Kolya and what he was prepared to give. It seemed to him there wasn't much point in being indirect.

'I can arrange for you to have Tesak's body, and I can share some information about his death, but I want information in exchange,' he said, getting straight to the point.

'Tesak? Well, between yourself and myself, Captain, he deserved what he got. You could have cut logs on that fellow's head, though he never knew it. But yes, we'd like to have his body; his woman is one of us still. The sharing of information is of more interest though. Is that authorized?'

'I'm authorized to speak to you, of course, but there are restrictions. Tesak's body is from myself. How he lived his life is for God to decide on, but you can bury him like a Christian, if that's what you do.'

Kolya nodded and gestured to a hay bale beside him.

'Sit then, Comrade Captain, and have a drink.'

They sat down and Kolya held up his hip flask, the silver flashing as he shook it gently like a fisherman's lure. Korolev looked at it and then at Kolya and, not for the first time wondered how the hell he'd ended up, at this moment in time, with this person, having this conversation. He sighed, reached for the hip flask and took a long drink, the spirit's warmth making him shiver.

'Either I'm cold or the Devil just walked over my grave. Drinking with you, I'm inclined to think it's the Devil.'

'I've been called worse,' Kolya said, chuckling. Korolev reached into his pocket and pulled out his cigarettes. They looked a little damp, but he offered the packet to Kolya anyway, who took one.

'So all this killing is to do with an icon?' Korolev said, exhaling slowly as he spoke and looking for any reaction to the question. He could feel the nicotine and vodka swirling down to his toes. Kolya nodded, but it was unclear whether this was agreement or something else.

'Tell me where you are with your investigation,' Kolya said. 'I'll make it worth your while from my side. You have my word.'

'And I trust you?'

'I'm not the type to run squealing to the Cheka, if that's what you're worried about, and it's in both our interests that you identify the killers, believe me.'

Well, the conversation had to start somewhere – Korolev didn't tell him everything, but he told him who the dead woman was, about Schwartz and the NKVD's interest in the investigation. In fact he ended up telling him more than he'd intended. When he'd finished, Kolya passed the flask to him once again.

'The torture – you think it was a professional?'

'Yes.'

'Cheka?'

'Who knows?'

'Did they talk?'

'Maybe. Possibly not the nun. She died from the torture itself. Tesak was shot, which would make me think they'd finished with him.'

Kolya seemed to consider the implications of Tesak having been broken. After a moment he shrugged his shoulders and spat on the ground. 'Tesak had a hard skin but a soft centre – I'd say he talked.'

He turned back to Korolev. 'Babel says you're a Believer.'

'I don't know where he got that idea.' Korolev couldn't help glancing towards the door of the stall, thinking that if he could see that damned scribbler now he'd give him a look that would singe the hair off his fat meddling head.

'And yet you have a bible underneath the floorboards in your room and talk about God deciding how Tesak lived his life,' Kolya continued.

Korolev rose to his feet, but Kolya waved him down.

'Once you began to investigate the Holy Sister's murder, and then Tesak's, we needed to know more about you. And that lock you have needs replacing – Mishka was inside in less than ten seconds.'

Korolev could feel rage pressing at his ribs, like the air inside a balloon close to bursting, but he held his tongue. Kolya's eyes were steady on his and they held each other's gaze for a long moment.

'This is important to us, this matter. Very important. The icon looks over us, from long ago. You might read in books that St Nicholas is the patron saint of Thieves, but Our Lady of Kazan is our true protector. That's our belief.'

'Our Lady of Kazan? The icon is *Kazanskaya*? But there are a million Kazanskaya icons – every newly-wed couple used to get one in the old days. Surely no one needs to die for such a thing.' Then he paused for a moment, catching the weight in Kolya's calm gaze, as he waited for the penny to drop. 'Tell me you're not talking about the Kazan cathedral icon. But it was destroyed back in the tsar's time – it's just not possible.'

Kolya sat in silence, watching him, as Korolev thought it through. In the Orthodox Church, icons had always been venerated almost as much as the subjects they represented. Kazanskaya was an icon of the Virgin Mother and the infant Jesus, named after the city of Kazan in which it had been miraculously discovered by the Blessed Matryona. Ever since its discovery, it had protected Russia in its hour of need – it had been paraded by Pozharsky and Minin before their victory over the Poles in the seventeenth century, as well as before the battle of Borodino when Napoleon had been sent packing. Hell, he remembered marching past it on his way to fight the Germans back in fourteen. There were indeed millions of copies – each house had had one in the corner before the Revolution – but the original, the miracle worker, had been stolen at the beginning of the century and then destroyed by the panicked culprits, or so he'd thought. But then he remembered the image of the icon on Tesak's body and it occurred to him that if anything was worth killing for, it was Kazanskaya – the icon that looked over Russia herself.

'My God,' Korolev breathed and had to bunch his hand into a

fist to prevent himself making the sign of the cross. 'I meant, hell's bloody bells,' he corrected himself. 'You kept it all this time.'

'Not exactly. You know something about us, I think. A *Ment* understands us better than a citizen. In our world there exists everyone else, and then us. We prey on the rest, but not on each other.' Kolya paused and considered this, after a moment raising his hand and twisting it from side to side, as if to say, 'Not too much anyway.' He took a drink and passed the flask back to Korolev.

'We have rules – more rigid than any legal code, believe me – and if you break them you suffer. Every Thief knows what is expected of him. For example, robbing a church is acceptable, at least it was when they were worth robbing, but killing a priest is a death sentence. We have our own honour; we are *right-thinking* people, judged by our way of thinking. Do you understand?' Korolev nodded in agreement. 'So the Thieves who stole the icon brought shame on each one of us. They were caught, of course. And the icon's cover was found.' He touched his heart. 'But then we heard they'd burnt the icon in their fear – well, if they were true Thieves they'd have killed themselves before doing such a thing. Instead they left us disgraced before the world and before heaven.'

He sighed and took the flask back from Korolev, inhaling on his cigarette. 'So, we laboured under a burden, maybe not all of us, but the men of honour, the Thieves-in-law, the keepers of the tradition – my uncles and my father amongst them. We wanted to shed blood to show atonement and so we hunted – the Okhrana had caught the men who stole the icon, but there were others. Men who had hidden them, women who had loved them, children who had been sired by them. We hunted them down.'

Kolya's words were flat, but Korolev had no trouble imagining the savagery involved. Kolya looked up at Korolev and smiled, as if he'd read his thoughts. There was no gentleness in the smile.

'Then we found it. Almost by accident. In a whorehouse,

believe it or not, hanging on a wall. The madame had been told to guard it with her life, but when faced with the choice she told us what she knew and we spared her. It was a miracle – we were forgiven. And we hid it, and have protected it for all the years since. When the priests were being shot in the street and Believers taken away to God knows where, when churches were being desecrated and worse, and cathedrals blown up with dynamite by Satan's minions with the blood star to mark them out for who they are, all this time we guarded it and kept its resting place secret. And then, two months ago, the Cheka found the hiding place. The Devil's work.'

Korolev wondered whether he was having his leg pulled. He searched Kolya's face. 'I don't believe this,' he said eventually, shaking his head. Maybe it was the alcohol that was making his mind feel sluggish, but he just couldn't take Kolya's story in.

'You saw Tesak's body? Where was his tattoo?' Kolya asked.

'On his arm, his right arm. The bicep.'

Kolya took off his waistcoat and opened his shirt, Christ's crucifixion spread across his chest. He pulled the shoulder of the shirt down along his arm, revealing an image of an icon, the Virgin and the Child, Kazanskaya, Our Lady of Kazan. 'Only the senior Thieves knew we protected her, but all our clan know she protects us.'

'What if it is the truth? What of it? What has it to do with me?'

'Maybe nothing. You want to catch the killer, am I right?'

'Of course. That's my duty.'

'Even if he's Cheka?'

Korolev considered yet again the course he found himself on and the insanity of it, the breath-stealing danger of it. But what choice did he have? He was a simple man and this was the road he walked. His job was to catch criminals and assist in the administration of justice – he wouldn't back away from his duty just yet.

If it came to a choice between duty and death – well, he'd make a decision then, if he still could.

'I'm investigating the murders,' he managed to say. 'If it's in my power, I'll bring whoever committed them to justice.'

'Soviet justice?'

'It's as good as any. The system may not be perfect – I'm not blind. These are eyes in my head. But we work for the future, a Soviet future. And it's as fair as any damned justice system the capitalists ever lied about.' He could feel his leg trembling against the bale of hay. Was it anger or some other emotion? He wasn't sure of anything any more. But if he didn't believe the leadership were working for the People's future – well, then where would he be? What hell would he find himself in then – if it all turned out to be a blood-soaked lie? He spat on the floor to ward off the thought, and then fumbled for another cigarette. He put it in his mouth, reaching for his matches, but Kolya had already extended a lighter.

'Thank you,' Korolev said, hearing the gruffness in his voice. He offered the Thief the packet.

'You're an honest man. And you are a Believer, aren't you?' Kolya seemed to be weighing him up.

'It's none of your business.'

'Maybe it isn't. But what if, at some stage, you have to decide between your loyalty to the Church and your loyalty to Comrade Stalin. How do you think you would decide?'

'I'm a loyal citizen of the Soviet Union.'

'But no Party member. Listen, our aim is to find the icon and see it returned to the Church. We don't know who stole it from the Lubianka, but we want to make sure it ends up in the right place – we can't keep it safe here, we know that now, and the icon is more important than our pride. But we're not the only people trying to find it, as you know, and they're the ones responsible for Tesak and the Holy Sister, and others besides. I have a feeling they are Cheka, these people, and they'll stop at nothing. After all, there's a lot at stake here – the icon is worth a great deal of money. But if we get to it first, we'll see it safe – out of the country. Now you've a decision. Do you tell your bosses what I just told you, or do you keep it quiet?'

'I can't see why I shouldn't tell them.'

Kolya smiled. 'Would you like to know the name of the Chekist commanding the search party? The one who took the icon from us?'

Korolev nodded, half-suspecting he knew the answer.

'Gregorin,' Kolya said and Korolev knew the time for choosing between duty and life had come.

Chapter Sixteen

THE THIEVES took them back to the stands just as another race finished and Korolev felt his Walther slipped into his pocket, saw Mishka tip his cap in ironic salute and then they were gone, swallowed into the swirling, half-drunk crowd as the last of the runners cantered past the post. Babel, meanwhile, had the inward-looking smile of a man committing to memory each detail of their encounter, and it made Korolev feel trapped, that small smile; as though Korolev were in the middle of a story still being written and over which he had no control. Perhaps it was that sense of powerlessness, or perhaps something more sinister, but he suddenly had a vivid sensation of imminent danger. Looking round the crowd, he could see nothing untoward, but the feeling persisted, and if seven years of war had taught him anything at all it was that such a feeling shouldn't be ignored. He took Babel's arm in a strong grip.

'We're getting out of here,' Korolev said and began to direct him towards the exit. The strength of Korolev's hold seemed to shock Babel and he threw him an indignant look, which Korolev chose to ignore. Instead, he shoved at the backs in front of them and dragged the writer along, observing Babel's confusion with some satisfaction.

'Watch where you're going, friend,' someone said, loudly enough for people to turn to see what was happening. The words weren't intended for a friend, however, Korolev realized, as he looked up at a worker in overalls fresh from the factory floor and with a nasty smile on his face. The giant, face etched with engine oil and dirt, had placed a filthy hand on Korolev's shoulder to hold him still and Korolev had an image of the fingers imprinting themselves into the fabric. What with the earlier razor cut, his only winter coat was having a hard day, and he felt a stab of irritation. He looked round at Babel, but the writer paid him no attention, his eyes fixed on the burly worker in expectant fascination.

'Leave the citizen alone, *Ment*. Damned filth – you're all the same. Pushing your weight around.'

Korolev was aware of a sudden quietness around them. He wanted Babel's attention and so he gripped his arm still harder.

'Now, Isaac Emmanuilovich, come on. We're getting out of here, like I said.' He intended continuing, but the worker now made to twist him round and Babel's eyes widened behind his bottle-thick glasses.

'Leave the *Moishe* be, do you hear me? We'll see what his business is later. Right now, I'm talking to you, you dirty terrier.'

The voice sounded slurred and Korolev turned with the grip, only more quickly than the man expected. A feeling of cold rage filled him as he lifted his hands to grab the man's shoulders while extending his head back to the limit of his neck's reach. In his peripheral vision he saw the crowd pulling back from the fight, and then caught a snapshot of the man's surprise just before the crunch of a breaking bone and the blinding pain in his forehead told him he'd cracked the fellow's nose like a nut. The worker rocked backwards a few paces, blood already spattering down his chin, but he managed to stay on his feet, his hands lifting to his face and then forward in defence. He stood there, legs apart for balance and seemingly mesmerized by the gobbets of blood on his hands. Korolev ignored his own pain and stepped towards him again, taking him by his collar this time and jabbing his knee upwards. The worker, still dazed, was too slow to protect himself, and the impact of Korolev's knee into his crotch brought a soft sigh from the watching crowd, a sound that seemed to combine sympathy for the injury with pleasure at its infliction. The worker leant forwards with a noise not dissimilar to a cow that hadn't been milked for several days, and Korolev raised his right fist high above his head and brought it down on the man's neck like an axe. That finished things. The man hit the ground like a bag of flour. Korolev could see the pointed brown caps and red stars of Militia uniforms pushing towards them, but his instincts were still screaming at him to get out.

'Hey, *Ment*, try that on me, why don't you?' came a voice.

'Look what he did to that poor fellow, for no damned reason at all. Come on, boys, let's get him.'

But Korolev was already twenty metres away with a bright-eyed Babel in tow and pleased to find Semionov beside them, looking calm, with one hand pushing out a gun-shaped bulge in his mackintosh pocket and the other clearing a path through the crowd. If the truth were told, the bang on the head was making Korolev feel a little unsteady on his feet, and when Semionov took Babel's other arm, it became more like Babel was dragging him along than the other way round. Somehow he staggered on with them through the entrance hall and then they were out on the street and clear. No one appeared to be following.

'Come on, to the car,' Korolev said, feeling a little better in the fresh air but still half-blinded by the pain in his forehead.

Semionov ran to the car and the engine was turning over by the time the others reached it. As soon as they were in, Semionov floored the accelerator and the car jerked forward, its tyres spinning in the wet.

'We're clear, we're all right. You can slow down,' Korolev said, looking over his shoulder at the receding Hippodrome and conscious at the same time of blood making its sluggish way down his face. He reached for his handkerchief.

'What the hell was that about?' Babel asked, beginning to laugh.

'No wonder they called you the Steamroller, Alexei Dmitri-yevich.' Semionov was grinning with delight. 'That was some demolition – Komsomol's word on that. Pow, pow, pow. Good-night and farewell.'

Korolev turned the rear-view mirror towards him and inspected the wound, hoping most of the blood belonged to the other fellow. There certainly seemed to be a lot of it. He wet his handkerchief with spit and began to clean it away.

'Maybe he was just a drunk hooligan or maybe he was something else, but I wasn't hanging round in the middle of a half-cut crowd of hungry workers to find out which.' Dark blood swelled from a deep purple cut. 'The Devil take it, I need stitches in this. Come on, we need to go to the Institute anyway. Chest-nova will fix me up.'

Semionov took the next turn to the right and they drove in silence. Korolev felt a little nauseous, and his head hurt like blazes, but he was also strangely elated. He thought back over the details of the encounter, the stale vodka on the man's breath, the rough feel of the collar in his hands, the eyes widening in surprise. He'd been in control of himself throughout, he was sure of that. He'd been angry, yes, but not at the worker so much as finding himself in the middle of this ridiculous case. Everyone pushing him this way or that – Popov, Kolya, Gregorin. Babel was at it too, in his own way – even now he was busy scribbling notes in the back seat. All of them pulling strings, laying false trails, observing him – setting him up for a damned big fall if he didn't watch out. Gregorin had never even had the politeness to pretend he wasn't using Korolev in whatever game he was playing, feeding him leads and scraps of disconnected informa-tion without, as it turned out, having the decency to tell him that he'd been the fellow who recovered the icon in the first place. And then some big ox of a mechanic decides to push him around? Well, no wonder it had felt good to crack the brute's nose. The grease monkey had picked out the wrong *Ment*, on the wrong day, to go pestering and putting his paws on. He dabbed at the cut again and hoped the bastard's nose was flattened to pulp.

'So what did Kolya have to say for himself?' Semionov asked.

'Some things which need to be checked, nothing very useful.' Korolev tried to keep his tone nonchalant. Split-open head or not, Korolev didn't like what Kolya had told him one little bit. It was the kind of information that could kill a man, and Semionov had his whole life ahead of him.

Semionov turned the car in through the gates of the Institute and then pulled in beside a muddy ZIS, which Korolev recognized from the Militia car pool. Several trucks were parked on the gravelled area in front of the entrance, their bonnets slick with rain. Chemical Warfare Defence Unit was painted in large white letters on each of their canvas sides. The drivers huddled beside them with damp cigarettes and a mutinous air, watching the Ford come to a halt as though it were bringing more bad news. There was a city-wide Civil Defence exercise the following day and these fellows must be part of it. The Fascists hadn't used gas in Spain, so far, but he supposed they would sooner or later.

'Larinin must be here,' Korolev said, gesturing to the ZIS.

'Who?' Babel asked.

'A colleague. Isaac Emmanuilovich – do you mind waiting here in the car? The autopsy area is restricted, so your presence would compromise Dr Chestnova. Vanya, do you mind keeping Comrade Babel company? I'll send for you if you're needed.'

§

He found Chestnova in her office, with her feet up on the desk, reading *Sovietsky Sport*.

'What happened to you?'

'I walked into a door,' Korolev said with a scowl. 'Can you fix me up?'

'Unlucky door. Here, let me have a look at it. Ah, it's not so bad. A couple of stitches and a bit of disinfectant.' She pointed him towards a small metal box with a red cross painted on its front that stood in the bookshelf beside the door. In the meantime she went to the sink in the corner of her office, where she washed her hands. Out of curiosity, Korolev opened the magazine the doctor had been reading.

'Don't worry, Alexei Dmitriyevich, I'm not planning to take up athletics.'

'It's never too late, I hear.' Korolev winced as she stretched the edges of the wound apart. 'Where's Larinin, by the way? I saw his car outside. You didn't slip him into the incinerator, did you?'

Chestnova scowled. 'Esimov is assisting your esteemed colleague. I thought it best to leave them to it. The magazine is Esimov's. Esimov gets to look at your colleague and the dead Thief for an hour or so, and I get to look at bare-chested Soviet athletes in their shorts. It's as good as a refresher course in anatomy that magazine, I can tell you.'

'It seems like a fair division of labour.'

'Ha. Now hold still when I do this, like a good Militiaman.' She dabbed at the cut with a piece of cotton wool impregnated with something yellow and strong. His eyes were watering even before it touched his forehead.

'There, it's not so bad, is it?' she said in a mischievous voice.

'Just put the stitches in and get it over with,' Korolev said, feeling sweat dampen his armpits and wanting to be somewhere else. For some reason he felt a strong desire to vomit.

'A moment, a moment,' Chestnova said, as she threaded a needle. 'Hold still, will you?'

'I am holding still,' Korolev said as he recoiled from the needle's point.

'That's better. By the way, an interesting body arrived in this morning. Found in a church that was being demolished. The explosives didn't blow and when they were checking the charges they found a dead drunk. I wondered if there might be a connection. Seeing as he was found in a church. Not the usual dumping spot – churches.'

'Are you finished?'

She patted his cheek and put the bloodied needle in a metal bowl.

'More or less. You should be careful for a day or so – that was a nasty bang. Have you felt dizzy at all? Nauseous? A headache?'

'I'm fine,' Korolev said, ignoring the spinning floor. He was damned if a bump on the head was going to slow him down.

Chestnova looked into his eyes for a moment, then held up some fingers.

'How many fingers?'

'Count them yourself. I'm fine.' Korolev wasn't about to admit there were six of them. Even in his state he knew that was too many.

'Concussion's no fun – it's up to you, of course.'

'I've had bigger knocks on the head, believe me.'

'Oh, that I believe,' Chestnova said with a smirk.

Chapter Seventeen

THE MORTUARY was empty when they entered and he followed Chestnova into the smaller of the autopsy rooms. The blinds had been lowered, but a grey light filtered in anyway – just enough to show a dead man on the stainless-steel table, his clothes covered in muck and blood. When Chestnova turned on the light, however, Korolev saw that the corpse's face was black with bruising.

'Could we clean him up a bit – see what he looks like?'

'Of course. Help me off with his clothes first.'

Chestnova had to cut the fabric of the military-style jacket in several places to remove it, and then do the same with the shirt underneath. As the shirt collar came unstuck from the blood-caked neck, she whistled.

'Well, well,' she said. 'He's picked up a bullet hole along the way. Strange – drunks don't often get shot in the back of the head. What do you think of that?'

She leant closer to examine the small dark wound. Enough of the crusted blood had been removed with the shirt to reveal a circle of burnt powder that had impregnated itself into the skin around it.

'The Devil,' Korolev said, his stomach making its presence felt. 'Let's see if he picked up any other interesting injuries.'

Chestnova nodded and, the dead man's upper body now naked, she began to clean it with the small hose.

'He's been beaten to a pulp, all right, and look – cigarette burns.' Chestnova pointed to some blackened circles – someone had certainly gone out of their way to cause the man pain.

'Do you think they did all this in the church?'

'Who knows?' Korolev said, angry that the uniforms had just dumped the body at the mortuary.

'Your colleagues were at the end of their shift and they needed the body out of the church before they demolished it,' Chestnova said, seeing the anger in his eyes. 'Nobody bothers too much about dead drunks these days. We get two or three in here a day. Often looking like this. Most of the time they died from what they drank, rather than a beating. The Militiaman who dropped him off was called Nikitin, if that helps. I'll have a record upstairs of which station he's based at.'

The dead man's mouth was missing several teeth, but his nails were clean and the palm and fingers soft – clerk's hands. Not that usual for an alcoholic, Korolev thought to himself. Then he saw that the wrists were rubbed and raw, just as the girl's had been, and that several of the corpse's fingers were twisted out of shape.

'Look at this – damn the man. No photographs or anything, and the crime scene now a heap of rubble. When do you think he died?'

Chestnova ran her finger over the corpse's skin and considered the question.

'No more than forty-eight hours ago – I'll have a better idea when I open him up.'

Korolev began to look through the jacket pockets, but found only the stub of a pencil. He turned back to the corpse and began checking the trousers. Nothing there either. He wasn't sure later what made him look at the feet, but when he did he immediately saw a shape in the corpse's sock. It was just an outline, but when Korolev peeled the sock back, he found a red identity book and groaned as he read the letters NKVD embossed on its cover in raised black print.

'He's a Chekist,' Korolev said in a quiet voice, as he opened it. 'Name – Mironov, Boris Ivanovich. Rank – major.' He compared the photograph to the dead man. It was definitely him.

'What do we do?' Chestnova asked. She had turned almost as pale as the dead man.

'I'll call someone. We'd better make sure nobody else sees him until we get firm instructions. Say absolutely nothing. To anyone.'

§

There was only one person to call in the circumstances, and that was Gregorin – no matter what Kolya had said.

'Korolev?' Gregorin's voice sounded flat on the fizzing line. 'What can I do for you?'

'I'm at the Institute, Colonel,' Korolev began, before explaining what he'd found in the mortuary. When he'd finished there was a long delay. He thought he detected heavy breathing in amidst the crackle.

'Anyone else know? Just you and Chestnova?'

'I'm here with Babel and Semionov, but they didn't come in. Some others may have seen the body, but even if they have, they think it was just a drunk kicked to death by his fellows.'

'Good. I'm on my way, but it will take a little while – I have to arrange a few things in the meantime. Let no one inside the mortuary until I arrive. And this is top secret, Korolev. You and Chestnova must understand the consequences if it isn't kept so. Understood?'

Before he could answer, the phone went dead in his hand, and Korolev replaced it on its cradle. His head felt as if it was about to split in two. Those damned Chekists – secrecy was like a sexual perversion for that lot.

Korolev helped Chestnova lock the mortuary and then positioned himself outside to wait for the colonel, sending Chestnova to her office. There was no point in her being around when Gregorin arrived. It hurt like blazes when he frowned, but he couldn't stop doing it, and his frown only deepened as Larinin turned into the corridor.

'Ah, Korolev. What's this? The mortuary shut?' Larinin seemed in a suspiciously good mood.

'Only for an hour or so. No one's to go in.'

Larinin nodded, not apparently interested in the reason, which suited Korolev.

'What happened to your head?'

'A long story – it's not as bad as it looks.'

'Good – it looks pretty bad. Although not as bad as poor Tesak when Esimov opened up his skull to get at the bullet, I can tell you.'

'Not that bad, certainly,' Korolev said, although if it got any more painful he'd begin to question that.

'Anyway, I've good news. Mikhail Mitrofaniyevich Smitin, also known as Tesak, also known as Priest. I found his record.'

'Mitrofaniyevich?'

'A deacon's son. His father died in the Zone in twenty-nine, but young Mikhail went to the bad long before that. Ran away from home and joined a Volga river boat before the war. He's dodged and ducked any useful contribution to society ever since. The files are on your desk.'

'Files?'

'Several. He's been a busy man, through the Zone three times for a start. He got off lightly the first time, appeared to have been re-educated but fell back into speculation and thievery once he was released. The second and third visits were for two years and five years. A senior Thief, as you said.' Korolev was surprised, not at the information – it was what he had expected – but at the way Larinin spoke, confident in his facts, proud even of the progress he'd made. It seemed the fellow was making a real effort for a change.

'And the car?' he asked, still bemused.

'Nothing, but I'm working on it.' Larinin's jaw took on a

determined line. He paused, looking at the closed door, a thoughtful expression coming over his face. 'You know, I didn't see many autopsies in the traffic department. Road accidents, yes indeed, and a tram will make a mess of a citizen when he's unfortunate enough to fall in front of one, believe me. But cutting open skulls and scooping out brains and the like? And all the time whistling? It's not right. Where is he, anyway? Esimov?'

'Not in there. Have you tried their office? First floor. Ask anyone – they all know where Chestnova sits.'

Larinin nodded his thanks and Korolev watched him walk towards the stairs. It seemed that the traffic cop had decided to take a stab at being a proper detective for once, and Korolev couldn't help thinking he might make a half-decent job of it.

§

Korolev sat back against the wall and thought about the dead Chekist. Beaten up and shot in the head. A coincidence? Unlikely. He'd bet his last kopek the fellow was involved in this damned Kazanskaya business. Was he one of Gregorin's people or one of the conspirators? That was the question. The body hadn't been meant to be found, that was for sure, not with a thousand tons of rubble on top of it. Kolya had warned him the killings would carry on until either the murderers were caught or the icon left the country.

He looked at his watch. Gregorin should be along soon. If the colonel wanted it kept quiet, maybe that meant they were close to catching the conspirators and bringing an end to all this. He could only hope.

As if on cue, the far doors opened and Gregorin entered the corridor, flanked by two large bruisers who looked as if they could stop tanks barehanded. Someone has been lifting weights in the Dinamo gymnasium, Korolev thought to himself as he stood and offered them the key. One of them opened the door and Gregorin looked in at the empty mortuary with no obvious emotion. Korolev handed him the small brown paper bag he'd put Mironov's papers in.

'His identity card. My fingerprints are on it, I'm afraid.'

'And they were in his sock?' Gregorin sounded a little angry at that detail.

'Yes.'

'I see – no one's been in?'

'No.'

'And Dr Chestnova?'

'Upstairs in her office.'

'Good. What happened to your head?'

Without really thinking about it, Korolev decided to keep his mouth shut about his meeting with Kolya, at least for the moment. The dead Chekist changed things and he needed to think the situation through.

'An accident, nothing serious,' he said, shrugging it off.

Gregorin nodded, and for a moment his detached manner slipped and Korolev thought he saw tiredness in the staff colonel's eyes. Not physical fatigue so much as weariness with the world.

'Thank you, Captain. You may go. We'll look after this from here. I'll be in contact later. Nothing about this in your report, obviously. And not a word to anyone – not even Popov. Understood?'

Korolev nodded, choosing to ignore the way Gregorin's colleagues looked at him. He expected that kind of examination from Gregorin by now, but from strangers it made him feel uncomfortable. They stared at him like butchers weighing meat on the hoof.

§

Outside the rain had stopped, but the sky was dark with more to come. Larinin stood with Semionov and Babel. They looked up as he approached and Larinin took a step forward.

'Listen, Alexei Dmitriyevich, can I take your car? I have to attend a Party meeting in twenty minutes and the ZIS won't start. Morozov's mechanic will be here in ten minutes at most, so even if it's past it – you can take his car.'

His voice tailed off as he seemed to conclude from Korolev's stern expression that his request would be refused, but Korolev had good reason to want to see the back of Larinin. He nodded after a moment.

'Of course, Comrade. Take it. We'll see you later.'

Larinin looked surprised at his agreement but had no hesitation in getting behind the driving wheel. Semionov wasn't disappointed to see the back of the Ford either, and was already prowling around the ZIS, inspecting it with unashamed enthusiasm.

'A great car. International class, you know. A real Soviet world-beater – that's the ZIS.'

The fact that it was temporarily out of action didn't seem to affect his positive view. Larinin, meanwhile, pushed at the Ford's broken windscreen with a look of disappointment but, seeing there was nothing else for it, pulled his hat low over his ears and pushed the collar of his coat up to meet it. Korolev didn't envy him the drive as rain drops began to spatter the ZIS's bonnet.

'Vanya, could you get us something to eat from the canteen? Whatever they have.'

Semionov looked at Korolev for a moment, then at Babel, before nodding in a mixture of agreement and understanding. They watched him walk past the chemical defence trucks towards the canteen's entrance.

'Isaac,' Korolev began, 'how do you know Colonel Gregorin?' As he asked the question, Korolev thought to himself what a good question it was. After all, what if Babel were Gregorin's informer? If Babel was an informer, though, he was worth his weight in gold; never had he met anyone more transparent. He was openly curious about everything and everyone, and yet he managed it with such charm that it was almost impossible to take offence.

You couldn't be like that and betray people's confidences. No, Babel might be an eccentric, but he wasn't a rat.

'I met him through an old friend, Evgenia Feinberg,' Babel said, after thinking about it. 'She has these parties I go along to, out of curiosity as much as anything.'

'Who is this Feinberg woman?' Korolev said, the pain in his head making his voice gruff.

'I know her from Odessa, we were friends once.' The way Babel lingered over the word 'friends' told Korolev they'd been more than that. 'And now of course, she's married to Ezhov, so you meet some really very interesting people at her place.'

'Ezhov? The new Commissar of State Security?'

'Yes, that's the fellow. In private he's a very pleasant man, and I must admit I like to observe these protectors of the State at close quarters. It can't be easy to do what they do, and yet you wouldn't know it from the way they stand with a glass of Abrau Dursov fizzing away in their hands. Refined, almost like they might be accountants for a State concern, but no more than that. All the interrogations and the rest, they barely show on them.'

Korolev found himself shaking his head, a reflection of the utter bewilderment he felt. No, Babel wasn't spying *for* the NKVD. Babel was spying *on* the NKVD.

'And tell me this, Isaac Emmanuilovich, just how well did you know Mrs Ezhov, in the past, when you were "friends"?'

Babel looked uncomfortable. It was an answer in itself.

'Does he know?'

Babel laughed. 'I don't think he minds much. It's all in the past, after all, and he's no wallflower when it comes to these things.'

'Does he know what you're writing?'

Babel turned to check they weren't being overheard. 'What are you talking about, Alexei Dmitriyevich? I never said I was writing anything.'

Korolev felt his eyebrows rise in disbelief. It hurt. Babel threw another nervous look at the building behind them.

'Just some notes, perhaps. You can't deny it's interesting. And the questions it raises. Can there really be so many enemies? What if the Chekists themselves have been infiltrated? What if the fear of the foreign interventionists, the spies, the Fascists and all the rest is self-perpetuating? You know, like a machine that, once you turn it on, can't be stopped – it just carries on until there's no one left. They tell me things, the Chekists, and they defy logic. They have quotas, Alexei Dmitriyevich. Like a factory. Each district has a set number of counter-revolutionaries and spies to identify. Do you know what that means? Suspicion isn't even necessary these days because there's a quota to be filled – and anyone will do. Not just filled, but exceeded if the local boss is to progress in his career, or avoid making up the numbers himself in the next quota that comes down the line. So maybe I am writing something, but only for the drawer. You could never even think of trying to publish it, of course, because the heart of the problem is that we are, as a country, genuinely in danger. Those trucks over there will be used one day, and it won't just be for an exercise. There's a war coming and we'll be in it. But a few words for the drawer can't hurt, can they?'

Korolev reached forward and put his hand to Babel's mouth.

'Never talk about this, Isaac. To anyone, do you hear me? Never say such things. Most of all not to me.'

Babel looked confused. 'But you're not the same as them.'

'You barely know me, brother. I'm a member of the Militia and a loyal Soviet citizen. Don't forget it.'

Babel smile was conspiratorial. 'Of course, I understand.'

'Good, let's be clear on that,' Korolev said, deciding to ignore the smile. 'I have another question. Did you ever come across a Chekist called Mironov at these parties of yours? Boris Ivanovich Mironov? A major?'

'The name is familiar. I could ask a few people.'

'Neither of us would want Gregorin to know you'd asked about this man, believe me.'

'You worry too much. I've come to the conclusion after the last few years that the more you worry, and the more you try to avoid the danger, the more at risk you are. They smell the fear on you. Then the phone stops ringing and friends cross the road to avoid you and then, bang, one morning there's a sealed apartment, red wax hanging from a string, and you're never heard of again. I thought it through. If they're going to take you, they'll take you. Why help them?'

Korolev looked at him in disbelief, but Babel was oblivious.

'Anyway, I think I know the fellow to talk to – a decent man, well connected within the organization, but not front line. I know him from the war; I can talk to him as one man to another and nothing will go further.'

'That would be just as well,' Korolev said.

Babel smiled at him, amused. Their footsteps crunched over the gravel as they returned to the Institute's entrance. Some orderlies were unloading stretchers from a truck – it seemed that the following day's exercise would be authentic.

THE DRIVER had come for him without announcement. A job needed to be done straight away and he was to be the back-up in case things didn't go according to plan. Not that there seemed to be much of a plan. The driver had a truck half full of rubble from somewhere, and an accident was to be arranged at the shortest of notice. He did as he was told, however, and climbed into the passenger seat. They drove across town and then parked on the side of the street. The driver went to make a phone call and, when he returned, handed him a photograph and explained what was to be done. 'It won't be long now,' the driver said, checking his watch.

After a little while a car had entered the gates across the street and the driver had nodded to him. Then, five minutes later, a different car had come out – a past-it looking Ford – and they'd followed it, from a distance initially. He was no saint – the Lord knew that – no one could have done the things he'd done and not be changed by it. But this smelt worse than anything up until now. By a distance.

He couldn't complain: he'd had a chance to refuse at the beginning, all those years before. There would have been no shame then, but he knew someone would have to say yes, sooner or later, and so he'd offered it up to the future; to the expectation of a new society where crime didn't exist, where the workers and peasants of the world would combine together in happy toil, where war and the exploitation of the masses were something students would study in history classes. He looked at the driver and felt weak with nausea. If this turned out to be a rogue operation, the very excuses he'd scorned from the State's enemies would be the only ones he could think of to justify himself. He hadn't meant to do anything wrong; he'd been misled by others; he'd believed he was acting in the best interests of the Party. He'd be better off saying nothing at all.

It was a tragedy, really. They'd taught him to work for the collective good – explained to him that the individual was weak but the Collective was a mighty force that could change history itself. But now it turned out that he'd been an egotistical individualist all along. He'd a choice all right, he could shop the rats, but it was no choice really, he'd be shot as well. Or given twenty-five in the Zone, which was the same thing. That long in the Zone wasn't possible. He knew how it was out there, men sleeping in the snow, frozen solid to each other in the morning, if they even survived the night. So much for theory – this was reality.

He probably wouldn't make it to a camp, of course, the other Zeks would have him on the train. They'd smell the Lubianka basement on him and he'd wake up with a hole where his throat had been. And his son? God might help the boy, if that villain still existed, but no one else would. He'd be lucky if he ended up half-starved and lice-ridden in an orphanage. More likely he'd be found dead under a bridge – another nameless waif to be tossed into an incinerator. This was the logic, Soviet logic. He was a traitor and his line would be eradicated, his family would cease to exist and no one would mention his name again. His fine apartment would be fought over by his former comrades, his belongings scavenged and there wouldn't even be a ripple to mark his passing.

They were behind the car now, travelling in the inside lane while the car stayed wide. There was only one man in the vehicle – it wasn't the boy and it couldn't be the writer, not in a Militia vehicle. The driver's face was white in the early evening light – his eyes were like black bullets and he could sense his physical excitement. Here was a fellow who enjoyed his work it seemed. A convoy of huge Metro trucks was rumbling towards them on the other side of the road, and he knew enough to brace himself.

THE HOLY THIEF

The trucks came closer, and the driver moved up alongside the car. So near were they that he could hear the rattle of the Ford over the roar of the truck's engine. Then the driver swung the truck, pushing the Militia vehicle up onto two wheels, and for a moment he stared down into the shocked eyes of the car's occupant, no more than three feet beneath them. There was a crash and a screech of tearing metal. Did he imagine the Militiaman's scream in amongst the noise? Perhaps. It all happened in milli-seconds. The Ford hit the lead truck of the convoy head on, collapsed like a concertina, and then the truck was mounting it and the car was being crushed as if it were made from paper.

He looked for the Militiaman in the rear-view mirror, but there was just a jumble of twisted metal, jagged glass and shredded fabric. The face stayed with him, though. And it wasn't the face from the photograph.

Chapter Eighteen

THE GENERAL stood in his usual place, looking down on Petrovka Street and smoking his pipe with a pensive air. The street light caught the squalling rain, turning the raindrops into falling white streaks that flew at the window, spattering the glass and leaving Korolev glad he was sitting here in the warmth and not outside, hunched into sodden clothes with his face streaming wet, stuck in a queue for bread that stretched for two blocks ahead of him.

'A terrible thing. Half the kids in from the country have never even seen a tractor, let alone a truck, back on their *kolkhoz*. Then they get a construction job in Moscow and they're put into one and told to drive it. Talk to the fellows in traffic – they can tell you stories that would make you weep. They might as well measure you for a wooden jacket when they give you a job as a truck driver in this town. Well, measure a pedestrian more likely.'

'The truck driver who hit him was experienced enough, the uniforms said. They think a truck on Larinin's side of the road ran him into the oncoming traffic and didn't stop to pick up the pieces. Mind you, that's all there was – pieces.'

'Why would he stop? He saw what happened behind him on the road, didn't he? And what he saw was ten years for sabotage under Article 58. Did anyone get a number plate? No? So it's an accident. Leave it at that. The fellow probably didn't even see Larinin from up in his cab and – who knows? – Larinin might

227

have been in the wrong. The traffic boys will look into it, don't worry. They'll poke around enough for all of us, and if something comes of the poking? Well, it's a different story then.'

Korolev opened his mouth to speak, but stopped when he saw Popov shaking his head and pointing to the ceiling. The general held up the day's report, a couple of pages only. It occurred to Korolev that the general's insistence that Larinin's death was an accident was a little overdone, but if he thought the office might be bugged, then that made sense. He nodded in understanding and the general turned to the first page of Korolev's skimpy update.

The report was brief for a reason – Korolev hadn't put anything in there about the dead Chekist because he'd been forbidden to. And as for the meeting with Kolya? He'd mentioned it, but only to indicate it had been a complete waste of time. In the end, the identity of Tesak was the only substantive piece of information it contained.

'So Kolya had nothing to say. Interesting he met with you at all.' Popov let the thought hang there for a moment, and Korolev shifted uncomfortably in his seat. 'So what next for our enquiry, do you think?'

'We'll do our best to track down the girl and the car. Keep looking for more local witnesses. Brusilov is still working his way through the Komsomol cell. We have a few known associates of Tesak's to follow up on. Maybe we'll get lucky and maybe not. Of course, State Security may take the matter over altogether.'

'Let's hope they do,' Popov said. 'The missing person bulletin has gone round the stations – that might produce something, I suppose.'

They looked at each other glumly.

'It feels like we're coming to a dead end,' Popov said.

'Maybe for the best. After all, we know there's a separate investigation going on.' Korolev realized they were both talking for the benefit of a microphone now.

'Agreed,' the general said. 'Well, nothing else to be done here tonight. Off you go home.'

Korolev rose to his feet and then sat down again as his legs gave way. The room's edges seemed soft all of a sudden and he had to swallow repeatedly to counter the nausea he felt. It felt as if all the energy in his body had dropped out through his feet.

'Excuse me,' he managed to say.

'What's wrong with you, Alexei Dmitriyevich? Are you all right?'

'Just a moment, Comrade General. Forgive me.' He felt the general's hand take his shoulder and, with some effort, he managed to focus his eyes on the table in front of him, while the rest of the room swayed about in his peripheral vision. A clammy sweat broke out on his forehead and he swallowed once again. Then it was as if the strength of Popov's grip provided him with a point of solidity round which he was able to pull himself together again.

'Thank you,' he whispered, after what felt like hours, 'I feel a little better now.' He understood, as he said it, that the general had been talking to him, but that he hadn't heard a word.

'Can you stand?' Popov asked.

Korolev leant forward to put his hands on the general's desk for support and then pulled himself to his feet. 'Good,' Popov said and patted Korolev's back, 'But I think I should give you a lift home. You look like a two-day-old corpse.'

Korolev wanted to object but the thought of fighting for the space to breathe on a tram changed his mind. 'Are you sure, Comrade General?'

'Of course. You're on the way. Pick up your things and meet me at the main gate. Will you be all right?'

'Yes, Comrade General,' Korolev said, already imagining the warmth of the car.

§

Five minutes later Korolev opened the door to the general's ZIS on Petrovka Street, and sat in. The general smiled at him as they pulled away from the kerb.

'Maybe the office is bugged or maybe it isn't,' he said, 'but my phone has developed a hissing sound that wasn't there three days ago.'

'I see. It could be nothing, of course.'

'Of course, but then there's another Party meeting tomorrow night.'

'I thought there was one today.'

'There was, but this one is specifically to address the Party cell's lack of vigilance and potentially counter-revolutionary failings. I'll be required to participate in the necessary self-criticism as a senior activist.'

The general's profile revealed no emotion when Korolev turned to look at him, and the way he spoke was matter of fact – but Korolev knew how these things went, most of the time anyway. It was like seeing a bear torn to pieces by dogs. The questions came thick and fast, aggressive beyond belief, and no one bothered too much about the answers. If you managed to deal with one dog, two others would be attacking another spot. And the crowd would shout them on, knowing that if they didn't, they might be the next in the chair.

'I'll admit my errors, throw myself on the mercy of the Party. Suggest I be assigned to other duties for my failures. I'm not going to fight. If it's the Party's opinion that Mendeleyev's loose mouth was a stab in the back at a time when the State is under threat, then I don't disagree with them. I liked Knuckles, a good worker, a tough cop – not a Party member but still a Militiaman who should have known better. If I'd been asked before the decision was made to punish him, I'd have taken his record into account. But would that have been the right thing to do? The Party thinks I've ignored the political and dealt only with the practical and they're right. I thought that was what I was meant to do, leave the political to the Chekists. I was wrong, of course.' The general's voice had grown rough and stilted and Korolev could see his knuckles were white around the steering wheel.

'I've shed blood for the Party more than once, Korolev, and I'll shed it again if it's needed. We all know the world situation. The Spanish Comrades are losing out against the Fascists, the Germans have crushed the Party there and are pushing out their borders, and the Italians are marching through blood in Africa. Sooner or later they'll come for us – they're already preparing the way with their spies and provocateurs. The Party knows this. We can't let our guard drop – they'll be on us like a flash if we do. If the Party needs an example to remind the department of this, I'm happy to be the example.'

Korolev didn't know what to say. It was true – even in the east the Japanese were pushing up against the Soviet borders, eyeing up Siberia. It had always been this way, of course. Enemies had encircled the Soviet Union since its creation, only now they were stronger than ever.

'It was a failure of mine as well.'

The general scowled, 'Don't start with that again. Leave it to the Party to decide, and in the meantime keep your head low. Understand?'

Korolev nodded in reluctant agreement and the general's scowl relaxed a little.

'Now tell me whatever it was you couldn't say upstairs.'

Korolev took a deep breath and then told him about Citizeness Kardasheva's opinion as to the profession of the Razin Street killers and that Gregorin might have led the raid that recovered the icon.

'I see. Still, Gregorin told you as much, that elements within the Cheka might be behind this whole mess.'

'He didn't tell me he led the raid on the Thieves.'

'No. But if he did, that might be why he's been assigned to investigate the case. What do you think? He wasn't responsible for this icon going missing from the Lubianka storerooms, surely?'

'No, I don't think so.'

The general considered the information in silence. Korolev wondered what he'd make of the dead Chekist or how he'd react if he told him that the icon was Kazanskaya. He'd probably crash the car.

'So what should I do?'

'Do? What can you do? You can't walk away from it, can you? Where would you go?' He turned the car into Bolshoi Nikolo-Vorobinsky and changed down a gear as the car struggled up the slippery slope. Mud had been washed down the alley by the rain and the car's bonnet twitched from side to side. The street's surface, despite being cobbled, was brown in the light of the car's headlamps. 'A bad night. The *rasputitsa* is upon us. Do you remember the autumn mud back in the war? I saw men drown in it. We can thank the Party for good roads and a lot else.'

Korolev nodded his agreement as the general came to a halt outside Number 4. The rain rattled on the roof of the car.

'Where's your driver tonight, Comrade General?'

The general shrugged his shoulders, 'Sick, or so he says.' He looked at Korolev. 'Now, listen. You have to proceed as if this is an ordinary investigation. It's the safest way. If there are traitors in the Cheka, they'll get their come-uppance soon enough and it sounds like Gregorin is hot on their trail as it is. Maybe you *are* a decoy, and maybe not, but either way you have to do your duty. You might even be the one to catch them. And, of course, it might just turn out to be a madman, and nothing more to it. Who knows? With a bit of luck we'll all come through in one piece.'

Korolev nodded and said his farewells, the general's hand enveloping his for a finger-crushing moment. The only madman anywhere near this case, of course, was anyone who thought it had nothing to do with State Security. Korolev watched him drive off, the car's wheels slithering through the mud. He could hear the blood pumping in his ears and wondered if he'd ever had such a headache. It felt as if he'd been shot, which would teach him to pick scraps with factory workers. At his age, that was ridiculous behaviour, although he felt a little surge of pleasure remembering the look Semionov had given him afterwards.

He stood there for a moment and then he felt the pavement shift under his boots. He took a step towards the door, but the street seemed to be closing in around him and panic made his nostrils flare. Now his stomach seemed to be squirming up towards his chest and instinct alone took him three slow steps over to the wall. He leant against it, ignoring the stream from a broken gutter that splashed down onto his arm, soaking his coat black. His stomach lurched again and he bent over, still clutching at the rough plaster for balance and then vomited against the wall, the stream of half-digested food immediately beginning to dissipate in the heavy rain. Two retches seemed to empty his stomach and any strength he had left. He could barely keep his eyes open, let alone stand, but somehow he managed to hold himself there and then, infinitely slowly, to lift a hand up to his face and wipe his mouth. He ran his tongue around his teeth and spat, the effort bending him over once again as his stomach heaved. The ground beneath him came in and out of focus and he wondered if he'd been poisoned, but he couldn't remember anything passing his lips in the previous few hours. He breathed deeply and put his free hand to his chest to try and control the shivering that was juddering throughout his body. He looked at the street lamp's reflection in the puddle beneath him. It seemed like the last light in the world. He swore, the words frothing on his lips, and began to edge towards the doorway, leaning against the wall, his arm banging against the plaster so hard was he shaking. At least, if he could get inside, he wouldn't drown like a dog in the street. He inched closer, feeling the weight of each thread of his sodden coat and praying for respite. 'Preserve me, Oh Lord,' he whispered to himself, the words growling out and tearing at the large ball of dull pain that mapped the contours of his skull.

When he heard the footsteps coming, he was too weak to lift his head and he cursed himself. Here it comes, he thought, the bullet with my name – and I welcome it, I welcome the release. But the last thing he remembered was someone putting an arm around him just before he fell.

Chapter Nineteen

THE LANDSCAPE was flat in every direction right up to the dark blue line of the horizon; one enormous field that flowed and ebbed in the wind, the wheat stroking his elbows as he walked slowly forward. It was like a sea, tossed and flattened by the strong breeze, golden and dark as the clouds moved over it, gusts marking their progress in long, rolling indentations. The only noises were the rasping caw of a circling crow and the swish of the swaying wheat.

The rifle was heavy, and he let it hang there at waist height, his thumb rubbing the safety catch and his finger light against the trigger. The Pole was here, somewhere ahead of him, crawling on his elbows and knees, no doubt, trying not to disturb the surface above him. Korolev searched for an anomaly that would signal the scout's progress. He'd be heading west – that was where he'd come from and that was where the rest of them would be. He wondered whether he was wounded. The Pole's horse was a hundred metres back, panting its life out, its eyes looking for the last time on the sky above, thick blood already drying on its chest where the machine gun had caught it. He stopped and listened, but all he could hear was the crow still circling the horse, calling its fellows to the feast.

Each step he took was careful, feeling for a quiet place to rest his weight before he swung the other leg forward. He could hear each stalk pop underfoot, but he couldn't hear the man ahead.

The Pole's rifle still hung from the saddle on the dying horse, but he could be sure the man had a pistol. Didn't officers always have pistols? How else could you shoot your own men?

He stopped and slowly turned his body to the left, shifting his weight as he did so. He'd heard something; very close. The bayonet rippled silver as it led the rifle's arc. Another noise and now he stood still, his thumb checking the safety catch was off. He thought about firing a bullet to smash a hole through the wheat just in case he might see a scrap of khaki cloth, but then up the Pole came, the sword first, then the arm, the cap, the eyes, the twisted grey teeth and the snarling mouth, the epaulettes, the dark polish of the Sam Browne belt, each gleaming button on the uniform coat, up they all came and straight onto the bayonet he'd pushed forward in a lunge. The point went in just above the buckle on the cross belt and slid through fabric and skin as if they were paper. The rifle twisted in his hands as the blade hit a rib and then another and then it was through, into the lungs, and then another rib as it searched for the daylight on the other side. The sword was still coming towards him though and instinctively he pulled the trigger, once, twice. The bullets flung the man off the end of the rifle, a look of surprise in his already dead eyes.

Korolev stood there, shaking, blood slick along the length of the bayonet, listening to the screaming and knowing it was his own voice.

§

'There, there. Quiet now. You're frightening the child.' The voice was deep and calm. He tried to open his eyes, but the lids seemed to be stuck together, and came apart only with difficulty. The resulting light was intense enough to hurt and he shut his eyes against it, as tightly as he could, feeling a familiar stab of pain in his forehead, and then opened them wide all at once. A pair of spectacles stared down at him.

'Concussion,' the spectacles said. 'That's what it is. Concussion.'

'Will he be all right?' a girl's voice asked. She sounded very young, interested rather than concerned. He felt relief there was no fear in her voice.

'Of course he will. Look at him. He's strong as a horse. He'll be fine.' The spectacles gleamed approvingly, 'He needs a good night's sleep and a little bit of care. But yes, he'll be all right. Don't worry yourself, young lady.'

Korolev blinked. He was in Moscow, in the new flat. The Polish officer remained in the past, just a memory indistinguishable from all the other bad memories from that time. He swallowed, his mouth dry, and someone put a glass to his lips. He swilled the water round his tongue before drinking it, feeling it work its way down his throat.

'There. You see, he's not so bad. Just a bang on the head. How many fingers, Comrade?' The man in the spectacles held up three fingers.

'Three,' Korolev said, his voice sounding broken and old. No energy for cleverness this time.

'Good. But, you need a day on your back all the same.'

'Can't,' Korolev heard himself say.

'Of course you can. I've never heard anything so ridiculous. Semion Semionovich?'

'At least a day. We have to preserve our best workers. That comes from the Central Committee directly.' He recognized Popov's voice but couldn't see him – the man with the spectacles was so close that he blocked out the rest of the room.

'There, what do you say to that?'

Korolev realized he was frowning. As far as he could work out, he was lying on the chesterfield in the shared kitchen. He managed to push himself up onto his elbow and then, with Spectacles' assistance, into a sitting position. He let his head hang and focused on the shifting floorboards at his feet until they steadied, and the urge to empty what little must be left in his stomach passed. Then he looked up at the people in the room. Shura was standing by the kitchen entrance, her face grave. To her side, Valentina Nikolaevna stood, her blue eyes searching his for something, her mouth a straight line. Her hand rested on a pretty young girl's shoulder. He presumed this must be Natasha, Valentina's daughter; about eight, dark blonde hair, her mother's eyes and a Pioneer's red scarf tied round her neck. She smiled at him shyly. Popov was standing by the window, rubbing his nose with his unlit pipe.

'What happened?' Korolev asked, still confused as to how he'd ended up back in the apartment surrounded by people – when the last certain memory he had was of being bent over double, spilling his guts onto a rain-drenched street with an assassin's footsteps fast approaching. But perhaps even that memory was uncertain.

'General Popov brought you,' Natasha said, her eyes on his, her wide face open and frank. 'He knocked hard on the door until I opened it. You were asleep on the floor. He told me you were ill and needed a doctor and then he brought you in here.'

'She came upstairs and I called up to Professor Goldfarb,' Shura said. 'He lives on the fifth floor. He came away from his supper and we carried you in here.'

'It will keep,' the professor said, taking off his spectacles to polish them.

'And the Comrade Investigator,' Shura asked, 'will he be all right? A nasty cut on his head he has, hasn't he?'

'As I said, he should be fine.'

'Your face was as white as a sheet of fancy paper, like a ghost's,' Natasha said with relish.

'What happened?' Valentina Nikolaevna took a step forward and reached out her hand as if to touch the stitching. 'It looks bad.'

'An accident,' Korolev said, waving away everyone's concern, although his voice sounded weak, even to him. 'Concussion is it?' he asked the professor, trying to adopt a man-to-man professional brusqueness.

Valentina Nikolaevna shook her head in bemusement. 'You should have seen the place when I came home, full of people and you in the middle looking like a corpse – it was like a scene from a play. Could you manage some food?'

Shura's head popped up like a gundog's and he hadn't the heart to refuse. 'Maybe a little soup,' he said and soon Valentina Nikolaevna and Shura were arguing quietly in the kitchen over its preparation. Natasha gave him a small smile as she placed a cushion on a wooden chair. Then she sat up to the table and opened an exercise book. Homework, Korolev thought to himself, and something about the child studying and the sound of the women in the kitchen filled him with a feeling of warmth and security. He leant back and closed his eyes for a moment and then opened them again to find Popov gazing down at him. He looked smaller than usual.

'How do you feel, Alexei Dmitriyevich?' Popov asked, his voice barely audible.

'I feel like someone filled my head with concrete, but not too bad, I think. Lucky for me you picked me up off the pavement.'

'Your notebook fell out of your pocket in the car. I came back to give it to you.'

'Thank you, Comrade General.'

The general waved his thanks away. 'The professor says you need a minimum of twenty-four hours' rest. I'll talk to Semionov and Gregorin tomorrow and we'll work out how to deal with the investigation. Whatever else, you're going to take it easy for a day or two.' Korolev opened his mouth to object, but the general raised a weary hand.

'An order, Alexei Dmitriyevich. Comrade Professor, please confirm your diagnosis.'

'Indeed. Concussion requires at least twenty-four' hours bed rest. Well, you don't actually have to lie on the bed, but certainly no going to work. You need a bit of quiet and a lot of sleep. Oh, and no vodka. Not even beer. Sleep is what you really need. Ideally there should be someone here with you the whole time. A precaution purely, but important. Valentina Nikolaevna?'

Valentina nodded without smiling, 'Of course, Comrade Professor. If it's necessary, I can rearrange my shift.'

Perhaps if the general hadn't looked so utterly worn, Korolev might have objected, but instead he allowed himself a grimace of annoyance for form's sake and nodded his agreement.

'Good,' the general said, rising to his feet. 'Well, we shall say our farewells, I think, Professor.'

'Yes. Goodnight. Valentina Nikolaevna, here's my number at the university tomorrow if you need to call me.'

The professor scribbled on a page from a small notebook, then tore it out and handed it to Valentina.

Korolev would have stood, but the moment he tried to shift his weight to do so he realized it was impossible. He made do with a nod of his head as they left and then slumped back.

'Here you are, Comrade Investigator,' Shura said, as she brought some soup to the table and placed it beside Natasha. 'Can I help you up?'

He nodded and Shura and Valentina Nikolaevna each took an arm and manoeuvred him to the table. The smell of the soup, cabbage with some scraps of chicken in it, brought saliva to his parched mouth and he picked up a spoon, blowing on the soup before sampling it.

'Is it too hot, Comrade Investigator?' Shura asked.

'I told you so,' Valentina Nikolaevna said. 'Here, let's give him some bread. He can dunk it till it cools.'

'It's fine. Please. Thank you both. It's very good.'

'I'm not allowed to dunk my bread,' Natasha said, turning indignant eyes from her copy book. 'How come he is?'

'Because he's an investigator, Natasha, and he needs to feed himself up to catch murderers and the like,' Shura said, with a mixture of conviction and reproof that seemed to satisfy the little girl. Natasha returned to her homework and the two women watched him finish the soup with satisfaction.

'A strong appetite, hasn't he, Valentina Nikolaevna – the Comrade Investigator?' Shura said when he tilted the bowl towards him to scoop up the last of the liquid.

'What happened to my clothes?' Korolev asked, aware that he was wearing an old sweater and his uniform trousers.

'You were soaked to the skin. Don't worry, we didn't look,' Valentina Nikolaevna said, causing a burst of laughter from Shura and Natasha which they hid behind their hands.

'No wonder he has such an appetite,' Shura said in a low tone, and Korolev felt his cheeks becoming warm. He wasn't used to having so many women around him – they weren't as cultured as people thought they were.

'What? There's no other entertainment in Moscow?' he said. 'Must all three of you stare at me like I'm a giraffe at the zoo?'

His anger wasn't false, but it seemed ridiculous in the context, both to the women and to himself, and they didn't bother to hide their laughter this time. He found a smile tugging at his own lips, which delighted them even more.

'I should go back upstairs,' Shura said, when they'd finished. 'Isaac Emmanuilovich will be home soon. But I'll come down later, Valentina Nikolaevna, in case you need me.'

They said their farewells to Shura and then sat looking at each other: Korolev, Valentina and the small girl. Natasha was the first to break the silence.

'I've finished my homework,' she said.

'Good,' Valentina said. 'Go and get ready for bed, Natasha. I'll be through in a moment.'

Natasha picked up her exercise books and her pen and, with a shy glance at Korolev, left the two adults alone. Korolev tried to look elsewhere but his eyes kept wandering back to Valentina's.

'Natasha did well,' he finally managed to say, after rejecting several alternative ways of breaking a silence that had become too intimate to bear. Valentina seemed to consider the statement, clenching her hands together, the knuckles white.

'She's old for her years. They all are these days. We demand it of them. You saw her Pioneer scarf? Even primary schoolchildren are being prepared for war.' She put a hand to her forehead and tapped a finger gently between her eyebrows. 'You mustn't misunderstand me, of course.'

'I don't, believe me. I know you to be a loyal citizen.' Which didn't come out quite how he meant it to, but perhaps all she wanted was reassurance.

She looked up at him and shook her head, as though at her own foolishness.

'I hope you'll forgive me if I say it makes me nervous, having you share the apartment with us. What if I were to say something in anger? Do you understand? I can see Natasha likes you, I don't know how or why, perhaps because she helped you. But it makes me nervous. Having you around all the time, it's like being watched.'

'I'm an investigator. I'm not a Chekist. I'm just a simple Militiaman.'

She laughed drily. 'You think the Militia don't get involved in internal security? That it's all handled by the Cheka? You must know that's not the case.'

He did. He knew that a large proportion of the arrests under Article 58 were carried out by Militia officers, usually under the direction of the NKVD, but often independently. He was able to ignore it, more or less, sitting in his Petrovka Street ivory tower, dealing with murder and mayhem and glad of it. But he was no longer surprised when witnesses to the crimes he investigated took the opportunity to denounce their neighbours, workmates and even family for political offences. The citizens on the street knew better than he did that the Militia handled political matters, even if he'd clung to the belief that he worked on purely non-political crime. He nodded in agreement.

'I understand. But what can I do? I'm assigned to this apartment. If another becomes available, then I'll move on. But you know how unlikely that is. I'll try to keep to my room. Don't worry – I'm not here to spy on you.'

She waved his words away. 'That's not what I meant either. You're here now, and that's that. I was just trying to explain –' she paused and considered him for a moment – 'I was trying to explain my reserve.' She stood, holding out her hand to shake his. It seemed a very manly gesture. 'I'm glad we spoke so frankly.'

He took her hand with a feeling of confusion. He really wasn't sure what the conversation had meant, but he nodded his head in agreement.

'You should go to bed,' she said. 'I'll stay at home tomorrow to keep an eye on you.'

'Thank you.'

'Natasha will expect me to; you're the stray dog she rescued from the rain. Would you like me to help you to your room?'

'I think I can manage.' He stood up from the chesterfield slowly, holding onto one of the chairs for support. He swayed for a moment, smiled at Valentina, and then made his way to the door to his bedroom with tentative steps.

'See? I'm fine.' He nodded a goodnight and then closed the door, leaning against it with his shoulder while his right hand felt for the round moulding of the light switch. Finding it, he hesitated. Instead he walked to the window and looked across the lane. The shadow of a man was clearly distinguishable in the gateway opposite. A round fur hat and a long coat that could be leather, judging from the way it reflected the light from the streetlamp. Who was he? A Thief? A priest? A Chekist? A foreign spy? If the devil was still there tomorrow, he'd pull a little surprise on him, but tonight he would be lucky to make it over to the bed. He pulled the curtain shut and, without turning on the light or taking off his clothes, walked to the chair where they'd stretched out his overcoat to dry. His leather holster lay on the seat and he took the automatic out, checked the safety was on, slipped it under his pillow and then rolled himself into the blankets.

For a few moments he was aware of the sounds of the building – conversation from Valentina and Natasha's room, someone walking around upstairs, the rush of water down a pipe – and then the room, the building and even Moscow itself spun away as sleep finally took hold of him.

Chapter Twenty

KOROLEV slept like a dead man, as his mother would have said had she not been dead herself for fifteen years. He slept past five o'clock and then past six. He wasn't woken by dawn squeezing itself round the edges of the curtain, and the cockerels calling to each other from street to street didn't wake him either. He slept through the pack of dogs that chased a cart down the lane and even the crack of the driver's whip as he tried to get rid of them. The factory whistles calling the workers to their shifts made no impression on his slumbering. For the first time in many years he slept past seven and then past eight. He didn't even stir when Valentina Nikolaevna opened the door with great care and listened to his gentle snoring. She and Natasha watched him for a moment or two, Valentina told him later, and then decided to let him sleep on. If neither of them mentioned the strange affection that darkened their faces in the half-light, it might have been because they were unaware of it themselves. Or perhaps a man sleeping soundly can make a woman of any age maternal, if she's so inclined. In fact, it was only when Babel looked in on him and, curious to see his reaction, shook him by the shoulder, that Korolev woke abruptly and, before his eyes had quite caught up with him, rewarded Babel with a close-up view of the business end of the automatic. Babel responded with a wide smile.

'It's me, Alexei Dmitriyevich. Babel. Is that a Walther? May I have a look? Where'd you pick up a piece like this? I had one many years ago, but it's long gone. Ah. 1917 – a Model 7, they stopped making them at the end of the war, of course. The Germans, that is. An officer's gun. Spoils of war?'

'A Pole.' And the flatness in his sleep-croaked voice pronounced a death sentence on the former owner, even to Korolev's ears. Babel blinked and handed the gun quickly back, then looked at his hands as though the dead man's blood might have transferred to them.

'Sleep well?' Babel asked, after a moment, looking over his shoulder to where an amused Valentina Nikolaevna leant against the door.

Korolev put the automatic back under the pillow, yawned and ran a hand across his scalp. He saw the daylight in the doorway to the shared room.

'What time is it?'

'Nearly ten o'clock.'

Korolev looked at his watch. He held it to his ear to make sure it was still ticking and felt the glass cold against the sudden warmth of his cheek.

'I don't normally sleep this late,' he said.

'Well, you don't normally try to crack people's heads open with your forehead, either. At least, I hope not.'

'Ah,' Valentina Nikolaevna said, putting disappointment, mockery and a tinge of reproach into the single syllable.

'It was self-defence,' Korolev said.

'You mean: "He started it," of course. Yes,' she said, shaking her head in wry disillusionment, 'I've heard that excuse before.'

Korolev was tempted to throw the blankets over his head and pretend his guests weren't there.

'Can a citizen not have any privacy any more? I support the Collective as much as anyone, but does it need to hold its meetings in my bedroom?'

Valentina Nikolaevna smiled at his discomfort and, touching

her forehead in salute, let the door shut behind her. Korolev turned his attention to Babel.

'And you? Will you let me have five minutes to myself?'

'Of course,' Babel said, settling himself into the chair he'd pulled up beside the bed.

'Well?' Korolev demanded, after the writer showed no sign of leaving.

'Well what? Do you want to hear what I have to tell you, or not?'

Korolev considered the question and then pointed to the window. 'At least give me a minute to change into a clean shirt.'

'You're shy? I was in the army as well, you know. There was no prudery on bath day in the Red Cavalry, believe me.'

'Look out at the street. Please, Isaac Emmanuilovich, I beg you.'

Babel grunted and stood up, before walking over to the window with a show of reluctance.

Korolev swung his feet down onto the bare floorboards. His vision took a while to catch up with the change of perspective and he breathed in deeply. He looked over at Babel, who was observing him with interest.

'You've gone quite grey, very suddenly. It's an interesting thing to see. Really, just like that. And you were so red only moments ago.'

Korolev managed to wave a hand in the writer's direction.

'I'm fine,' he said, without much conviction, 'just look out of the window, if you don't mind.'

The damned writer would end up describing his flabby arse in *Novy Mir* if he wasn't careful. And, anyway, a citizen *should* be entitled to a moment or two to himself, housing shortage or not. He reached out for the chair and pulled himself to a standing position, feeling the blood plummet to his toes. He rested for a moment and then took a couple of steps over to the wardrobe.

'You look even more unwell now; would you like me to give you a hand?'

Korolev discovered that keeping the contents of his stomach where they belonged required all his concentration. Speaking was out of the question, as was even the tiny turn of the head necessary to give the irritating interloper a stare that would melt his spectacles to his damned nose. Instead he made do with a feeble flick of the hand, which he hoped conveyed his dismissal of the writer's annoying interruptions adequately. With one final step he grabbed hold of the wardrobe with both hands and allowed his cheek to rest for a second or two against the smooth wood. The smell of varnish seemed to revive him and something resembling energy began to seep back up his body and give him hope that the danger of being sick had passed, for the moment at least. With a grunt, he pulled the jumper off over his head, undid the buttons on the trousers and allowed the clothes to form a pile at his ankles.

He took his last clean shirt, put his arms through the sleeves with a bit of difficulty and fastened a respectable number of buttons, then he pulled on a fresh pair of trousers by leaning against the wall and stepping into the legs one at a time. He slipped the braces over his shoulder.

'There, that's better.'

'You're meant to be looking out of the window.'

'I'm a writer – we're interested in moments like this. How you walked, the colour of your face, the way you put your shirt on. I'm making mental notes.'

Korolev tried to summon that spectacle-melting glare, but it seemed to be a harder task than he was capable of at that particular moment in time. Instead he sat down on the nearest chair.

'So what did you find out?'

'Not too much, I'm afraid. The fellow I spoke to knew Mironov's name – but all he said was that he was Seventh

Department and that asking questions about the Seventh Department wasn't sensible these days.'

'The Seventh Department?'

'The former Foreign Department.'

'I see,' Korolev said. Everything he'd ever heard about the Foreign Department had been whispered. He knew that it was responsible for the Soviet Union's intelligence operations overseas and had a reputation for ruthlessness and obsessive secrecy above and beyond even the NKVD's high standards. Interesting, though. The Foreign Department loses a man in the same week as an American émigré shows up dead and half of Moscow is searching for an icon that might well be heading outside the State's borders.

'There's a purge coming, you know,' Babel said. 'Not that that's news. The Chekists are nervous as hell.'

'They removed Yagoda's statue from Petrovka Street the other day. Smashed it in the process.'

'They say he's to be arrested any day. In the meantime he sits in his office alone and the phone never rings. He walks like a ghost through the corridors of the Ministry and no one seems to see him. And this was the most feared man in Russia just weeks ago. When he falls, he'll fall hard, and the Chekist factions are running round trying to make sure they don't go down with him. Which brings me to Gregorin.'

'What did you find out about him?'

'Well, he's not loved by the Georgians, that's certain, despite being a Georgian himself. Half a Georgian, anyway – his father was Russian. There's bad blood there: I've an idea he may have stepped on a few toes back in Tbilisi. And, of course, he was a protégé of Yagoda, which is no longer healthy. Still, Ezhov seems to like him, so he might be all right even if the Georgians do come out on top. And they probably will. Well, they're close to Stalin, they sing the same songs. It seems likely they'll win in the end.'

'He gave me the impression he was working directly for Ezhov, maybe even higher.'

'It could be, it could well be. But I got the feeling he's not in a very good position at the moment, although not in immediate danger. He's the same as everyone else, in other words.'

'More research for the drawer?'

'As you say – a very secret drawer.' Babel lifted himself off the windowsill on which he'd been sitting and stretched his arms. 'I must do some writing before the exercise this afternoon. Who knows if I'll be able to do anything after half an hour in a gas mask.'

'Better a mask than a lungful. I've seen men gassed and I hope never to see it again.'

'No, and I don't think the Fascists will be dropping bouquets from their bombers if it comes to war. It's as well to be prepared. I hear Stalin ordered the Metro stations to be dug as deep as they are because of air raids. Well, if we're prepared for bombs – why not for gas?'

'Do you really think they'll come?'

'They're already on their way, my friend. We're shooting at them in Madrid and they're shooting back, and it won't stop there.' He shrugged his shoulders. 'Stalin sees it. He's making sure we're ready.'

'Yes,' Korolev agreed, thinking about the man of steel, who expected everyone else to be made of steel also.

Babel said his farewells and left, and for a moment Korolev felt every one of his forty-two years of age. The thought of another war, and the horror and the hardship it would bring, was like a weight pressing him down onto the mattress. It had been bad enough against the Germans and the Austrians: he could see the faces still of dead young men, each one of whom could so easily have been him. Thousands of them – millions by the end of the Great War, and then twice as many again in the Civil War, and it would be worse this time, with the new tanks and bombers, and machine guns that could kill an entire battalion in two minutes flat. He'd serve, of course, when it came to it. He knew his duty as well as the next man.

§

Perhaps he drifted off, because the next thing he knew Valentina Nikolaevna was standing in the doorway, her hair turned golden by the pale sun as it streamed in through the open window. She looked as though she'd just stepped down from a cinema poster.

'How are you feeling?' she asked.

'Not too bad. Better. I'm not used to lying around like this, but I think I can get up now.'

'Good, I'll bring you some tea from the samovar. Your colleague Semionov is on his way over. And Colonel Gregorin called as well – he hopes you feel better soon.'

'Thank you,' he said, wondering how Gregorin felt about his puppet being off its strings.

'All you men need looking after from time to time. I don't mind.' She smiled and turned to leave the room and, as the door shut behind her, he allowed himself to think about holding Valentina Nikolaevna in his arms. How small she would feel there, yet strong as well. Her hair would smell of flowers and her skin of fresh bread, he was sure of it.

The tea that she brought him was the turning point – he stood and walked to the window, pleased that the room and the floor were both holding steady underfoot. He crossed his arms and looked out at a blue sky empty of any cloud. Beneath the window a long line of Civil Defence handcarts was being pushed by gas-masked women in loose-fitting boiler suits and heavy rubber gloves. The handcarts seemed to be full of some kind of white powder. He wondered what the powder was – in his experience the best counter-measure against gas was to run as fast as you could; and gas masks weren't much use against mustard gas, that he did know. Whatever that stuff in the handcarts was, he hoped it worked.

His regiment had been in reserve when the Germans had dropped mustard-gas shells on the Russian trenches back in seventeen. At first the troops had thought the Germans were making a mistake – hundreds of shells crashing through the forest, splashing into mud, but no explosions. The only hint they'd had of the trouble they were in was a slight smell of garlic. A few hours later and blisters covered every inch of exposed skin. Not only exposed skin, though, the gas wormed its way through their uniforms to crotches, armpits, chests, stomachs – everywhere. Who knew how many had died? There'd been thousands of blind soldiers, begging aloud for help, wandering the battlefield. The Germans shot them like rats, and those were the lucky ones. His regiment had been sent to plug the gap, and maybe God had forgiven the few Prussians who fell into their hands, but they hadn't.

The building shook as a squadron of bombers flew overhead, and one of them momentarily filled the sky above the lane – so low he could see the individual rivets on its open bomb doors. The glass rattled in the window frame and a dog ran howling for safety. The raw power of the aeroplane lifted Korolev's spirits, even as it sent a shiver down to the soles of his feet. This time they would be prepared for anything the Fascists threw at them.

He took a deep breath and walked over to the desk, leaning on it for support. He looked at the blood on the collar of his coat and the case wormed its way back into his thoughts. It occurred to him that if the traitors were trying to sell the icon abroad, that might explain why Mironov was involved – who better to help get it out than a major in the Foreign Department? But again, perhaps he had been trying to prevent the icon going to the West. He cursed Gregorin. Korolev didn't mind being led up blind alleys and manipulated as though he were an idiot if it was for the greater good, but Kolya's revelation that Gregorin had led the raid that recovered the icon had unsettled him. It occurred to him that Gregorin might be using him to try and track down the icon because he'd been the one responsible for losing it, through incompetence or worse. Well, if that was the case, it would come to light sooner or later, and if Korolev was still alive when it did, then he'd hunt the vermin down and rip his heart out with his own bare hands.

He was still contemplating the bare hands in question when there was a knock at the door and Semionov entered.

'How are you, Alexei Dmitriyevich? The general said you have concussion. Are you feeling better?'

The smile on his face seemed more teasing than sympathetic and Korolev gritted his teeth. What had he been thinking of after all – head-butting some giant *kulak*? He should have been more mature, given a better example to the youngster. He was supposed to be showing Semionov the ropes and yet here he was, his head cracked open and unable to pull his weight. It was humiliating.

'I'm fine,' he growled. 'Sit down, take the weight off your feet. Stop standing there like a lamp post and tell me your news.'

'Well, first things first. I bring Comrade General Popov's greetings to his favoured shock worker.'

'Look, you little squirt, I've a head that's splitting in two, so, if you know what's good for you, you'll leave your provocations until tomorrow.'

Semionov raised an eyebrow and Korolev wondered if the youngsters of today gave a damn about anything. *And* he was wearing that blasted mackintosh again. He looked like a corner boy in it, his hair slicked back with some kind of cream. It occurred to Korolev that Semionov would fit right in with the touts selling marked-up train tickets over at Kiev station.

'Come on, Alexei Dmitriyevich, don't feel sorry for yourself. It could have been worse – think of poor Larinin. I've seen the Model T – two trucks ran right over it, one after the other – it's like a pancake. They had to cut Larinin out of it piece by piece. And poor Pavel Timofeevich is mourning the Ford like a lost daughter. So if you don't feel sorry for Comrade Larinin, then you should feel sorry for Comrade Morozov. Poor Larinin – cut down at the peak of his career as an investigator, mourned by his fellow workers.'

'Really?' Korolev found himself saying, the disbelief apparent in his voice. 'Mourned?'

'Not exactly,' Semionov allowed his straight face to break into a small smile before resuming a more serious expression, 'although, for myself, I would say I'm grateful he took the car. Maybe the brakes were shot or a tyre popped. Whatever happened, it could have been us, not Larinin, spinning into the oncoming traffic. So I remember him fondly on that account. I'll say no more on the subject.'

Semionov pulled at the cuffs of his shirt so that they poked out from the sleeves of his mackintosh. 'Of course, it's still regrettable that Comrade Larinin was run over by the two trucks,' he added after a moment.

'Indeed,' Korolev said, his tone flat enough for Semionov to give him a searching look.

'But better him than us, right?' Semionov said with a shrug.

Korolev considered his younger colleague and noticed the uncharacteristic uncertainty in his demeanour. It made him wonder whether the younger man was entirely sure the crash had been accidental. There was just something in the way he had set out the possible explanations – the brakes, the tyres – that made him wonder if Semionov wasn't looking for reassurance from him. Well, he could look elsewhere. Whether they were in the shit or not, they still had to keep swimming. He sighed and rubbed at the bandage that swaddled his head.

'Despite a head that feels it belongs to someone else, I can only agree, young Vanya. It's not so bad, being alive. What other words did the general have for me?'

'For us,' Semionov said, his expression serious, once again. 'We're off the case.'

It took a while for the news to sink in and Semionov watched him for his reaction.

'Has someone else been assigned to it?' Korolev said eventually, more to break the silence than anything.

'Paunichev. We're to be assigned a new case on Monday morning. It's because of your injury, the boss said. He didn't want the case to lose momentum. He took the file and all the reports from me this morning.'

'Who did?' Korolev said, finding it difficult to concentrate on what Semionov was telling him and conscious of a vein pulsing in his forehead. He forced himself to keep his voice calm, but he could feel his stomach filling with acid.

'Comrade Paunichev. It was the boss's orders, Alexei Dmitriyevich. There was nothing to be done. Also the general told me to keep quiet about the second American. If something comes of the missing person enquiry, then the general will decide what to do.'

'Were you allowed to tell Paunichev anything? About the woman Smithson having been a nun? Schwartz's information? Gregorin even?'

Semionov shook his head and Korolev slammed his right fist into his palm.

'Then they've got away with it. Did Popov really order you not to tell Paunichev any of it? What words did he use? Exactly what words, please.'

'He said that all information acquired from Colonel Gregorin has been designated a State secret. Under no circumstances are we to give that information to anyone without express permission. He didn't tell me not to tell Paunichev – he told me not to tell *anyone*.'

'And what Schwartz told me?'

'The same. We're ordered off the case, Alexei Dmitriyevich. I would have thought you'd be pleased.'

Korolev leant back in his seat and looked up at the ceiling. There was a cobweb in the corner of the room and in the middle of it a spider sat, no doubt looking down at him and thinking, 'All I need is a bigger web.' To his surprise, a burst of laughter came from somewhere inside him.

'You're right. We should be pleased. And Paunichev will find someone that fits for the murder in the church. It won't be the right person, of course, but the statistics won't care.'

Semionov was looking at him as though he'd farted at the ballet. Korolev tapped his head in apology.

'Forgive me, Vanya. I still have some pain – I'm probably not in the best of moods to hear this kind of news.'

'You don't need to apologize, Alexei Dmitriyevich. They say that's why you're a good detective – the other investigators. They say it's because you treat each case as if the victim were your mother. But if you'll permit me to make the suggestion, you must harden your heart, Comrade. The path of the Party is not always clear to ordinary folk like us, but it must be followed.'

'Stalin?'

'No, Comrade – you.'

Korolev smiled in bleak acknowledgement – the case was in the past and that was all there was to it. So they drank a cup of tea, washing the unpleasantness away, and spoke of other things. Semionov had been out to Gorky Park with some friends and climbed to the top of the parachute tower. For a few kopeks, the attendants had strapped him in and he'd floated down to the ground beneath, just like a real parachutist. Except the parachute itself wasn't really that white any more, Semionov remembered with a touch of disappointment; more grey after the recent rain and snow. These days it seemed everything in Moscow became dirty after a little while.

They sat for a while in silence, listening to a convoy of military trucks rumble up the lane towards Vorontsovo Pole as the exercise continued around them. Semionov shifted on his chair.

'I have another message for you,' the younger man said. 'The works meeting is this evening and the general orders your non-attendance.'

The words hung there like a bad odour.

'What do you think will happen?' Korolev said in a voice that sounded as though it belonged to someone else.

'It's difficult to know. The general is much respected, but Mendeleyev is a black mark against the department and "vigilance" is the word of the hour. My impression, and I accept I'm inexperienced in these matters, is that the activists are afraid of things spiralling out of control – Andropov's accident shocked people. The good news is I detect no external pressure either way – so I would say that public self-criticism should be sufficient. Any more Mendeleyevs, however, and the situation would be different.'

The strange thing was that, as he spoke, Semionov seemed to acquire five years in age and his voice dropped an octave. Korolev was aware the younger man was a Komsomol activist, but the information he had seemed to come from a higher level than that. And he spoke with the clarity and confidence of an insider. It never occurred to Korolev to question what Semionov was saying, but he made a mental note that the young man was no ingénu in the ways of the Party.

'And you? Will you be going?'

'Yes, I've been appointed the Komsomol representative on the committee. Yesterday. I'll support the general, if the situation requires it. Of course I will. But you must rest here. Otherwise you'll be too tired to go to the game tomorrow.' Semionov smiled. 'It will work out fine, Alexei Dmitriyevich. Trust me. What time shall I pick you up?'

'The game is at two.'

'And the American?'

'I don't see why not. We have Gregorin's permission to take him and it's our duty to show him how Soviet sport surpasses

257

that of the capitalist countries. Babel will come too. We'll make a day of it.'

'Morozov said he could let us have a car.'

'But we should take the tram. He should have the full experience.'

Semionov sighed at the missed opportunity to drive. 'The tram it is. Morozov wasn't very keen to be honest – I think he blames me for the Ford. He was never going to fix the windscreen, you know – we'd have frozen to the seat in January. Perhaps it was for the best, in that regard.'

§

When Semionov left, Korolev sat in silence for a while, and then stood, going over to run a finger along the spines of his small collection of books. He stopped when he reached the faded gold lettering of *A Hero of Our Time*. With a feeling of pleasant anticipation he opened the cover and read the first line:

> I was travelling post from Tiflis. All the luggage in my small springless carriage consisted of one valise half-stuffed with notes on my travels in Georgia. The greater part of them, luckily for you, has been lost; while the valise, with its other contents, luckily for me, remains safe.

Korolev nodded to himself with satisfaction. Now, Lermontov, whatever else they might say about the fellow, was a man who knew which end of a pistol to point where, and how to start a novel.

Chapter Twenty-One

KOROLEV woke the next morning at the usual time, refreshed and with much of his old energy restored to him. The sky was still dark outside, but he didn't immediately turn on the light. Instead he walked to the window – the alley was empty and, with a mixture of regret and relief, he felt the case becoming a memory. Gregorin had called the night before, thanked him for his efforts and wished him well, and that had been that. The colonel hadn't asked him anything about the previous day's report, or about Kolya, nor had he commented on Larinin's mysterious death. It was as though Gregorin had lost all interest in the matter, which was a relief as Korolev was certain that the colonel would have smelt a rat the moment he'd opened his mouth. Now, as long as Gregorin maintained this lack of interest, Korolev could forget the whole thing, and particularly the icon.

It was deflating to walk away from an unsolved case, but, strangely, he found himself humming a tune as he began his morning exercises – perhaps he was not too disappointed after all.

The lane was beginning to see the first traffic of the day by the time he'd finished his final piece of stretching and was tying the laces on his battered but still sturdy summer shoes. He'd get another year out of them, with a bit of luck, and they were fine for wearing around the house – but he'd have to start asking around about a new pair soon enough. He hadn't seen shoes in the ordinary shops for months, which didn't mean there weren't any – it just meant that finding a pair that was available and fitted him would take time and effort. As for leather boots to replace his felt ones? Well, perhaps he would have to ask the other Militiamen how to go about it. There was obviously a way, perhaps not entirely above board, and maybe he'd just have to swallow his pride if he wanted dry feet this winter.

§

It was a cause of some embarrassment to Korolev, later, that when Babel arrived to collect him, Valentina Nikolaevna should be in the middle of insisting on his wearing a scarf belonging to her dead husband, which Korolev didn't consider necessary.

'Isaac Emmanuilovich,' she said, with no respect for Korolev's dented pride, 'keep an eye on poor Korolev today. I know what these football matches can be like. He's to stay out of trouble, no fighting with factory workers. And he's not to take off this scarf.'

'I can look after myself.' Korolev scowled at Babel, whose face was bright with suppressed mirth.

'Don't worry yourself, Valentina Nikolaevna, it will be my pleasure to keep Comrade Korolev under the closest of observation.' Babel bowed in Korolev's direction. 'Would you like to take my arm on the way down the stairs, Comrade Korolev?'

'The Devil take you, I can manage myself. And take that damned smirk off your face, you rotten scribbler!'

'See, Valentina Nikolaevna, the injury has made him disgruntled, but I forgive him,' Babel said, the picture of indifferent innocence. 'I shall see you downstairs, Alexei Dmitriyevich. Don't forget the scarf.'

'Rat,' Korolev muttered as the door closed behind the writer. Valentina Nikolaevna raised an eyebrow. 'Forgive me, Valentina Nikolaevna, I was rude. It's just I think he was making presumptions.'

As soon as the words were out of his mouth he wished he could catch them and push them back in.

'Presumptions, is it?' She produced the word like a rapier from its sheath. Her imperious blue eyes looked at him in artful confusion and he felt the net close around him.

'Ah, to hell with this!' he growled, more to himself than her. 'I'm destined to be provoked all day long I can see.'

He clumped to the door, insofar as anyone can clump in felt boots, and tugged the handle towards him, half-disappointed that it offered no resistance.

'Well, goodbye then, Valentina Nikolaevna,' he called behind him and did his best to ignore what sounded very much like laughter from the kitchen, where he'd left her.

§

Semionov was waiting for them outside and, after a brief discussion, they decided to walk. It was a sunny day with a bite to the air that was pleasant on the skin after the rain and snow of the preceding weeks. They proceeded at Babel's pace as he exchanged words with vagrants, kiosk vendors, street sweepers, ticket touts, as well as actresses and Party officials. Korolev took the opportunity offered by the writer's distraction to ask Semionov about the works meeting.

'It went well. I myself took responsibility for my failure to observe anything untoward about former Party member Mendeleyev's attitude and it was accepted that the lack of vigilance was a collective error.'

'But you hardly knew Knuckles.'

'So I ran no great risk,' Semionov acknowledged with a small smile. Korolev found his arm resting on the young man's shoulder as they walked along, and it seemed quite natural. It occurred to him, however, that the relationship was not quite the paternal one he might have thought a few days before. Semionov was a handy lad; quite how he'd landed himself on the committee after only a few weeks was something of a mystery. He glanced at him out of the corner of his eye. Of course, he looked the part with those clear blue eyes and his golden hair. But it was more than looks alone – the youngster was a solid fellow to have behind you in a scrap, for certain. In fact, it astonished him that Semionov had so little experience – he often carried himself like a man who'd been around the block once or twice at least.

When they finally arrived at the Metropol, Korolev was reassured to discover that it had lost none of its opulence over the previous few days. It occurred to him that foreigners must be equally impressed with this living embodiment of the great socialist dream. And it was open to everyone, unlike in the capitalist countries, where some lackey with a whip would no doubt send an ordinary man like him packing with a bloody stripe across his back for a souvenir. He turned with proprietorial pleasure to observe the reactions of Semionov and Babel, but was disappointed. The writer seemed uninterested in his surroundings, tapping a cigarette against an open enamel case and looking less animated than he had all morning. Semionov at least had the courtesy to look interested by the swimmers in the pool, but Korolev suspected that was for carnal rather than aesthetic reasons. Babel he could understand – the writer visited Paris every other month by the sound if it – but Semionov was yet again a surprise. Perhaps he'd been here before, with his Hercegovina Flor-smoking girlfriend.

Schwartz was sitting in the restaurant, perusing *Izvestia* with an expression that suggested he was reading it for amusement rather than political education. He rose as Korolev approached, looking slightly guilty and putting the paper behind him.

'Comrade Captain, good to see you. It looks like a great day for a sporting event.' He'd dressed down for the occasion; wearing a black jumper under a short blue overcoat with a turned-up collar, but the grey trousers were so precisely cut they looked as though they belonged in a museum of tailoring. What the Spartak fans would make of a crease like that could only be imagined. Schwartz pointed at a peaked cap on the table.

'I even got myself a hat. Think I'll fit in?'

Korolev looked at the hat, wondering where he'd managed to buy it. One of the currency stores, no doubt.

'That's a fine hat. Practical. You'll need it – it's brisk enough outside.'

Korolev didn't feel he should add that he also thought the hat would look very well on his own head. Schwartz smiled in acknowledgement, then lowered his voice and leant forward, his face serious.

'And the case? Any progress?'

'I'm no longer working on it,' Korolev said, indicating his bandaged forehead. 'I had to take a few days off, so they transferred it to someone else. I've some good news for you, though. We identified the victim and it wasn't your friend. Of course, if she contacts you, let me know – she might have some useful information.' But he could hear no conviction in his voice. After all, if the Chekists got their hands on an American nun traipsing round Moscow on a false passport, her original Intourist trip would be extended by a long visit to Siberia. Then something else struck him – Schwartz showed no relief or surprise at the news. He merely nodded in gratitude for the information. Did he not care about his friend from the train any more?

'If she does get in touch I'll certainly advise her to contact you,' Schwartz said, with the careful intonation of a diplomat. 'By the way, our previous conversation?'

'Remains between the two of us, of course,' Korolev answered, surprised how easily the lie slipped off his tongue. A thought occurred to Korolev, and he looked around to see whether Babel and Semionov were within listening distance. 'In fact, I would like to extend that conversation if you don't mind – now that I know which icon we're dealing with.'

Schwartz seemed to consider how to respond. Again he didn't look surprised, merely mildly perturbed. 'I thought you were off the case?'

'For the moment, yes, but on Monday I will probably return to duty.' Well, who knew what Monday would bring? 'A few minutes of your time is all I ask.'

Korolev was sure from Schwartz's reaction that he'd already known the dead nun wasn't his friend, Nancy Dolan. Now how could that be? He couldn't press the matter because of the American's importance to the State's finances, but it seemed clear it was his duty to see if the American would tell him anything useful about the icon. He was sure the general would understand – well, almost sure.

'I don't see why not,' Schwartz said, after he'd considered the proposal for another lengthy moment, 'provided we keep to the same terms as before.'

'Agreed.'

They turned to watch Semionov and Babel looking with salacious smiles into the swimming pool, from which sixteen legs, slick with water and with red-painted toenails, pointed up at the huge central chandelier. The mysterious limbs looked, for a moment, as though they should be hanging from hooks in an abattoir.

'After the game?' Schwartz asked.

Babel looked towards them, indicating his watch. Korolev nodded to Schwartz.

'After the game will be fine,' he agreed.

§

'I've never travelled on a tram before,' Schwartz said, as they walked out onto Teatralnaya Square. 'Not in Moscow, anyway.'

'That may not change today,' Babel said, looking at a passing red and white tram that seemed in danger of exploding outwards from the press of people inside. Young men hung from the door handles, their feet wedged onto the running plates and their Spartak scarves mimicking the huge red flags that fluttered from either side as it charged past the crowd waiting at the stop across the street.

'The bandit isn't even stopping!' Semionov said, echoing the rest of the queue, who were cursing the driver and waving clenched fists at the conductress, who shrugged her shoulders helplessly in response.

'Should we walk?' Schwartz asked, apparently nervous at the idea of risking his life by hanging onto the outside of a hurtling tram. Others had already started to look around for alternative means of transportation, and Korolev was on the point of suggesting they join them when another tram approached. Like the first it was bedecked with banners and slogans celebrating the imminent anniversary of the October Revolution, but it also looked as though it might stop.

'Order, citizens, order,' shouted the conductor in vain as people surged forward. Korolev decided it was every man for himself and pushed and pulled his way on, conscious that Schwartz was right behind him, and together they managed to squeeze their way into the muggy travelling compartment. Korolev found himself pressed up against a window facing Semionov on the other side of the glass, the youngster's knuckles white around a chrome handle on the side of the tram.

'It looks like Vanya is taking the scenic route,' Schwartz said. 'Not a bad idea,' he added, trying to turn away from the armpit of an inebriated soldier with his hand stretched up to the roof for balance. Babel wormed his way through to join them and then the tram groaned forward, the passengers breaking into good-natured chatter.

They rumbled onwards in the direction of the stadium, cheering when the tram driver narrowly missed separating a green bread van from the two tired horses pulling it, singing songs and loudly discussing the merits of the various players. The mood was one of excitement, although Korolev knew things could change quite suddenly, particularly at a game like this, where the newly constituted Union-wide league could be decided in Spartak's favour. Sure enough, when they arrived at the ground, several scrappy fights were already under way between rival supporters. Chants of 'MEAT, MEAT, MEAT!' from the Spartak fans, were answered with equally loud shouts of 'RED ARMY, RED ARMY, RED ARMY!' Mounted Militiamen patrolled the area in pairs, occasionally inserting themselves between opposing groups. In all the excitement, getting off the tram was nearly as hard as getting on it.

'Why do they chant "Meat"?' Schwartz asked.

'The Spartak sponsor is Promkooperatsya, the food workers' union. So the fans chant, "Who are we? We are the Meat." It's a good thing.'

'But sometimes the opposing fans call them "the Pigs",' Babel added.

'Only if they are uncultured hooligans. And who are you supporting today, Isaac Emmanuilovich?'

'Why Central House of the Red Army, of course. As an ex-Red Cavalryman it's my duty.'

'I was a soldier too once, but I was from the Presnaya long before that,' Korolev said, feeling slightly offended.

'Even pigs can choose to leave their sty,' Babel replied with an innocent smile.

Korolev was about to respond in kind when he saw a group of determined-looking young men arrange themselves in front of the gates, each holding onto the belt of the man in front with one hand, with the two biggest and hardest-looking in the front.

'Jack, we should wait for a couple of moments now.'

'Yes,' Babel agreed. 'The train is about to leave the station.'

Schwartz looked at the crowd and smiled. 'They're going to crash the barriers?'

'Yes, it's called "the steam engine". Ah, the ticket collectors have spotted them.'

But the ticket collectors were too late to marshal an effective defence and the snake of men charged forward, kicking and punching, knocking bystanders and defenders out of their path and, in the case of one, trampling him underfoot. The chain remained unbroken until two of the collectors and a Militiaman, furious and blood-smeared, grabbed the last of them by an arm and detached him from his colleagues. Their triumph was short-lived, however, as the captured gate-crasher's fellows gathered themselves into a tight wedge and returned to the fray, snatching the captive back and leaving one of the ticket collectors sitting on the ground spitting blood into his hand. The crowd waiting outside cheered and the youths raised their arms in triumph before retreating in the face of approaching Militia reinforcements. Then the crowd cheered once again as a darting rabble of wild-haired street children launched themselves at the same place, squirming and diving around the distracted ticket collectors' legs. A tiny girl was caught by the hair and flung back through the gates, where she landed in a crumpled heap. The crowd growled and stepped forward in unison, eyes fixed on the perpetrator, a Militiaman with the build of a wrestler and a face like a squashed cabbage. Korolev took Schwartz's arm.

'Perhaps we'll try another gate,' he said, as the first brick clanged off the metal fence and, with a roar, the crowd charged. The last thing they saw of the Militiaman was his panicked face just before it disappeared in a tumble of flat caps and flying fists. The other uniforms would have their work cut out to keep the fellow out of the morgue, Korolev thought to himself without much sympathy, as men ran from all directions to join in the mayhem.

'They seem fond of children,' Schwartz said.

'Fonder, I think, of the opportunity to put a Militiaman in hospital,' Babel replied. That was true, Korolev thought. In fact, they'd probably run straight over the girl to get at him. He recalled a splash of red hair in amongst the scrabbling rush of children and wondered if it had been Kim Goldstein's gang of ragamuffins charging the gates.

Korolev was relieved when they arrived safely in the relative calm of the south stand. He couldn't imagine, after all, that the general would forgive him, let alone Gregorin, if he managed to get Schwartz caught up in a football riot. They sat down on the concrete benches and watched players kicking the ball back and forth and occasionally test the goalkeepers. The Spartak players were at one end of the field in red shirts with a thick white hoop around the chest, while at the other were the Army players, wearing blue shirts and red shorts. The Army players looked big.

'They'll give our lads a good battering, if I'm not much mistaken. I hope Alexei Starostin has put on an extra pair of socks.'

A middle-aged man walking along the bank of seats immediately beneath them looked up and then stood for a long moment with an expression of astonishment. He wore no colour to indicate his team preference and Korolev was confused as to how he might have offended him. He pointed at the largest of the Red Army players.

'Come on, brother. You don't think the horse-washers brought along a lump like him for his footballing skills, do you?'

The man nodded in acknowledgement, but still looked shaken. There wasn't much to the fellow, Korolev thought, probably a clerk in a factory or a minor bureaucrat, but there was some strength to his face once you looked at it a second time. He sat down in front of them alongside a young boy, about ten years old. The clerk began to point out the players to the lad, reading their names from the programme. His voice sounded constricted and the boy looked up at him with a question in his eyes, but the clerk didn't stop reciting the names. Korolev turned to Babel and shrugged his shoulders. It was an unusual reaction from a stranger, but perhaps the bandage on his head made Korolev look like a hooligan. Babel examined the clerk as though trying to place him, but shook his head after a brief pause. Then, as if to change the subject, the writer produced a silver flask of brandy and they drank to a fair game – Schwartz joining in with enthusiasm.

By now the stands were crammed and, as if on a signal, the crowd rose as one and Korolev said farewell to his seat and joined in the cheer as the whistle blew for the game to start and Spartak passed the ball out wide.

§

It was a hard-fought first half. As Korolev had predicted, the Army defenders gave no quarter in the tackle, but then nor did Spartak when it was their turn. The game ebbed and flowed with Spartak appearing to dominate, until just before half-time when a well-placed cross allowed a tall Army player to head the ball into the back of the Spartak net. The Spartak supporters roared with anger while the Army fans in the north terraces cheered themselves hoarse. Spartak charged downfield, but they had nothing to show for their efforts by the time the first half finished, and the Spartak supporters muttered darkly about Army transgressions and a weak referee.

Korolev looked at the crowd packed in like logs in a woodpile and volunteered reluctantly to make his way to the buffet for some meat pies. The American should have the real Moscow sporting experience, and in Korolev's view that meant meat pies – but he regretted his decision as soon as he descended beneath the stands. The room where the buffet was located stank of unwashed bodies, urine and stale *papirosa* tobacco, and the second half had started by the time he managed to get to the front of the queue. Then on his way back the small red-haired figure he'd seen earlier appeared beside him. Kim Goldstein gestured for Korolev to follow and he did, conscious of other children moving in the same direction through the crowd. Not more than a minute later they stood in a quiet spot behind the stands where the boy held out his hand.

'Ten roubles,' he said, determination hardening his jaw.

'Ten roubles. What have you got for me that's worth ten roubles?'

'We found the woman you're looking for, Comrade Investigator.'

Korolev looked around at the other children. The young girl he'd seen thrown through the air was with them, a streak of blood running down her neck and her eyes red-rimmed. He nodded to her as he tried to digest what Goldstein had told him. Again, surely it was his duty to establish where this Nancy Dolan was? Case or no case.

'Where is she?'

'Arbat. Ten roubles you said. We'll take you there after the game.'

'All right.' Korolev nodded. 'Here's five on account. I need to take a foreigner back to his hotel, but I'll meet you there with the rest of the money. Do you know the Prague cinema?'

'Of course. We know it well.' The children shared a smile and Korolev guessed they'd found a way to slip in the back.

'Six o'clock then,' Korolev said, counting out five notes. 'Will you be there?'

'At your command, Comrade Investigator,' Goldstein said, giving him an ironic salute.

§

Korolev was wondering how he would ever make it back to his seat when the press of people in front of him reduced so suddenly he almost fell over. The explanation was out on the pitch, where hundreds of spectators had broken through the cordon of stewards and were spreading across the green of the grass like a muddy tide. The players moved to the centre circle, where they stood around the referee as if to protect him. The crowd, however, was not hostile and it seemed the stands had simply reached capacity and were overflowing onto the pitch.

When Korolev reached the others he found Babel standing on

his seat to get a better view as a line of mounted Militia began to push the crowds back to the touchlines. One of the Militia horses was completely white and Korolev found himself following its slow and patient progress along the length of the football field, as the dark-clothed crowd gradually retreated to mark out its edges.

'Will they be able to finish the game?' Schwartz asked, squinting into the afternoon sun that now cast long shadows across the pitch.

'I think so. It just needs a little patience from the *Ments* – sorry, Alexei Dmitriyevich, I meant the Militia. At least they're being comradely about it. See – they have most of them on the sidelines now.'

The crowd began to clap the Militia, which was so unusual that Korolev and Semionov exchanged a glance.

'Nicely done,' Schwartz said, joining in the applause. As if on cue, the announcer began requesting the crowd's cooperation in a friendly voice and a wave of good humour spread around the stands, extending even to the players, who began to shake hands with each other. Korolev handed round the pies and pretended he didn't see Schwartz's expression of mistrust.

'See, Jack, it's the Soviet way. Play hard, but always in the proper spirit.' Korolev said, wondering if perhaps the man had never seen a meat pie before. Then there was more applause as the spectators on the touchline linked arms to provide an unbroken human barrier around the playing area. Korolev felt his chest fill with pride and he turned to beam at his friends.

Play began again with a sustained Spartak attack that yielded a goal to Alexei Starostin. The crowd surged again and the Army goal collapsed sideways, leading to another delay as ground staff pushed the upright back into place. Korolev could see the referee discussing the situation with the captains and the coaching staff in the centre of the pitch and he could imagine what was going through their minds. The crowd was well behaved enough for the moment, but if the game was abandoned the mood would more than likely turn ugly. Even he could feel anger welling up inside at the thought that Spartak might have to wait until a rematch to win the league. But after another flurry of handshakes the game was on once again with the Spartak players returning to the attack. The volume of cheering rose higher and higher as the crowd willed them on and, when the goal came, it was as if the crowd, rather than any one player, propelled the ball into the corner of the net. The Spartak fans embraced each other, stamping their feet and chanting, 'MEAT, MEAT, MEAT'. The clerk's son threw his cap in the air and his father searched desperately for it on the ground. Korolev retrieved it from the row behind him, but when he touched the clerk's shoulder the man whipped round as if he'd been hit, before blushing bright red when he saw the cap in Korolev's hands.

'Thank you, brother,' the man said, his eyes sliding away. Korolev, delighted with the goal, ruffled the boy's hair.

'My pleasure. One more to be sure, eh? Best keep this in your pocket in the meantime, youngster. It'll be a long winter with no hat.'

'Yes,' the man replied with a half-hearted smile, 'one more for safety.'

Just before full-time, the wished-for third goal came and, to the absolute delight of the Spartak supporters and the rueful acknowledgement of the Army fans, the game was won. The referee allowed another minute of play but with red and white waving all along the touchline, and the thinly stretched Militia-men looking more and more nervous, he blew the whistle and the second pitch invasion of the day took place, far rowdier and more joyful than the first, with the white hoops of the Spartak players visible above the crowd as they were borne around the field.

§

As they walked away from the stadium, Korolev considered how best to approach the new information Goldstein had given him.

The logical thing to do, of course, would be to get hold of Paunichev and let him deal with it, but that would mean disobeying the general's orders, as he would have to explain to Paunichev who Nancy Dolan was, and how she was relevant to the case. He could haul Semionov along with him, but it was too dangerous to involve the youngster. Or Babel for that matter. And he didn't even consider calling Gregorin. There, Korolev thought to himself, Kolya had his answer. His loyalty to the State was not, it seemed, absolute. He could always go to Arbat on his own. Hopefully, a quick look at the situation would tell him whether it was worth involving anyone else and, with luck, who that person might be. After all, Arbat was a safe area; he couldn't imagine anything happening there that he couldn't handle. Then he thought over the last few days and reconsidered. Maybe he would call Yasimov. He lived nearby.

'So,' Schwartz said, interrupting Korolev's deliberations, 'would you men like to come back to the Metropol for a celebratory drink? So I can say a comradely thank you for an authentic Soviet experience in such excellent company?'

'If you put it like that, it's impossible to say no,' Babel said cheerfully.

'I agree, Comrade Babel. We are honour bound to accept.' Semionov's open smile was contagious and so, at Schwartz's insistence, they hailed a taxi and headed back to the centre of town. It wasn't long before they took their seats at the Metropol bar and watched a white-jacketed barman pour beer from a silver tap into improbably tall glasses. Behind them a jazz band was tuning up for the evening's performance. Semionov nodded over to them.

'They're not bad these guys, they're Utyosov's players, although the man himself refuses to perform in hotels. A real artist, you see – theatres only for him.'

Semionov caught the eye of one of the band and raised a hand in greeting. The musician gave him a quick grin in response and Semionov excused himself to go and talk to his acquaintance.

Korolev looked around the bar. Babel had wandered off to find a toilet and they were alone.

'So Jack, is it true? About the icon? That it's the original Kazanskaya?' He spoke in a low voice, too low for any microphone to pick up with the band playing in the background.

'Possibly,' Schwartz said, after a moment's consideration. 'I won't know anything until I see it, and even then I'll probably only be able to date it, more or less. And, hopefully, say where it might have been painted. The quality will be the crucial thing. You've got to understand it's been copied since the very beginning, millions of times. But if the quality is there, and I can date it back far enough – then I'll know there's a good chance it's what they say it is.'

'So you still haven't seen it,' Korolev said, and Schwartz gave him an enquiring look, as if guessing why Korolev had asked the question. Korolev tried to keep his face blank.

'Come on Alexei Dmitriyevich, fair's fair. What's going on?'

Korolev shrugged; he was in enough trouble that a little indiscretion like this wouldn't make any difference. And he would be interested to see Schwartz's reaction.

'I understand the icon has gone missing again.'

Schwartz looked puzzled and then pulled a piece of paper from his pocket.

'Well, I have a viewing tomorrow. Their representative called while we were out.' There was something in the way that Schwartz used the word 'representative' and his puzzlement that caught Korolev's interest.

'Isn't he one of your usual contacts?'

Schwartz opened his mouth to respond and then stopped, considering the question.

'No,' he said, after a brief pause. 'Not one of my usual contacts, but he's a full staff colonel in the NKVD. I normally deal with more junior ranks. But this is beyond the limits of their authorization, which is understandable.'

'A staff colonel?' Korolev repeated, a thought occurring to him. He tried to stop himself saying the name, but it seemed to come out of his mouth of its own volition. 'Gregorin? Staff Colonel Gregorin?'

'You know him?'

'I've come across him. A very capable fellow,' Korolev managed to say.

'He seems that,' Schwartz went on. 'He drives a hard bargain, that's for sure.'

'What kind of hard bargain?'

'One million dollars, cash.'

'What's that in roubles?' Korolev asked and Schwartz laughed.

'A lot. An awful, awful lot.'

Chapter Twenty-Two

BEFORE Korolev left the Metropol he showed his identification card at the reception desk and called Yasimov's number. He had to wait for a couple of minutes while Yasimov was summoned to the communal phone, but his old friend agreed when Korolev suggested that they meet at the usual spot for a drink, and didn't ask any questions when he told him to bring along his best friend. 'An investigator's best friend is his pistol,' was something Yasimov said at least once a week and their usual spot for an after-work drink was the Arbat Cellar, a late-night bar which was convenient for the Prague cinema and which would be empty at this time of day. Even if someone was listening to the telephone conversation, Korolev doubted they'd make much of it.

Stepping out into the square, Korolev crossed the street and took a tram in the direction of Arbat. He was reassured by the solid presence underneath his armpit. It had seemed silly bringing the Walther to the football game, but now – well, at least he'd have a chance to put some holes in anyone who looked like they were planning to do the same to him. He jumped off the tram a few stops early, having decided to use the network of passages, alleyways and courtyards that existed just off the main thoroughfare to throw any tail and as he walked, keeping to the shadows and constantly changing direction, his mind went backwards and forwards like an abacus in a bread shop.

If Gregorin was rotten, things were not good, and Korolev's

gut was saying Gregorin was rotten to the core and, what's more, that he'd played Korolev for a dupe. He clung to the hope that it was impossible that such a senior Chekist could be behind the murders, and inconceivable that he could have had anything to do with the theft of the icon, but there were just too many coincidences, too many indicators to the contrary. Every instinct he had was telling him Gregorin was a dirty traitor, out to stab the Party and his fellow workers in the back. He cursed the fellow's black heart.

He entered a courtyard festooned with washing that hung across the open spaces almost up to the height of the roof, and then ducked into a low archway leading to another alley. How had he ended up in this mess? He realized he'd asked the question aloud when he drew a glance from an old man unloading coal from a handcart into a shed. The man turned quickly away when he saw Korolev's face and he realized he must look like a madman, bursting out of tiny archways with a bandaged head, muttering to himself. If he'd any sense, he'd go home, make himself some dinner and, if necessary, drink himself into a state where he forgot all about it. But then, if he did that, Gregorin could be off to Berlin or Paris or some other capitalist Gomorrah to spend his illgotten gains. And a staff colonel of the NKVD would be a fine fish to catch for a foreign intelligence service. The Judas would no doubt have many a State secret he could sell if he so chose. The fiend had guarded Stalin, for the love of God; they'd welcome him like manna from heaven.

Korolev looked at his watch; he had a few minutes before he was due to meet Yasimov, so he slipped into a doorway from where he could watch both ends of the narrow lane he'd ended up in. If he was being followed by anyone, and it was by no means certain that he was, they'd be scurrying around trying to catch up with him after all his jinks and turns, and that meant it was a good time to stop, lie low and let any search pass him by.

It would also allow him a little time to gather his thoughts. He lit a cigarette and considered the situation.

Of course, the possibility remained that Gregorin was straight, in which case everything was fine. However, if that wasn't the case, what had driven the colonel to murder and the theft of valuable State property? A million dollars in roubles wouldn't be worth much if he was in the Zone. Korolev exhaled a wispy trail of smoke. Start at the beginning, he told himself. The first victim had been the American nun, Mary Smithson. Everyone agreed her presence in Moscow was because of the icon; Gregorin had said as much, and Kolya seemed to have confirmed it. Even Schwartz's story about Nancy Dolan backed it up. So why had she been tortured to death? Well, obviously whoever did it must have wanted information. What kind of information? What else could it have been other than the location of the icon? Kolya and Gregorin, and Schwartz as well, all confirmed that the Cheka had been in possession of the icon after the raid on the Thief's hideout. There would have been no point in torturing the girl if it had still been in the Lubianka, would there? So it really had been stolen and whoever had tortured her must have thought the Church was responsible, or at the very least knew where the icon was located. But judging by the level of violence and the loss of blood, if the Holy Sister had known the icon's location, she'd been stubborn about revealing it to the killers. Korolev thought back to the scene in the sacristy and shivered.

The motive for Tesak's torture, and his subsequent murder, was also probably information. Tesak probably *had* talked, but whether he'd taken the killers closer to the icon was another question. Kolya had said the Thieves were trying to make sure the icon was returned to the Church, but he'd denied that they knew the whereabouts of the icon. The killers, however, seemed to believe the contrary, perhaps with reason. He wouldn't put it past Kolya to have lied to him on that point, although strangely he did believe much of the rest of his story. He wasn't sure where Mironov, the dead Chekist, fitted into this, if he did at all. He'd been killed in a different way, but he'd also been tortured, and he'd been found in a church. So it was more than possible that his death was linked to the others. Korolev's guess was that the link was something to do with Mironov being a member of the Foreign Department.

So who were the killers? It could be Kolya's lot, but it seemed unlikely the Thieves would kill a nun, or one of their own, without good reason. On the other hand, if Mironov was indeed involved in this mess, Korolev could well imagine Kolya doing away with the Chekist for his own purposes. The dead Chekist aside, though, Kolya seemed to be in the clear; nor could Korolev believe the Church would ever be responsible for butchering people in sacristies and the like. So that left the NKVD. Gregorin had said the NKVD were looking for the icon, which was to be expected. But was it really possible that the NKVD were torturing people in churches and leaving bodies scattered around Moscow to be found by ordinary citizens? It didn't make sense. Tesak and the nun could have disappeared into the Moscow prison system and no one would have ever heard of them again – secrecy wasn't an issue for the Cheka. What's more, if it *were* the NKVD, why would they rush things when they had the facilities and the time to carry out interrogations and dispose of prisoners at their leisure?

Korolev felt a chill run down his spine. If it hadn't been the NKVD, it could still have been Chekists – the conspiracy that Gregorin had referred to. The only question was whether the colonel was involved in that conspiracy, and Korolev was beginning to think there was a good chance he might be. He took a last drag and then stubbed the cigarette out against the wall. It was a bad situation. Very bad, because if Gregorin *was* a traitor, and planning to defect with the cash from the sale, that meant the icon, and the staff colonel, were going abroad. It didn't take a fortune teller to predict how the Chekists would react if Kazanskaya turned up in New York with tales of heroic nuns martyred to recover her from Soviet oppression. Not only that, but with a senior Chekist in tow. Anyone associated with Gregorin's treachery would have some explaining to do, and that meant Popov, Semionov, Babel and, most importantly, one Captain Alexei Dmitriyevich Korolev. Stalin himself would give instructions on how to deal with the matter and Korolev had no illusions that the General Secretary would be measured in his response.

All in all, he needed to talk to this Nancy Dolan, to get to the bottom of the whole mess. He pulled out the Walther and checked the magazine. He had a full clip. Five minutes had passed and no one had come poking down the alley looking for him, so the chances were he could move. He slipped the automatic back into his shoulder holster and started towards the meeting spot.

§

Descending into the Arbat Cellar was a little like going down into an underground cave. It was dark and reeked of damp and years of spilt alcohol, sweat and cigarette smoke. The walls, once white, were, after countless thousand *papirosa*, covered in an orange-brown film that you could write your name in, if you had the inclination. In the corner of the room an emaciated elderly black man was performing half-familiar tunes on a battered piano, his fingers like spider's legs as they travelled along the keys and his eyes focused on another place. Another foreign Comrade washed up on the Moscow beach, thinking of the place he'd left behind and wondering would he last another winter in this 'worker's paradise'. The Cellar was not at its best in the early evening, but later it would liven up. After all, it had the advantage that it stayed open late and served real vodka from a factory, not something made in a back room.

At the bar Yasimov signalled for two drinks as Korolev took the stool beside him. They saluted each other and drank them down in one gulp.

'I should go home soon, Lena's sister is visiting us from Tver. On the other hand, I need a drink after listening to them gossip all day long.'

Yasimov nodded to the barman and the glasses were filled again, this time accompanied by two slices of black bread.

'It's a little job, nothing much really,' Korolev said, hoping that he was telling the truth.

'I see.' Yasimov raised an eyebrow. 'You're in trouble, I take it?'

'Maybe. I just want you to follow me. Don't intervene, just watch. If something happens – tell either Popov or Semionov. They know the full picture.'

'You want me to just walk away?'

'Yes. Don't get involved. Absolutely not.' Korolev hesitated as he broke off a piece of bread. 'There's a chance it might be political. I need to find out, which means taking a risk.'

'And this?' Yasimov patted his coat pocket where a gun-sized bulge stretched the fabric. He had indeed brought along his best friend.

'For yourself, not for me. I have the Walther. There are undesirable elements involved. Thieves. If one of them comes at you, then shoot him and ask questions later. There may be State Security around as well, but they don't walk the same way.'

Yasimov smiled. It was true – Thieves had a stylized walk, a sort of shuffle with toes turned inwards. It was their version of a Mason's handshake. Korolev signalled the barman to bring Yasimov another drink and laid roubles on the counter to cover the cost.

'I'll be at the Prague cinema at six. Just follow and observe. Semionov and Popov will put the pieces together. If you know nothing, you run less risk.'

Yasimov nodded. 'You've saved my hide more than once, so I owe you, brother. But if things turn out badly, you never saw me or spoke to me. Promise me that, for Lena and the boys. I'll see that Semionov and Popov get word.'

Korolev nodded his agreement and they shook hands. There was no need for further discussion. As Korolev walked out, he caught sight of Yasimov's pale face reflected in a mirror, downing the drink the barman brought him and gesturing for another.

§

It was dark outside and the street was busy. Pedestrians crowded the pavements, shoulder to threadbare shoulder, as they searched the Arbat stores for something to buy. An open shop window had busts of Lenin and Marx and dusty cardboard boxes but nothing, apparently, to sell. Outside the Prague a long line of Arbat youth slouched along the wall waiting for the next show, the lads shivering in their mackintoshes and plus fours and the girls ignoring the cold that whipped their bare knees red. They looked thin and hungry in the blue light cast by the Prague's electric sign.

Korolev leant against a street lamp on the other side of the street and tried to resist the urge to smoke a cigarette, instead examining the film poster while digging his hands deep into his pockets. *We Are from Kronstadt* was showing; three noble sailors faced a line of bayonets with defiant chests braced to meet the blades. Things didn't look good for them, and the rocks hanging by ropes from around their necks suggested that things might even get worse. He gave in to the craving and pulled the packet of Little Star from his pocket. There was only one cigarette left, and after lighting it up he went to the kiosk on the corner to buy more. The transaction complete, he looked down to see a small girl, about seven years old, pretty, with a bow in her hair and not looking at all like one of the Razin Street Irregulars. She tugged at his coat.

'Hold my hand,' she said with a smile, and he reached down,

feeling her warm little fingers take his as she led him away from the cinema. They walked along Arbat, a father and his daughter out for a stroll on a Friday evening. They weren't the only ones and he thought to himself, not for the first time, that Goldstein was a clever little runt, destined to have a long and successful career – if he managed to survive. The girl stopped beside a narrow archway leading to a small square and he saw Goldstein's red hair at the far end of it. The little girl turned and skipped away.

'There's a man following you,' the youngster said as Korolev approached.

'Thinning hair, small moustache, heavy black overcoat?'

'That's him.'

'Nothing to be concerned about.'

Goldstein's eyes flicked back to the alleyway Korolev had come through.

'Are you sure? I'll tell you this for free, Comrade Investigator, there are a lot of blue fingers hanging around the neighbourhood this evening. You should be careful.'

'Thieves?'

'They're not Pioneers, I know that much. Take the first right. There's a big white apartment building with a green door and beside that a smaller wooden house with two trees in the front garden. She's in there, on the ground floor. But there are some real bandit types outside, so be vigilant.'

Korolev produced ten roubles from his pocket. It was more than they'd agreed, but if things went badly, he wouldn't have much use for the money.

'Thanks.'

Goldstein took the money without surprise or gratitude. 'I'm just concerned for our future business relationship, that's all.'

'Well, I'll see what I can do to ensure that it's maintained.'

'That's all I ask,' Goldstein said with a grave expression and saluted him with the bank notes before walking away. Shapes moved in the shadows and the rest of the Irregulars congregated around him, moving in silence and with purpose. Korolev felt reassured; Goldstein would have a plan for the winter, he was sure of it. They'd make it to spring – most of them, anyway.

§

When Korolev turned the corner of the lane, he found three likely-looking lads clustered round an oil drum, warming their hands on whatever was burning inside. Their faces were red above the flaming fire and their black eyes shone as they looked up at him. Korolev recognized Mishka, and the Thief nodded in greeting as Korolev approached, the young tough's thin-lipped smirk a dark crescent in the flickering light.

'What a coincidence, *muchachos*, the Comrade Captain strolls into view. And what brings you to this neck of the woods, old friend? As if we didn't know.'

'Just out for a walk, same as yourselves I expect,' Korolev said as he came closer to them. The other two Thieves moved slowly to either side and so Korolev patted the pocket he'd moved his Walther to.

'Stay in front of me, lads – where I can see you. We're all friends here tonight. Right, Mishka?'

The Thieves looked at Mishka, who nodded.

'So,' Mishka said, slipping his own hand into the pocket of his coat.

'So, indeed,' Korolev replied and waited. He felt his eyes itching with the effort not to blink. Mishka held the stare with his usual dead expression before eventually bestowing a lazy smile, and motioning with a blue-inked thumb towards the house with the two trees in the garden.

'I suppose you want to go in there?'

'Perhaps. Will you try to stop me?'

'Why would I? It's a free country, right? A socialist democracy is what they say. You can do whatever you want here, I expect.

285

None of us will try to stop you, that's for sure. It would be uncultured. Anyway, you've an appointment.'

'I see,' Korolev said, and then walked on towards the house, an unpainted wooden building made from heavy, rough-cut timber logs, wondering how on earth the Thieves had known he was coming. He could feel every stitch of the fabric across his back as he turned away from them but he wasn't going to look over his shoulder, he was damned if he was going to do that.

The front door was old and wooden, in keeping with the house itself, but solid. Korolev knocked three times and only then allowed himself to look back at Mishka and his goons. They were watching him, sure enough, and Mishka raised a hand in salute. Korolev kept his face hard and straight and turned to the door as he heard footsteps coming.

'Hello?' a woman asked. The voice sounded elderly and genteel.

'Captain Korolev of the Moscow Criminal Investigation Division, Citizen. Please open up.'

There was a pause and Korolev looked at the hinges, wondering if he could kick his way in. It seemed unlikely and he didn't think it would do his feet much good to try, seeing as he was wearing felt boots.

'Citizeness?' he asked.

'Yes,' the reply came. The woman didn't sound scared.

'I don't want to have to break the door down.'

'I don't want you to either.'

'Then perhaps you would be kind enough to open it,' Korolev said, allowing a trace of honey to sweeten his words.

'What do you want?'

'To talk to the Holy Sister, that's all. I came alone. I'll leave alone. Just a talk.'

'Just a talk?'

'That's right. It's important.'

'I'll go and ask. Korolev, you say.' Footsteps walked away from the door, there was the sound of a conversation and then the footsteps returned, a key turned in the lock and the door swung open. A thin woman, about sixty years of age stood there. She looked calm, but she had no smile for him.

'This way, please, Captain.' She gestured along the corridor to where the yellow light of an electric bulb was framed by a doorway.

Inside the kitchen a woman sat at a table, looking up at him with a tired curiosity. If his memory of the visa photograph was correct, it was the second American nun, Nancy Dolan. She seemed older than in the visa photograph, and had lost the cheerful disposition he thought he'd detected in the picture, but a week in Moscow could do that to a person. Behind her, leaning against the wall, was Count Kolya. Kolya nodded a greeting, but his left hand was hidden in his pocket and Korolev decided it was safe to assume that it held a gun.

'Greetings, Captain,' Kolya said, 'Have a chair. A glass of tea? Or something else perhaps?'

Kolya indicated the samovar that sat on the table, a thin ribbon of steam emanating from its spout.

'I'll take a glass, why not?' Korolev said. 'Do you mind if I sit down, Sister?'

'Please,' Dolan said. 'Pelagia Mikhailovna, will you keep watch on the street?' Her Russian was perfect, but the pronunciation was that of an older person. Today's Russian was more pragmatic, more comradely. Hers was the kind of accent people disguised these days.

'She knows nothing about all this,' Dolan said as the old woman shut the kitchen door behind her.

'Of course not,' Korolev replied, wondering how naive this American thought he was. 'I'm not after old ladies, Citizeness Dolina. I'm not even after you, in particular.'

Korolev put an emphasis on the word *citizeness*. The nun opened her mouth to speak, but no words came. She must know she was a long way from America now.

'I spent some time with Jack Schwartz today,' Korolev continued. 'I think you met him on the train from Berlin.'

'The train from Berlin?' Dolan seemed to consider denying all knowledge of the journey, but then she lifted her eyes to meet his, calm again. 'How is Jack?'

'I'm sure he would have sent his regards if he'd known I was meeting you. We thought for a while that the Holy Sister who died in the church on Razin Street was you. He was pleased to hear it wasn't.'

She flinched, and Korolev was struck by how small she seemed alongside Kolya's solid bulk.

'Can you tell me what happened to her?' she asked, her eyes a clear blue. 'I know she's dead, but no more than that. Kolya said it was best that way.'

Korolev looked at Kolya, who shrugged.

'She was tortured to death, Sister,' Korolev said, deciding Dolan should know what she was mixed up in. 'There are better ways to die. I'd like to find the fellow who killed her, truly I would.'

'I see.' Her right hand made the sign of the cross. 'God rest her soul.'

'And one of Kolya's men here was also tortured and murdered, probably by the same persons.'

'Yes, he told me there had been others.' The nun seemed listless almost, or perhaps just resigned to her fate.

'And one of my colleagues died – in a car accident, which maybe wasn't an accident. Then there's a dead Chekist – Major Mironov. All in all, there's quite a trail following you around Moscow.'

'It's not following me. I'm not what they want.'

Kolya shifted, enough to draw Korolev's attention. 'Listen

Alexei Dmitriyevich, if we didn't want you to be here, you wouldn't be. That *moishe* brat Goldstein knows where the sun sets, and that he wouldn't see another if he turned me in. So let's speak like friends.'

Korolev nodded – perhaps he was being a little aggressive. And if Kolya had a gun pointing at him from that pocket of his, then maybe that wasn't sensible.

'Is it here?' Korolev asked. 'The icon? You must know they're closing in on you. We've been pulled off the case, and I don't think that's a good sign.'

'It's safe,' Kolya said, 'but if you're not on the case, Korolev, do you mind my asking what you're doing here?'

'I want to finish what I started – to get to the bottom of things. Let's face it, we're all in this together now. In a way.'

Kolya didn't disagree. Instead he gave a small nod as if to acknowledge the point and to consent to the questions.

'Did you kill the Chekist, Mironov?' Korolev asked, deciding to get straight to the point.

'No,' Kolya said. 'My conscience is clear on Mironov.'

'God rest his soul,' Dolan whispered.

'But he was involved in some way? Am I right? I see his death must be to do with the icon, but how exactly? It didn't look like he was killed by the same person as the others.'

'Major Mironov was a Believer,' the nun said in a quiet voice. Kolya looked at her in surprise, but didn't interrupt. 'He recovered the icon on behalf of the Church. The same people killed him who killed the others. Maybe not the same person – but the same group of people.'

'Were they NKVD?'

'Yes, but they aren't in this for the love of Stalin,' Kolya said. 'Gregorin and his crew are in it for themselves.'

'How can you be sure it's Gregorin?' Korolev asked. Even though it was as he'd suspected, it still shocked him to have it confirmed.

WILLIAM RYAN

'Comrade Gregorin is close to Yagoda – not good news now this fellow Ezhov has taken over. Then the icon falls into Gregorin's lap. One of the fellows caught in the raid must have blabbed and he couldn't believe his luck. He made enquiries, found out what it could be worth, and decided it could be his ticket to the West. Mironov worked in the Foreign Department and so Gregorin approached him with a view to securing a safe exit route. Major Mironov didn't believe him, so Gregorin took him to the storeroom, and there it was – Kazanskaya. So Mironov agreed to help with the exit visas in exchange for a cut. Originally Gregorin was going to sell the icon to the Church, which would have been all right, but then another party became involved. When it looked like the icon might be sold to the highest bidder the major acted.'

'He took the icon from the storeroom,' Korolev guessed.

'Yes,' the nun said.

'So Gregorin was the traitor all along. He played me for a mug.'

'Correct,' Kolya said, 'although there must be a few of them in it – they've been tearing Moscow apart. Believe me, the deaths you know about are only part of it. I've lost two others. That's it – now you know everything.'

'But you said it was safe. Why then has Gregorin promised to show Schwartz the icon tomorrow?'

'When did he say this?'

'Earlier today, I think. Schwartz wasn't specific.' Korolev saw a look on Kolya's face that was as close as a man like him was ever likely to come to concern. The Thief digested the information, exchanging a glance with the nun. He looked as if he might say something, but was interrupted by a knocking at the front door – two quick knocks and then a pause before a final rap. Kolya's pistol came out of the pocket.

'We must go, Little Mother,' Kolya said gently.

'Where to?' Korolev began, rising to his feet.

'I'm sorry, Captain. You won't be coming with us.'

He heard steps behind him and caught Kolya's nod to whoever had entered the kitchen. The last thing he saw was the nun's eyes opening wide in shock.

Chapter Twenty-Three

WHEN Korolev awoke it was the intense light he was first conscious of – it seemed to press down on him, even through his closed eyelids. He moved his head to the side and lay there, feeling the ridges of a brick wall against his cheek, and cursing the pain that seemed to stretch his skull outwards.

He knew where he was, he didn't need to open his eyes. Prisons always smelt more or less the same – a mixture of piss, mildew, rotten cabbage and the stench of unwashed, frightened men. He mightn't know which, but he was in one, that was for certain. He swallowed carefully, tasting blood in his mouth and, eyelash by eyelash, broke apart the crust that held them shut. Then he cursed again. He was in a small cell, about three metres long and two wide, at the far end of which a tiny table and stool were bolted to the floor. The walls were painted a light, glossy blue, the smooth surface of which was scarred down to the brick with names, dates and messages. He didn't need to read them to know where he was. The small wooden tiles barely visible under a layer of grime gave him the answer. The Lubianka had been the head office of an insurance firm before the Revolution, and its parquet flooring had famously survived when the panelled offices had been ripped out and replaced with cells and interrogation rooms. He'd known this case was cursed from the start.

Angry with himself, and uncomfortable, he pushed down at the filthy floor, rolling onto his shoulder and then his back and eventually releasing his left arm from beneath his body. The arm was utterly numb, as though it belonged to someone else. He lifted his hand with difficulty and flexed his fingers, feeling no sensation at all to start with, before an itchy tingle told him the blood was coming back. With another effort he pushed himself to a sitting position against the wall, feeling a dizzy nausea as he did so. There was a bench long enough to sleep on, folded up against the wall and getting up onto it was the objective he had in mind, but his whole body hurt, most particularly his head, where a mess of hair had crusted around a fat sticky bruise. Some dog had given him another crack on the skull and he couldn't imagine that was going to do his concussion any good. His belt was gone and his winter coat and felt boots were missing as well. He hoped that dirty brigand Kolya hadn't made off with them, and then smiled at the thought. Kolya wouldn't bother with a patched-up, moth-eaten rag like his. Not in a million years. Only honest men wore coats like Korolev's. The boots and the coat would be waiting for him if he got out of this in one piece, no doubt of it. And if he didn't make it out, he'd have no need of them.

The metal plate that covered the Judas hole slid back and a pale blue eye examined him. Korolev instinctively raised a hand in greeting, but the metal plate was already sliding shut. He listened to the guard walk along the corridor, his keys jangling and the sound of other metal plates sliding back and forth. Well, at least they knew he was awake. Perhaps something would happen now. He allowed his eyes to shut.

§

When he came round for the second time, he found he'd enough energy to stand and then push down the wooden bed so he could sit on it. There was a thin blanket on the table which he hadn't noticed before, and he placed it between himself and the wall to lean back on. A bucket stood in the corner, ringed with dried piss and more solid substances that he didn't want to think about, so he didn't. Anyway, he'd no need of it as yet. He sighed – the Lubianka, no less. Not the Butyrka, nor the Novinskaya. Not Lefertovo or any of the other Moscow prisons. The Lubianka. They only sent senior Party bosses here or foreigners. Zinoviev. Kamenev. The fellow who'd assassinated poor Kirov. British spies. That was the kind of traitor who ended up in the Lubianka – Central Committee types and foreign agents – not some half-dead Militia captain. He supposed he should feel privileged. It was enough to make him smile, although not with much humour.

And what the hell had happened back at the Arbat house? One of Kolya's men had slugged him from behind, most likely, but Kolya couldn't be responsible for him being here, could he? The only connections Kolya had with the Organs were the kind that would put Kolya in prison himself. No, Kolya's lot must have knocked him out cold and then left him in the house. Then he'd been found and brought here. That wouldn't have happened if it had been Militia or even ordinary Cheka – they'd have asked questions and, even then, he wouldn't have ended up in the Lubianka. It must be Gregorin behind it. At least he hadn't been shot, for the moment anyway.

The metal grate scraped open and the blue eye stared in at him once again. Korolev looked back, but the eye remained expressionless. Then the grate slid back into place and the keys moved off down the corridor to another cell. He stood up slowly and leant his hands against the facing wall and stared at the painted bricks in front of him. 'Forgive me, my darling wife,' some poor bastard had scrawled and he thought of Zhenia and the boy in Zagorsk. Maybe Yasimov would be able to look out for them. Or maybe not. The boy, of course, would suffer. Having an Enemy of the People for a father would be a burden on the youngster, even if he hadn't seen the poor mite in the best part of a year. But then it occurred to him that, if it was Gregorin who'd found him, there'd be no judicial proceedings. If he was alive now, and here, it was for a reason. He'd want to know what

Korolev knew and that would be that. He couldn't let him go free. Not with what he knew. The thought sent cold sweat trickling down his spine – that was why they'd brought him to the Lubianka. To mine him of whatever information he had and then finish him off.

As if on cue, footsteps approached the cell, keys sounding their discordant tune, and the door squealed open. Three guards stood there. Two of them were young fellows, strong shoulders and broad faces – almost identical in fact – but with eyes that reminded Korolev of dead fish. The twins entered the cell and lifted Korolev to his feet. The third was taller and older, his skull shaved to a grey shine and softened by rolls of fat that pushed out his ears like cup handles. He, at least, had some expression in his eyes, even if it was contemptuous. The bald guard examined a file he was carrying and then looked up at Korolev.

'Prisoner, you will not speak unless asked a question, in which case your answer should be brief and to the point. For preference, use "yes" or "no". Any attempt to speak to the guards otherwise will be treated as a physical assault and dealt with accordingly. Understood?'

Korolev was surprised that the guard had the voice of an educated man, even if he looked like a brute. He considered trying to tell them about Gregorin, but dismissed the idea. He'd get his beating soon enough, no point in asking for one in advance.

'Yes,' he answered.

'Can you walk?'

'I think so.'

'Yes or no, prisoner.'

'Yes,' Korolev said.

'I'll lead, one beside, one behind. Handcuff him first. Eyes front at all times, prisoner.'

The twins turned him to the wall, cuffed his hands behind his back and then pushed him out into a narrow corridor that was painted the same light blue as the cell. Heavy metal doors lined both sides of the passage, lit by single high-watt bulbs that dangled from the ceiling at regular intervals. In one of the cells someone was sobbing like a child; an unreal sound, as if it were happening on the radio in another room. The bald guard checked their positioning and then they started off, the lead warder jangling his keys like a bell as they walked. The brownish streaks on the painted floor and walls looked like dried blood to Korolev. In the circumstances he was surprised he didn't feel fear. Instead, after the initial shock, he felt quite calm.

They entered a stairwell and descended four flights. The windows were blacked out to allow no light or noise to come in from the outside so, as a result, it felt like being underwater, the only solid sounds being those of their own footsteps, and even they seemed distorted. There were other sounds, but they were smothered and remote, from elsewhere in the building, and, like the sobbing from the cell, had an unnatural quality. Korolev half-wondered whether this might all be a dream, and it was almost a relief to be led into a plainly furnished room with a solid metal chair in front of a desk, thick leather straps hanging from its arms and legs. The room had the harsh rasp of reality to it.

'Sit in the chair, prisoner.'

He sat and the twins took off his handcuffs before buckling the leather straps on, tight as tourniquets. The only part of his body he could move was his head and he began to look around him to see what kind of a place he'd ended up in.

'Eyes front, prisoner.'

'But,' Korolev began and got no further. One of the twins hit his left ear with a blow that exploded inside his head like a pistol shot. For a moment he didn't know where he was, but then his vision cleared and the room settled into something resembling focus. He thought he was deaf for a moment, until the bald guard spoke. It was if the blow had never been struck.

'Hood the prisoner. You, wait with him until the major comes.'

Some kind of small sack was put over his head. It stank of

vomit and something worse which took him a moment to identify. Then he had it – rotting flesh. For a moment he was back amongst the broken, decomposing bodies scattered along a recaptured trench somewhere in the Ukraine. He gripped the arms of the chair and tried to breathe through his mouth. Korolev started to count, anything to distract himself. At first all he could hear was his own breathing and he felt like screaming or trying to throw the hood off but he knew he'd just be beaten for his troubles. He forced himself to concentrate on the counting. Seventy-five, seventy-six. He'd reached four hundred and sixty-two by the time the door opened.

'You may go. You've been told that you are never to discuss the prisoner, under any circumstances, not even with the other guards or your superiors. Please confirm you understand, and commit to fulfil this duty to the State.'

'Confirmed, Comrade,' the guard replied.

'He is secure?'

'Yes.'

'That will be all. This corridor is to be sealed until further instructions are given.'

The guard took care shutting the door, so that all Korolev heard was a quiet click, footsteps receding and then another door, far away, shutting with a metallic clang, and finally nothing except the sound of pages being turned.

'You know why you're here, prisoner?' The voice was quiet, putting a small emphasis on the word 'prisoner', which succeeded in conveying resigned disappointment.

'I haven't committed any crime.'

'Everyone has committed a crime, prisoner.' The voice sounded bored. 'It's only a question of discovering which one. Would you like me to take off the hood?'

'Of course I would.'

'Well then, perhaps you could tell me what you were doing

lying unconscious in the apartment of a known proponent of the Orthodox cult.' There was that rustle of papers again.

'I was making enquiries with regard to a criminal case, in the course of which I was attacked.'

'What case is this?'

'A series of murders. One of which was the murder of Citizeness Kuznetsova, also known as Mary Smithson, an American nun. I've been working under the direction of Staff Colonel Gregorin of the NKVD.'

He could hear the interrogator approach him and braced himself for a blow, but instead he felt hands pulling at the hood and then the stark light of the interrogation room flooded in.

'It's not very pleasant, the hood,' the interrogator said, his disinterested voice coming from behind Korolev. Korolev knew better than to turn to look. 'Deliberately so, of course. It's often as effective as more traditional methods. You know how it goes, being an investigator – a brutal interrogation is exhausting. It leaves some people in as bad a state as the prisoner. But the hood works well.' The interrogator sounded as if he were speaking to himself.

'I don't beat confessions out of prisoners. I find such measures counter-productive.'

A hand patted Korolev's shoulder – it wasn't clear whether in approval or sympathy.

'Now, who do you say assaulted you?' The voice had moved to Korolev's left. It was disconcerting, having no one to look at. But then it was probably deliberately so.

'I didn't see him. He hit me from behind. Why am I being held, Comrade? I've done nothing wrong.'

There was silence while the interrogator walked to the desk and then turned. With a shock, Korolev recognized him. It was the man from the football game. His watery blue eyes looked tired and his face seemed greyer than Korolev remembered, but it was definitely him, and now in the uniform of an NKVD major. He smiled when he saw he'd been recognized; a small upward spasm of the lips; the smile of a man unaccustomed to the act.

'Yes, a strange coincidence,' the major agreed. 'I was surprised to see you at the game.'

'You knew who I was?'

The major considered the question and then shook his head as if deciding it couldn't be answered safely.

'To business. Prisoner, we're here to determine the extent of your involvement in a conspiracy concerning the theft of State property. The priority of the investigation at this stage is directed at recovering the property in question.' He paused for a moment and then added, almost as an afterthought, 'The extent of your guilt will be determined at a later stage. But your cooperation will be considered a mitigating factor.'

'A conspiracy? I've been involved in no such conspiracy and no such theft,' Korolev said, feeling anger boiling up inside him. The major considered him for a moment and then nodded towards the file. He displayed no emotion except, perhaps, melancholy. He spoke like an accountant might speak about a factory's output of shoes; calmly, with the remorseless weight of facts to back his words.

'Let me put it this way,' he said, quiet to the point that Korolev, with his damaged ear, had to lean forward to hear him. 'You can tell me what I want to know freely, or I'll break you like a frozen branch. And then you'll tell me all I want to know anyway. And then you will be shot, your ex-wife will be sent to the Zone and your son will end up begging on trams. Your friends will also suffer.' He looked at his notes for a moment. 'Popov, Semionov, Chestnova, Yasimov, Babel, Koltsova . . .' In a flat voice, he recorded the names of friends, family and acquaintances, his voice becoming quieter and quieter. When he slapped the file down on the table, the sudden sound seemed as loud as the guard's punch.

'Do I need to go on?' Anger burned in his eyes for an instant and then his voice returned to a whisper. 'There are fifty names there; you must know how this works. They'll be arrested and imprisoned, and then *their* families and friends will suffer, and so on and so on. It will be a ripple across Moscow, one by one by one. Hundreds of people. All because you didn't cooperate. What advice do you think they would give you, were they here beside you? Would they tell you to keep quiet? To defy the State? To fly your little flag of selfish honour from your besieged individualist castle of sand? Be sensible, prisoner. In fact, be merciful. Their lives are in your hands.'

The major shook his head and it seemed to Korolev that the light caught a glint of moisture in his defeated eyes. Then he reached into his pocket and pulled out a packet of cigarettes. Hercegovina Flor. The cigarettes from the snowy football pitch where Tesak had been found. The major lit one and then walked over and put it into Korolev's mouth. Korolev inhaled and watched the major light another. Korolev nodded to the empty stenographer's desk, speaking from the corner of his mouth.

'No typist? This isn't an official investigation, is it?'

The major sighed. 'Come on, Captain. I ask questions, you answer. This isn't a conversation. Do I have to beat that into your thick skull? Cooperate, Korolev, for your own sake. You will in the end, believe me.'

It was the first time since he'd found himself in the prison that he'd been addressed by his name or rank. It felt almost intimate, and the half-smile the major gave him opened a chink that Korolev aimed for, almost without thinking.

'With electricity? Like you did to Kuznetsova?' It wasn't exactly a shot in the dark, but the words surprised Korolev almost as much as they seemed to surprise the major. Of course, it was a possibility – here was a man threatening to torture him who knew him by sight, in front of an empty stenographer's desk, with a packet of Hercegovina Flor on the table beside him – but yet the major reminded Korolev more of a priest than a psychopath.

However, any doubts vanished when the blood seeped away from the major's face. Korolev watched him in fascination; he looked like a hunted animal. Eventually he seemed to control himself and began to speak in a furious whisper, two red spots appearing on his blanched cheeks.

'What are you talking about? What foul nonsense is this? How dare you accuse a Chekist of such a crime? You dog. You filthy, rotten, slanderous dog. I'll rip your skin off inch by inch.' He rose to his feet and jabbed a finger at Korolev, his voice rising to a scream. 'Shut your dirty mouth, do you hear?'

But Korolev was, temporarily at least, past intimidation.

'A strange reaction, if you don't mind me saying so, Comrade. I suppose the State property you're looking for isn't a certain icon either? That's why you tortured her. Isn't it, traitor? To find the icon?'

'You know where the icon is, prisoner,' the major replied, calmer now. 'And you know who the real traitor is as well, you black-hearted dog.'

'What will your lad make of it when you arrive in America? To find out his own father's a traitor to the Soviet People. It will be difficult for him. I could see how he looked up to you. A Pioneer, isn't he? Will you pack his red scarf for the journey?'

The major's eyes narrowed in confusion for a moment, then Korolev's words seemed to give him some comfort and he relaxed, waving Korolev's barbs aside.

'You fool, I'm not going anywhere. You, on the other hand, will be shot this very hour if you refuse to cooperate. To hell is where you're going.'

'Maybe I am. But why did you shoot your Comrade, Mironov, from the Foreign Department? Because he didn't go along with the plan to sell the icon to the highest bidder?'

The major again blinked in surprise, and then it occurred to Korolev: perhaps the fool didn't realize the conspiracy was Gregorin's. Perhaps he was a dupe as well.

'You don't know about Mironov, do you? Major Mironov? They went to him to arrange the visas. But no visa for you, it seems. You'll be left to face the music, while they salute the Statue of Liberty with French champagne from the deck of an ocean liner. At least I got wise in time. If I'm going to be shot, let me be shot with my eyes open.'

'What the hell are you talking about?'

'We're the dupes, brother. The icon was recovered from Thieves in a raid led by Gregorin, and then it was stolen again right from this very building. You know this much, am I right?'

The major shrugged an acknowledgement. At least he wasn't threatening to peel his skin off, Korolev thought to himself. That was progress, he supposed.

'What you don't know is that the icon was a secret. Only Gregorin and a couple of others knew about it. He never told his superiors its significance – instead he made contact with foreign enemies, looking to sell it. Mironov was to help them with visas, but he took the icon for his own purposes, so they had to get it back. They knew the nun had entered the Soviet Union, and that there was a chance she was here for the icon – so they sent you after her in case she had it. With me so far?'

The major still wasn't stopping him, so Korolev carried on, the pieces fitting into place as he talked.

'So, when she was found, us poor Militia investigators, we thought it was just another murder. Then Gregorin started taking an interest and told us there was an ongoing Cheka investigation into stolen artefacts and that the crime was probably connected. It was Gregorin who pointed us in the direction of the icon. We worked out the dead woman was a foreigner from her fillings and her clothes, but without him we'd never have identified her as a nun or had a clue about the icon. So you were pursuing your line of enquiry, using your methods, and I was pursuing mine, following you, but we're both looking for the icon and both of us dancing like puppets on strings pulled by Gregorin. Now do you see?'

The major looked at his fist for a long time. Eventually he lifted his head and frowned.

'No. Everything was authorized, of course it was, and at the highest levels. Sometimes a Chekist has to perform unpleasant tasks, but we're the Party's sword and it isn't for us to decide the nature of the blow we must strike. No one likes the wet jobs, but sometimes they're necessary – to exact retribution without judicial process. And this Mironov? What is he to this? A Chekist dies – there are many of us ready to do as much. There's no connection to this matter.'

'But there is.' Korolev considered for a moment and then became resolute – after all, if Mironov had been murdered, it was because Gregorin already knew he'd taken the icon. 'They offered to cut Mironov in, in exchange for the passports and visas, but instead Mironov stole the icon and handed it over to the Church. That's why the nun was here. That's what was confirmed to me by the cultists this evening. Now do you see?'

'Mironov?' The major seemed to be considering the name. 'I've heard nothing about a Chekist being killed. When do you say this happened?'

'He was found four days ago. When he was killed is another question. But his body wasn't meant to be found. They put it in a church due for demolition. By chance, someone came across it and, by another chance, I identified it. Gregorin took the body from the morgue and my guess is it's buried deep in the forest by now.'

The major shook his head with a frown and, in the silence, Korolev heard a metal door down the corridor creak open and footsteps approaching. The door opened behind him and the major stood to attention.

'Well?' the voice asked.

'As you predicted, Colonel. He was turned by the cultists.' The major looked at Korolev with a disgust that chilled him to the core. Korolev tried to turn, but the chair held him tight. Then the colonel walked into his line of sight, a sad smile making his expression almost gentle. Gregorin. Korolev would have given a lot for a free right hand and room enough to swing it.

'Poor Korolev,' Gregorin said with a sympathetic smile. 'You became confused, didn't you? Political matters are complex – shades of grey, whereas you see things in black and white. You swam into deep waters and the Party's enemies were waiting. The Party warns of this over and over again. "Be vigilant!" they tell you. "They're not fools, these counter-revolutionaries." No, indeed they're not – they're adept at deception and deceit and yet citizens are always surprised at their cunning ways. So and so was a Party member for thirty years, Lenin's right-hand man, how could he have been a traitor? Because we're fighting a many-headed hydra, Korolev, with infinite patience and incomparable self-control and its agents are everywhere. Your Mendeleyev, for example, an apparently useful contributor to the Revolution for many years and then he's spreading Fascist lies dressed up as humour. A dupe perhaps, or was he simply in hibernation, waiting for this time of crisis to unleash his poison? And what about you? Were you a willing participant in this attempt to steal from the State or were you cynically manipulated without even being aware of it? What's Korolev's son's name?'

The major looked at his file.

'Yuri.'

'Yes, Yuri. Poor child. You know about State orphanages, don't you? They're in transition, of course. In time, ordinary children will be envious of orphans who are cared for by the State. But these days, I'm afraid, things aren't so good. Did you hear about that little boy who was crucified for wetting his bed? Crucified? Nailed to the wall in the dormitory as an example to the other children? Nailed, I ask you. Of course, the perpetrators were punished when it was discovered, but even so these things happen more than we would like. And he's a good-looking boy, your son. It's a shame, but some of the staff are degenerates. They slip in, no matter how hard we try. Well, one can only hope for the best.'

'Why isn't there a stenographer, Colonel?'

Gregorin smiled, his teeth white, and Korolev was not for the first time reminded of a predator toying with its prey.

'I told you, Korolev. This is a confidential matter. And that comes from the top. The very top. You know how the peasants are about icons – we can't have them getting upset about Kazanskaya now, can we? Not the same year the cultist cathedral named for her in Red Square is blown to smithereens. I don't think that would be very sensible. Do you?' His voice lost its amused tone and became hard. 'So no stenographer, and no mercy if you don't tell us everything we need to hear. Not to you or anyone who knows you. That isn't a threat, Korolev. It's a sacred oath.'

'Explain Mironov to me, that's the one I don't understand. Why did you kill one of your own?'

The colonel's eyes slid sideways to look at the major – enough to confirm to Korolev that Gregorin was a crook, and that the major probably wasn't.

'Mironov was part of the conspiracy – it had to be resolved expediently and quietly. I can't say anything else – Major Chaikov here isn't cleared for the information, and you most certainly aren't. Suffice it to say that Mironov had betrayed the Party's trust for far too long and got what he deserved. Still.' Gregorin smiled. 'I took my hat off to you when you came up with his body. You may not be very bright, but you have the Devil's own way of being in the right place at the right time.'

'I don't believe you. Mironov may have been working for the cultists out of misguided belief, but you're even worse. You're just after the money.'

Gregorin shook his head in disagreement. 'No, Captain. I followed orders. You were given orders – to stay away from the case – and you ignored them like the petty individualist you are. Your clumsy bumbling messed up the Arbat operation. We burst in on that damned house hoping to find the icon and a pack of traitors. Instead all we found was an unconscious, blundering fool lying on the kitchen floor with a bump on his head. Presumably they turned you, got the information they wanted, and then knocked you out cold. Perhaps you really did think you were getting something useful from them. Who knows? We may still be able to find it in our hearts to forgive you – accept that you were stupid rather than criminal. We could even spare your friends and family. If you cooperate fully and with an open heart.'

Korolev sat there, conscious of the two men's cold eyes on him, and decided he'd run out of cards to play. As he'd listened to Gregorin's explanation, he'd been half-convinced. It was just possible he'd been mistaken – even if his instinct was telling him louder than ever that Gregorin was a crook of the highest degree. But Chaikov seemed to have fallen for it hook, line and sinker, and that meant Korolev's room for manoeuvre was limited. It was time to roll over. After all, who was he protecting by keeping quiet? Kolya, who'd left him to be found? The nun – a woman he'd met once? He owed it to Yasimov and Babel to keep quiet about their parts in the affair, but the others could go hang. At least his son and his friends might have a chance this way. So he told them what had happened in the Arbat House . . .

§

'Come, Korolev,' Gregorin said, when he'd finished, 'this is all very interesting, but where is the icon? It was there, of course – but where did they take it when you warned them we were coming?'

'I didn't see the icon. It may have been there, but I saw none of it. I've told you the conversation I had with Kolya, word for word, and that's as far as I got. If I knew who had it, I'd tell you. To me, it's just a wooden board with some paint on it.' Which wasn't entirely true, but this wasn't the time to expand on the nature of his religious beliefs.

Gregorin considered him and there was no charm in his expression now, only calculation. It occurred to Korolev that, without the veneer of charm, Gregorin's features had the cold malevolence of a snake. Gregorin scowled and turned to the major.

'He's lying. Break him.'

'Yes, Comrade Colonel.'

'You've four hours. Don't bother telling me it's not enough. We have to find this damned piece of cultist chicanery before they smuggle it out of the country. Don't fail – there can be no excuses. My office will know where to find me.'

He turned to Korolev.

'The major here is skilled at what he does. For your own sake, Korolev, tell us now. Where's the damned icon?'

'I don't know, Colonel.'

'This isn't a game, Korolev. The major isn't just going to beat you. He'll destroy you – you'll be praying for a bullet by the end.'

Korolev didn't doubt it, and he felt his body trying to back its way into the chair, but he couldn't tell them what he didn't know.

'One thing, Colonel Gregorin,' Korolev said, as Gregorin turned away from him.

'Yes?' The colonel turned, impatient.

'What happens if you haven't got the icon by tomorrow? Will you have enough money for the visas? Is the net closing in? Is that why you're rushing? You won't get a million dollars for a promise.'

The colonel was a sturdily built man and his knuckles had calluses from where he'd hit others before, so perhaps Korolev shouldn't have been surprised at the force of the punch that sent his head slamming back into the headrest and warm blood coursing from above his eye, blinding him even as he tried to blink it away.

'You fool, you deserve everything you're about to get,' Gregorin hissed. 'When you've finished with him, Chaikov – Room H.'

The door slammed as he left.

Once the far door shut as well, the major walked over and, bending down, cleaned the blood from Korolev's forehead with a handkerchief. His touch was gentle on the raw cut. He held Korolev's head back and stared into his eyes.

'You have concussion.'

'Everyone keeps hitting me.'

'Perhaps you provoke them.'

'Look, I know nothing, but if I did, I'd rather shoot myself than cooperate with a devil like Gregorin.'

'Fuck that Georgian rat,' Chaikov whispered, pulling the handkerchief down Korolev's face with an almost dreamy expression. 'Fuck his mother. Fuck his sister.' The handkerchief was soaked with blood now. 'I had suspicions, but I ignored them. I let him lead me by the nose – like a pig to the slaughter. What will happen to my own son? Answer me that.'

Korolev stared at the man in amazement, wondering if this was some ploy to soften him up. A single tear rolled down the major's face. 'See what I've become. Look at me. He's turned me into an enemy.'

There was the clang of the far door opening and then running footsteps in the corridor. What the hell was going to happen now, Korolev asked himself, as the door crashed open behind him.

'Up against the wall, one move and I fire. Hands high, hands high.'

Chaikov looked up calmly, smiled and reached for his pocket. Instantly there were three loud explosions and the major was thrown over the table by the force of the bullets hitting him.

'Damn,' an easily recognized voice said, through the ringing in Korolev's ears.

Chapter Twenty-Four

KOROLEV'S head hurt a great deal. A dense, tooth-grinding pain, with not much variation for the individual injuries. It occurred to him that nearly everyone he'd met over the last few days, whether Chekist, factory worker or Thief, seemed to have left a lump on his skull as an aide-memoire. Perhaps as a side effect of the constant battering his cranium had taken, he remained slightly unsure that he really was sitting in a warm office, in a comfortable chair, with a glass of vodka in his hand and faces surrounding him that, if not all particularly friendly, didn't seem to want to cause him any harm either. But, if the reality was something else, he didn't want to have anything to do with it.

The stitches the doctor was putting in the cut above Korolev's eye were a good reason for suspecting that this wasn't a dream, of course, as he could feel each millimetre of the needle as the doctor pushed it through his skin. Semionov, sitting on the desk watching the doctor work, seemed genuinely concerned, which was gratifying, but as Korolev had been wrong about him all along, he couldn't trust to that either. Like now, for instance – Semionov had just put three bullets into a fellow Chekist, yet here he was, cool as a cucumber.

Semionov's real boss, the fat, aggressive Colonel Rodinov, was clearly only concerned at how long the doctor was taking.

'Aren't you finished yet?' Rodinov barked.

'Last stitch – one moment – there.' The doctor wrapped a bandage round Korolev's head to protect the wound then stood, examined his work, and nodded his approval. Korolev was just pleased he'd finished.

'Leave,' the colonel said and pointed a stubby thumb towards the door. The doctor, a man of about fifty, began to bow before recollecting where he was and, rather than continue with a bourgeois gesture that could get you five years in a camp, walked with long steps and a hunched back to the door, reminding Korolev of an ostrich.

'Carry on where you left off,' the colonel said. He was a rosy pink in colour and his round, bald head shone with a thin sheen of sweat. Korolev had told him pretty much everything he knew already, except for the fact that the icon was Kazanskaya. That was information Korolev had decided to keep to himself. As far as he was aware, everyone who knew the identity of the icon was either dead or had good reasons for keeping their mouths shut. And Korolev had a feeling that if Rodinov knew that the icon was Kazanskaya, things would escalate out of control very quickly.

'So you see,' he said, searching for another piece of relevant information and finding nothing, 'Gregorin guided us through the whole affair. Step by step. And all for his own ulterior motives. Or those of the conspiracy, if there turns out to be one.'

'It's a damned conspiracy all right. He's had no orders from anyone other than himself. When Semionov started telling me about your investigation I thought it strange, but often there's a need for secrecy in our work.'

He paused as if considering something, then picked up the phone, listening for a moment before speaking.

'Rodinov. Tell Sharapov to call me with news.' He put the phone back onto the cradle. Obviously social niceties were unnecessary if you were Colonel Rodinov. He turned his cold gaze back to Korolev.

'Chaikov, though – that man has waded through blood for the Party. Gregorin I can believe, but Chaikov. No gun, of course.'

'He was used by Gregorin. Once he realized he'd been manipulated and had contributed to a crime against the State – well, maybe he wanted to be shot.'

Rodinov shook his head. 'I'd never have believed it. I've seen that fellow go through three pistols in a day liquidating enemies – wore out the barrels, one after the other. I don't know why he didn't just put up his hands. Lack of vigilance, yes, but what a worker.' Rodinov shook his head sadly. 'Well, Captain, it seems your actions may have uncovered a nest of vipers. And yours, Semionov. If you hadn't come to me when Gregorin took Comrade Korolev here, we'd never have got to the bottom of this. Commissar Ezhov himself is asking for hourly updates. Once we have Gregorin in our hands we'll find out the true extent of it – it's only a matter of time now.'

'I knew it was inconceivable that Captain Korolev could be a traitor, Comrade Colonel.'

'If there's to be an arrest—' Korolev began.

Rodinov raised an eyebrow. 'You'd like to be involved?'

'If it were possible.'

'We'll see. We have to find him first. It's a Cheka matter, but I doubt Commissar Ezhov would object in the circumstances. Yes, I'm sure you have some things you'd like to say to him. I certainly would have in your shoes.' He turned to Semionov. 'A tough bird, this investigator of yours, Semionov. Look at his forehead – it's like a railway junction with all that stitching.'

'Comrade Korolev has taught me a great deal in the few months I've been with the People's Militia, Colonel. I've been impressed with his dedication to duty and his logical and practical approach.'

'High praise, Korolev – from a young man Comrade Ezhov himself has his eye on. High praise indeed.'

§

Dawn was colouring the silhouetted domes of Moscow's churches when Semionov drove Korolev home. It would have been earlier, but it took some time to find Korolev's belongings and he'd refused to leave without the winter coat or his felt boots. Eventually one of the twins, now himself beltless and barefoot and wearing an expression of terrified bewilderment on his heavily bruised face, guided them to a cardboard box which contained Korolev's belongings, including his Walther and papers. Korolev considered giving the twin a dig or two – his ear was still ringing from the guard's blow – but he decided fate had revenged him sufficiently. Anyway, it might have been the other twin who'd swung the fist.

'It's like old times driving this Ford,' Semionov said, as the Lubianka became smaller in the rear-view mirror – the Model T they were driving in was remarkably similar to the car in which Larinin had met his end.

'Watch out for trucks,' Korolev muttered and Semionov smiled. He looked uncomfortable, and Korolev didn't feel the situation was entirely normal himself, so they drove in silence. It was the morning of the October Day Parade and the early trams and buses were covered with placards extolling the successes of the Five Year Plan, the might of the Party and the wisdom of Stalin. Work parties were clearing the streets and a column of soldiers had halted in formation on Yauzski Boulevard, holding huge balloons in the shape of *kolkhoz* buildings. Here was the cooperative store, there the Party office, behind that a smithy – altogether there were forty or more swollen structures swaying in the light wind. The soldiers' breath and cigarette smoke made it look as if a village were floating on a thin mist. Further along there were massed squares of Pioneers in overcoats and red scarves, their flags and banners touching the last autumn leaves on the trees, and behind them a line of brown tanks, their exhausts belching black smoke as they turned their engines over. Korolev wondered how the teachers would keep the Pioneers quiet in the hours they'd have to wait before the parade moved. Perhaps the tanks were there to maintain order amongst the little Comrades.

'Were you surprised?' Semionov asked.

'That you turned out to be a Chekist? Yes, although when I look back, maybe I should have suspected something. You look young but you've an old head on your shoulders.'

'I was following orders. I know it may seem I didn't behave in a comradely way – concealing my identity – but my orders demanded it.'

'I'm sure they did. Whatever you were up to, announcing you were an NKVD operative would no doubt have defeated the object. I'm not complaining, Vanya. A junior lieutenant in the Militia couldn't have sprung me from the Lubianka. I'm grateful you turn out to be a Cheka captain.'

'Thank Yasimov. He called me with the registration number of the car. Once I'd tracked it to Gregorin I asked Rodinov to look into it. Gregorin's story came apart almost immediately – he was riding his luck, hoping people would be too frightened to ask questions. If it hadn't been for Yasimov, though, we'd never have found you. When Gregorin told Chaikov to send you to Room H, it meant you were to be shot immediately.'

Korolev hadn't focused on how close he'd been to death – he'd been conscious of it in the interrogation room, but since Semionov and the other rescuers had broken in on them the time had been filled with explanations and activity. Now he allowed himself to consider how close-run a thing it had been, and it was much too close for his liking.

'Yasimov's a good friend, I'm thankful to you both,' he said, grateful beyond words if the truth had been told.

'I wasn't lying when I spoke to Rodinov earlier. I learnt a great deal from you.'

Korolev wasn't sure how to respond to that. The affection he'd had for the old Semionov still existed, but he kept on remembering his own indiscretions, wondering if they featured in the younger man's reports. And what about the questionable things Semionov himself had said from time to time? Had they been designed to trap him and others into making disloyal statements? He didn't want to know what Semionov had been up to in Petrovka Street, but he must have been spying on the Criminal Investigation Division in some way.

It was as if Semionov had read his mind. 'I spoke up for Mendeleyev, by the way, and I told Rodinov that I'd uncovered no evidence of serious disloyalty or dissent within the Criminal Investigation Division – only the usual mutterings that informers such as Larinin are always keen to pass on. Popov took the right approach, thorough self-criticism and an apology to the Party. Rodinov's no hothead – he'll recommend no further action is taken, I'm sure of it. Especially after this.'

Korolev held up his hand to stop him speaking.

'Please, Vanya—' he paused, considering whether the diminutive form of Semionov's name was appropriate, and then deciding to continue anyway, 'you saved my life back there, everything else is irrelevant. Believe me – when we meet again, it will be as friends.'

Semionov turned towards Korolev and the pleased smile on his honest, open face belonged to the old Semionov. But Korolev suspected the NKVD would soon change him into something harder, crueller probably as well. If it didn't, then the likelihood was the boy would become a victim himself.

Semionov turned into Bolshoi Nikolo-Vorobinski and parked the car in front of Korolev's building. He extended a hand.

'Friends then, Alexei Dmitriyevich.'

'Friends, Ivan Ivanovich.'

There was nothing else to say, and so they smiled at each other. Korolev knew his was genuine, in thanks and in the memory of the three months they'd worked together, but he couldn't help wondering about Semionov. Who knew what he thought about anything after the way things had turned out?

Chapter Twenty-Five

IT WAS a weary Korolev who opened the apartment door as quietly as possible, just in case Valentine Nikolaevna was still asleep. He hadn't taken more than two steps inside when he felt something cold and metallic being pressed just above his left ear.

'That's a gun against your head, Captain Korolev. Not a word now. Hands above your head, please, and then take one slow step forward.'

Korolev did as he was instructed and the gun barrel moved with him, just as if it were glued to his hair. He could hear the click of the door being closed behind him and, as his eyes adjusted to the gloom, he saw Gregorin sitting on one of the chairs. The pale morning light that slipped through the gaps in the curtains gave a slight polish to the leather jacket the colonel was wearing. Gregorin regarded the policeman with distaste.

An expert hand ran itself up and down Korolev's body, quickly locating the Walther and removing it. Then he was pushed forward into the middle of the room. Gregorin nodded in greeting.

'Korolev. I was beginning to wonder whether you would come home at all, but it seems the wait was worth it.'

Korolev allowed his eyes to sneak sideways. The man holding the gun was Volodya, Gregorin's driver.

'Luck's an amazing thing. If you have it, you're unstoppable, really – even a fat, incompetent pedant like you. Isn't that right?'

'If you say so, Colonel.'

317

'I do say so. I said it when Volodya here ran your car off the road and it turned out to be some other fellow. I said it when you stumbled across Mironov's body. Now fortune has favoured you again – it's quite extraordinary. Sure as hell there's no intelligence involved, you just have the Devil's own luck. But it's run out this time.'

Korolev said nothing – what was there to be said when a man the size of a bull was holding a gun to your head? If he hit Volodya with the table, the table would come off worst.

'Chaikov, was it?' the colonel mused. 'He'd never have co-operated if he'd known, but I thought once he was in so deep he'd have no choice. It was always a risk if he found out.'

'Not just him, I was followed by a colleague to the Arbat house. He took the number plate of your car. Once people started asking questions about why you'd taken me into custody, things fell apart for you.'

'I take it I'm being searched for high and low.'

'Yes.'

Gregorin shrugged. 'Well we're not done yet, although this does make things more difficult, it's true. I'm surprised it took so long to come unravelled, in a way, but once the icon went missing we had to move fast. Yagoda's incriminated me, so I'm told, and I wasn't going to wait around for the axe to fall. The icon was heaven-sent, and I'm not even a Believer.'

'You were never going to get away with this.'

'Wasn't I? It was just another icon as far as everyone else was concerned. I was the only one who knew what it was, initially at least. I couldn't believe what I was hearing when the Thief we caught in the raid told me, and it wasn't hard to imagine what the icon might be worth. A great deal, of course, and I knew the people to talk to. Mironov was the only fly in the ointment.'

'So you killed him – not Chaikov.'

'Volodya did, in fact. Chaikov could be pointed in a direction,

318

but even he would ask questions if he was interrogating an NKVD major. Fortunately Mironov wasn't strong like the American nun. A few broken fingers and he sang like a nightingale.'

'So the nun Dolan has the icon, after all?'

Gregorin sighed. 'Don't try and play me for a fool, Korolev. I'm tired and I don't have any time to waste. You spoke to the nun, you told me that, so you must know where it is. Tell me.'

Volodya pushed the muzzle of the pistol hard against Korolev's head, making Korolev wince, partly from the pain and partly from the fact that Volodya's hand seemed to be shaking. He hoped the big man had the safety catch on.

'I don't know where it is, I told you that back in the Lubianka and it's true.'

'Please, Korolev, don't take me for an idiot.' Gregorin extracted an automatic from his pocket, the grey metal an oily shine in the half-light. He pointed the gun at Korolev and then nodded to Volodya.

'Bring them out.'

Volodya pocketed his own gun and entered Valentina Nikolaevna's bedroom. First he brought out Natasha, who looked tiny in Volodya's massive arms. She struggled, although she was bound hand and foot, but the big man paid no attention and sat her on the chesterfield. She was gagged and her eyes were wide with fear. Next he dragged out Valentina Nikolaevna, his hands under her arms. Korolev could see a purple bruise down the side of her face which vanished beneath the white cotton strip that pulled her mouth back in a blood-smeared grimace. Volodya sat her down as well, as though arranging dolls for a tea party.

'Look, Korolev, I think I know you by now. You're a tough fellow, but you have a soft heart. You probably believe I'm going to shoot you in any event, so you'll likely tell me to go to hell if I threaten you. But these two could still come out of this in one piece.' Gregorin leant over and stroked Natasha's face with his automatic. The girl made a low buzzing sound through her gag, while Valentina Nikolaevna's head bowed in supplication, tears rolling from her eyes.

'The girl first, I think. Understand me, Korolev, I don't do this from pleasure. You're forcing me into it. That icon belongs to me now, and I will have it. If I make it out of this damned country, I don't plan to live in penury. Nor does Volodya. Do you, Volodya?'

Volodya's gun was back at Korolev's head now and he pushed it in affirmation. Valentina had now turned towards Korolev and her eyes seemed to be begging him for mercy. He'd no choice in the face of eyes like that.

'Schwartz has it. In his room at the Metropol.'

'What?' Gregorin said, in something close to shock. Then he began to think about it, and the anger was soon visible in his face. 'The bastard. Of course – he strung us along the whole time. Used you to mislead us as well, no doubt.'

'The nun told me.' It occurred to Korolev, as he was speaking, that Schwartz's involvement in smuggling out icons for the Church sounded more than plausible, even though he was making it up as he went along. 'Schwartz told me the Church approached him in America, remember? He's been working with them all along.'

Gregorin seemed to be thinking hard, then he looked up at Korolev and from him to Valentina Nikolaevna and her daughter. He seemed to consider the relationship for a moment and then to come to a decision and pointed his gun towards Valentina Nikolaevna.

'You'll go and fetch it for us then. If you fail, or try some trick, your daughter won't just be shot. Look at Volodya, he hasn't had a woman in hours. The girl's perhaps a little young for him, but he's not choosy. You won't mind, will you, Volodya?'

'No,' Volodya said, the deep voice sounding half-amused.

Natasha was crying now and Valentina's purple bruise was

vivid against the shocked pallor of her skin, her pupils large black discs. The tension was like an electric force, humming from person to person. When the creak in the corridor outside the apartment's front door came, it sounded like the crack of a whip.

§

At first everything froze. A cart bumping down the cobblestones outside sounded like a tank in the silence. Then there was another noise from the corridor, as if someone were very carefully advancing towards the door. Gregorin's eyes were now as round as Natasha's had been and his arms stretched forwards as he gradually stood from his chair. He gestured Korolev towards the corner with his gun, away from the door, and then nodded to Volodya, miming turning an invisible handle. Volodya moved across the room in preparation, while Gregorin aimed his weapon. Korolev, crouching against the wall, wished he were a lot smaller than he was. Everyone waited.

When the door smashed in, it pulled Volodya's wrist with it, and for a moment he was jerked forward. Korolev dropped to his knees as guns fired repeatedly, splashing yellow on the walls of the darkened room again and again. In the flashes Korolev saw Volodya thrown to the floor, his gun tumbling towards the still standing Gregorin, while Valentina tried to cover Natasha with her own body. Then the only sounds were Natasha's sobbing and a strange muffled banging – like a drum being hit with a sock.

The smell of cordite was sharp as Korolev stood up, watching Gregorin move his gun towards him as he did.

'Stay where you are!' Gregorin's voice came to Korolev from a distance. The gunfire had half-deafened him. 'No. Go to Volodya. But keep your hands in the air.'

Volodya was lying on his side, facing Gregorin, his left leg kicking against the wall in involuntary spasm. That accounted for the noise. The driver's eyes, caught in a dusty ray of light from the window, looked up at Korolev in confusion. There were bloody black holes in his coat and a dark puddle was slowly spreading around him.

'How is it?' the big man whispered to Korolev. Korolev didn't answer, his attention caught by Semionov, who'd been thrown against the opposite wall outside in the corridor. Blood was pumping down his chin from a long red gouge that revealed the white of his jawbone. He'd also been hit in the shoulder and chest and his breath bubbled red in his open mouth. He didn't look as if he'd last long.

'How is it?' Volodya said, a little louder. 'I can't feel my legs.'

Korolev looked down at him and shrugged.

'Not good.'

'Damn it,' Gregorin said. 'Back to where you were, Korolev.'

Korolev stood up and retreated towards the corner with slow backward steps, not taking his eyes off the colonel. Gregorin walked over to Volodya, pausing as he did so to pick up the stricken man's weapon and put it in his pocket. He moved heavily, favouring his right side, and when he dipped to pick up the gun Korolev could see that his left leg was damp with blood. Good for Semionov, thought Korolev – he'd clipped the rat.

When Gregorin reached his driver, Volodya looked up with a calm expression and then breathed out slowly.

'Do it. There's no way you can get me out like this, I know that. There's only one way this ends for me now.'

Gregorin looked down at the driver for a long moment.

'I'm sorry, brother,' he said, then pointed his gun, closed his eyes and fired. Volodya's body jerked once and the kicking stopped. The red puddle around him spread a little faster.

Korolev's back, meanwhile, had found the wall and there was nowhere further for him to go. He straightened up and began to pray in silence that the Lord would forgive him his sins. Then the muzzle of Gregorin's gun was a black hole aimed straight between his eyes.

'This was all your fault,' Gregorin said.

Korolev closed his eyes and waited for the bullet. He hoped he'd feel nothing and that the Lord would hear his prayers and spare Valentina and Natasha.

Click. Click. Click.

Korolev opened his eyes at the sound of the trigger pulling on empty chambers. The colonel was looking at the gun in mild confusion, then he looked at Korolev and shook his head in disbelief. After a long moment the colonel dropped the empty gun onto the floor and limped to the door. As he left the apartment, Korolev saw him pull Volodya's gun from his pocket and hold it straight down his wounded leg. In the distance a Militia whistle shrieked, and Korolev wondered why on earth the colonel hadn't shot him.

§

He stood absolutely still, listening to the receding footsteps and then the sound of the colonel going down the stairs. It wasn't fear that kept him immobile so much as amazement that he was still alive. But he was, and that meant he had to do something. He shook himself, then walked into the kitchen and reached into the drawer where Valentina kept a sharp knife.

'Valentina Nikolaevna, pay attention,' he said as he cut the cord that held her wrists, and then pressed the hilt of the knife into her freed hands. 'I need you to do some things for me.'

She nodded, although her eyes were still wide with terror.

'First, you have to call the Lubianka and ask for Colonel Rodinov. Tell him that Colonel Gregorin has shot Semionov. Ask him to send an ambulance. Inform him Gregorin may be making his way to the Metropol and I've gone after him. Then, and only then, see to Semionov and Natasha. Understood?'

'Yes,' she managed to say when he pulled the gag off, and the effort of speaking seemed to calm her. He touched her face for a moment and she moved her head around so that her lips rested against his wrist. They held each other's eyes for a moment and then he stood.

With a grunt of exertion, Korolev managed to turn Volodya's body, and he pulled his Walther out of the dead driver's coat pocket. Semionov lifted a hand as he left the apartment and he stooped down to him.

'His car. Emka. On Vorontsovo Pole. That's how I knew. To come back.' The words came out in bubbles of blood that left Semionov's lips crimson.

'Help is coming, Vanya. Hold on, friend.'

Korolev went down the staircase four steps at a time. White faces stared from half-open doors as he hurtled past and then he was out of the front door, looking up the alley towards the church for which the street was named. He thought he saw Gregorin turn the corner but couldn't be sure. Two Militia uniforms were running towards the building and he held up his identity card.

'Korolev. Petrovka Street. You, come with me. You, there's a wounded man on the first floor. See he gets taken care of. There's a dead one, too.'

One of the Militiamen ran into the building while the other stood there with his hand on his holster. Korolev turned to the four or five curious neighbours who'd emerged from the surrounding buildings and raised his voice.

'A dark-haired man in a leather coat came out that door not more than a minute ago. Who saw where he went?'

The elderly Lobkovskaya, his downstairs neighbour, stepped forward from the group and pointed up the lane towards the church.

'He went off that way, Alexei Dmitriyevich.'

There was no sign of the limping figure, but then Korolev spotted a trail of dark red drops along the lane.

'Your gun, Sergeant. Make sure it's ready for use.'

The uniform's nervous fingers moved to the flap of his leather holster as he followed Korolev. The church sat in its cobwebbed splendour on the right-hand side of the alley, and he tried to think ahead as he ran towards it, his Walther pointing skywards and the safety catch off. Semionov would have turned left at the end of the alley if he were driving back towards Petrovka Street, or the Lubianka, he decided, so that's where he must have passed Gregorin's Emka. The colonel must be heading for the car to make his getaway. He sure as hell wouldn't walk far with a bullet in his leg.

Korolev duly moved to the left-hand side of the alley as he approached the junction. There were already numbers of pedestrians heading along the bigger street towards Red Square for the parade, and a line of slogan-slung parked buses and trucks had parked up to the right, having dropped their loads of activists and workers. A group of drivers stood, and one of them pointed at him as he stopped at the corner. The Militia sergeant arrived beside him, breathing heavily.

'What's this all about, Comrade?' the uniform asked in a low voice.

'A bandit. He killed a man back there and wounded a Chekist – he mustn't get away.'

There was silence as the sergeant took the information in. In the meantime, Korolev lowered himself to his knees and let his Walther lead his head round the corner. In his peripheral vision, he sensed the drivers backing away and pedestrians moving quickly into doorways as the presence of men with guns finally registered.

When the rest of the street came into view, Korolev saw an Emka parked about thirty metres down the street, a figure hunched in the front seat. But there was no sound of an engine. He turned to the sergeant.

'There's an Emka just to the left. I think it's our man.'

The sergeant nodded. He was about Korolev's age, a broad face underneath his peaked cap, his blue eyes calm as he squinted across the street. He indicated a kiosk with his revolver.

'How about I make a run over there, Comrade? That way we'll have two angles of fire.'

'I'll cover you,' Korolev said and took a bead on the Emka, although now the hunched figure was gone, the driver's door hanging open. He stood up to get a better view and then, when the uniform was in position, advanced along the wall towards the car, his Walther out in front of him. The car was empty except for broken glass and smeared blood on the driver's seat. Of course, Volodya would have had the key. He waved the uniform forward and was just turning round when a bullet thwacked into the wall behind him, spraying fragments of plaster and stone. He dropped to his knee, trying to work out where the shot had come from and then heard the uniform's pistol bark twice. There was another shot and he heard a shout of pain from behind him. The uniform was clutching his right arm, his heavy revolver lying at his feet, and his face twisted in pain. He'd taken cover behind the kiosk.

'On your side. There's a yard entrance. About forty metres,' the uniform shouted, and Korolev nodded in acknowledgement. He could hear running feet and turned to see more Militiamen coming at a brisk trot, their guns out. He waved to them to keep low and then ran the few metres to the parked car and crouched behind it, feeling it vibrate as a bullet clanged into its side.

Further down the road Militiamen scattered for cover and the street was suddenly empty, the only noise that of an idling truck engine. He slipped to the ground and lay flat, looking towards the yard entrance, spying a knee-high boot with a dark stain running down its length. He aimed carefully and fired, seeing the boot and its twin jump away from the cloud of dust that erupted on the wall beside them. He stood up to take another shot and felt a bullet whip past his ear, and the simultaneous sound of breaking glass behind him. If he were a cat, it occurred to him as he dropped to the ground, he'd be down to his last couple of lives.

In the quiet that followed he heard the uniforms working their way closer and also the stop-start rhythm of a limping man's boots as they broke into a run. He lay there and thought about leaving the uniforms to it when it occurred to him – if Gregorin made it as far as Yauzski Boulevard, he might well slip away into the crowd. It was enough to get him up. Gregorin was moving away at a surprisingly quick pace and, as Korolev stood up from the ground, he looked back and raised his pistol. Korolev was already moving but he fired in Gregorin's direction, to remind the colonel that he was there, if nothing else, and was gratified to see him duck. But Gregorin was already close to the column of soldiers, and the inflatable *kolkhoz* village strained against its ropes as white faces turned in the direction of the gunfire. Gregorin fired again and panic began to buckle the orderly ranks. There was another shot from behind Korolev and the village's smithy lunged upwards as two of its anchormen fell flat to the ground. The remaining men struggled to hold the balloon, but another shot weakened their resolution and the smithy soared with surprising grace towards the morning sky.

Korolev threw himself into an already occupied doorway as Gregorin lifted his gun to fire once again, still moving away as he did so. Curses greeted Korolev as he crashed in on top of a well-fed man in a fine fur hat. The curses stopped when Korolev's Walther went off in his hand, causing lumps of plaster to drop down onto the doorway's occupants.

'Sorry, Comrades,' Korolev muttered as he stepped back out into the street. Ahead of him Yauzski Boulevard was in chaos, the entire inflatable village now bumping its way up through the trees and along the side of the tall apartment buildings that lined the road, and brown-uniformed soldiers were scattering in all directions. Korolev ignored the chaos and took careful aim at the limping colonel, missing him and seeing men and women fall to the tarmac around the fleeing man, their hands over their heads as they crawled on their elbows towards more substantial cover.

Korolev's shot must have been close because Gregorin stopped and turned, lifting his weapon. Korolev made no effort to take cover and aimed the Walther at the traitor's chest. He saw the blaze of Gregorin's shot even as he pulled his own trigger, and pain surged along his right arm as his body was shoved sideways by the impact of a bullet. He was hit, yes, but still standing and he still had the Walther in both hands – so he clenched his teeth and looked for Gregorin, ready to fire again.

But the colonel was just a crumpled heap of clothing lying motionless where he'd fallen.

Chapter Twenty-Six

SEMIONOV'S open coffin had been laid out in the Komsomol club, of which he'd been a member, attended by an honour guard of six of his young Comrades. It wasn't until he'd arrived that Korolev had realized that the club was one he was familiar with, located as it was in the church where Mary Smithson's body had been found. Even more extraordinarily, the coffin had been placed on the very same altar on which the nun had died. Visible stains still marked the white marble, despite the wreaths and flowers that surrounded the coffin. For a moment Korolev wondered whether the symmetry was deliberate but then dismissed the thought. This was a mis-communication, that was all – because of the special circumstances surrounding the funeral. No one had that dark a sense of humour – not even the Chekists.

He stood at the entrance to the sacristy, conscious that his appearance was causing a stir. He wasn't surprised, his winter coat had had most of the blood cleaned out of it by Shura, and the rip caused by Gregorin's bullet had been neatly sewn up, but it had been shabby to start with and now looked shabbier still. If he'd been allowed to wear his Militia uniform, he might at least have looked presentable but, even then, with his bandaged head and his arm in a sling, he suspected he'd still have drawn stares. He sighed and consoled himself that at least beneath the knee he was resplendent, wearing, as he was, a pair of the finest boots he'd almost ever seen, even if in a way the boots were causing him the greatest discomfort of all.

It wasn't just the blisters on his heels, although the new boots felt as though they'd rubbed their way down to the bone on the walk to the church. It was more the mystery of how he'd found them, wrapped in brown paper, when he'd opened the apartment door that morning. There was no explanatory note accompanying them, but his name had been on the package. And when he'd unwrapped them, and seen them standing there in the early sunlight that came in through his bedroom window, one name came to mind and that was Kolya's. So the smell of new leather wafting up to him caused him as much guilt as pleasure – but what was he to do? Give them away? It was a relief when Popov arrived and, without a word, took his arm and walked him over to the side of the room.

'The Devil, Captain. I've seen healthier-looking corpses.'

'I got knocked about a bit, it's true.'

'How's the arm?' Popov asked, pointing his pipe at the sling in which Korolev's right arm hung.

'The bullet went straight along it, from elbow to shoulder; a flesh wound.' He stopped for a moment, remembering that any mention of the 'incident' had been forbidden by Colonel Rodinov when the NKVD man had visited him in the hospital. On the other hand, he couldn't exactly pretend he hadn't been injured, so he continued.

'My arm was stretched out, so it ran the length rather than hit anything. I was lucky.' Korolev tried not to think about what would have happened if the bullet had been half an inch better aimed, not while he was in the same room as Semionov's corpse anyway. Nor did he want to think about the sound of the trigger hitting the empty chambers of the colonel's gun, nor the inexplicability of the colonel leaving the apartment without finishing the job. The Lord had been merciful – that was all there was to it.

They joined the queue to view the corpse. This being a

Bolshevik funeral, there would be no priest, nor any ceremony as such. Popov and others would make speeches at the graveside, of course, but there was no set form to mark Semionov's passing. The only thing that was certain was that Korolev's involvement would be minimal. He was under strict instructions in that regard.

'You're not speaking, are you?' Popov asked, as if he could hear Korolev's thoughts; the question sounded more like an order than anything else.

'I've been advised that my health does not permit it.'

'Indeed,' Popov said, running his finger absent-mindedly down a mosaic. 'I've been told to keep it short, myself.' He nodded towards the stained altar and the coffin. 'If I'd been consulted, of course, I might have advised against holding it here. Did you know?'

'No.'

'Nor did I – just a number and the street on the announcement. You'd have thought he would have mentioned he was a member here when we found the nun – but then he didn't tell us much, as it turns out, did he? A pity, this whole affair – he'd have made a useful investigator if he'd been allowed to continue with us.'

Their conversation had led them to the coffin and Korolev found himself contemplating Semionov's grey face, thinner than he remembered and now soft, almost flabby, except where the cheekbones and nose held the skin taut. He leant down and kissed the boy's forehead, and then pushed a loose hair away from the smooth skin. Without a soul, Semionov's body was nothing – an empty box that smelt like the sea at low tide. He felt a tear itch the corner of his eye and wondered at the futility of such a young life coming to a full stop.

The room had filled up, he saw, as he moved on from the coffin. And he couldn't help but notice the grim-faced men in good-quality military-style tunics muttering in the corners – Chekists, Korolev presumed.

'There'll be a medal for him. And for you. They're trying to decide what.' The general smiled. 'They want to reward you for unmasking the traitors, but quietly. The shoot-out on Vorontsovo Pole never happened, as you know.'

'Colonel Rodinov informed me.'

The general sat down in one of the ranked chairs and pointed Korolev to another.

'You're to forget about the whole business. The NKVD will be tying up any loose ends. And this time, Alexei Dmitriyevich, please understand this is an absolute prohibition.'

'I understand,' Korolev said, although there was one loose end he planned to deal with personally, whatever anyone said.

'Good. You don't know how lucky you are, Korolev. Ezhov wanted everyone concerned with the case shot – just to avoid contamination. If God existed, which of course he doesn't, I'd say he was on your side. Do you know what happened? Stalin was out walking in the Kremlin gardens when the *kolkhoz* village floated overhead and it amused him. That's all. That was the dividing line between life and death. If it hadn't amused him, or if Gregorin had run the other way, or if the soldiers had held onto the ropes, or if a hundred other things had or hadn't happened – well, you'd be dead. And so, almost certainly, would I.'

Korolev tried to imagine Stalin laughing at an inflatable village floating across Moscow and found it difficult.

'We were lucky a breeze blew up later on, though,' the general said, almost to himself. 'He probably wouldn't have stayed amused if they'd had to cancel the air force's contribution to the parade.'

Korolev nodded, remembering squadron after squadron of bombers flying above Moscow – a demonstration of Soviet strength on the nineteenth anniversary of the Revolution. They sat in silence, contemplating the ridiculous nature of fate.

'What happened in the end? To the village?' Korolev asked.

'They shot most of it down. Apparently one building got

away. There are sightings of it. They say it's heading towards Finland.'

'I wonder if it will make it,' Korolev said, thinking of Gregorin's plans to cross the Finnish border.

There was a shuffle of movement near the entrance and they followed everyone's gaze to see who had caused such a stir. Korolev recognized Rodinov immediately and, at first, thought the reaction of the crowd was for the colonel, but then he noticed the small man beside him, walking with a swagger that seemed out of keeping with his diminutive size. Commissar of State Security Ezhov's bony face peered out from under a military cap and his yellow teeth flashed in a smile that didn't reach his eyes. Everyone rose to their feet, but Ezhov waved them back down with that special gesture Stalin used – modest, but aware of his power.

Rodinov leant to whisper in the commissar's ear, and Ezhov nodded his agreement and took a seat at the back next to a pretty brunette in mourning black. A man joined them and Korolev felt a shiver raise the hairs on his neck as he recognized Babel. The writer nodded to him, and Korolev could have sworn he saw a twinkle in his eye as he turned his attention to Ezhov's wife.

Rodinov had by now reached a small lectern beside the coffin and set about unfolding a sheet of paper from his pocket. He was dressed in a suit that looked specially bought for the occasion.

'Comrades,' the colonel began, looking up, 'thank you for coming here today to mark the passing of the loyal Komsomol and Soviet citizen, Ivan Ivanovich Semionov. I thank you on behalf of his family, his Comrades and his fellow Komsomol members.'

There was a sob and Korolev turned to see a middle-aged woman buckled with grief. He recognized an echo of Semionov's features in her tear-streaked face, and prayed he would never have to bury his own son.

'What more can be said about our beloved Comrade, other than that he was a cultured man, a true believer in the historical imperative of international socialism, a diligent worker in the construction of the Soviet Union, a true and loyal Komsomol who lived in a genuine fashion?'

There was more it turned out. Much more. But eventually Rodinov folded his sheet of paper and turned to the Komsomol guard of honour with a nod. The young men looked at each other in momentary confusion that closely resembled terror, and then one of them made to lift one end of the coffin lid with a questioning look. Rodinov nodded again, this time with visible irritation and, with fumbling hands, his Comrades shut poor Semionov away in his lonely pine box for ever.

Chapter Twenty-Seven

PEOPLE stopped in the street to watch the young Chekist's coffin pass, surrounded by the guard of honour, who clung to the timbered sides as the truck bounced over pot-holes. Some took their hats off and one or two crossed themselves. More looked at the long cortège of shiny black cars that followed it with open curiosity. Korolev couldn't help but smile. This was a secret funeral for a Bolshevik hero and yet it couldn't have been more visible.

Ezhov didn't come to the cemetery. At some point his car must have turned off and taken the commissar to a more important engagement. Of the hundreds who'd attended the dry Bolshevik funeral ceremony in the church, not more than eighty persevered to the graveside.

There were some additions to the mourners, however. Schwartz stood, slightly removed from the main group, and Korolev spotted Valentina Nikolaevna by the graveside, along with Shura and Babel's wife Tonya, and wondered where poor Natasha was – the girl had barely spoken since the terrible events of two days before. At least Valentina Nikolaevna seemed composed – and he cursed himself for the hundredth time that morning for the horror he'd brought into their lives.

It was also apparent that not one of the presumed Chekists was still in attendance, and that the atmosphere had changed as a result. Women sobbed openly and a gaggle clutched at Semionov's mother, whether to support her, or be supported, it wasn't clear. It was Popov's turn to speak now, and he stood in the priest's spot at the head of the grave. He organized the guard of honour with quiet instructions, so that they slung thick canvas bands underneath Semionov's coffin and, when the general nodded, began to lower the body slowly into the grave. As Semionov descended, inch by inch, Popov began to speak.

'Life continues, Comrades. We are nothing more than a stage in the evolution of history. If we wish to remember our fallen Comrade, let us do so by continuing Ivan Ivanovich's work for a better future for the proletariat. Let us carry on that struggle, and let us be prepared to give our lives for our Comrades, as Ivan Ivanovich was prepared to give his. His memory will remain alive in our efforts. We will finish what he, and many others who have given their lives for the Revolution, began. He was of the People, and the People move forward with his shining example to guide them.'

Popov's voice was a deep rumble, remorseless and yet gentle, not dissimilar to a priest's voice in fact, and when he'd finished, Korolev saw more than one of the mourners make the sign of the cross.

He turned, to see Schwartz standing beside him.

'Hello, Jack,' Korolev said in greeting.

'Alexei. I'm sorry about Vanya. He was a good kid.'

'He was a good man, in the end. You should be grateful to him for that.' Schwartz's brow crinkled in enquiry. 'If it hadn't been for him, Gregorin would have visited you in the Metropol. He wasn't a happy man – seemed to think you'd double-crossed him. That you'd stolen his icon.'

Which wasn't entirely true, but he was curious to see Schwartz's reaction. If there was one, it was well enough hidden for Korolev to miss it. But, of course, that in itself was revealing.

'The icon?'

'Oh, come on, Jack. If I wanted to cause you trouble, you'd be in a Lubianka prison cell. And that's somewhere you don't want to visit, believe me.'

Schwartz took a slow look around, as though he suspected he might be caught in some kind of trap.

'I don't know what you're talking about. Is this why you left the message at the hotel today? To question me again?' Schwartz's face remained calm, however, and anyone watching would have thought they were having a solemn conversation about poor Semionov.

'My questions aren't official, Jack – but when a man nearly gets himself killed as many times as I have in the last week he becomes interested in the reasons why. And perhaps I owe it to Vanya to get to the bottom of it all.'

'And you think I can help you to do that?'

'Call it an investigator's hunch. You've told me yourself the Church asked you to buy the icon, you travelled on the train from Berlin with Nancy Dolan, and the late, not much missed, Colonel Gregorin was trying to sell the icon using your services. In a way you link the main actors in this drama as much as the icon does. It wouldn't surprise me if you turned out to be Count Kolya's brother-in-law, to top it all.'

Schwartz shrugged his shoulders in a dismissive gesture.

'And you haven't asked me about the icon either. If I were in your shoes –' and here Korolev couldn't help looking wistfully down at Schwartz's sturdy brogues – 'it would be my first question.'

'Do you know where the icon is, Alexei?' Schwartz asked drily, and Korolev wondered if he was making a joke.

'No, Jack, but I've an idea I might just find it if I whistled up twenty Militiamen and started doing a bit of poking round in your vicinity. Would you like me to do that?'

'I'm guessing that might make leaving the country tomorrow a little difficult.'

'So you're leaving us? That also makes me curious. Why would you be leaving if there was still a chance of purchasing the icon?

I presume you take a percentage of the purchase price – don't you? Even a small percentage of a million dollars must be worth waiting round for.'

Schwartz frowned.

'Is that what you want, Alexei? Money?'

'Money, Jack? I don't think so. Kolya was right, I'm not quite the Soviet citizen I thought I was, but I'm not for sale either. I just want a few answers. Just for myself. My discretion is evidenced by the fact that you're not being questioned by less polite people. Not to mention that the city isn't being torn apart brick by brick to find her.'

Schwartz smiled, as if at a half-forgotten joke, then nodded. 'I have a car by the main gate. Why not come back with me to the hotel?'

Korolev nodded. 'Give me five minutes.'

'Of course,' Schwartz said.

Korolev watched him walk away before approaching the grave. Two diggers – thick-handed peasants from some far-off province – were filling it in with shovelfuls of earth and he watched the last visible corner of Semionov's coffin disappear.

He felt sadness, he supposed – not only for Semionov, but also for himself. To lose a friend and kill a man were both hard things, and he'd done both in the last two days. He didn't regret Gregorin's death, but he wished someone else had pulled the Walther's trigger. It hadn't even been a good shot – Korolev had been aiming for Gregorin's chest and hit him just above his left eye – but it had snuffed out the colonel like a candle all the same. To end a man's life so suddenly – well, it made you think about your own mortality, and that was never a comfortable thing to do.

Perhaps it was the memory of Semionov lying dead in the corridor that made him do it, he couldn't rightly say afterwards, but his right hand raised up as if of its own volition and executed a perfect sign of the cross, for all the world to see, and, for a moment at least, he felt no fear of the consequences, and a total peace.

Chapter Twenty-Eight

THEY DIDN'T speak in the car – partly because of the driver's presence but also because there didn't seem to be much to say – nor did conversation start up when they entered the Metropol. The silence was only broken when Schwartz opened the door to his room.

'After you,' he said.

Korolev walked inside and, despite the shadows within, he was able to make out the huge bed, the elegant lines of a pair of chairs, a writing desk, dark wallpaper, the pile of packing crates that stood in front of the window, and the faces that stared up at him from the floor.

Icon after icon after icon leant against the high skirting board that circled the room, golden halos reflecting the weak sun that streamed through the half-closed curtains. Korolev turned slowly, his eyes running round the wall at devout renderings of Christ at every age, saints and, of course, the Virgin Mother herself.

There were nearly twenty representations of the Virgin – in many of the traditional forms – but, of these twenty, five were Kazanskayas. They all had the appearance of great age and he looked at them in silence for several moments, intrigued by the small variations and then seeing how the thing was to be done.

'Clever,' he said in a low whisper.

339

Schwartz nodded in confirmation.

'I'm packing them up now – they'll come with me by train to Hamburg, and from there I sail to New York.'

It was brilliant – what better way to hide an icon than amongst icons? He looked at the Kazanskayas once again.

'And?'

'We'll never know for sure. It's a question of belief not truth – it always has been. But there's enough truth here to base belief upon.'

Korolev felt the eyes of the Mother on him as if she were in the room. He wanted to ask which icon was the one, but he didn't. He didn't need to. There was no doubt in his mind – there was only one of them that it could be. The one that looked into his soul. But he didn't kneel, or cross himself, or pray. 'But what will they do with her in America?'

Schwartz considered the question. 'D'you know, my guess is they'll do nothing. Wait, I think, until things change.'

Korolev considered the icon, nodded and then held his hand out to the American.

'Have a good trip, Jack. Perhaps we will see you again in Moscow. One day.'

'Perhaps,' Schwartz said, and then Korolev was closing the door behind himself as he left.

§

He took his time walking back, rehearsing what he'd say when he arrived. He had it all worked out by the time he opened the door and saw Valentina Nikolaevna standing by the table, as if she was waiting for him, and so he came straight to the point.

'Valentina Nikolaevna, I've thought it over. I can't forgive myself for being the cause of those men coming into your home, and for what happened here. I've decided the best thing will be if I leave this apartment. I can stay with my cousin and I'll say nothing to Luborov or anyone else. You'll have the whole place to yourself, if I'm still down as living here. It's not enough, I know it, but it's something at least.'

She considered him for a time and then shook her head.

'Thank you for your offer, Alexei Dmitriyevich. It's kind of you, but unnecessary. It wasn't you that brought the men here, they came themselves. You're not responsible for the evil of others.'

'But—' he began.

'Enough, please. I mean what I say. And anyway, Natasha wouldn't hear of it. She will only come out to Gorky Park this evening if you'll be there as well. So, you see? I can't do without you.'

And then she smiled at him.

Authors Note

I've done my best to recreate 1930s Moscow accurately in this book, but it should be remembered that it remains a work of fiction and that I've allowed myself some flexibility from time to time, particularly with regard to the interiors of buildings. For any inaccuracies that aren't deliberate, I apologize.

Those curious about the period might find the following of interest:

Anne Applebaum. *GULAG – A History of the Soviet Camps.* Allen Lane, 2003.

Danzig Baldaev (and others). *Russian Criminal Tattoo Encyclopedia,* Vols 1–3. Steidl/Fuel, 2003; Fuel, 2006; Fuel, 2008.

Robert Edelman. *Serious Fun – A History of Spectator Sports in the USSR.* Oxford University Press, 1993.

Orlando Figes. *The Whisperers.* Allen Lane, 2007.

Sheila Fitzpatrick. *Everyday Stalinism.* Oxford University Press, 1999.

Sheila Fitzpatrick. *Tear off the Masks – Identity and Imposture in Twentieth-century Russia.* Princeton University Press, 2005.

Véronique Garros, Natasha Korenevskaya and Thomas Lahusen. *Intimacy and Terror – Soviet Diaries of the 1930s.* Trans. Carol A. Flath. New Press, 1995.

Jukka Gronow. *Caviar and Champagne – Common Luxury and the Ideals of the Good Life in Stalin's Russia.* Berg, 2003.

Jochen Hellbeck. *Revolution on My Mind – Writing a Diary under Stalin.* Harvard University Press, 2006.

Marc Jansen and Nikita Petrov. *Stalin's Loyal Executioner – People's Commissioner Nikolai Ezhov.* Hoover Institute Press, 2002.

David King. *Red Star over Russia – A Visual History of the Soviet Union from 1917 to the Death of Stalin.* Tate, 2009.

Hiroaki Kuromiya. *The Voices of the Dead.* Yale University Press, 2007.

Catherine Merridale. *Night of Stone – Death and Memory in Russia.* Granta, 2000.

7Simon Sebag Montefiore. *Stalin – the Court of the Red Tsar.* Weidenfeld & Nicolson, 2003.

A. N. Pirozhkova. *At His Side – the Last Years of Isaac Babel.* Steerforth, 1996.

Vitaly Shentalinsky. *The KGB's Literary Archive.* Harvill, 1993.

Frederick Starr. *Red and Hot – the Fate of Jazz in the Soviet Union.* Oxford University Press, 1983.

I was fortunate enough to complete a Masters in creative writing at St Andrews University and remain indebted to Douglas Dunn, Meaghan Delahunt, Don Paterson and John Burnside for their patience, insights and guidance, and, above all, to A. L. Kennedy, who not only taught me a great deal about the nuts and bolts of writing but also included my short story 'Denmark' in a German collection she edited – which was tangible encouragement when I very much needed it.

I'm also thankful to David Wilkinson, Kuhan Tharmananther, Jonathan Thake, Sue Turton, Bryan Hassett, Ken Murphy, Ed Murray, Ian Iqbal Rashid, Melanie Richmond and my wife, Joanne – all of whom read the book at various stages – and Larisa Ivash, who proved an invaluable source of information on subjects as diverse as pre-war Soviet cigarettes and the starting motor of the GAZ M-1. My agent Andrew Gordon at David Higham Associates helped make this book much better than it once was, as did my editor Maria Rejt and my US editor Lindsay Sagnette at St Martin's. Their suggestions have always been valuable and their corrections always correct, and Maria's attention to detail and care have made me weigh each word, which is probably how it should be. Thanks also to Liz Cowen for her precise and careful copy-editing.

Above all though I'm grateful to my wife Joanne. This book is dedicated to her in acknowledgement of her patience, and other things.